Shattered
Souls

Shattered Souls

by: Patti Keno

Shattered Souls is a fictional novel. Any real persons, real places or actual events mentioned within are used in a fictitious manner. All other persons, places and events were created by the author. Any resemblances to real places, actual events, or people living or deceased are purely coincidental.

First Edition: July 2015

Cover Design: Cheekycovers.com

Clip Art found on clker.com

Final Edit done by: Jennifer Friess

ISBN:0692493247

Dedication:

Although many people were involved in the production of this book, there are two that were instrumental in its conception and completion

To My Aunt Bonnie:

Who taught me that my stories did not have to be completely serious and that magic can exist in fiction. She opened my eyes to a realm of possibilities that I had not known before.

To my dear friend Kreishna:

Who had the patience to listen to the entire story read in one day while we walked through Ann Arbor, MI. Her excitement for my words kept me writing. She inspired me to continue with the story even though I had my doubts. I can only wish you the reader will love it as much as she did.

Inspiration:

I wanted to include the inspiration for this novel because it is quite funny. I was in the bathroom at work and I overheard two ladies talking one said: "I've never experienced anything like that before" I got to thinking what could happen to someone to make them say something like that and that is how Shattered Souls was born in a bathroom at Borders.

1

The Boardwalk:
Josh & Maggie

Maggie whimpered softly in pleasure as Josh's hand gently touched the back of her neck. His lips were soft and so exquisite. He kissed Maggie so passionately that she almost forgot that she had only just met this man. Tears began to well up in her eyes, as she realized this was exactly what she had wanted to do since the moment she first laid eyes on this beautiful stranger. She whimpered once more in sorrow as he finally pulled his lips away.

Maggie gasped for air, surprised that she had been holding her breath for so long. She looked into his eyes and saw a rapture that echoed her own.

"That…was…amazing," she whispered, still trying to catch her breath. She had never been kissed so deeply; so passionately before this moment. "I never…" She tried to speak the words that were in her mind, but they melted away before she could. She struggled to explain what she felt inside, but stopped as she noticed the tears in his eyes.

"What is it, Josh?" Maggie touched his cheek gently. "You felt it too, didn't you?" Her words were soft, but full of urgency. How could he not have felt the chemistry between them?

Josh nodded slowly, a tear rolling down his cheek. "You don't remember do you?" he asked cryptically.

"Remember what?" Maggie wiped away his tear.

"I'm sorry," Josh whispered painfully.

Those words filled Maggie with confusion, sorrow, and rage. She started shaking her head. "No," she protested softly, knowing what was coming next –rejection– the only thing, in Maggie's eyes, that could ruin this perfect evening. "Don't say you're sorry," she begged, still shaking her head.

She hadn't noticed him moving until his lips touched hers once more. She whimpered again at the raw passion behind his delicate kiss. Slowly, he kissed his way to her ear. The feeling of his stubble against her cheek and neck made her knees feel weak.

"I really loved you," he said, his warm breath tickling her ear and sending chills down her spine.

Again, his lips found hers and she was swept away with emotion; swept away with love and lust for this man she had just met. It felt as if that missing part deep inside of her had finally been found. How could she love this stranger so much? How could she have such feelings for a man she had never met before?

His tongue began to explore every part of her mouth; she caressed it gently with her own tongue and found herself melting into the arms that held her. She was lost in his kiss; his tongue, her tongue–there was no difference. They had become one in the passion of the kiss.

As his tongue probed deeper into her mouth, she could feel it rubbing against her molars. She began to suck his tongue passionately as she longed for his hand to move to her breast. She hadn't felt like this in so long. She hadn't been kissed like this in….well, she'd never been kissed like this before.

All at once, she began to feel something much deeper than anything she had ever felt. It was something more primal than sex or lust. His kiss had awakened an insatiable longing deep inside her soul. It was as if with his kiss, Josh had touched the very core of her soul.

Once again, her knees went weak with the glory of the rapture that filled her. Thankfully, Josh's strong arms supported her as her knees gave way. She began to cry openly, no longer caring what happened to her as long as she could remain in Josh's arms forever.

She felt his hot tongue pushing deeper still into her mouth. She inhaled his tongue with a needy desire, unable to control herself anymore. She was accepting him, accepting anything he wanted to do to her.

She heard his voice once more, but this time it seemed as if it were coming from inside of her own mind. Somehow they had connected so deeply that they could communicate mind to mind. Maggie couldn't even stop to think about the impossibility of that idea. The voice inside her head pushed all thoughts out of her head. "I love you," Josh's voice echoed through her mind. It was raw and aching with real emotions.

She was not surprised when the orgasm overtook her. She wanted to scream out in sheer ecstasy of his kiss. She dug her nails into Josh's back. The leather of his jacket almost felt like flesh as it gave way and gathered under her fingernails.

She was pulsating in pleasure as she was pushed even further past the point of orgasm, pushed to a point of perfection that could never be matched. She had never imagined that there was anything better than an orgasm.

She felt as if her soul had lifted out of her body and taken flight. This had to be love. It had to be the real thing. Josh had to be the one. After spending only a few hours with him, she knew she wanted to spend the rest of her life with him. Anyone who could bring her to orgasm with a simple kiss was not to be given up, but why was he so sorry? He couldn't still be thinking of leaving, especially not after this kiss.

Suddenly, pain ripped through her soul. She shuddered in horror as she tried to pull away, but Josh's hand held her locked to him in an iron grip. He would not let her break the kiss.

The pain was exquisite, sensual and raw. Maggie couldn't help but to give in and let go. She let the pain sweep through her entire body. She was sobbing now, but Josh didn't care. He continued to force the kiss upon her.

She felt like she was spinning faster and faster accelerating at an alarming rate. She longed to open her eyes and see if she actually was spinning, but she no longer had control of her body. 'Is this death?' she wondered, as she lost all feeling in her body. Her soul began to panic as she realized that Josh was killing her. He was suffocating her with his kiss. He was sucking the very air from her lungs. She couldn't move, she couldn't breathe. She was surely dying. She wanted to scream out in horror and pain, as the sickening sensation of vertigo swallowed her

She began to lose herself once more. This time she lost all touch with reality as she spun endlessly. Just as she thought she could no longer take it, the feeling disappeared. Her soul snapped back to reality so fast that she thought she might vomit.

She dropped her arms, rejoicing that she could finally move again. She found herself standing on the boardwalk, gasping madly for air.

His lips were gone and his arms pushed her away. The kiss was finally over and she was still alive. She had thought she would never breathe again. Her lungs were burning as she sucked the sweet autumn-chilled air into them. Her entire body throbbed and ached with the power of his kiss. She licked her lips sensuously, savoring his taste on them. It felt odd as she did this. Something felt different, felt wrong. It felt as if somehow the kiss had changed her in some way.

"Wow." Her voice sounded strange; maybe she hadn't said anything at all. Maybe it was Josh who said it. She opened her eyes. She was filled with the sudden urge to see his eyes. She had to know if he had felt it too. She wanted to know if what she felt was real or if she had imagined it all.

As her eyes adjusted to the dark night around them, she noticed that somehow her vision was crisper. She could see things so much clearer than ever before. She started to feel nausea creeping up into the back of her throat again as she focused on the person standing before her.

Instead of seeing Josh standing there, Maggie saw a girl. In fact, the girl was a mirror image of herself. She smiled, but the mirror image's face remained still.

"I'm sorry, I didn't mean to," the mirror image whispered. Her eyes lifted up to look at Maggie. She was shocked to see Josh's essence staring up at her from behind her own eyes. This was not just a mirror image of Maggie; standing before her was a complete duplicate of her body.

"What the hell?" Maggie exclaimed. Josh's voice came out of her mouth. Realization dawned on her and she felt as if the world had just dropped out from under her. This couldn't be real... The body standing before her was not a mirror image and it was not a duplicate. It was her body. Her own body stood before her with Josh looking out of her eyes.

Maggie began to panic. Her breathing sped up until she was literally gasping for air. She looked down at her chest and found Josh's chest heaving in time with her breathing. She felt as if she were hyperventilating. She couldn't seem to catch her breath...his breath.

"What happened?" Maggie asked in a pitifully small Josh-voice. "What did you do to me?" she demanded without conviction. She was crying again. She moved her hands to touch her chest, and Josh's hands moved at her command. This was real, somehow. Josh was inside her body and she was in stuck in his.

"Put it back...put it back," Maggie began a feeble chant. "Put it back...put it back...put me back...put me back," she demanded between sobs.

The mirror image...Josh...stood before Maggie. He toed a crack in the boardwalk with Maggie's cross trainer-clad foot. He was staring intently at the lake. Josh bit Maggie's lip trying to stop the tears welling up in his stolen eyes.

Josh turned his gaze onto his former body. He stared deeply into the eyes that used to be his. He was staring directly at the part of the man before him that was Maggie. Josh reached Maggie's hand up and touched the face that used to belong to him. Maggie recoiled from his touch...no, her touch.

"I'm sorry," Josh repeated through Maggie's lips.

"No, it's not real," Maggie argued. The masculine voice she heard was hoarse from crying. "This is not happening," Maggie moaned. "This can't be happening."

"I'm sorry," Josh repeated. "I love you, I really do." Maggie felt the body she now occupied trembling as she heard her own former voice whispering his words.

Maggie watched in horror as her body moved closer. She panicked again as Josh placed Maggie's own hands on her new Josh shoulders. The reality of the situation hit harder with the touch of her former hand. Maggie's breathing sped up again. She wanted to scream, but all that came out was a sob.

Still in shock, Maggie stood frozen as the lips that once were hers kissed the hollow of Maggie's now unfamiliar cheek. Josh lingered, softly breathing into Maggie's new ear. Maggie whimpered, crying as she heard Josh's voice whimper instead of her own.

Josh backed away slowly, regretfully even. He reached up and wiped the tears away from Maggie's new cheeks. Josh smiled a small, sad smile. He shook Maggie's head and opened her mouth as if to speak. Suddenly, he turned and ran, leaving Maggie to deal with the situation alone.

"WAIT!" Maggie screamed in a desperate Josh voice. "JOSH! COME BACK!" She started crying again…no… He started crying. Maggie knew no amount of tears could ever change what had happened, as strange as it all seemed.

All she wanted was go home and go to sleep. Then, when she woke up in the morning, this entire nightmare would be over. She would be back in her own body again. 'This has to be a nightmare,' her mind rationalized. 'It just has to.'

She took a few steps forward getting used to his footing, a few steps more to get used to his stride. Then she started to run, pumping his legs as fast as she could. She needed to go home. Everything would be fine, if she could just make it home.

2

Maggie's Apartment:
Emmy & Maggie

Maggie stopped in front of her apartment building, automatically reaching for her keys. She didn't have them; they must have fallen off somewhere. No matter, she would just buzz the buzzer and Emmy would let her in. She pressed the buzzer to her apartment and waited. Nothing happened, so she pushed it again, holding it down longer this time.

'Come on, Emmy. Wake up,' she thought to herself, in her own girl voice. She heard footsteps inside the building, heading towards the apartment unit's door. The door opened slightly and Emmy's sleep weary face appeared in the crack.

"What do you want?" Her voice was seething with irritation.

"Let me in," Maggie shuddered as Josh's voice spoke her words. She had forgotten who she was until she spoke.

"No!" Emmy's voice turned angry, but Maggie could tell she was scared. "I don't even know you."

"Emmy, it's…Maggie," Josh's voice cracked with desperation as she spoke her own name.

"What's wrong with Maggie?" Worry filled Emmy's eyes as she clutched at the door frame for support.

"Nothing, I…I'm Maggie," Josh's voice whispered sadly. It was hopeless; Emmy was not going to believe her. No one would.

"Look mister, I don't know what kind of sick game you're playing, but Maggie's not here." Her voice was laced with ice. Her eyes returned to that weird mixture of fear and anger once again.

"But…Emmy…I…," Maggie tried to protest, but Emmy cut her off.

"No! I don't want to know how you know my name or Maggie's. I don't care! I just want you to GO AWAY!"

"Emmy," Maggie breathed, she was too close to tears for any other words to come out.

Emmy's face softened a little when she heard the sadness in the strange man's voice. She sighed. "It's four o'clock in the morning. You woke me up, I'm tired and I just want to go back to bed. Do you want me to take your name or something?"

"M…." Maggie paused, her heart breaking a little as she gave Emmy the only name she could. "M… My name is Josh. Could you tell her to call me, if she comes home?" Maggie shoved Josh's hands into his back pockets.

"I'll tell her to call you *when* she comes home," Emmy corrected Maggie. She seemed to be waiting expectantly for something. "Do you have a number, Josh?" She emphasized the name Josh as if she didn't believe that was his real name. She was losing her patience again.

"She knows it," Maggie replied. She hoped Josh would bring her body back here sometime soon.

"Well, goodnight then," Emmy dismissed Maggie with such finality that there was no doubt the conversation was over.

"I'm sorry," Maggie paused at how familiar those words sounded with Josh's voice. "I'm sorry that I woke you."

"Thanks," Emmy started to close the door.

"PLEASE!" Maggie panicked and stuck Josh's foot in the door. Emmy's eyes filled with terror. "You have to believe me! This is not a sick joke. I *am* Maggie," she pleaded. She could hear how stupid those words sounded when Josh's voice said them.

"I've got to go, my boyfriend is waiting for me," Emmy lied, fear raging in her eyes.

"Don't you mean girlfriend? Kaitlin is a girl." Maggie couldn't stop herself. It wasn't often that Emmy hid her homosexuality.

"How did you... NEVERMIND!" Emmy yelled, "Leave me alone, before I call the cops!"

Maggie's heart broke at the coldness of her best friend's voice.

"Emmy!" she cried out, she had to believe her "Help me!" she begged, grasping at the doorframe.

"I mean it you freak! GO AWAY!" Emmy showed her other hand that had been hidden behind the door. Her cell phone was in it. Maggie could see that she had already typed in 911. All she had to do was press send and the police would be on their way. Maybe Maggie should let her call the cops. Then she could explain to them what happened, maybe they could fix it. No, if Emmy didn't believe her, what chance did she have that the police would?

"Wait! I'm sorry, I'll go," Maggie felt dejected. "I'm sorry." She pulled Josh's foot back and let the door shut.

Maggie wiped the tears from his eyes and shoved his fists into his jacket pockets, trying to hold back her tears.

"His wallet," she whispered and withdrew his hand from his pocket. She opened up his wallet and looked at his driver's license, "my home."

She turned away from her past life and walked toward the unknown.

3

Josh's Apartment:

Maggie

Maggie walked in the general direction of Josh's address. She didn't want to think about it. She was still in shock and denial; this couldn't be happening, this couldn't be real.

The rain started falling as she reached the boardwalk where it happened. She rolled Josh's eyes, one more horrible thing to cap off a horrible night. The rain helped her though as it soaked Josh's hair; it cleared her mind, made her think straight. She had to think this through, sort it out, and analyze her situation.

What did Josh do to her and why? What motivated him to steal her body and leave her in this one? How was it even possible? Body snatching? That was the stuff of horror movies, not real life. Was this all just some crazy nightmare? Was she going crazy? The most important question of all was where did Josh run off to with her body?

As Maggie walked and thought about it, she realized this had to have been his intention. Josh had been planning this out since the beginning of the evening, perhaps even before that. This was all part of his master plan and that's why he was so sorry. That's why he kept apologizing. He had planned to take her body from the beginning.

Who was he really? And why did she feel like she had known him before? What did he want with her body? What was he going to do with it? Would she ever get it back?

He loved her; she knew that he did. She felt it in his kiss, in his words. It was more than that; Josh had told Maggie without words during the exchange that she was the only one he had ever truly loved.

She wiped a tear from Josh's cheek. "Men don't cry," Josh's voice scolded her and it frightened her even though she was the one who spoke the words. 'But I'm not a man,' Maggie thought desperately. She pulled out the key that she found in Josh's pocket. She hoped it was his apartment key and not a car key. She sighed in relief as the door unlocked with the key. She pushed the door open and leaned against the frame for a moment. She was exhausted.

The first thing she saw upon entering the apartment was the living room. A brown leather couch stood against the wall in front of her. The place was messy as if a single man occupied the apartment, but the décor had a bit of a woman's touch to it.

She shrugged out of the wet leather jacket that he was wearing and let it fall to the floor. She stepped towards the couch. Taking slow, deep, breaths; she reached Josh's hand out to touch the couch. Somehow, she felt it would validate this nightmare. It would make it real. His fingers came in contact with the cool leather and she felt it as she would if her hand had touched it. She was truly in this man's body, she was now a man. Maggie dragged his hand across the arm of the couch, feeling every bit of it. She was trying to find a mistake, something that told her that this was a nightmare and not real. It couldn't be real. She heard a cat hiss and quickly she pulled Josh's hand back.

A large, orange, longhaired cat sat regally on the back of the couch. The cat eyed Maggie viciously. Maggie laughed a little at the sight of such a fat cat. He barely even fit on the back of the couch. Maggie made a fist, holding it out for the cat's approval.

"You can tell I'm not Josh, can't you?" Maggie whispered softly. Immediately at the sound of Josh's voice, the cat attacked, biting the fist she held out to it. "Hey!" She jumped back and rubbed the fist, more startled then hurt. "You don't have any teeth, do you?" she asked the cat, but it only hissed in reply.

Just then a flashing, green light next to the couch caught her attention. The light was coming from his answering machine…a message. She stumbled over to it and pressed play.

"Maggie?" a woman's voice asked. "Maggie, it's me. I'm sorry; I didn't know… I shouldn't have…" It took her that long to recognize that it was her own voice coming from the machine. "I can't let you… Oh my God…," Maggie's real voice said quietly as the phone clicked off suddenly.

"Josh?" Maggie grabbed for the phone. '*69 will work,' she thought. She would much rather hear her own voice inside her head than to hear Josh's voice coming from her lips again. She dialed the numbers and as she waited to be connected, the recorder continued to play messages.

A heavy breathing filled the room; she searched frantically for the volume and turned it down slightly. "Where are you?" A voice followed the breathing. "Where are you? WHERE ARE YOU? YOU SON OF A BITCH! I'M GONNA KILL YOU!" Maggie jumped as a male voice screamed from the answering machine. The man took a moment to calm himself. "I am going to find you. You are going to fix this and then I WILL KILL YOU." Maggie stared at the machine, horrified. Then in a whispered voice just before the machine cut him off, he said, "You'd better watch out." Maggie started shaking. So this is why Josh did this to her. Someone was trying to kill him and now that person was trying to KILL HER!

It took a moment of the phone ringing for her to remember what she had just done, a split second more for logic to spell it out for her. 'If you dial *69, it automatically calls back your last caller. If your last caller wants you dead, it's probably not a good idea to dial *69,' she thought, yelping out in terror as she quickly disconnected the line. She threw the phone across the room as if that would make everything better.

She sat down slowly on the couch, in front of the toothless cat. She needed to think this through. She had to find a way out of this mess. She looked down at her hand, but it was Josh's hand she saw. She raised the hand and slowly touched her lips, Josh's lips quivered slightly beneath her touch. Hs bangs had fallen into his eyes so she pushed them back and ran her hand through his short cropped hair.

"Jesus, Josh," she whispered with his voice. "What the hell did you do to me?"

The cat, which had almost fallen asleep, jumped awake at the sound of Josh's voice. He hissed and swatted a giant paw at her. Maggie was startled by the cat's violent reaction. She jumped off of the couch and backed away from the cat that didn't seem to have claws either.

She tripped over the wooden coffee table and struggled to stay upright. The cat hissed at her as she lost her balance and fell over backwards. She sat up, looking around the room stunned. Josh's forehead had smacked against the corner of a bookshelf on the way down. The cat hissed at her again.

"Shut up," she snarled at the cat. She held his hand up to the fresh cut on his forehead.

She stood up slowly, hoping she hadn't just given this body a concussion. She wandered around the apartment until she found the bathroom. Dazed, she stood in front of the mirror and used toilet paper to clean the small cut. The bleeding stopped almost immediately, but she found herself still staring at the reflection before her.

She stared into the eyes in the mirror and she could see herself. She could see Maggie staring back at her, but the rest of the body was all Josh. She laughed a little as she realized if she stood really still she could almost believe that Josh was actually standing in front of her. She could almost believe that she wasn't trapped in his body. She watched as the man lifted his hand and pinched his arm. She flinched in pain. There was no doubt that she was in this body, this body that was not her own.

She sighed. Josh's clothes were soaked and she needed to take them off. She slowly pulled off his tight shirt. She watched every move to make sure none differed from what she tried to do. She dropped the shirt to the floor. Josh was definitely a handsome man. He was well-built, but not too muscular. His chest was hairless and there was a tattoo just above where his heart was. It was a name in Old English style writing: Erik. She traced his finger over it.

"Must be an old lover or something," Maggie winced again at the voice that she heard.

She placed both of his hands on his chest and ran them down his finely-toned body to his pants. It felt strange to her not to cup breasts as she touched this body. She smiled slyly as she unbuckled his belt and unbuttoned his pants. She let them drop to the floor. She stepped out of them and kicked them to the side.

She reached his hand underneath the elastic of his underwear and gently caressed the soft skin just above his penis. She began running his fingers gently up and down his pleasure trail. That movement alone began to arouse her. She found herself picturing naked women and she was hard. Pulling down his underwear she smiled and looked down at it in the mirror.

That was when she noticed the envelope taped to the bottom of the bathroom mirror. The words written across it read:

You don't belong here.

Immediately, all sexual thoughts left her mind. She reached for the letter, watching in the mirror as Josh's penis slowly became limp again.

She paused just before she actually touched the envelope. His hand started shaking. What if it was a death threat or a note stating that the killer was already in the house?

"Too many horror movies, Maggie," she said, clearing her throat trying to make her voice sound right, even though she knew no amount of throat clearing would fix her voice. She looked into the mirror. "Josh," she corrected herself. She couldn't keep referring to herself as Maggie. She was not Maggie anymore.

She pushed back her fear and carefully pulled the envelope from the mirror. She ripped it open and unfolded the letter inside.

Dear "Josh",

Consider yourself lucky... I'm giving you and only you a crash course in my nightmare realm. Consider this your instruction manual. You're Josh now, so act like it. The best thing you can do is quit fighting and give in to the urge to lose yourself in Josh. It's the only way. If you don't, you'll die. It's as simple as that.

You don't belong here. I know this and you know this, but hey, LIFE SUCKS! You're Josh now and you're just going to have to learn to deal with it. Maybe this won't be permanent... Maybe I can fix it, but don't get your hopes up. You're useless to me now. Just be Josh and everything will be so much easier.

Yours,

E

P.S. A warning: don't tell anyone! Besides who would believe you anyway? I know I wouldn't.

She whimpered softly, holding back tears of frustration and anger. This wasn't real; none of this was real, it couldn't be. Shit like this didn't happen in real life. She ripped the letter to shreds and threw it in the trash. She could deal with this. She was a strong woman; well she used to be, anyway. She was an actress. She could play Josh. She could definitely play Josh.

The phone rang, startling her. She looked at Josh's watch; it was 6:36 AM. She walked into the living room afraid to pick up the phone. She listened as the recorder answered it for her.

"Hi this is Josh…," the voice on the recorder said. It was the voice she now owned.

"And Lauren. We can't come to the phone right now…," a perky female voice said. Maggie wondered where this Lauren person was.

"So leave a message," Josh's voice finished.

"Lauren," a desperate voice moaned after the tone sounded. It seemed familiar to Maggie. After a heartbreakingly long pause, the man continued. "SON OF A BITCH!" the voice screamed. Maggie immediately knew it was the voice from the last message. "YOU BASTARD! YOU MURDERING BASTARD." The voice paused. Maggie could hear the desperation in the voice. "Where are you?" he asked in an exasperated tone. Then the dial tone sounded.

Shaking, Maggie made her way to Josh's bedroom. What was she thinking? She couldn't handle this. Nothing could have prepared her for this, nothing. She lifted his covers and crawled into his bed. What was she doing here? How could this have happened to her? How could this have happened at all? These thoughts ran through her head with such violence that it was painful. She curled his body up into the fetal position and covered his ears with his fists.

"What am I gonna do? What am I gonna do?" she repeated over and over again. "How the hell did I get myself into this mess?" She hated the sound of every word she heard. She whimpered as sobs began to shake the masculine body she now wore. They wracked Josh's body so hard, sometimes she couldn't even force it to breathe. She wasn't even sure she wanted it to breathe.

Finally after what seemed liked hours of howling and sobbing, she fell into an exhausted sleep.

4

Lilly's Apartment:

Eon & Lilly

Shaking, Eon hung up Maggie's cell phone. He caught a glimpse of his reflection in the darkened shop window. He smiled and Maggie's face smiled back at him.

Eon reached her hand up and caressed the face he now wore. He could almost imagine he was caressing Maggie. Her fingers found her lip and Eon ran her finger across it. How could he have done that to her? Something had gone horribly wrong. He had only wanted to kiss her. He wanted her to remember another time. A time when he was in another body loving her; loving this body. Oh, what had he done?

He sighed and dragged his eyes away from Maggie's reflection. He turned and watched as a woman fidgeted with the keys to the apartment building. It couldn't be. Another past love here in this city?

"Lilly," he said softly, with a hint of sadness in his voice. He was filled with desire and longing for the woman he had married so long ago. Lilly knew all about Eon and what he was. Maybe she could help him. He stepped out of the shadows of the shop's doorway and walked towards the building.

After she unlocked the door, Lilly glanced back as if she felt someone watching her. Eon slid into the shadows of the building next to Lilly's. He laughed a little, knowing she wouldn't have recognized him anyway. Satisfied that no one was following her, she stepped inside the building.

Eon broke free from the shadows and ran towards her building. He stood outside the door and read the names on the intercom directory. The fifth one down read Dr. Lillian Mae. He traced one of Maggie's fingers across the name. That name cut him like a knife. Why would she do that? Why would she choose such a last name?

He moved his finger across to the button and waited a few minutes to make sure Lilly made it to her apartment. He scanned the list of names until he found a woman's name. He pushed Lilly's button and double checked the name he had chosen from the directory.

"Yes?" Lilly was out of breath and her voice was full of suspicion. Her voice was the same and it cut Eon. He was reminded of that night so long ago; when she was screaming at him and demanding he leave.

"Lilly?" Eon asked. He was afraid she would hear this voice and somehow know it was him. He shook his head. She wouldn't know. That was not possible. If she were looking in his eyes she could tell, but just hearing his voice, whatever that voice was at the time, recognition was impossible.

"Yes." He could still hear that suspicion in her voice.

"Hi. It's Valerie from 2B. I lost my keys. Can you buzz me in?" he asked. He was resting Maggie's hand on the door handle; sure that Lilly would help someone in need.

"Sure," relief echoed in her voice. Little did she know, she was letting in the very person she was hiding from.

"Thanks a bunch," Eon tempered his voice with mock relief.

"No problem."

The door buzzed, Eon opened it and quickly slipped into the building. He walked over to the elevator and pressed the up button. He noticed a mirror hanging next to the elevator and he couldn't resist looking at Maggie's face once more. This time he leaned forward so close he could feel the cool smooth surface of the mirror against his soft skin. He stared into Maggie's eyes wishing he could see her staring back at him and not his own essence echoed in them.

The elevator buzzed and startled him. He felt like Maggie's heart would jump out of her body. He pressed her hand to her breast and willed her heart to stop racing. He took a deep breath, entered the elevator, and pressed the button for the fifth floor. Lilly was staying in apartment 5C. How long had she been living here right under his nose?

Eon paused outside of her door. He stared for a moment, wishing that he could see through it; wishing that he could see her. He knocked twice. Lilly opened the unlocked door almost immediately.

"You're not Valerie," she pointed out slowly. She stared deep into his eyes. "Eon? Is that you?" she asked with a hint of fear in her voice. Eon couldn't blame her for being afraid. He felt guilty for all that he had put Lilly through, but he didn't let any of that show on his face. A lot of practice over the last few centuries left him very good at hiding what he was really feeling.

"Lilly," Eon breathed out. He hadn't realized how tired he was until just now. "Something went wrong," he leaned heavily against the doorjamb. "I switched..." He swallowed back tears. Tears? He hated being a woman. It was much harder to control the emotions they felt. "I switched without wanting to. It was out of my control," he confessed.

"And the girl?" Lilly stood angrily barring his entrance, any trace of fear she had shown earlier was hidden. She too lived long enough to learn how to hide her emotions, except when she was taken by surprise.

"She lives," Eon assured her, staring deeply into his wife's eyes.

"But for how long?" The question was rhetorical; she knew that Eon didn't really care. He never had and most likely he never would.

Eon ignored her. He didn't want to hear her lectures right now. "Please let me in, I'm tired and hungry." He tried to look contrite, but he could tell she wasn't buying it.

She stared at him for a few moments, a war raging within her. She wanted nothing to do with him. She wanted to turn him back out onto the street, but she couldn't, she loved him. "Fine," Lilly gave in, opening the door for him. She couldn't help feeling like she had just invited a vampire into the sanctity of her home. "The kitchen's over there." She pointed to it as she closed the door and locked it. Eon couldn't help but notice there were seven locks on her door.

"Expecting trouble?"

"Yeah, you," Lilly replied sullenly.

Eon laughed. "And yet here I am." He walked towards the kitchen.

Lilly resisted the urge to punch him. She knew that whatever body he was in, he had the strength of ten men. She had seen the aftermath of that strength before. She followed him into the kitchen "Why Maggie?"

Eon froze mid-step and turned back to face her. "How do you know about Maggie?"

She ignored him for the moment and poured herself a glass of wine. "I'm not stupid, Eon. I keep tabs on you," Lilly informed him, sitting down at the kitchen table, wine in hand.

"You do still love me," he smiled, joining her at the table with a container of cottage cheese.

Lilly blushed, his smile brought back feelings that she had long forgotten, even on this new face that he wore. She looked away from Maggie's dazzling smile. She was ashamed that she still felt that way after everything he'd done to her. She nodded reluctantly. "Why Maggie?" she repeated. She was not letting him leave until she had an explanation. He had never, to her knowledge, revisited his past, except for her. He always seemed to find his way back to Lilly. She was the only person in the world that knew about his ability and his horrible past.

"I told you, it was an accident. I didn't mean to do it. I just wanted to kiss her and then it just happened. I couldn't stop it, Lilly. I really didn't want to hurt her."

Lilly laughed. "You always hurt the women you love."

"This isn't funny, Lilly," Eon warned through a mouth full of cottage cheese.

"Oh, but it was funny when you killed our daughter?" Lilly demanded. She slammed her wine glass on the table a little harder than she had wanted to. She smirked a little on the inside as Eon jumped. It was good to know that she could still startle him, even if she couldn't actually put real fear into him.

"I see you're still angry about that," Eon set the spoon inside the empty container, a smug look crossing his face, hiding the pain and guilt he actually felt for what he had done.

"Still angry? STILL ANGRY!?" Lilly was enraged. "You killed Mae, OUR DAUGHTER, and you put me in HER BODY! You think I would have forgotten that? You think I could ever forgive you for that?"

"I didn't want you to die." The truth slipped out before he could stop it.

"I would rather have died if it meant that Mae lived," Lilly said through clenched teeth.

"There wasn't any time. I couldn't save you both. I chose to save you" He placed his hands on hers.

"You chose wrong." She ripped her hands away from the strange hands he now wore.

"I didn't come here to make you angry." He stood up, pushing his own anger deep inside. It would not help his cause if he got angry now. He carried the empty container over to the sink.

"And yet, you did." She chugged the rest of her wine and followed him to the kitchen. She gently placed the glass in the sink. "Why did you come here, Eon?" She turned and leaned her weary bones against the counter.

"I needed your help." Eon really looked at Lilly as he stood by the fridge. She was a lot older than she had been that last time he had seen her.

"Just like always," she scoffed.

"Your hair is turning gray," Eon pointed out.

"Well, I am 157 years old," she said sarcastically. This body that she now wore was only 69.

"Thanks to me," he said, grinning proudly.

"Thanks to you," she replied, not bothering to return his grin. She was not pleased to be as old as she really was, not with the price she had to pay for it.

5

Maggie's Apartment:

Maggie

As Josh's body slept, Maggie dreamt…

In the dream, Maggie smiled into the mirror that reflected her own image back at her. She finished applying lipstick to her lips and smacked her lips together.

She was so excited she was almost shaking. This was going to be her first date since she broke up with Julie. That relationship hadn't lasted very long. She frowned as she realized that had been over a year ago.

She did one final check in the bathroom mirror. Her face smiled back at her. Her brown hair was highlighted with blond streaks. It was piled on top of her head in a waterfall of curls. She wished she had the time and the job that would allow her to dye her hair again. Light green hair would match this outfit perfectly. She sighed. She was an adult now, almost 30; even though she didn't feel like she was any older than 19. It was time to stop doing childish things like dying her hair green.

Maggie walked into the kitchen where Emma, known as Emmy, her best friend and roommate for two years, was making dinner.

"So, how do I look?" Maggie asked smiling at Emmy's girlfriend, who was sitting at the table reading a magazine.

Emmy's light mocha-colored skin was positively luminescent. She was in a great mood because Kaitlin had just returned from a two week business trip to Europe. She smiled brightly, holding a spoon in one hand. "You look great, Mags," Emmy complimented her.

"No, Emmy," Kaitlin corrected as she set the magazine down on the table. "She looks hot!" She smiled and winked. "So, where are you going? What's she like?"

"I'm sorry to disappoint you, but this time it's with a man. I don't know anything about him at all. Sue from work is fixing me up. I have no idea where we are going either. She said that they would pick me up at..." She glanced at the clock above the stove. 'Shit... Now!" she exclaimed. "Where are my shoes? Where are my shoes?" Maggie began to panic. Emmy pointed next to the front door. "Thanks," Maggie yelped as a horn honked outside their apartment building.

"Well, that's them. Wish me luck!" Maggie smiled up at them as she strapped on her shoe.

"You'll need it if Mark is going too." Emmy made a face; she didn't get along with Maggie's brother very well.

"Are you sure this doesn't make me look like a hooker?" Maggie asked as she stood before the mirror in the living room.

"Only if you were wearing black thigh high boots," Emmy joked. Maggie glanced down at her fancy sandals; her toenail polish was the exact same shade of green.

"I do look good, don't I?" she smiled at herself in the mirror, as the horn repeated.

"You look radiant," Emmy assured her opening the door. "Now go, before they send Mark up to get you," she laughed as Maggie grabbed her purse and raced down the stairs.

"Bad news," Sue announced, turning to watch as Maggie carefully climbed into the car. "He couldn't make it, I'm sorry," she apologized. "Do you want to go to a movie instead?" she offered.

"Dressed like this?"

"Sure, why not?"

"I guess." Maggie shrugged. "Hi Mark." She waved to her brother.

"Hey Maggot," he waved back.

"Did I ever tell you how disgusting it is for you to be dating my brother?" Maggie asked Sue.

"Many, many times," Sue started the car and backed out of the parking spot.

***

Saddened by her failed date, Maggie unlocked her apartment door and walked in. Kaitlin and Emmy were wrapped in each other's arm's sleeping on the couch.

"Aww, cute," Maggie whispered as she covered them up with a blanket.

"How was your date?" Emmy mumbled.

"He didn't show," Maggie frowned.

"You alright?" Emmy tried to force her eyes open.

"I'm fine. Don't wake up. Go back to sleep."

"G'night," Emmy replied sleepily, as she snuggled deeper into Kaitlin's arms.

"Goodnight," she kissed Emmy on the top of her head.

The way they were laying brought back a bitter memory of Dylan. They had fallen asleep like that many times before, but that seemed like a whole lifetime ago. Dylan had been dead for over four years now. Every time she thought she was finally over his death, sadness would rear its ugly head and threaten to swallow her in memories.

She walked into her room, still thinking about Dylan. She suffered from insomnia and it would be a long time before sleep came for her, if it came at all. She washed her face, getting rid of every trace of make-up that had been there, and changed into her jogging clothes. She picked her spare key and connected it to her jogging lanyard. She pulled on her little blue hooded sweatshirt, zipped it up, and left her apartment.

For her, jogging was a great way to relieve tension and a way to forget about everything. This was another activity Dylan had gotten her into. She sighed, wishing it didn't still hurt whenever she thought of him.

She walked out of the apartment building backwards, slowly closing the door so it wouldn't slam. She hated when people let it slam. She turned around, preparing to leap off of the porch and into a jog. A man was standing directly behind her, blocking her path. She just barely suppressed the urge to scream.

"I'm sorry," the man apologized smiling. "I didn't mean to startle you."

Maggie could tell he was trying hard not to laugh.

"No Prob," Maggie said, pushing her way past him.

"Wait!" he called out to her as she started to jog away. "Maggie?"

She had made it as far as the parking lot. She stopped dead in her tracks at the sound of her name. "How did you know...?" Her voice trailed off as he held a bouquet of flowers out to her. "You're the blind date?" she asked. He nodded, still smiling. She began to feel self-conscious as she realized she was meeting the blind date in her dirty old jogging clothes. "I was just heading out for a jog," she explained, smoothing down her hair. At least she hadn't taken it down yet. She began jogging in place, hopefully giving him the impression that she wasn't really comfortable meeting him without Sue.

"I'm Josh," he introduced, offering his hand out to her. Maggie stopped jogging. She could see now that getting rid of him was not an option. She walked back to the porch and shook his hand.

"Maggie, but then you already knew that." She smiled.

"I wanted to apologize for not showing up tonight. Something...came up."

"That's alright. I don't really like my brother tagging along on dates anyway."

"Your brother?" he asked.

"My brother is Sue's boyfriend," she explained, taking the pre-offered flowers. "Well, I should get these in a vase." She paused, trying to decide the best way to tell him she'd be right back. She definitely was not ready to invite him up to her place. "Could you maybe wait down here? My roommate is sleeping in the living room and I don't want to wake her."

"Sure," Josh said, biting his lip in a nervous gesture. Maggie could tell he was afraid that she might not come back down. She smiled reassuringly at him and let herself into the building.

She ran up and put the flowers into a vase, then scribbled a note on the fridge note pad:

"Date showed up... Be back soon. Love M"

She ran quickly down the stairs and out the door, gently closing it behind her. Half of her hoped he was gone, while the other part was hoping he'd stay with her forever. She just met this guy, why was she thinking like that? It felt like they had known each other for a long time, even though they hadn't exchanged more than a few words. Feeling like that about a total stranger freaked Maggie out.

"That was fast," he said softly, trying not to startle her.

"I know," she smiled, glad that he was still there.

"So, instead of a jog, do you just want to walk? Maybe we could get some coffee or something?"

"Dressed like this?" she asked, gesturing at her baggy clothes.

"I think you look beautiful," his compliment took her breath away.

"I... Uh... Thanks," she stammered. It had been a long time since a guy had complimented her. "Let's go to the boardwalk," she suggested, directing Josh's attention away from her.

Josh nodded. If only Maggie knew what was going to happen on that boardwalk a mere two hours later, she would have found an excuse not to go anywhere with this stranger.

6

Josh's Apartment:

Maggie

Maggie awoke to the sound of the phone ringing; automatically, she reached out to answer it. She didn't remember the events of last night until she heard herself say "Hello" and it wasn't her voice. The lump of fear and sadness grew once again in her throat as she remembered everything.

"Josh? Baby, it's time to get up and come to work," a female voice on the other end coaxed. "You told me to call you and wake you up."

"I told you to call me?" Maggie asked, shaking his head.

"Yes, you told me you were going to be partying all weekend and for me to call and wake you on Monday. You said you were going to be doing as many drugs as you could to make you forget who you are," she explained, with a hint of sadness in her voice. "Did you forget?"

"Yes," Maggie answered. Leave it to Josh to have everything planned out ahead of time. "Where do I work?" Maggie asked, hoping the question wouldn't sound too strange.

"Lanaway's! Don't you remember anything?"

"No."

"What drugs did you take?" the girl asked.

"I don't know... I don't remember." Josh's voice was breaking up in tears again.

"Josh, are you alright?"

"No."

"We'll talk when you get here. Don't be late…. And don't call off, Josh. Frank will fire you."

"Frank?" Maggie asked.

"Your boss. Oh, shit! I have to go; Table 14 looks angry. See you when you get here. I love you," and with that, the receiver went dead.

Maggie looked sadly around Josh's bedroom. She got up and found a Lanaway's uniform that looked mostly clean. All of Josh's drawers were empty and there were clothes all over his floor. "What a slob," Maggie stated, as she stepped in front of the mirror. She tried to do something with his hair, but she didn't know what she could do.

"Whatever. It's not like I'm actually here," Maggie told Josh's mirror image. "This can't be real, it just can't be."

She ran out the door and stumbled into a man in a trench coat.

"Sorry," she said in a gruff voice, barely even glancing at the man. Luckily, there was a cab waiting outside the townhouse. She jumped in the cab and buckled her seatbelt.

"Lanaway's, and quick," she requested of the cab driver. It would be just her luck to be late for work on her first day of being Josh. She laughed out loud at how stupid that thought was. The cabby glanced in the rear view mirror at Josh. Maggie smiled and winked at him. Obviously, the cabby thought the man in his cab was crazy, and maybe unstable, because the man in the back seat was crying now. The cabby applied a little more pressure to the gas pedal.

"It's out of my hands," Maggie declared, not knowing why she said it or even what she meant by it. She wiped away the tears and laughed again.

The cabby's knuckles were turning white as he clenched the steering wheel. He kept throwing fearful glances at the strange man in the back seat of his cab.

By the time the cab driver stopped in front of Lanaway's, Maggie was feeling sorry for him. "Sorry if I scared you," she apologized, pulling out Josh's wallet. She paid him extra, hoping a big tip would make up for her erratic behavior.

Maggie walked towards the building and smiled; this used to be her and Emmy's favorite hangout. The last time she was here was about two weeks ago.

Maggie wondered what exactly it was that Josh did here. She stopped in front of the building, more than a little afraid to go in. She couldn't pass herself off as Josh, even if she did look like him now. Anyone who knew him would realize something was different; they would know something was wrong.

Before Maggie could even think about turning around and leaving, a blond girl in her twenties, opened the door. "Josh, get in here!" She reached out and grabbed Josh's arm, Maggie didn't even try to stop her. "I punched you in already. Go on into the back."

"The back?" Maggie was a bit dazed.

"You're bussing tonight."

"Bussing?"

"Dammit, baby, quit repeating everything I say. You're bussing tables and washing dishes from now on; Frank's orders," the girl explained. Her nametag read: Sunshine.

"Why?"

"Frank says you're scaring the customers. You have got to quit touching people. Some people just don't like to be touched, especially by a waiter."

Those words struck something in Maggie's memory. The last time she had eaten here, a waiter grabbed her arm and said, "You, I know you." He smiled slyly and said, "You're Nessa." That waiter had been Josh. Why hadn't she remembered that? If she had, she would have never talked to him. The whole incident was rather traumatic. Maybe she had blocked it out. She didn't really remember what his face look liked, but she would never forget his eyes. That was even truer now because those eyes were now hers.

"I've got a present for you, Josh. Let's punch out for break. Come on, quick." Sunshine grabbed his hand and led Maggie into the back room.

"But, I just got here." Maggie protested. Sunshine ignored her as she opened a door that seemed to be an office of some sort and pushed Maggie into the room.

"Frank's gone for the day. Aren't you going to wish me a happy birthday?" Sunshine asked, locking the door behind her. She smiled seductively.

"Wait," Maggie pleaded as she watched Sunshine unbutton her uniform. "Sunshine, wait, I'm not who you think I am."

"How many times are you going to say that to me, Josh?" Sunshine asked, letting her uniform fall to the floor. "I don't care who you are right now. It's my birthday and I want you," she slowly took off her bra. Maggie could feel Josh's body responding to the stimuli. All of a sudden, Maggie was filled with so much lust she couldn't stop herself. She grabbed Sunshine and pulled her to his lips.

She reached his hand down into Sunshine's underwear. "Oh Josh, baby, what's this?" Sunshine breathed in response. "You've never been concerned about my pleasure before." Sunshine shuddered in pleasure as Josh (Maggie was no longer in control of Josh's body) led her to the couch. Maggie watched in amazement as Josh's arms gently laid Sunshine on it. This was the way she had always wanted to be treated by a man.

"I told you, I'm not who you think I am," Josh's voice whispered seductively into Sunshine's ear, as he lowered himself down on top of her.

"I like this you, Josh.... OH!"

7

Lilly's Apartment:

Eon & Lilly

Lilly smiled in post-coital bliss. "Why can't it always be like this?"

"It can, my love, it can," Eon assured her. "I can be a woman more often."

"No, that's not what I mean," Lilly groaned as the past came rushing back to her. It was always like this. Every time she helped Eon, he would have sex with her, use her, and then he would leave. "Why can't you stay here with me and be one person?" Lilly asked.

"I'm working on that," Eon explained. "I am so close to finding The One."

"You're never going to find the 'one' Eon. The 'one' doesn't exist." She had heard it all before, his lies, his endless quest. She was sick of it, all of it.

"How dare you?" He slapped her across the face. "It does exist!"

"Eon! How dare you!" Lilly raised her hand to her face in shock. Eon had never hit her before, not in all the years he had lived with her as one man. Not in all the fractured years he had lived with her on and off as so many different people. She stood up and ran into the bathroom.

"Lilly, I'm sorry." Eon jumped up and chased her toward the bathroom. She closed the door mere seconds before he reached it. He stopped and leaned Maggie's head against the closed door. "I'm sorry, Lilly. I didn't mean it."

"No, Eon. You're not sorry, that's your problem. You're never sorry. You don't care. You don't care how many people die for your stupid game!" she yelled through the door.

"It's not a game, Lillian!" he shouted in anger, pounding his fists against the door once. Then he turned around so he wouldn't be tempted to tear the door down just to get to her. "It's not a game. It's what I deserve! It's what they took away from me!" He walked across the room as something caught his eye.

"Who, Eon? Who took what away from you?" she asked, exasperated. Eon always talked about this mysterious betrayal that happened at some time in his past. He always talked about getting revenge against the traitors that had hurt him. "Eon?" she asked when he didn't answer her question. "Eon?" she repeated, opening the door. She gasped at what she found. He was standing next to her desk reading something on her laptop. It was her journal; the journal that she had been tracking Eon's movements in.

Eon looked up at her with rage in his borrowed eyes. "You little bitch!" he yelled, slamming the lid of the laptop closed. "What is that? What? You've been spying on me?" he demanded, grabbing her by the hair on the back of her head.

"Eon, please," she grabbed at his hand and tried to pry it off the back of her head. Why was he being so violent? He had never treated her like this before, never.

"What is it, Lilly?" he repeated, pulling her neck backwards so far she could barely breathe. With her free hand she reached behind her, grabbing whatever she could of Maggie's flesh and squeezing.

"WHORE!" Eon screamed. He threw her forcefully on the bed. Lilly lay there for a moment trying to catch her breath. She wasn't as young as she used to be and all this excitement was causing her asthma to flare up.

"It's my penance!" She stood up and stared venomously at her husband. "You son of a bitch! You brought me into this; you made me do things...bad things." She ground her teeth, trying to push back the tears of anger and frustration building in her throat. "I had to do something. I had to help them somehow. You can't just fuck up someone's life and leave them to fend for themselves." She raised her hand, but could not bring herself to actually hit him. "You have to be held accountable! These are people, Eon! Living, breathing people, they're not clothing you can take off and toss on the floor. They have families, people that love them." She lowered her hand, her anger waning.

"Don't you dare lecture me, Lilly!" He moved Maggie's face so close to hers that she could feel his angry breath burning her face. "Who chose the men that I took over back then?" He stood before her, Maggie's eyes looking back and forth between both of Lilly's eyes. The movement made Lilly dizzy so she focused instead on his lips. Spit was dripping out between Maggie's soft lips. They were curved up in a wicked smile. "Who was it, Lilly? It wasn't me. I could care less. It was you, once you found out what I could do. You wanted to try one of every color, size and shape. How many men did you go through, Lilly?"

Lilly shook her head. Who was this person that stood before her? It wasn't her Eon. It wasn't the person she had loved for so many years. "I hate you." There was so much conviction in her voice that she knew Eon would believe her, because she meant it. She hated him. She would never get over everything he had done to her. She would never forgive him.

"What did you say?" Eon cocked Maggie's head to the side as if that would help him hear her better.

"I. Hate. You." Lilly stared him down as she spoke the words slowly.

She was not expecting what he did next; no one really would expect it. He whipped Maggie's head back and head butted her as hard as he could.

She heard his words as she sank into darkness. "I hate you too, bitch." Unlike Lilly though, his words held no conviction. He didn't hate her. In fact he loved her more for standing up to him, but he wasn't going to let that stop him from exacting his revenge upon her.

8

Lanaway's:

Maggie & Sunshine

Maggie looked up from mopping the floor. She was remembering her encounter with Sunshine again. She needed to quit thinking about it. This day had gone by quite fast after the excitement at the beginning. She had pretty much cruised through the rest of the day on autopilot. Josh's body seemed to know what to do.

Sunshine smiled as she walked by Maggie.

"I'd like to see the new you again sometime, Josh," she whispered seductively.

"We may be able to work something out," Maggie assured her in Josh's sexiest voice.

"Tonight?" Sunshine asked a hopeful gleam in her eyes.

"Maybe," Maggie answered, "text me later."

"This you knows how to please a woman. I like that," Sunshine explained walking away.

"That's because I am one," Maggie mumbled under her breath. As much as she wanted to have sex with Sunshine again, she didn't think she would that night. She just wanted to sleep and pray that when she woke up, she'd have her own body back.

Maggie left the closed restaurant and walked to the boardwalk. She stood, staring out into the lake. "This is where it all began," she whispered, desperately wanting the voice she heard to be her own.

"Where what began?" a female voice asked. Maggie jumped, startled by the sudden voice. Adrenalin from the hope that it was Josh in her body pulsed through Josh's veins. She turned to find Sunshine standing beside her.

"What do you want?" Maggie asked, angered by Sunshine's persistence.

"I want you, Josh," Sunshine replied, stepping in front of Maggie and placing her hands on Josh's chest. "I need you," she cooed, caressing Josh's face. Maggie shivered at her touch.

"Can you just leave me alone for now?" Maggie asked.

"I can't, I.... I think I love you," she whispered the last words, almost as if she was afraid to say them at all.

"You don't love me! You don't love Josh! If you loved him, you would see that I'm not him. I'm not JOSH! These shoes...this shirt...the pants.... They're not mine. They're Josh's. Everything is Josh, except in here," Maggie pointed at Josh's head.

"What are you talking about?" Sunshine asked in shock.

"Can't you see? I'm not Josh. Just look into my eyes. I'm not who you think I am. I can never be who you think I am," Josh's voice sounded panicked.

Sunshine looked deep into Josh's eyes and saw something....saw Maggie maybe. She stiffened. "Who are you?" she whispered, reaching up to touch Josh's face again.

"I'm not Josh," Maggie replied.

"I know," Sunshine nodded.

Maggie kissed her on the cheek and turned to leave.

"Where are you going?" Sunshine asked.

"My home," Maggie answered with tears in Josh's voice.

***

Maggie paused in front of her apartment building. She couldn't bring herself to buzz the buzzer. She didn't want to wake Emmy again. She didn't want to hear that cold tone in her voice. So she just stood, staring up at her bedroom, wanting the light to turn on, wanting Josh-in-her-body to be in there. Her bedroom light never turned on. She stood underneath the window for hours, just waiting and wishing she could just get inside. She foolishly thought that if she did then everything would return to normal. Finally, she sighed a deep sigh and headed back to Josh's apartment.

Maggie walked in and dropped his keys on the table next to the door. She headed into his kitchen and opened the fridge. She grabbed a beer and twisted the lid off. She didn't usually drink beer, but when she needed to calm herself anything alcoholic would do.

She paused in the hallway between the kitchen and the living room. Maggie stared at Josh and Lauren's wedding picture on the wall. A deep sadness was stirring inside of her. Dylan…she missed him so much. She felt a dizzy sensation in the back of her mind when she thought of him. She walked over to the couch, thinking if she sat down the feeling would pass.

That was when she noticed the flashing light on the answering machine. She was afraid to play the message. She knew whose voice she would hear once she pressed play and she never wanted to hear that voice again.

She smiled as a new thought struck her, what if it was Sunshine. She walked over to the machine. She pushed the button and closed her eyes, praying that Sunshine's cheerful voice would fill Josh's dreary apartment.

"I'm gonna get you! You murderous bastard! I am going to get you SOON! Oh and by the way…. Whatever you do….don't look in the bathroom."

Panic swept over Maggie. She found it hard to breathe. She wanted to get out of there. She wanted to run. She held back the urge to scream, but she couldn't hold back the tears as the bathroom door slowly swung open. A man in a familiar looking trench coat stepped quietly into the living room.

"So, how are you going to fix this?" The man's voice and the one from the answering machine were the same. This was the killer.

He didn't look like much. Maggie figured that if Josh was still in this body, Josh could probably take this man. He was shorter then Josh, by almost a foot. He had dark hair and almond shaped eyes. He looked Hawaiian to Maggie. There were dark circles under his eyes and his skin was pale and ashen. He stared at Maggie intensely, his eyes full of hatred.

"Wh-what?" Maggie stammered in confusion.

"Don't give me that stupid act, you son of a BITCH!" the man screamed at her.

Fear took hold of Maggie; she was going to die now. This man was going to kill her and she was going to die alone in someone else's body. She was never going to see her family again. Shit, she wasn't even going to see her own body again, much less be in it. 'Forget that!' she thought. She wasn't going out without a fight. She started to move Josh's body into attack mode. The man ran towards her before she even had time to prepare herself for the oncoming fight. The man rammed his fist into Josh's stomach, catching the lower part of Josh's ribcage. Maggie screamed out at the sudden pain. She felt Josh's body crumple to the ground.

Josh's instincts took over and Maggie felt his body scrambling to escape, trying to run even as the man kicked his steel-toed boot into Josh's side. Using the coffee table Maggie pulled Josh's body up off of the ground, only to feel the man's fist connect with Josh's cheek. Stars exploded across Maggie's vision, she lost herself in the darkness that those stars left behind.

When she came to, it seemed to be seconds later, but Maggie wasn't quite sure. She had only one thought in her mind: 'Get away, I have to get away.' The man in the trench coat had stopped his brutal attack. He wasn't even in the room with Maggie anymore. She tried to turn Josh's head to look for him, but she felt disconnected. His body wouldn't seem to listen to her commands anymore.

She could hear the man moving around in the bedroom muttering to himself. Now was her chance. If she were going to survive this, she needed to get Josh's body to pay attention to her commands.

'*GETUP*!' she thought to herself, directing the command as hard as she could to Josh's body. '*GET UP! HE'S GOING TO KILL YOU! HE'S GOING TO KILL ME!*

HE'S GOING TO KILL US! GET UP!' Maggie screamed within the confines of the flesh prison she was trapped in. '*HE'S GOING TO KILL US! PLEASE, GET UP!*' she begged to the immobile body. That moment of begging seemed to rekindle the connection between Josh's body and her mind. She felt his body moving to get up.

'*Come on, you can do it,*' she encouraged softly. Finally, she was in control again. The transition was so quick it left her blinded for a second. She reached forward to steady his body with the arm of the couch. She paused to let his eyesight clear. Then she pushed off of the couch and broke for the door. She made it out of the apartment before the man even noticed she had woken up.

She felt dizzy and tired, but still she ran. Running with all the life she had left in this male body she now owned. When she finally stopped running, she found herself outside of her old apartment building. She stopped herself just as she was about to ring upstairs.

She couldn't ring the buzzer. She couldn't turn to Emmy anymore. That part of her life was over now. She was a man…Josh…and like the note said, he would have to deal with it. Maggie was gone; she no longer existed. It was time to face the fact that *she* was now a *he*.

He was covered in beer and blood. All he wanted to do was go home to shower, change clothes, and sleep. But he couldn't go back to that apartment either. That life was gone too.

So, if he couldn't be Maggie and he definitely couldn't be Josh, then who was he supposed to be now?

He sighed and turned away from both of his lives to begin something new. He headed towards a motel not too far away from where he was.

In the daytime, the city was a wondrous, safe place, but at night the city seemed dark and ominous. Its dirty streets were a haven for all sorts of criminals just waiting for their next victim. As a woman, Maggie would never have been caught dead in this area. Even now, he shivered slightly in fear. He hadn't been in this body long enough to know how to fight with it. The thought hadn't crossed his mind that not too many people would want to mess with a six-foot-four man, with blood all over his face. He hadn't even thought to wipe it off.

He walked into the shabby motel's lobby. "I need a room," he practically croaked.

The woman behind the desk was visibly shaken. Her hand moved towards the phone.

"Don't...please," he begged her. "I drank a little too much....got in a fight....need a room.... Don't think I should drive in my condition," his slurred speech helped his story. He wondered when his jaw had taken a blow; he could barely move it. He pulled out his wallet and took out a credit card. He hoped that it would work.

"Right away, sir," the frightened women said.

The look in the woman's eyes reminded him of Emmy's eyes. She had that same look of fear. He wasn't quite sure that it was only the blood on his face that was scaring her. He wondered if his new body was really that threatening to people. He closed his eyes. Maybe somewhere deep inside, people knew something horrible had happened to him. Maybe they even knew that they could be next. It must have frightened them too much to even comprehend what they were actually afraid of. That would explain why Emmy was so cold to him. The mere sight of him frightened her so much that her defenses went up immediately.

Why couldn't Emmy just have known who she was? Why couldn't she see Maggie deep inside Josh's eyes? Why couldn't she have said, *'Maggie is that you? What happened to you? Come on in and I'll put on a pot of coffee and we'll figure this all out. We'll have you back to normal in no time.'*

"Are you alright, sir?" the woman's voice broke through his stupid fantasy.

"No," he replied, automatically. His voice sounded desperate and achingly raw. "My wife left me," he lied.

The woman softened immediately. Almost all the fear left her eyes, as she held the key out to him. He reached out his hand to take it. She placed the key in his hand and clasped his hand between hers. "I'm so sorry," she sympathized looking directly into his eyes. "You really should go to the hospital." She gestured to his face.

"I'll be alright. My wife's new boyfriend packs quite a punch," he stated, lifting his hand to his split lip. "At least the bleeding's stopped."

She nodded. "Your room is up the stairs, to your left, and it's the first door. Snacks are just down the hall," she informed him, finally letting his hand go. As she pulled away, he felt a bit of energy tickling his hand. He reached back out and grabbed the woman's hand. She jumped and the fear returned to her eyes. Immediately, he regretted it. There was no energy in her hand. What was he thinking? It was probably just static electricity.

"Thank you," he whispered. He pulled her hand slowly up to his broken lips and kissed it softly. She melted at the touch of his lips. "I may be staying here awhile," he murmured and winked.

She smiled and winked back.

He turned and walked slowly out the door, hugging his body as he walked. The part of him that was still Maggie longed to feel the warmth of a man's body holding her, but her body was gone. All that was left was this battered shell of a man that she never wanted to be. All that was left was one pitiful, lonely man.

He closed the door behind him and locked all the locks on it. He turned and looked at the shit hole of a room. That's when the reality truly sunk in: Maggie was trapped alone in a world that he barely understood anymore, with no money, no food, and no friends. He was utterly alone. He leaned against the door and started sobbing. He had a lot to learn about being a man. Especially how they could go through something so horrible and still not cry. He stumbled his way across the room to the bathroom.

He pulled off all of his clothes and stepped into the shower stall. He didn't bother to adjust the water; he just turned on the hot water and stepped under it. Maggie felt the pain of the water scalding his skin. He didn't care anymore. All he wanted was his own body back and if he couldn't have that then he'd rather be dead. He thought about it and if there was a way he could…he would have killed himself right then, but there was no way. He could have thought on that subject more, but he was too tired.

He turned off the water and toweled his body dry; Maggie barely even noticed what he had been so eager to look at the day before.

He crawled underneath the covers on the well-worn bed. He lay in the motel room from hell, naked, and he cried himself to sleep again.

9

Lilly's Apartment:

Eon & Lilly

Lilly woke feeling sore and stiff. Her shoulders were aching and she wanted to move them, but when she tried to, she couldn't. Eon had bound her wrists and tied them to the headboard.

"Eon?" she called out. Her voice was scratchy and weird sounding. Come to think of it everything felt strange...different. She could feel the after effects of the exchange tingling through her body. "No!" she whimpered as realization crashed upon her. She looked in the mirror at the end of her bed. She was no longer Lillian Mae; she was Maggie Reynolds. Eon had done it again. Against her will, he had gone and done it again.

"God damn it, EON!" she screamed, but no answer came to her.

She jumped as she heard a groan coming from next to her on the bed. "Who's there?" she asked.

"Shadow," the body on the bed whispered. It was her body, the one she had lived in for over 50 years. "My real name is Alex," the person whispered. "Where am I?"

Lilly could tell the spirit in her old body was a young boy, just by the way he moved.

"At my home," Lilly answered.

"What happened?" The boy sat up and rubbed his eyes. He looked first at her then down at his own hands. Almost as if he was checking to see if he too was tied up. "What's wrong with my hands?" He looked at Lilly accusingly. He cleared his throat and coughed. The same thing everyone did after the exchange. They tried to make their new voice sound like their old voice; it never worked. "What did you do to my voice?"

"It wasn't me." Lilly gave him the most sympathetic look she could muster in her current situation. He turned from her and noticed the mirror.

"No, don't look in the mirror," Lilly warned futilely as the boy moved closer to the mirror to see his face. "Try the glasses on the nightstand." Tears saturated her voice. This was the part she hated. This was the part that urged her to stop Eon.

The boy reached over and grabbed Lilly's glasses. He looked at them doubtfully, but placed them on anyway.

"What the...," he started, staring at his new face in the mirror. "WHERE AM I?" he screamed. "Where's my face?" He touched his new face with both hands repeatedly. "What happened to my face?" He turned to look at Lilly. "Who am I? Who are you? WHO ARE YOU? Who am I?" He turned back to the mirror, touching his new face again.

"Calm down," Lilly soothed. She was afraid he was going to pass out or go into an asthma attack.

"Calm down? Calm down?" he repeated, panicking. "How can I calm down? I'm an old lady! I was not an old lady before! I'm a man! GOD DAMN IT! I'M A MAN" He screamed at the face in the mirror.

"You're not that old," Lilly scoffed sullenly.

"What?" he turned to look at her. Her words seemed to break through his panic.

"I said: My body's not that old," Lilly repeated.

"Your body? This is your body?" the boy gestured to the body he now wore. "Where's my body? What did you do with it?"

"I don't know," Lilly answered. "You have to untie me."

"Why?" He looked at her suspiciously. "How do I know you're not the one who did this to me?"

"Because, I'm tied to the bed," she tried to hide her exasperation and stress the urgency of the situation. "Come on, we have to get out of here before he comes back."

"Who? Before who comes back?" the boy demanded.

"The man who did that to you. The man who took your body."

"Who is he? What is he? How could he do this? WHO IS HE?"

"Him," Lilly pointed her finger. The boy in her old body turned to look where she pointed. A teenage boy stood in the doorway, with Eon's essence staring at her.

"You? You're me." the boy in Lilly's body gasped. "What are you? What the fuck did you do to me?" he begged.

"Good, you're both awake." A wicked smile crossed Eons face as he completely ignored the newcomer. "Now we can have some real fun." He rubbed his hands together slowly.

"No, Eon, please," Lilly begged, as Eon shoved the boy-in-Lilly's-body back onto the bed.

"Please," the boy whimpered. "Don't," he begged, trying to fight back, trying to push Eon off of him. The elder woman was no match for the teenager that was holding her down.

Eon smiled a horrible smile that Lilly had never seen before on any of the faces her husband wore. Something had changed with Eon. He no longer seemed human anymore. The look she saw in his eyes was nothing short of demonic. He grabbed the nightgown on Lilly's old body and tore it off.

"No, oh God, no," Lilly whispered as she realized what he was going to do. "Don't do this, Eon. This isn't you. You're better than this."

"No, sorry Lilly, I'm not," Eon laughed a wicked laugh that seemed to echo through the room.

"Do you realize what you are doing?" She tried to reason with him. She tried to reach the part of him that was still human. "You're using that boy's body to rape his soul. You can't do this. It's depraved. You're depraved."

"I know. It's ingenious isn't it? I'm just helping him to accept his current situation." Eon glanced over at Lilly as he held the boy-in-Lilly's-body down. "I should have started doing this sooner." He turned back to the task at hand. "Don't even think about closing your eyes, Lilly." His voice had some tiny bit of power to it and Lilly found herself unable to look away or even close her eyes.

"Who are you?" Lilly asked sobbing.

"I'm Eon," he glanced back at her. "I'm you're Eon." Lilly could almost see the man she used to love in the eyes that stared at her.

"You are not my Eon," Lilly said in defiance. "You're a monster!"

10

Motel Room:

Maggie

When Maggie awoke, his head was fuzzy and sore. He stretched and yawned crying out in pain, both his jaw and his ribs ached with the effort. He scratched his face and realized that a beard had started to grow there. He felt as if he had been asleep for a hundred years, but he knew it must have been only a couple hours.

"What do I do now?" he asked himself as he got out of bed and walked over to the window. It was a dreary day outside. All he wanted to do was call Emmy. She had been Maggie's best friend for so many years. She had been there for Maggie when her parents died. She had been there for her when Dylan died. Mark was the only blood relative she had left, but Emmy had been more of a sibling to her then Mark had ever been. Thinking of Mark now made her regret that she hadn't been closer to her brother.

She sniffed back tears as she realized Maggie was gone and nobody would even miss her. That must be why Josh chose her. There she was, thinking about herself as a woman again. Referring to this man's body as a her…no…she was a man now.

He knew he couldn't call Emmy for help, as much as he wanted to, but maybe he could call Sunshine. He walked over to the phone and called Information. Information gave him the number to Lanaway's. He dialed the number hesitantly, not knowing what to say.

"Lanaway's. Can I help you?" a man's voice asked.

"Can I speak to Sunshine, please?" Maggie tried to disguise Josh's voice.

"Sorry, she's not working tonight," the man replied.

"Do you by any chance have her home phone?" Maggie asked, feeling stupid for asking for it.

"Actually I do, but I can't give it to you. It's against company policy. Now if that's all, I need to be getting back to work now."

"Yeah, sorry to bother you," Maggie was getting sick of apologizing to everyone.

He hung up the phone and picked up his jeans, the underwear still inside them. He pulled them both on, and as he buttoned them a thought occurred to him. Guys never clean out their wallets; Dylan's wallet had always been full of crap. He had even had a couple phone numbers of girls he had dated before he married Maggie.

Maggie took the wallet out and spilled the contents of it on the bed. Feeling like he was snooping, he sifted through a bunch of useless scraps of paper. He picked up a worn photo of the woman from the pictures in Josh's apartment. On the back in beautiful handwriting were the words 'I love you'. Underneath those words, there was a heart and the name Lauren. Maggie felt a single tear roll down his cheek. 'Lauren's dead.' The words echoed through Josh's head and somehow he knew they were true. For a split second, Maggie could remember two separate pasts: his past as a woman and his past as Josh. He had to sit down on the bed until the wave of nausea that came with the memories passed. Finally, after what seemed like an hour, the only past he could remember was his past as Maggie. His memory was back to normal, as normal as it could be for a man named Maggie.

When he sat down on the bed, a lone scrap of paper fluttered to the floor. He picked it up and immediately knew it was Sunshine's number. There was a small sun drawn in the corner of the paper.

Quickly, he grabbed the phone and dialed the number. It rang about five times and then her answering machine picked up. He almost hung up the phone, but he couldn't... He searched desperately for a phone number he could leave on the machine. He found some stationery in the nightstand. The motel's phone number was in the letterhead.

"Sunshine?" he asked after the beep. His voice came out as whisper. He wasn't even sure if the machine caught the voice. He cleared his throat, ready to try again.

The machine clicked off and Sunshine's voice came across the line. "Josh, is that you?" she asked.

"Yes," Maggie answered through gritted teeth. He wasn't Josh and he was tired of pretending that he was.

"Where are you?" Her voice was frantic. "Did you know that Frank's gone and fired you? You missed two days of work. Two no call-no shows is a fireable offense. You know that!" she scolded him.

"Maybe I can talk him into giving me my job back." It was a half-hearted response; he didn't want that job anyway.

"No way, Josh! That was your third time. You've had six no call-no shows. Frank was letting you slide because of Lauren, but he's tired of cutting you slack. Add that to your weird behavior lately, and he's glad to see you go. He used to like you, but now he can't stand you. Josh, what is going on with you? What's going on with us? What, were you just going to disappear without even saying goodbye?"

"What are you talking about? I just saw you last night!" Maggie shook his head. Trying to make sense of the avalanche of words he had just heard.

"That was three days ago, Josh." Sunshine's words broke through his confusion.

"Three days!!" Maggie cried out. How could three days have gone by? Had he really been sleeping for that long?

"Yeah, what were you doing? Did you find another girl?" He could hear the rejection in Sunshine's voice.

"No, Sun, nothing like that. I got my ass kicked, I must have been unconscious"

"Oh God, Josh. Are you OK?" Concern replaced the rejection in her voice.

"I don't know, maybe I should go to the hospital." Maggie touched his tender lip.

"You don't have insurance, remember? I can take you to the clinic," Sunshine offered. "Where are you?"

Maggie gave her the name of the motel and the room number, and then he lay back down on the bed. He closed his eyes and fell asleep.

11

Sunshine's Apartment:

The Man in the Trench Coat

The man in the trench coat pushed his way through the underbrush in the woods behind Sunshine's apartment complex. He sat down and waited. He had seen the two of them together many times since Lauren died. If the bastard went to anyone, he would run right into sweet little Sunshine's arms. Patiently, he opened his trench coat and pulled out a sawed off shotgun. He put the scope to his eye and looked at Sunshine's window. He could see her running around inside. She was frantically filling a suitcase.

Quickly, he made sure the gun's safety was still on and shoved it back into his coat. She was packing a suitcase for *him*; maybe she was in on it too. Maybe she was the one who tipped him off about Lauren. He pulled himself out of the underbrush and ran to his car, his gun hidden under the trench coat her wore. If he followed Sunshine, she would lead him to the bastard who killed Lauren. He took his shotgun out of his jacket, checked that safety once again and shoved it under the bench seat.

He put his car in drive and turned it around stopping next to the driveway to her apartment complex. But he was too late, her car was gone. He screamed in fury and slammed the palm of his hand into the steering wheel.

He needed Lauren, more than anything. He just wanted to feel her touch again, and if he couldn't feel that, then someone was going to pay.

He turned his car around again and left. He headed to the freeway towards the cabin where he had been staying for the past couple of days. Then he thought better of it. He turned just before the freeway entrance and pulled off the road in front of a cemetery. He paused, taking a moment to breathe in the fresh air. He thought about his shot gun, but he knew he wouldn't need it here.

He started to get out of the car, but stopped as a memory came to him. It was a memory of his mother that stopped him, but it wasn't his mother, was it? Then the pain hit him like a train, he doubled over, grunting. The pain seemed to be getting worse, every time it happened. He leaned over to reach his glove box and opened it. Inside, he found a switchblade. He expertly flicked out the knife's blade.

The pain was getting worse. The images of his mother and another woman were bombarding his brain. He pulled up the sleeve of his trench coat to reveal an arm covered in shallow slashes. He placed the knife against his skin and pulled. Nothing happened; the memories and the gut wrenching pain were still tearing through him. Pressing harder on the knife, this time a thin red veil of blood trickled down his arm. The pain seemed to ooze out with the blood and the man sighed in relief. He reached into the glove box again and pulled out a roll of gauze. He wrapped his arm in it and settled the trench coat gently back into place. He closed his blade and shoved it into the pocket of his black jeans.

Shaking, he lifted himself out of the car. He glanced around hoping no one else was in the graveyard. He hated coming here. He wished he didn't have to. He stopped walking and ran his hands through his oily hair. He couldn't remember the last time he had showered.

Why did he keep coming here? He wished he could just close his eyes and when he opened them, the world would be right again. He wanted this nightmare to be over. He shook his head and lowered his arms. He needed to stop thinking like that. This was his reality now. He glanced down at his hand. It was shaking again. The tremors were getting worse. He had to find the man that did this to him and make him pay, but first...

He walked towards the grave. He collapsed to his knees next to the grave and picked a rose out of the bouquet someone had place in front of her headstone. He held the rose tightly in his hands.

"Lauren…," he whispered softly as the thorns pierced his skin. "I will get the bastard that murdered you, Lauren. He will pay for what he did to you; for what he did to *us*!" He dropped the rose next to her headstone and pressed his face against the cool stone. He traced his finger across the engraving. "Lauren," he whispered and placed a single kiss on the picture of her encased in glass and set into the stone. He didn't want to leave her here in this place all alone, but he couldn't join her, not yet. He had a mission. After the mission was completed he would join her, by his hand or by whatever sickness was ravaging this body. His only hope was that he could complete his mission, before the sickness finished him. He had to fight. He had to keep himself alive and aware until it was over; until that bastard was dead.

He stood up from the ground using the tree next to her grave for balance. The roots of this tree were probably near Lauren's casket. He imagined them cradling her and guarding her. In a fit of emotion, he pulled out his switchblade again and carved into the tree: "Josh loves Lauren."

12

Motel Room:

Maggie & Sunshine

Maggie woke up to the sound of someone pounding on the door. Immediately he thought of the man in the trench coat. He got up quietly and moved stealthily towards the window. Slowly, he pushed the curtain aside and peeked out.

Sunshine was standing outside the motel room, pounding on the door, with a look of fear on her face. "Josh, it's me. Open the door,"

Maggie knocked on the window. Sunshine turned to look at him and he smiled as much as his broken lip would allow. Her whole face brightened once she locked eyes with him. He watched as all the fear seemed to melt away. A smile spread across her face and it touched Maggie's heart. It was the kind of smile that could light up even the darkest of days.

Maggie rested his forehead against the glass and took in the beauty of her. She pushed back her blond hair and pressed her forehead against the glass opposite his. She lifted her hand and placed it on the glass. He matched her hand and smiled again. She smiled back and laughed. Maggie's heart soared as her laughter grew louder. He reached over and unfastened the locks to let Sunshine in.

Sunshine walked in and set down the suitcase she had been holding. Her smile disappeared as she noticed his bare chest. He followed her gaze and saw so many bruises; they blended into one big bruise. His entire side was blue and purple. He looked up with tears in his eyes, his lip trembling. Sunshine had tears rolling down her face. She smiled a sad smile and spread her arms to take him in. He wanted to cry in her arms, but he was all cried out. He pulled back and smiled at her.

"You're a mess," she commented.

Maggie nodded. "I know."

"What happened?" She ran her finger tentatively across the bruise on his jaw.

"I was mugged." Maggie didn't know how to explain what happened, so he lied.

"I packed a suitcase full of stuff you would need," Sunshine gently kicked the suitcase at their feet. She wore delicate sandals with straps that wound up her legs. They reminded Maggie of the heels he had worn on his last date. She was wearing a beautiful red sundress with a white sweater over the top of it.

"Where did you get the stuff?" he grabbed her shoulders. "Please, tell me you didn't go to my townhouse."

Sunshine shook her head. "It's all the stuff that you brought over to my apartment," She turned and picked up the suitcase. Maggie shut the door and followed her to the bed where she opened the suitcase. "I got shirts, pants, undies...you name it. I also brought an electric razor, just in case. It definitely looks like you need it," she placed her hands on Maggie's cheeks and Maggie melted. He had to sit down on the bed; his legs had turned to jelly. Sunshine pushed aside the suitcase and sat down next to him on the bed.

"What's going on, Josh?" she reached out and brushed a lock of hair off of his forehead. "Do you still want to go to the clinic?"

Maggie shook his head. "He'll find me there. I have to hide from him."

"Who will find you?"

"The man who did this," Maggie gestured towards his chest. "I think, he thinks, I killed Lauren."

"What?" Sunshine exclaimed.

"I don't know!" Maggie clenched his fists and began to pound them against his temples.

"Stop it, Josh!" Sunshine grabbed his arms to still them. "You didn't kill Lauren, that Erik guy did. Not you."

"I don't know what's going on," Maggie admitted. "I'm so lost."

"It's OK," Sunshine soothed, staring intently into Maggie's eyes. "Listen, we'll get you cleaned up and fed, and then we will sit down and try to figure this all out, OK?" She raised her eyebrows and seemed to stare directly at the part of Maggie that was still Maggie; still a woman.

Maggie nodded, a tear rolling down his cheek.

"What's wrong?" Sunshine reached up and wiped the tear away.

Maggie reached up and caught her hand. He pressed it to his lips. "You are everything I needed."

Sunshine nodded and leaned forward to kiss Josh's lips.

Maggie's heart seemed to jump as he felt the energy again, like a bolt of lightning against his lips. It was the same feeling he had when he had brushed the clerk's hand. This time the energy was so much more powerful. Maggie felt as if he were swallowing fire as the energy burned down his throat and across his chest. He pulled away taking a deep painful breath.

Sunshine gasped. "What was that?" she asked, licking her top lip in pleasure.

Maggie stared in shock at Sunshine's lip. A tiny crack had broken through her lip, exactly where Maggie's lip had been split.

Sunshine lifted her hand to her lip and looked at the blood.

"What the…?" she asked, fear filling her eyes once more.

Maggie shrugged and shook his head. "I don't know, Sunshine. I don't know."

13

A Diner:

Maggie & Sunshine

Josh and Sunshine were sitting at a corner table, in the back of a small diner in the nicer part of town. Josh was clean-shaven and dressed in fresh clothes. He was beginning to feel like a man after shaving and showering. He had even stopped thinking of himself as Maggie. He was just Josh now, a man in love with the woman who sat next to him; the woman who brought sunshine with her wherever she went.

The suitcase of clothes and toiletries was sitting under the table at their feet. Sunshine insisted Josh leave that shithole motel and find a new one. She wanted Josh to come and stay at her apartment, but he refused. It was too dangerous there.

They were waiting for their food to arrive and pondering the events that led them here.

"So," Sunshine began a little shyly. She turned in her seat so she could see his face better. Her hand twitched a little in Josh's grip. She stared at their hands lying clasped on the table in front of them. "If you're not Josh, then who are you?"

Josh blinked at her in surprise. "How do you know that?" Josh asked suspiciously.

"Remember the other night at the boardwalk. I saw you…not Josh. I saw the real you."

"I thought that was a dream," Josh explained, his thumb beginning to trace little circles on the skin between her thumb and her index finger. She shivered in delight at his touch.

"You wouldn't believe me if I told you." Josh lowered his head. "Hell, I don't even believe me."

"Look, Josh...or whoever you are, I promise you. Whatever you tell me, I will believe you. I've known Josh and Lauren for a long time. I know that something happened to him when Lauren died. He changed, I mean totally changed. I don't think it was just grief or loss that changed him. It was something else; something physical or spiritual that changed in him. For a while he was cold, uncaring and well...very um...sexual," she paused, a small, sly, smile spread across her face. Josh felt a tiny bit of jealousy as she talked about having a past with the body he was now in. "And now, you...you are completely different than both of the other Joshes. You are beautiful and caring and sensitive. I know you're not the real Josh and...," she stopped, looking away nervously.

"And?" Josh prompted her.

"I know...well at least, I think I know...that you are or were...a woman," she said, flinching as if Josh would hit her or something.

"Is it that obvious?" Josh asked softly.

"No, I can just tell, because I know you. It was mostly the way you made love to me. You touched me exactly the way I wanted to be touched. You knew spots that most men don't know about. So, basically, you know too much about a woman, to be a man." She laughed a soft lilting laugh.

"I am...I was a woman," Josh admitted softly, choking a little on the last word.

"How did it happen?" It was her turn to caress the skin on his hand.

"I don't know," Josh looked sadly to the side, trying to avoid Sunshine's eyes. "My name was Maggie, but I guess now, you can just call me Josh." A tear rolled down his cheek. Sunshine reached up and wiped the tear from Josh's cheek. Josh flinched away from her touch; he was still in shock from his attack.

"Sorry," he whispered feebly.

"Does it hurt that bad?"

Josh nodded. He didn't want to explain that he was afraid of her touch because of the beating he took.

Sunshine pulled her hand away from his and put her arm around Josh's shoulders. She scooted closer to him and wrapped her other arm around him in an awkward hug. Josh's body relaxed into the circle of Sunshine's arms. This was all Josh wanted; someone to hold him. Even before he had become Josh, he had wanted that. The last person who had held him like this had been Dylan. It was all he could do to keep from crying. "Thank you," he whispered into her hair.

Sunshine pulled away from Josh and looked deep into his eyes. "You are so beautiful," Sunshine whispered.

Josh smiled. "Me or Josh?" he laughed sadly.

"You, Maggie," Sunshine whispered, she cupped his cheeks in her hands. "You are so strong, not many people would be able to handle what you've gone through." She smiled. "You're amazing."

Josh was taken aback as Sunshine kissed his lips passionately. It was very sensuous and soft. He knew that Sunshine wasn't kissing Josh; she was kissing Maggie.

"I love you," Josh murmured before he could stop himself. He was surprised that he said it, but he was even more surprised the he meant it.

"I love you too...," she replied and then she smiled. "Maggie," she whispered.

14

Boardwalk:

Maggie & Sunshine

"This is where it all happened, that's what you said, 'It happened here'." Sunshine pointed out softly as they approached the boardwalk, later that same evening.

Josh nodded sadly. Sunshine reached out and took his hand and squeezed it gently in support. Josh had told her everything he knew about what happened to him that night, while they ate their meals at the diner. After they left the diner, Sunshine got him checked in to a hotel closer to her apartment.

Josh looked up at Sunshine and gave her a half smile that didn't reach his eyes. Sunshine tried to take her hand away, but Josh stopped her. Instead, Josh interlocked his fingers with hers. Sunshine looked up with tears in her eyes.

"What's the matter?" Josh asked, after they'd been walking in silence for a while.

"You're so much more special than any of the other Joshes. You make me feel like a person. The first Josh was just a friend and then after Lauren died, he was a sex partner, but nothing more. He wasn't very nice to me at all."

Josh nodded. "I know how the first Josh felt losing the one he loved. I lost my husband almost four years ago, but it still hurts; it still aches."

"You were married? How old are you?" Sunshine asked.

"29," Josh replied. "I was married for four months, but we dated for about 2 years," he said sadly.

"That's so sad," Sunshine commiserated. "I'm 21. I hope the age difference doesn't bother you."

Josh shook his head. "My license says I'm 24."

"I've never been in love...until now," Sunshine said quietly. She turned quickly to gauge his reaction.

Josh stopped, turning to face her. She looked nervous. Josh kissed her lips softly. They kissed, standing in the middle of the sidewalk for a few moments.

"You know, it's quite strange walking down the street holding a woman's hand and not getting funny looks or even worse trouble."

"You've done this before?" Sunshine asked.

"Yes, once or twice. I'm bisexual. I hope that doesn't bother you."

"Not at all."

"How 'bout you?"

"Oh me, I'm as straight as they come...until now." Sunshine smiled again. "That is, if you consider this a lesbian relationship," she laughed nervously.

"I don't even know what to consider it," Josh sighed as they arrived at the hotel. The hotel room was cold when they entered it. "It's cold in here," Josh pointed out, stating the obvious.

"I know how to warm us up!" Sunshine replied seductively.

"I'm sure you do," Josh replied.

***

Waking up after a tiring session of love making, Josh rolled over to face Sunshine.

"Again?" he asked.

Sunshine smiled in delight. "You are so naughty. I like that."

As their lips met for what seemed like the thousandth time that night, Josh started to feel the strange energy building up inside him. He tried to pull away from Sunshine to break his connection with her, but she pushed herself against him again. He could feel the energy spreading as they kissed. Not only did he want her body sexually, but he wanted her body physically too. He wanted to be a woman again. Sunshine let out a muffled gasp of pain, but Josh couldn't seem to stop himself. He felt the energy spreading through his lips and into Sunshine. She was practically screaming now, but he couldn't force his hands to let go of her.

He began to feel dizzy again, like he was lifting out of his body. The feeling snagged a memory deep inside of Maggie's spirit and he realized what was happening. Violently, he shoved Sunshine away.

Sunshine lay at the bottom of the bed gasping for air. Josh curled up in the fetal position and began rocking.

"What was that?" Sunshine's voice was breathless and soft.

"It must be contagious. I tried to take your body," Josh stopped rocking and looked at her.

Sunshine still looked a little pale, but her breathing had returned to almost normal. She sat next to Josh and reached out to touch his face.

"NO!" he screamed and pushed her away so hard that she fell off of the bed and landed on the floor with a thud.

"Josh, what's wrong?" a look of fear filled her eyes.

Josh hated seeing that fear in her eyes. He wished he could take it away from her, but he knew he was the one who was it.

"Don't touch me," he warned in reply to her question. "You can't touch me anymore. I want your body too much."

Sunshine laughed, the fear draining out of her face. She smiled. "I want yours just as much," she whispered seductively.

"No, you don't understand. I want to be inside your body. I want to be you. I want you to be in this body" he pounded his chest for emphasis "and I want to be in there. I want to be a woman again," Josh paused, taking a big breath. "I can make it happen. I can trap you in here, but I don't want to. I love you too much to do that to you," Josh couldn't stop the tears from falling.

The fear entered Sunshine's eyes again, but this time it was distant and overshadowed with love. "It'll be OK,

Maggie." She crawled her way across the carpet to the head of the bed as she spoke. "It really will, we'll find out who did this to you and we'll get your body back." She reached out to brush back the hair from of Josh's eyes.

"Don't touch me, not yet," Josh whispered. "It's still there. I can feel it." The energy was slowly turning into a simmering pain deep inside of Josh's skull, like an old wound opening up again.

"Oh Maggie," she said, stopping just before she touched his face.

"Stop calling me that!" Josh yelled. "I'm not *her* anymore. Maggie's dead! There's only Josh here."

"I don't believe that! I can't believe that!" Anger filled her eyes. Josh didn't see the anger there because his eyes were closed tight. If he saw her right now, he knew that he wouldn't be able to stop himself from taking her. "Why would you want my body? Unless you were still Maggie wanting to be a woman?! Maggie's not DEAD and don't ever say that again!" She jumped up off of the floor and started searching for her clothes.

Josh was in so much pain, that he could only lie there listening as Sunshine got dressed and grabbed her car keys.

"It's true," he assured her through gritted teeth.

Sunshine stopped at the door barely able to stop herself from running back to Josh's side...Maggie's side. She swung around to look at him. "If that is true, and Maggie is dead like you say," she started calmly, pausing to search for the right words. "If Maggie is dead, then so is our love!" She slammed the door and left Josh, who was now staring at the door, with red, swollen, eyes and a throat raw from crying.

15

Sunshine's Apartment:

Maggie, Sunshine &

The Man in the Trench Coat

The man in the trench coat watched from his car as Sunshine's car pulled up in front of her building. He was filled with excitement at the prospect of possibly getting his hands on the bastard who killed Lauren. He was let down once again as Sunshine exited the car alone. The light from the slowly rising sun played across her face in speckles as she crossed the street to her apartment. That is when he noticed her face; her lip was split and her eye was bruised.

He was filled with rage that the bastard would hurt his friend. He would wait for her to return to the bastard, even though deep inside he was hoping she wouldn't. He would get that bastard back for both of the women that had once been part of his daily life, his wife Lauren and their friend Sunshine. He would have the bastard fix everything and then he would make the bastard pay for all the pain he caused.

He blinked in surprise as he realized that Sunshine was staring directly at him. She started to walk towards his car. He opened the door and climbed out, careful not to bang his aching arms.

"Sunny," he greeted her, relieved to see her, forgetting that he now wore another man's body.

"SCREW YOU!" she returned. "You killed Lauren!" she accused.

"I didn't!" he argued, his voice unconvincing. He realized now that he was in the body of the man that killed Lauren. To Sunshine, and everyone else in the world, he was the murderer. He *was* the man that killed Lauren.

"Get out of here!" she demanded. She shoved him against his car. "GET OUT OF HERE AND DON'T COME BACK!" she screamed. "I DON'T WANT TO SEE YOUR FACE EVER AGAIN!"

"Sunshine...," he begged. "I have to tell you I'm really J..." She cut him off.

"Sorry? Is that what you were going to say? You're SORRY!" she screamed. "You killed my best friend and now you're telling me you're sorry." She closed her mouth and stared at him. "As if that would fix everything, I'm supposed to forgive you for killing her and ruining Josh's life?"

He was trying to make his mouth work; trying to think up an answer. He was trying to think of a way to explain what had happened to him.

Sunshine narrowed her eyes. "You deserve to rot in jail for what you did."

"I didn't do it. I didn't kill Lauren," he begged her to believe him.

"Don't you dare lie to me!" Sunshine shook her head. "I was there, Erik. I saw everything."

"It wasn't me. I swear," he whispered in futility. "I love Lauren. I love her with all my heart."

Sunshine couldn't stop herself from slapping him. "You don't deserve to love her," she spat out.

"Sunshine," he begged, raising his hand to touch his face where she had slapped him. She ignored him.

"You have until I get into my apartment before I call the cops," Sunshine turned and ran to her building. She scrambled to get her keys out. She was too afraid to look back and see whether he was following her or not. She let out a sigh of relief when she heard his car start.

"I didn't do it!" he called through the open window of his car. "No matter what you saw, I didn't do it. The man who you think is Josh did it! He won't hesitate to kill you too!" He paused as Sunshine stared back at him like a deer in the headlights. "He's a dangerous man, Sunshine. Look what he did to your face."

Sunshine squeezed through the door and slammed the door behind her. She fell to the ground, just inside her door. She found herself wishing she had rented an apartment that had an outer unit door. It would have doubled her protection right now. She stood up and locked all of the locks on her door, including the chain latch that she never used. She looked around her apartment and it seemed cold and empty. All at once she started to regret the words she had screamed at Josh. She dug through her purse until she found the number for Josh's new hotel. She picked up her phone and called the number.

"Sunshine?" his voice asked in a hoarse whisper.

"Yeah, it's me, Josh. I'm scared," she sat back down in front of the door.

"What happened?" Josh sat up in his bed.

"Erik, the guy who killed Lauren was here. He was waiting outside my apartment. He threatened me, Josh, and I'm so scared. He was at my home."

"Is he still there?" Josh was afraid for Sunshine's safety. "Can you come back here?"

"I think he's gone. I told him I was going to call the cops."

"Well, wait there for a little while to make sure that he's really gone and then come back over. I want you with me so I can protect you," Josh instructed.

"OK," Sunshine was glad that Josh was concerned about her. There was no way that Josh could kill her. No matter what that man said. He was crazy anyway. She thought she remembered someone saying that he was going to use an insanity plea at the trial.

"Keep talking, Sunshine. I like hearing your voice."

"I'm so scared, Josh," she whispered into the phone. "He knew my name. He called me Sunny, like he was glad to see me. I think he's the same guy who's after you. He told me to stay away from you. He said you were dangerous. He said that you killed Lauren, but I know it wasn't you. He told me to look what you did to my face," she babbled as she stood up and walked over to the mirror. "I don't know what he meant... HOLY SHIT!" she couldn't help crying out as she stared at her reflection in the mirror.

"What's wrong Sunshine? What's the matter?" Fear began to fill Josh's mind. "What's going on?"

"I'm OK. I just need you to do me a favor," she tried to calm his fears. "I need you to look in the mirror, OK?"

"For what?"

"Just do it!" Sunshine demanded, more forcefully than she had wanted to.

Josh stood up and walked over to the dresser. He stared at the mirror in awe. His face was completely healed. He had no cuts, no bruises, nothing. His chest was smooth and healthy looking. He poked experimentally at his side where his bruises had been; there was no pain whatsoever.

"Sunshine, unbutton your dress."

"Josh, this is no time for that..." He heard a cry from the other line and he knew what he suspected was true. "What the hell is going on, Josh? I have bruises all over my chest." She gasped in pain and Josh knew that she had touched one of them.

"I don't know. I think maybe it's a side effect of what happened." Josh paused, staring into his own eyes trying to see the Maggie that was hidden deep within. "It looks like I gave you all of my pain. All of my bruises are gone. Everything is; I'm completely healed," Josh explained sadly. "I'm sorry."

"I don't understand,"

"Neither do I," Josh admitted. "Just come over as soon as you can. I'm going to go take a long hot bath. Just come on in when you get here. You have the key, don't you?"

"Yes, I do. Maybe I'll take a bath too,"

"OK, I'll see you in a while."

"I love you."

"I love you too," Josh hung up the phone and rubbed his eyes. He had been napping when Sunshine called. He walked into the bathroom and took off the jogging pants that he had pulled on after Sunshine left. He didn't like the feeling of being naked. It made him feel vulnerable, although going around topless was such a wonderfully freeing sensation to the woman that was buried deep inside the man.

Josh turned on the water in the tub. He placed a towel on the toilet seat and sat down on it, closing his eyes as he waited for the tub to fill.

The bathroom door was still open and so were the curtains in the main part of the hotel room. Even though Josh's room was on the 18th floor he was still afraid someone might be watching him. He just didn't have the energy to get up and close the curtains. Suddenly, the bathroom door slammed shut and he could hear the curtains being drawn.

"Sunshine?" he called out automatically.

He reached down for his jogging pants and pulled them back on. He opened the bathroom door and examined it closely. He felt the air around the door for breezes that could have blown it shut. Then he moved over to the curtains and examined them closely, but found nothing unusual. No one seemed to be in the room with him. He sat down on the bed trying to figure out how the door and the curtains had gotten closed.

He decided he was too creeped out to take a bath. Immediately after he thought that, the water turned off. Was he causing this somehow? Was he making this happen? His head was beginning to ache, but he tried to concentrate on the hotel pen on the nightstand. He called it to his hand and it came automatically as if it were attached to a string.

"What the hell is this all about?" he asked aloud. He focused his energy on a few other things in the room and found that he could move them too. Finally, he was so tired and headachy that he couldn't even keep his eyes open. He collapsed down on the bed and fell asleep.

16

Lilly's Apartment:

Lilly & Shadow

"Eon?" Lilly moaned as she woke up. Her body was sore and aching. He had raped her too. After he was finished with the boy, he raped her. Her own husband raped her. He wasn't her husband anymore. He was nothing to her; nothing at all.

She rolled over, for the first time realizing that she was no longer tied up. "Shadow?" she asked, turning over the body lying next to her. There was no answer from Shadow. She felt for a pulse and found it. "Shadow, wake up," she begged.

"I'm not Shadow," the voice whispered softly.

"Who are you?" Lilly asked in fear. Had Eon switched them again?

"My name is Lilly," the voice whispered.

"No, Dammit! Don't give in. Do not give up. You're Shadow. Your real name is Alex," Lilly reminded the boy trapped in her old body.

"No, I'm Lilly," the boy insisted.

"No, I AM LILLY!" Lilly said forcefully. The boy cringed as if Lilly would hit him. "You're Shadow, a teenage boy."

"I am?" the boy asked, looking around nervously as if expecting to see Eon reappear in the boy's body. Lilly thought to herself, 'This is the worse form of autophobia there is.' Most people, who suffer from fear of self, don't really have to be afraid of their actual body coming to rape them or worse: kill them.

"Yes," Lilly urged.

"I am," the boy agreed.

"We have to get out of here."

"We do?"

"Yes," Lilly said, looking deep into the boy's eyes. He was in an extreme state of shock. He was probably suffering from posttraumatic stress disorder. He stared back at her with no emotion in his eyes.

"If we stay here, he'll come back," she explained to the boy.

The boy started shaking. "No." He looked around quickly. "We have to go."

"You need to stand up now. Slowly, you have arthritis," Lilly warned the boy.

"I do?"

Lilly nodded, blinking back tears. Even though she hated what happened here, she still couldn't help feeling enormous relief and joy that her arthritis was gone.

"I hurt,"

"I know," Lilly replied, trying to put clothes on the boy. "We have to hurry."

"No, it doesn't matter, we're dead anyway."

"NO!" Lilly yelled. The boy jumped. "I'm sorry. I didn't need to yell. It does matter. We need to find him and get your body back."

A look of sheer terror filled the boy's borrowed eyes. "No...no, no, no, no, no," he began chanting. "I don't want to go back. I don't want to see him again," the boy cried, clinging to her.

"OK, OK, we won't find him. We'll just run away. We'll go somewhere safe."

"Safe," the boy repeated. Lilly wiped away tears from the boy's borrowed face.

"Let's go Miss Mae."

"Who is that?"

"You are," she whispered with tears in her voice.

"I'm Mae?" the boy asked.

"Yes, you're my Mae," Lilly said, choking back more tears. She knew this was the best thing for the boy. His essence was too fragile to try and accept what was really happening. She told herself it was only for the boy's sake she did this, but in truth it was mostly for her own sake that she did it. She missed her daughter more than anything and she knew deep down this body remembered its original owner.

"Are you my mommy?" Mae asked.

Lilly nodded. "You don't look like her."

Lilly shook her head. "Daddy put me in a new body," Lilly told Mae. She knew this wasn't her Mae, but it didn't matter. It was Mae back in her own body.

"Daddy is a bad, bad, man," Mae seemed to have reverted back a younger version of herself.

"Yes, he is," Lilly sobbed. "A bad, bad man," she repeated.

17

Hotel Room:

Maggie & Sunshine

"Josh, honey wake up," Sunshine's voice intruded on his dream.

"I had the worst dream," he groaned. "I dreamt I was a vampire. But instead of blood, I ate souls."

"It's over now," Sunshine soothed. "I'm sorry about what I said. I'll love you no matter who you are." She wrapped her arms around him.

"Thanks. I'm sorry too, but it was for your own good. I don't want to …eat…your…soul," Josh said slowly, as he connected his dreams with reality. "Oh God, am I a vampire?"

"No, you're not! You're Josh,"

"But I wasn't before."

"No, you weren't," she agreed. "But you are now. You're not some silly vampire. You said it yourself, you were trying to take my body, not eat my soul," she reminded him.

Josh nodded. "I don't want to hurt you anymore."

"You won't," she kissed him gently on the lips. This time the pain stayed away. He kissed her back, until she pulled away.

"I have an idea," Sunshine announced.

"What kind of idea?"

"I'll call your house…. Maggie's house and ask for her. Maybe, whoever took your body went back there. Maybe your friend, what's her name?" She paused, waiting for Josh to supply the name.

"Emmy."

"Right, Emmy. Maybe Emmy will know where your body is," she smiled. "Then we can get you back in your real body."

"Sunshine?"

"Yes."

"Will you still love me if I go back? Will you still love me when I'm a woman again?" Josh was afraid that the answer would be no.

Sunshine thought for a few minutes. "It may be a little hard at first, but I can't see myself living without you in my life," she replied honestly. "Are you feeling alright?" she asked, noticing for the first time how pale he looked.

"Yeah, I just have a really bad headache," Josh answered. Then he remembered what had happened after she called. "Hey!" he yelled out, startling her.

"What?" Sunshine laughed

"I can move things with my mind. Want to see?" he asked, sitting up.

"Sure," Sunshine answered skeptically.

"Watch the pen," he instructed. He tried to call the pen to his hand like he did before, but it didn't work. All that came to him was a pounding ache in his head.

"Maybe, it was just a dream," Sunshine suggested after he tried for a while, with no results.

Josh was completely stumped; he knew it wasn't a dream. It was real, just like the bruises that were now on Sunshine's body.

Josh gave Sunshine Maggie's phone number and he continued to try and move the pen. His headache was getting worse with every try.

"OK, Emmy said that Maggie hasn't called or come home in over a week and she's really worried about her. She filed a missing persons report and gave them your description as a 'creepy character' lurking around asking questions about Maggie. She told them she thought you had something to do with her disappearance," Sunshine explained after she hung up the phone.

"Great! Not only is someone trying to kill me, but now I am also wanted in suspicion of my own kidnapping,"

Josh rubbed his temples with the palms of his hands. "If it wasn't for you, Sun, I would seriously be thinking about suicide."

"You wouldn't," Sunshine whispered in disbelief.

"Yes, I would," Josh asserted softly, reaching out for her hand.

"Maybe you should call there and pretend that you've heard from Maggie and she told you to call Emmy or we could write Emmy a letter or something," Sunshine suggested, taking Josh's hand and placing it against her heart.

"No, it doesn't matter anymore," Josh's voice was filled with sorrow. "Maggie's as good as dead anyway."

"Don't start that again, please," Sunshine begged.

"Think about it, love. Do you really think I'm ever going to get my body back? Because I don't," Josh admitted sadly.

"You have to have hope," Sunshine urged softly. She raised his hands to her lips and kissed them gently.

"Why? All I want to do is give up. I want to go away with you and start a new life. I can't handle this anymore, Sun, I just can't."

"Well I'm here with you now and if you even think about suicide again... I'll kill you," she whispered, just loud enough for Josh to hear her.

"Isn't that the point?" Josh asked, pulling away from her and standing up.

"I'll do something bad. I will," she threatened. She stood up and wrapped her arms around him again.

He laughed a hollow laugh. "I can't promise that I won't."

"Just don't," she begged. "Now get dressed, I'm hungry. We should go to the park for a picnic." Sunshine untangled her arms from around Josh and then slapped his butt. "Let's go!"

Josh smiled and resisted the urge to kiss her.

He watched her disappear into the bathroom and then he pulled out a black tee shirt from the suitcase she brought for him. He turned to look out the window at the daytime city below. This was, by far, the nicer part of the city. He could almost see the boardwalk from his window. It was so small and distant from so high up. He wondered idly what it would feel like to fall all those stories down to his death. As he stared down at the ground, he was filled with vertigo. Peering down made his knees weak. He felt himself falling and falling; spinning through the air.

Sunshine came out of the bathroom just then and ran over and caught him before he hit the floor.

"Josh?" Sunshine said, struggling to hold him up. "Josh? What happened?"

Josh blinked up at her. He stood up to his full height and stared down at her. "I just got dizzy that's all. I'm OK now."

"Where were you?" Sunshine asked.

"What do you mean where was I?"

"It was like you were gone," Sunshine tried to explain.

"Gone?"

"Daydreaming."

"Oh, I was just remembering,"

"Remembering what?"

"Josh," he lied. "I was remembering the Josh that stole my body."

She startled him by wrapping her arms around his chest. "I love you," she said in an almost singsong voice.

Josh turned to face her. Sunshine loosened her grip just enough for Josh to turn around, but kept her arms locked tight. Josh was swept away by the emotion filling him. He had to kiss her. He had to respond in some way to her overture, but in the end he knew he couldn't. He knew if he kissed her; if he even touched her bare skin, the temptation would be too great. If the energy built up again, he wouldn't be able to stop it…not this time.

"I can't," he whispered, seconds before their lips touched. He pulled away as far as her arms would let him go. Sunshine's eyes filled with tears and she dropped her arms.

"Why won't you kiss me? Don't you love me anymore?" she begged.

"I do love you. That's why I can't kiss you. I don't want to hurt you anymore." The words seemed familiar to Josh for some reason. He felt as if he heard them before, back when he was still a woman, back when he was Maggie. While he pondered those words Sunshine took advantage of his dropped defenses and kissed him. The kiss was long and passionate.

"See, you won't hurt me," Sunshine assured him in a luscious voice.

"Not now, but maybe next time I will. I can't control it," Josh whispered desperately.

"FINE! Then don't kiss me anymore!" Sunshine stalked across the room. She stopped in front of the mirror staring at her blackened eye. She touched it and flinched in pain. "Look what loving you has done to me," she said absently, more to herself than to Josh.

Josh moved across the room to where she stood in front of the mirror. He gently moved her silky, sweet smelling hair and placed a soft kiss on the inside of her neck. Suddenly, Josh could feel the power again. He felt it building up deep inside, but he couldn't seem to stop it. He just wanted to take all of Sunshine's pain away. He didn't want her to live a life of love not shown. His entire body tensed as he kissed her again, roughly, biting a little. He could feel her heartbeat quicken just underneath her skin. He felt like the vampire from his dream getting ready to have a juicy meal.

"Stop it Josh!" she yelled and shoved him away. There was a panicky fear in her eyes as she stared at herself in the mirror. Josh followed her gaze to find that her face was once again clear of bruises. "I saw it," she gasped in horror. "I watched it! You took my pain away and the bruises on my face went away and now they are back on yours," she stuttered, her voice shaking in terror. "What are you?" she begged. "What the hell are you?" She started to back away from Josh. Involuntarily, he held up his hand and commanded her to stop.

He concentrated and pulled her towards him using his newfound powers. She stumbled forwards to him. He reached out and caught her, before she fell. She cringed at his touch.

"You're not human," she whispered. "You're not human…not anymore!" she accused and pushed past him. She ran towards the door. Josh tried to stop her again, but he couldn't make his power work again.

Sunshine's words stung Josh. They ached with a truth that he didn't want to believe. He wasn't human anymore. He was a monster.

Josh shook himself out of his daze and chased after her. He ran down the hallway, but she reached the elevator first and closed the door before he reached it. Josh sprinted for the stairs. He dashed down them three at a time.

Josh exploded out of the lobby in a fury and ran smack dab into Sue. "Sue?" he asked, helping her stand up again. He knew this was Maggie's oldest friend and her brother's fiancé. Sue looked up at him in surprise.

"How do you know my name?" she demanded.

"Don't you remember? It's me, Josh. You fixed me up with your friend Maggie." Josh explained.

"I never fixed you up with Maggie."

"Are you sure?" Josh's skin began to crawl as he realized that this 'Josh' guy was indeed a total stranger.

"Of course I'm sure. I fixed her up with Graham from Accounting and you don't look like Graham from Accounting." Sue's eyes seemed to be looking past him. "Oh my God!" Sue whispered as her eyes opened wider in shock. "LADY, LOOK OUT!" she screamed. Josh turned to see why Sue was yelling.

Josh looked just in time to see Sunshine running across the street. He watched in horror as a car slammed into her, throwing her into the air like a ragdoll.

"NO!" Josh screamed out. "SUNSHINE!" He ran towards Sunshine's broken body. It was twisted in such a way that Josh was sure there was no way she would survive.

He fell to his knees next her, rocking back and forth. His voice seemed to be stuck repeating her name in the most pitiful voice he'd ever heard. He had to look away from the empty eyes that stared back at him.

"I love you, Maggie," Josh heard Sunshine's voice whisper in his ear, even though the corpse's lips never moved.

He turned his head to look towards her voice but there was nothing there. She was gone. The only person who knew who Josh really was, now dead and gone.

Josh looked around at the crowd gathering around him. "Who did this?" he asked, expecting to hear Maggie's voice, but he was surprised when Josh's angry, sorrow-filled voice repeated the words over and over. "Who did this?" he growled, focusing on the nearest gawker. Sue was standing next to the person he was staring at. The gawker shrugged sadly.

"Josh?" Sue asked, unsure of whether she had the correct name or not. "I'm so sorry. I tried to warn her, but the guy didn't stop. It looked like he sped up to hit her." Sue accused.

"Where is he?" Josh growled. "WHERE IS HE?"

Sue looked around. "He's gone. He never stopped."

"WHERE IS HE?" Josh screamed again, nothing was left of Maggie. All that was left was a man filled with so much rage and anguish he couldn't contain it. He had to find Sunshine's killer. He had to find him and make him pay.

With tears streaming down his face, he looked down at Sunshine. He stared into her glassed over eyes and saw not only Sunshine lying there, but Maggie too. His past self was dead and gone. All that existed now was a lonely, angry man named Josh.

He reached down with a shaking hand and closed Sunshine's eyes. "She's gone," he whispered softly and looked up at the crowd. "She's gone!" he said, louder this time, for all to hear. He bent down and gently kissed her lips.

"I love you Sunshine," he whispered into her ear. "I love you," he inhaled deeply. The scent of blood was so overpowering that could barely catch the scent of her hair.

He stood up slowly, not wanting to leave his love behind. He wiped away his tears and ran. He ran away from Sunshine's corpse; away from the crowd; away from the sirens screaming through the air. He ran away from it all. He remembered when he used to enjoy running, but now he only ran to stop thinking of her death. Running was the only way he could stop the scene of her death playing over and over again in his head.

18

On the Street:

Eon

Eon tried the doors on every car parked on the street until he finally found one that was unlocked. He didn't know where he was going, but he knew what he needed to do. This body was already rejecting him. He had to find another one, and fast.

He opened the door and climbed in, checking the usually hiding spots for spare keys. Finding none, he proceeded to hot wire the car. It was a useful skill he picked up years and years ago. Sometimes if the body he wore had a latent ability he could use that power to start the car, but this body had none.

He paused as his vision doubled and the pain in his stomach began. He couldn't deal with this, not now, not while he was in the process of a crime. He slapped his face and pushed the pain down deep inside.

He pulled out into traffic and started to cruise. He was trolling for specimen. Any strong healthy man would do; he needed a man. He was tired of women. He never wanted to be a woman again, but he knew necessity dictated his choices, not want.

He blinked in disbelief as he saw Maggie. Well, he saw Josh, but he knew Maggie was in there. Maggie was standing there talking to a woman. Eon was so busy looking at Maggie, that at first he didn't see the other woman crossing the street. He saw the woman Maggie was talking to point and scream first. He looked back just in time to realize he was about to run over a woman…not just any woman. Sunshine stood before him, like a deer frozen in headlights.

He paused for a split second as his foot hovered above the brake. This woman had always been suspicious of him. She knew what he was; he was convinced of it. He moved his foot back to the gas and pressed the pedal down. Sunshine would never again give him pleasure and surprisingly, he found that he didn't care. Lilly was right; he didn't care. The only two people he actually cared about were himself and Maggie, in that order.

The car seemed to buck backwards as he collided with the sultry blond. The engine sputtered and almost died, but luckily kept running. He squealed his tires as he tore off into the city. It felt good to kill randomly, something he had never intentionally done. Anytime someone died from the switch, that wasn't his fault. He didn't actually kill them; their bodies just gave way. There was only one guy he actually did try to kill, but that was long ago.

If Lilly had been following his every move, she might have known about that. She might have written it in her vicious little journal of hatred. Eon couldn't risk that laptop falling into the wrong hands. Lilly could turn it in to the cops or worse; she could turn it in to The Guardians. Lilly couldn't do that, she didn't know about The Guardians. He never told her about them.

He had never told anyone about The Guardians. Who would ever believe that a small army of magic users protected the human race from evils like him? So far in his massive life, he had managed to fly under the radar of The Guardians and he hoped that it would stay that way. He did not need the added stress of The Guardians chasing him.

He had to get that laptop. He had to kill Lilly. Could he actually kill her, his wife of over 130 years? He wasn't sure if he could, but he was going to try. He parked the car in an alleyway and got out. He pulled a picture out of his pocket. It was a picture of Erik and his precious Angel. He chuckled as he dropped the picture in the stolen car. Chalk one more murder up to Erik Summers.

19

The Boardwalk:

Maggie

Josh stopped running as he reached the boardwalk, the place where his life had changed forever. He threw back his head and wailed in sorrow. Why did this have to happen to him? What had he done as Maggie to ever deserve the hell he was going through now?

He was jobless, penniless, and homeless. He was tired, hurt and angry, but most of all, he was alone. No one knew who he was or who he had been. At least with Sunshine, he could forget all that and concentrate on being in love: on the sunlight in her hair and the dimples that appeared whenever she smiled. Sunshine alone made this hellish nightmare bearable. But now she was gone and he was alone, so utterly alone.

He couldn't see himself living much longer without her, without his Sunshine. He had to do something, find out who killed her. No, he didn't need to find out who killed her. He already knew. It had to have been the man in the trench coat, the man that was stalking both Sunshine and him. What did Sunshine say his name was? Erik? He knew who her killer was, but what could he do about it? He couldn't go to the police, not without proof, not without telling them everything. How could he stop the man from killing him? How could he keep himself safe, when he couldn't even protect Sunshine from the man's wrath?

He screamed out in anger. He wanted to destroy something. He wanted to kill someone. He wanted the man to pay for what he had done.

There was nothing left for him to do but run. He would run his anger and sadness off. He would run until he didn't feel anything anymore. He turned from this horrible spot and ran into the woods. He ran so far and so fast that he lost himself. There was nothing left, but the ground at his feet and the wind through his hair. He ran until he was so lost, he would never find his way home.

He finally collapsed and rolled next to a tree. His body was heaving and shaking with sobs. He was shivering in the cold air of the nighttime forest. When had night arrived? He didn't know. He couldn't breathe from sobbing so hard. He closed his eyes and slowly fell into a deep sleep.

***

Josh awoke quickly to a pain, like fire, racing through his body. He cried out, but the cry was muffled. Something was in his mouth. His stomach began to cramp up; all of his muscles began to follow. He screamed as loud as the gag in his mouth would let him. The pain was similar to menstrual cramping, only it wasn't localized in his ovaries...her ovaries...his...hers... It didn't matter anymore, not with this pain. Nothing mattered, except for the fire in his brain.

"You know this pain," a familiar voice whispered into his ear. "You've felt it before."

Josh vaguely remembered when he was Maggie; this was the pain she felt when she was first trapped in this body. It was a pain that felt like her entire soul was being ripped out.

"Oh yes, you know what this feels like. It's your body rejecting your soul; a soul that doesn't belong. YOU SON OF A BITCH!"

Josh remembered the voice then, but it didn't matter. The pain was gone as he dropped into the dark oblivion of unconsciousness.

20

Lilly's Apartment:

Lilly & Mae

Lilly anxiously chewed on her borrowed nails, as they waited for the elevator to reach the lobby. This was not the first time she had to run away from Eon. Lately she had been running after him not away from him. Trying to keep up with him was hard enough. Trying to keep away from him should prove easier. She helped Mae out of the elevator.

"I'm going to put you in a home," Lilly explained. "You'll be safe there. Daddy won't be able to find you."

Mae nodded. "Safe," she whispered, clutching her handbag to her chest. "Momma will keep me safe," she nodded again. Lilly stared at her in wonder. It was always so strange to her how completely the soul changed. The boy had been so traumatized that she could not even see a remnant of him within Mae's body.

"You know I love you, right?" Lilly asked, still staring into Mae's eyes.

Mae nodded. "I love you too, Mommy. I missed you; I was gone for a long time wasn't I?"

"Yes you were, my love, but it's time to go now." Lilly led her out onto the street. They made it to the street corner when an alarm on Mae's wristwatch went off.

"Shit! Give me your purse," Lilly instructed. She took the purse and started digging through it fervently. "Where is it? Where is it?" she asked. "For the love of God, don't tell me I forgot to pack my insulin. I mean your insulin." Of course it was easy for her to forget now that she wasn't in that body, now that she was in a healthy young body.

"Insulin?" Mae asked.

"Yes, baby, remember your shots?" She hated to remind Mae of them since they were not something Mae had been fond of as a child. In fact Eon would have to hold the screaming child down while Lilly injected her. It was a hereditary condition and what had eventually killed Lilly's original body. She cringed as she remembered that part.

"We have to go back for them, you won't survive without them." She handed Mae her purse and grabbed her hand heading back to the apartment building.

"But, I don't want to go back," Mae begged her sadly.

"We have to, my love. You will get very sick if we don't," Lilly explained.

Mae shook her head. "I don't care!" She planted her feet and refused to move.

"Mae!" Lilly stopped and looked at her young daughter in an old body. "I am your mother," she whispered. "You have to listen to me!"

"You don't look like my mommy," Mae pointed out.

"I am. You remember what daddy does, don't you?" Lilly took both of her hands gently, remembering the arthritis in her joints.

"Daddy is always a different person," Mae answered.

"Exactly and how can you tell who daddy is?" Lilly was getting impatient. She didn't have time for this. They needed to get out of here before Eon found them.

"Look into his eyes and I'll know Daddy by the way his soul looks," Mae responded.

"Very good," Lilly opened her eyes wide and stared into Mae's. "Now look into my eyes just like that and you'll see me."

Mae obeyed and searched Maggie's eyes for the soul of her mother. "There you are," she laughed. "I found you."

"Good, now we need to go back to my home and get your insulin."

"No.," Mae stood her ground.

"Why not?"

"I remember what he did to us. He took my body and gave it to you. He's not my daddy anymore. He killed me."

Lilly's heart broke at the words her daughter whispered. How could she remember that? Her mind must have supplied her with Lilly's memories.

"I remember everything he ever did to you," she confirmed Lilly's guess. "I just don't want Daddy to hurt me ever again."

"Don't worry, he won't hurt you. I promise. He won't even be there."

"You promise?"

"I promise," Lilly vowed, hoping that she could keep that promise. Mae finally began walking with Lilly back into the building.

21

Unknown Location:

Maggie &

The Man in the Trench Coat

Slowly Josh waded through the darkness of his oblivion. He could feel warmth and smell the smoke of a fire nearby. He tried to move his body closer to warm his frozen bones, but he couldn't move at all. His hands were tied behind his back and his ankles were attached to the legs of the chair he was sitting in.

"Where am I?" He opened his weary eyes and tried to focus on the room he found himself in. His head hurt when he tried to move it. He now knew the reason he blacked out and why he had a splitting headache. His captor had hit him with something. He groaned loudly; his back was sore. Everything was sore, though was not as painful as the last time he woke up. He wondered how long he'd been out.

"OK, let's try this again, *Josh*! How are you going to fix this?" his captor asked.

"Fix what?" Josh asked, tears in his voice. He finally realized where he had heard the voice before. It was the man that had been in Josh's apartment "Don't kill me, please," Josh begged.

"I'm not going to kill you," he assured, grabbing a handful of Josh's hair and pulling his head violently back. "You have something I want," he whispered harshly into Josh's ear.

"I don't have anything, I swear," Josh whimpered.

"Don't you dare play that game with me!"

Josh sucked in air as the palm of the man's hand slammed into his Adam's apple. When his voice finally returned Josh howled in pain.

"Please," he wheezed. "I don't know what you're talking about," Josh rolled his head forward so that the man couldn't hurt his neck again. He soon learned there were other more vulnerable places on his body that needed protecting. The man planted his knee in Josh's crotch.

"Ahh... Uhhnn," Josh's howl turned into a groan.

"So, you think you're something, do you Erik?" the man roared. "Well, I'll tell you something. You are nothing but a murderous thief!"

"Who's Erik?" Josh asked in a small voice.

"Cut the crap!" Josh's head shifted violently backwards as the man slammed his fist into Josh's cheek. Stars filled Josh's vision and he tasted blood. This time the man continued to pound on him until Josh thankfully slipped back into oblivion.

*＊＊

He was crying when he felt her touch upon his head. Excited, he looked up, hoping to find Sunshine, but instead he found another girl. She looked so familiar, but he couldn't quite place where he'd seen her before.

The girl kissed him gently on his forehead.

"I thought you were dead," he whispered.

"I thought you were dead," the girl responded. She put her arms around him. "Dylan," she whispered softly, with tears in her voice. Suddenly, she pushed away from him. "No," She turned her head and looked off in the distance as if expecting to see someone there. She placed a finger across her lips. She turned then and began to walk away.

"Wait!" he called out, struggling to remember her name, struggling to remember anything about her at all.

"Josh! WAIT!" he screamed out the only name he could think of, trying to stop her. Something seemed so familiar about those words, but the woman didn't stop. She kept walking into the darkness until she finally disappeared.

***

"Wake up!" the voice commanded. A hand slapping his face dragged him back to reality.

"What the hell do you want?" Josh growled loudly. Then an idea struck him. "You killed Sunshine, didn't you?" he accused. "You wanted to hurt me. You're a murderer."

"Murderer? Murderer? *You're* calling *me* a murderer?" the man laughed. "I didn't kill anyone, you lying bastard," he said through clenched teeth.

"Neither did I."

"YOU SON OF A BITCH!" the man screamed and proceeded to whale on Josh.

Josh cried out in surprise at the sudden attack.

"Please, PLEASE!" Josh screamed, "Please just kill me. Stop hitting me and kill me," Josh begged. "I'm not who you think I am," Josh explained, knowing that the man wouldn't believe him.

Immediately, the man froze. He stared at Josh in wonder. Realization crossed his face as he backed away from Josh.

"Oh God, you're not him anymore are you?" the man asked.

Josh shook his head emphatically.

"I'm so sorry for hurting you," he sat down on a bed across the room from Josh.

"Thank you," Josh whispered, "for believing me." He paused, making connections in his head. "Are you...?" he began not sure how to word the question. "Who are you?"

"I'm Josh," the man replied, "Well technically, my name is Erik," he pointed to his head. "But in here, I'm Josh." He smiled sadly and looked at his hands. "I didn't think he would do it again. I didn't think he could. I thought this was just a fluke." He looked up at Josh with sad eyes. "How long have you been...?" The real Josh trailed off, not knowing quite how to finish.

"That night, when you kicked my ass in your house?" Josh looked confused for a second and then continued, "That was the second night."

"What's your real name?" the real Josh asked. Josh smiled and began to say the word; began to say his real name. It was on the tip of his tongue, but he couldn't remember it. His smile turned into a frown and tears filled his eyes. "I can't remember." He took in a shaky breath. "I don't remember anything beyond these past two weeks. I can't remember anything at all about my old life," he mumbled.

"Well, I can't call you Josh," the real Josh complained. "I'll have to call you something else."

"Dylan," Josh answered automatically, not quite knowing where the name came from.

"OK. Dylan, you can call me Josh." The man now named Dylan nodded. He was beginning to hate the name Josh. He was glad to finally be rid of it.

"Josh?" Dylan asked.

The real Josh nodded.

"Could you untie me please?" Dylan begged. He just wanted to sleep on the bed that the real Josh sat on.

"Oh, yeah, sorry," Josh stood up and walked over towards Dylan. "It's just so strange that you can't remember your own name. You've only been in there for about two weeks."

"I've been through a lot of trauma," Dylan replied, resentfully.

Josh crouched down to untie Dylan.

"I said I was sorry about that," Josh looked up at Dylan suddenly. "Did you say Sunshine was dead?"

Dylan nodded sadly, tears flowing freely now. Nothing could make him forget the love that they had shared. If only he could remember what the last thing she whispered in his ear was.

"What happened?" Josh asked. Dylan looked up at him with pain in his eyes, rubbing his wrists idly.

"Someone...," he paused, swallowing back tears. "Someone ran her down...on purpose." Dylan took a deep shaky breath and then began again. "She was the only person who knew me for me. She loved me and I loved her." Somehow, that declaration of his love for her made him stronger and he was able to fight back his tears.

Josh chuckled. "Sorry, I don't mean to laugh. It's just funny to me because I never thought of Sunshine like that. I mean, she was always just a friend…more like a sister," he smiled sadly. "She was Lauren's best friend. I hope they're together again now."

"That's not how the Josh that was in here before me treated her," Dylan explained, "From what she told me, he just used her for sex."

"That would be Erik, that bastard." Josh closed his eyes, thinking for a moment. "You said you told Sunshine about who you really were. Did she believe you?"

"I didn't tell her, she already knew."

"And she knew about the other Josh… Erik?"

Dylan nodded.

"He killed her," Josh speculated. "She knew too much and he killed her."

"He didn't seem like that kind of person. He didn't look very ruthless to me." Dylan argued in a small voice as he moved over to the bed. Josh stood up and walked over to the fireplace. He picked up a poker and pushed the logs around.

"He killed my fiancé. Believe me, he's more ruthless than you can ever imagine."

"What does he want?" Dylan curled up in the bed and pulled the blankets over him. "Why is he doing this?"

"I don't know, Dylan," Josh turned back to him. "I know just about as much as you do."

"Could you tell me how it happened to you?" Dylan was staring at Erik's body through half closed lids. He could almost see an aura of complete darkness surrounding the body that Josh was in. He wondered if he had the same aura surrounding him.

Josh didn't answer. His face had gone pale and his teeth were clenched. He fell into a sitting position next to the fireplace ledge. He groaned loudly and Dylan suddenly remembered the searing pain he felt earlier. What had Josh told him it was…. his body rejecting its soul?

Dylan threw back the blanket and rushed to his side to try and help Josh. He put his hand on Josh's shoulder.

"Don't touch me!" Josh shoved him away. "It'll go away. Just don't touch me," he mumbled as he rocked back and forth in agony.

Dylan returned to the bed and curled up in it. He was frightened, very frightened. He didn't like not knowing who he was. He didn't like being trapped in a room with a lunatic that had only just stopped trying to kill him. He began to cry, wishing Sunshine was here to hold him. He never felt this lost and alone with her there.

"Hey man, you doing alright? Did you catch the rejection from me?" Josh's tentative voice came from beside him.

"No, go away!" Dylan snapped. "You can't give me what I want!"

"What do you want?"

"I want someone to hold me like she did. I want someone to tell me everything's going to be alright. I want someone to tell me that we are going to get my body back…our bodies back," Dylan added, remembering that there were two of them in this predicament now. "I want to be back in my body at my home and I don't even know where that is." Dylan's babbling couldn't break through the shield of indifference that Josh had built. Josh wanted people to think he was invincible, that nothing could hurt him.

"I can't do that."

"Why not?"

"Because, I don't believe it, we aren't ever going to get our bodies back. I just want to find the bastard and kill him. I don't care about my body anymore."

"That's bullshit! If you didn't care, you wouldn't be fighting it. You would have just let Erik's personality take over," Dylan pointed out. "I don't care what you say. You do believe it."

"I can't do it," Josh repeated.

"Why not? Can't you just hold me at least? Even if you don't believe?"

"No."

"Why not?"

"I'm not gay."

"That has nothing to do with it. SCREW YOU! Just get out!" Dylan demanded in anger. "Dylan was the name of my husband. Just think of that next time your homophobic ass looks at me. GET OUT!" Dylan screamed.

"Whatever!" Josh slammed the door as he walked out of the room.

The emptiness of the room swallowed Dylan. The only thing that soothed him was the soft noises of the fire.

22

Lilly's Apartment:

Eon, Lilly, & Mae

Lilly paused at the doorway to her apartment. She was afraid to go in again. She was afraid that Eon was waiting inside for her. She dialed 911 on her cell phone.

"911, what is your emergency?" the operator asked.

"I think someone is in my apartment." Lilly whispered into the phone. She wasn't sure if Eon was in there, but she wasn't taking any chances.

"What's your address? Are you safe?"

"I'm in the hallway, I haven't gone in yet." Lilly explained and gave her address.

"Thank you. Listen to me, whatever you do, do not go in. Wait for an officer to arrive. There is a patrol car very close to you. Stay on the line OK, Miss."

Lilly nodded. "OK."

"Do you know who it is?"

"It might be my ex-husband Eon Reynolds. My name is Lilly. We had a fight. He attacked me," Lilly sighed; it felt great to finally tell someone the truth.

The door swung open. Lilly lowered her phone, but didn't disconnect.

"Well, are you coming in or are you just going to stand out here like idiots?" Eon grabbed on to Mae's hand.

"Oh God, no!" Mae screamed, trying to pull away.

"Eon, let her go," Lilly demanded calmly, "I'm the one you want. Just let her go." She could hear the operator's calling out her name, but she ignored it.

Eon laughed. "I'm not leaving witnesses anymore."

"For the love of God, Eon, just let her go," Lilly grabbed Mae's other hand.

"There is no God," Eon growled, pulling Mae into the room. Lilly stumbled in after her. She dropped her cell phone and let go of Mae's hand to catch herself before she slammed into a wall.

"You promised," Mae whimpered, staring at Lilly. "You promised me."

"I'm so sorry, sweetie." Lilly righted herself and looked at Mae. "I thought he was gone."

"She's so sorry, sweetie," Eon aped. "Isn't that cute." He caressed Mae's cheek mockingly.

"Don't you hurt her, Eon!" Lilly screamed.

"I'm not going to hurt her. I'm just going to kill her," Eon declared. The words felt amazing on his lips. "I've played it safe for far too long. I am so close to the 'one' that it doesn't matter if The Guardians find me."

"Who are The Guardians?" Lilly asked.

"Well, they aren't the ones that are going to save you," Eon growled. He shoved Mae into the bedroom.

"LILLIAN!" Eon roared as Lilly tried to bolt. His booming voice sounding strange coming out of the teenage body he wore. He grabbed her around the waist and threw her into the bedroom, slamming the door behind her.

"Mommy?" Mae whispered.

"We'll be all right," Lilly whispered back. "The cops are coming, they will save us."

"I'm scared," Mae whimpered.

"So am I, Miss Mae," she paused, remembering the reason they came back to the apartment in the first place. She swallowed back her fear. "Let's find your insulin."

Mae nodded. "Are we safe?"

"For a little bit, my love, for a little bit." She pulled her insulin kit out of her nightstand and prepared the injection.

23

The Cabin:

Dylan & Josh

In Dylan's dream, she returned; the sweet soft girl...no, she was a woman. She was the same woman who had been haunting his dreams since Sunshine died. She walked towards him on soft footsteps. He tried to call out to her, but he had no voice.

She smiled and lay down beside him on the bed. She put her arms around his borrowed body. He cried into her shoulder as she held him. He slept quietly then, with no dreams swimming in his head. He was at peace, with her arms around him.

Little did Dylan know, she was beginning to return. Maggie was tentatively trying to return, but she was still so scared and heartbroken. For now, she was willing to let whoever was now in Josh's body have it. She was sick of it. In the morning, she fled back into the darkness, far back into Dylan's consciousness where the other presence couldn't see her.

"I'm sorry about last night," Josh's voice startled Dylan awake. He looked around for the woman that had been holding him, but she was gone.

"What?" Dylan asked, still sleepy.

"I said: I'm sorry about last night," Josh gave Dylan an angry look. "Don't make me say it again."

Dylan shook his head. "I won't."

"Get up, we have to get moving," Josh demanded.

"Where are we going?"

"We have to buy you some new clothes." Josh said, handing him a black tee shirt from the dresser. "Here, put this on, it'll be tight, but at least it isn't covered in blood."

"Why can't we just go back to the apartment and get some clothes?" Dylan asked as he picked up the shirt.

"Apparently, you haven't heard yet. The day after you ran away from the apartment, Josh was evicted. Seems our good buddy Erik, in my body of course, failed to pay the rent and now the apartment and everything in it is gone."

"What about the cat?"

"Who cares? I hated that cat," Josh admitted, with a hint of sadness in his voice. He watched as Dylan carefully took off his shirt, his torso was covered with bruises from his more recent beating. Those bruises covered older bruises that had barely healed.

"God, I'm so sorry about that, man," Josh apologized, gesturing to the bruises.

"It's no problem," Dylan inhaled painfully as he hit a particularly tender bruise.

"Did you do that?" Josh asked, pointing at the tattoo.

"Not me. It was like that when I got here."

Shocked, Dylan watched as Josh lifted his shirt to show him Erik's hairless chest. Tattooed in the same spot in the same old English style were the names Angel and Lauren. "I thought he did it to punish me. That's why he did everything else."

"Tell me about what happened," Dylan requested again.

"Let's get some clothes and food first."

24

Lilly's Apartment:

Brad, Cheyenne, Eon,

Lilly, & Mae

"Open up, this is the police!" Officer Cheyenne Beswick shouted as she pounded on the door of apartment 5C. She pressed her ear to the door, trying to hear if anyone was inside.

"YOU DUMB BITCH!" a voice screamed from inside the room.

Cheyenne nodded and stood back. Her partner Brad kicked at the door.

"Eon Reynolds, open up!" Cheyenne yelled between kicks. The door finally swung open. The living room was empty.

"No wonder it was so hard to break it down," Brad said, gesturing his weapon at the multiple locks.

"Where are they?" Cheyenne whispered. Brad shook his head and gestured towards the two doors. "Which one?" she mouthed.

Brad cocked his head to the left. Cheyenne nodded. They moved towards the door on the left and prepared to enter the room.

"Eon, please, no," a woman's voice begged, from behind the other door.

"Over there," Cheyenne pointed to the door.

Brad nodded and moved closer to the door. It swung open and a woman ran out.

"Please help me!" she cried out. "He's got a knife. He's going to kill our daughter." She ran directly into Brad's arms. Brad caught her and held her up.

"Lilly?" he asked. She nodded. "We're here to help; you did a good thing calling before you entered." His voice was soothing and it calmed Lilly down. She nodded again. "He's got our daughter in there." She pointed to the room she had just run out of.

"Eon Reynolds, drop your weapon and come out with your hands up," Cheyenne demanded.

"I'm coming," Eon responded. "I'm coming." He grabbed Mae around the waist and led her out of the room with the knife pressed against her neck.

"Drop the knife," Brad demanded.

"Where's the child?" Cheyenne asked.

"What child?" Eon asked and turned to Brad "You drop your gun."

Brad looked over at Cheyenne. She nodded. They both placed their guns on the floor.

"Lilly, grab the guns," Eon instructed.

Lilly shook her head. "No, Eon, I will not help you; not this time."

"You will help me, you always do."

"Not this time. It's over between us," Lilly declared defiantly.

"LILLIAN!" Eon flung the knife he was aiming at Lilly, but the knife embedded itself in the policeman's neck.

"Brad!" Cheyenne screamed. Forgetting the perp, she ran over to her fallen partner. She checked for a pulse. It was weak and thready. He needed help. As long as the knife stayed in his neck, he might make it. She lifted her hand to her radio; she needed a bus. He needed medical attention immediately. A hand closed around her hand and squeezed it.

"I wouldn't do that if I were you," Eon warned, allowing his strength to crush her hand. Cheyenne cried out in pain as the radio exploded with the force of his hand. He let her hand go and grabbed the handle of the knife.

"No!" Cheyenne begged. "You'll kill him!"

"That was the point." He pulled the knife out of Brad's neck. Cheyenne and Lilly both screamed as the blood sprayed out of the wound.

Eon took the knife and wiped it on Cheyenne's uniform.

"What are you?" she asked, staring into Eon's eyes.

"I'm your worst nightmare," Eon replied. "Lilly, grab that boy before he gets out."

"Run!" Lilly screamed, throwing a lamp in Eon's general direction.

"YOU TREACHEROUS BITCH!" Eon screamed as the lamp shattered next to him.

Lilly ran for the door, grabbing Mae's hand as she went.

Eon ran faster and beat them both to the door. He grabbed Lilly and threw her against the wall. He grabbed Mae and without thinking twice, he slit her throat.

"You BASTARD!" Lilly screamed, throwing herself at him, before he had a chance to aim the knife at her. She knocked it out of his hand. "You killed our daughter!"

"That was not our daughter!" Eon argued.

"It was our daughter. The boy gave up his soul. He became her. HE WAS OUR DAUGHTER!" Lilly screamed. She couldn't stop pounding on him. She couldn't stop hurting him. He had taken Mae away from her again.

25

A Diner:

Dylan & Josh

"It happened in a place a lot like this one." Josh began, gesturing Erik's hands around the small diner where they ate their dinner. "It was the place where Lauren and I first met. When we met, she was a waitress there, but then she left to work with me at Lanaway's. We'd been going out for five years on the day it happened. We'd lived together for three of the five years.

"I proposed to her that night on the anniversary of our first meeting. It was all beautifully romantic, just the way she wanted it." Josh paused and took a sip of his coffee. Dylan could tell there were tears in his eyes.

"I proposed and she said yes. I asked her to dance. She told me I was crazy and I told her that I was crazy in love with her. She loved it. Her face lit up with such joy. I will never forget that look of joy." He sniffled and wiped at his eyes, angry at them for betraying him with tears.

"We were so happy. Everyone thought we were insane dancing through a diner, but we didn't care. We were in love." He paused again, swallowing back anger. "That's when he came along, that bastard," Josh said, spitting out the words with such distaste that Dylan hated the stranger immediately.

"He tapped me on the shoulder to cut in. I'd never seen him before, but what could I do? So I let him dance with her. I never should have let him do that. Never," Josh paused to wipe an angry tear away. He took another sip of coffee. "Then he...he...kissed her," he struggled to get the words around his tears. "He…kissed her passionately for a long time. I remember how she lifted onto her toes in pleasure; pleasure from *his* kiss. Then her whole body stiffened and she tried to pull away. She was struggling. She was trying so hard to get away from him and then suddenly, she went still. The man…Erik…turned to me with this look of sheer horror in his eyes. 'Josh,' the guy whispered. 'Help me.' Then he yelled 'HELP ME!' Lauren was still in his arms and she started shaking and convulsing. She grabbed his face. He screamed out my name again, but it was Laurens voice that I heard in my mind. She was in Erik's body…this body and I couldn't do anything to help her. He was inside her body and it was dying. So using her body, her lips, he kissed his lips and then she was gone. Her body died and Erik ran off. That's how he killed my Lauren."

"Oh my God!" Dylan exclaimed. His hatred for Erik growing with every word.

"It's not over yet," Josh stated. "I called an ambulance and the police. I described him to the police and went with Lauren's body to the hospital, but it was too late, my baby was gone. They had her on life support, but there was no brain activity. They were waiting for her parents to get there and decide what to do. I was standing alone in the hallway outside her room, when I heard a voice behind me.

"'I didn't mean to kill her,' the guy says. 'I just wanted her body, but I guess yours will do.' I yelled then for the police, screaming that the killer was there. I had the killer. He bolted, but I tackled him. We wrestled a bit as I waited for the police to arrive. Somehow, he ended up facing me. I tried to pull away, but he kissed me and I…. I liked it," Josh said in disgust. "I liked it a lot. Then I felt like I was spinning and then there was the pain…like no other, a ripping sensation that…," Josh tried to describe what he felt.

"I'm familiar with the feeling," Dylan admitted.

"Yeah, I keep forgetting. Anyway, the next thing I know the cops are hauling me away and I'm screaming, 'You got the wrong guy!' The last thing I saw was him in my body, smirking at me and I heard his voice inside my head saying 'that'll teach ya'.

"They arrested me for Lauren's murder. The days in jail after that went by in a blur. After I'd been in there for two months, Erik's mom finally paid the bail. I'm supposed to go back for the trial, but I'm not going to do that. I'll kill myself before they blame Lauren's death on me."

"So, wait... If I have the name Erik on my chest...," Dylan started.

"My chest," Josh corrected angrily. "Don't forget the body you're in doesn't belong to you."

"Sorry. If Erik is written on this chest, and Angel and Lauren are written on that chest, then maybe he's keeping track of where he's been. Maybe each person has the name of the person he was last in tattooed on their chest."

"So," Josh picked up where Dylan left off. "We can find each person and see how far back it leads us and maybe, we can find out who he really is."

"But, how do we even start?" Dylan asked.

"We could go talk to Erik's mom. Maybe Angel is someone Erik knows."

"But, what if she's not? You said, you didn't know Erik and I'm pretty sure I didn't know you."

"Dylan, it's all we've got." Josh assured him. "We've got to at least try it. It's not like we can chase him; you not knowing who you are and all."

26

The Hospital:

Lilly

Lilly cleared her throat and opened her eyes. She found herself in a hospital room with four people crowded around her. "Where am I?" she asked. She tried to lift her arm to rub her eyes. She found an IV in her right hand so she lifted her left hand instead.

"Maggot?" the man sitting on her right asked. "She's awake." He turned to the others in the room. The three other people rushed to her bedside.

"Where's Mae?" she asked.

"I think that was the old woman," a light-skinned black woman took her hand. She was so beautiful; Lilly couldn't take her eyes off of her.

"Who are you?" Lilly didn't recognize anyone standing around her bed.

"I'm Emmy," the woman answered rubbing Lilly's hand. "I'm your best friend."

"Who am I?" Lilly asked.

"You don't remember?" one of the other women asked.

Lilly shook her head. She did remember who she was, but she had gone through this situation before, so many times thanks to Eon.

"You're Maggie," the man explained. "My sister, my Maggot,"

"Don't call her that, Mark," one of the women said angrily.

"Sorry Sue. I just thought she would remember me more if I called her that."

"Why am I here?" Lilly asked.

"You were kidnapped. They found you at that murdered woman's house."

"Murdered woman?" Lilly asked.

"The one that you called Mae, she died," Emmy whispered as if she was afraid to say the word.

"Yes, that bastard killed her," she growled through clenched teeth.

"You remember what happened?" Sue asked her.

"No...a little, but not really," Lilly lied to them. She had to get out of here. She had to track Eon down.... and kill him. She would wait until visiting hours were over and then she would get out of here.

27

Mrs. Summers' House:
Dylan & Josh

"What if she recognizes me and blames me for getting her son arrested?" Dylan asked nervously.

The two men were standing on Erik's mom's porch.

"Don't worry about that, she's pretty senile," Josh rang the doorbell.

"Hey Ma!" Josh exclaimed as Erik's mom opened the door.

"Erik, is that you? You look so different."

"What do you mean I look different?" Josh pursed Erik's lips.

"Something about your eyes, they're different somehow…. Oh well. Come in, come in." She moved out of the way for the two men to enter.

"She adopted Erik when she was in her 50's," Josh whispered to Dylan. "He was three, I think." Josh looked around the room. "I gathered that from the pictures last time I was here."

"Twenty-seven years old and you can't even find time to come and visit your poor old mother."

"I'm here now, aren't I?" Josh asked.

"Sure, but where were you when I needed to go to the hospital last month," she asked, sitting down in a chair across the room from where they stood. "Sit down, sit down," she suggested, gesturing towards the couch.

"I was in jail last month, remember Ma? You bailed me out. We have to go to court."

"Oh yeah, that's what Millie said." Erik's mom nodded.

"Who's Millie?" Dylan asked.

"Her dog," Josh replied, smiling.

"How is she going to tell us anything that we need to know?" Dylan whispered, exasperated.

"Don't worry about it," Josh turned back to Erik's mom. "Hey Ma, do you ever remember me talking about someone named Angel?"

"Angel, your sweet little girlfriend? Yes, of course, I remember her. Millie told me she was in the hospital."

"Which hospital?" Josh asked.

"Millie knows everything, don't you, Millie?" she asked, patting the poodle that was lying in her lap.

"I wish we could talk to the dog," Dylan whispered.

"Time for your medication, Mrs. Summers," a perky young woman walked out of the kitchen and into the living room. "Erik! How are you doing?" she exclaimed when she caught sight of Josh. She placed a tray on the table next to Erik's mother.

"Uh hi," Josh blushed, apparently, he knew this woman.

"Who's your friend?" She eyed Dylan. "He's gorgeous," she complimented, checking out Josh's body. This time it was Dylan's turn to blush.

"This is Dylan. Dylan, this is Ami. She's my mom's nurse."

"Do you know Angel?" Dylan blurted out.

Ami's eyes turned from flirty to sad in an instant. "She's in a coma, didn't anyone tell you, Erik?" Josh shook his head.

"Is she OK?" he asked adding a deep concern to his voice. Dylan was impressed at his acting skills. He almost believed that Josh was really upset to hear that Angel was in a coma.

"She's as good as she could be in her situation. You should go visit her, sometimes hearing from loved ones helps to bring a patient out of the coma." She placed her hand on Josh's arm. "I can't believe no one told you."

"Where is she?" He placed his hand on hers and looked up into her eyes.

"She's at our hospital." Ami placed her other hand on top of his.

"Which hospital is that?" Dylan placed his hand on Josh's back as Josh bowed his head, pretending to cry.

"St Louise's," Ami clarified.

"Come on, J...Erik, let's go," Dylan had to stop himself from calling Josh by his real name.

Josh stood up, wiping away his pretend tears. Dylan stood up and patted him on the back.

"Ma, we're going to go see Angel, OK?" Josh turned back to look at Mrs. Summers.

"OK," she nodded, patting the poodle and staring off into space. "Oh yeah, and boys?" she called out as they reached the door. Both men stopped to look at her. "If you see my son, my real son, tell him to come home, please," she said, staring directly into Josh's eyes.

"MARTHA!" Ami yelled. She ushered the men out the door. She stepped out onto the porch and closed the door behind her. "I don't want to worry you too much, but she is getting worse," Ami informed them sadly.

"She's better than you think," Josh assured her.

Dylan spoke up before she could reply. "It was nice meeting you, Ami," he offered his hand for her to shake it. She pushed it aside and gave him a hug. She turned and gave Josh a hug too.

"Goodbye. You guys take care and help Angel, if you can." She smiled. "She needs you, Erik."

Josh nodded.

Ami turned and walked back into the house.

"Lana, those boys are up to no good," Martha informed Ami with a matter-of-fact tone to her voice.

"I'm sure they are Martha." Ami watched as the two gorgeous men climbed into their car and drove away.

28

The Hospital:

Josh & Dylan

"Erik!" A female nurse ran over to Josh and Dylan. "I'm so glad you're here! Angel's been waking up lately. She's been asking for you." She paused to take a breath. "How are you? I heard about your 'thing'. You didn't kill that girl, did you?"

Josh shook his head. "I'm doing fine and I didn't kill anyone," Josh assured her. "Where is she?" He let fake desperation fill his voice.

The nurse led the way to Angel's room. She left them at the door. Dylan and Josh stood in the doorway looking in at the pale woman lying in the bed.

"I can't do this," Josh whispered.

"What do you mean?"

"I'm not Erik. I don't know anything about this girl."

"Just pretend it's Lauren," Dylan suggested, regretting it instantly. Before Dylan could even react, Josh grabbed a hold of Dylan's shirt and slammed him against the wall. Dylan cringed in anticipation of the punch that never landed. Josh seemed to calm himself and he let go of Dylan and turned away from him.

"Don't mention Lauren's name, ever!" Josh ordered.

"Don't worry, I won't." Dylan stalked away from Josh and into the room. He stopped at the end of Angel's hospital bed. "You know, the way you treat me, I don't know why I don't just leave. I could, you know. I could just walk out and leave you behind."

"No, you couldn't," Josh argued.

"What do you mean, no, I couldn't? Yes I COULD! I don't need you!"

"Let's put it this way!" Josh spoke slowly as if he were speaking to a child. "You have my body. I'm not letting you or it out of my sight until I get it back. So until then, we're best friends. Everywhere you go, I go. Everything you do, I do. Got it?" he asked. "So we can hole ourselves up in a hotel and pine about our lost Sunshine or we can figure out what the hell happened to us," he growled through clenched teeth.

"Shut up!" the girl in the bed moaned. "Leave me alone!"

"Angel?" Dylan asked. "I know you don't know me, but I'm a friend of Erik's," Dylan lied to the girl in the bed.

"No, you're not," she mumbled. Dylan could see it was hard for her to talk.

"Angel?" Dylan asked again, as she seemed to fade back into slumber.

"Erik," her voice whispered. Dylan looked up to find Josh still lingering in the doorway. He gestured for Josh to come in and talk to Angel as Erik.

"It's OK. I brought him. He's here with me," Dylan assured Angel softly.

"You're not my friend," Angel argued, opening her eyes to look at Dylan.

"I told you, I'm Erik's friend," Dylan corrected.

"NOT MY FRIEND!" she insisted angrily.

"Angel calm down," Dylan soothed.

"ERIK!" she screamed.

Finally, Josh ran to her side and grabbed her hand.

"Angel?" Josh asked tentatively. She was still very weak and it was difficult for her to turn her head away from Dylan.

"Erik." She looked up at the man holding her hand. "My name is Erik." Angel corrected Josh, as her eyes focused on Josh, her face filled with shock. Her eyes opened in horror.

"Who are you?" she begged. "What are you?"

"Shh! Angel, calm down," Josh soothed, glancing at the heart monitor and noticing her heartbeat increasing.

"I'm Erik! I'M ERIK! I'M ERIK!" she pleaded with Josh until her eyes rolled back into her head and she fell back into unconsciousness.

Just then the heart monitor's alarm went off. Quickly, before the doctors could rush in, Dylan reached over and pulled down the hospital gown to look at the name on her chest.

"Tori," Dylan read out loud. As he drew his hand away from Angel, he started to feel the familiar tearing pain inside of him. "Uh-oh," he gasped softly.

"What?" Josh asked, grabbing his arm and pulling him out of the doctor's way and into the hallway.

"PAIN!" Dylan explained through clenched teeth.

Josh led him to the waiting room.

Dylan moaned softly. "Let go, let go, let go," he begged. He needed Josh to quit touching him. Josh sat him down in the waiting room.

"What is it, Dylan?"

Dylan shook his head vigorously.

"Rejection?" Josh asked, not knowing what else to call it.

Dylan nodded. "It won't go away," he groaned in pain. He leaned forward in his seat until his stomach was against his lap. He was trying not to make any sound, but he couldn't help it, the pain was so much worse this time.

Suddenly, he felt a soft soothing touch on his forehead, as if someone were checking him for a fever. He looked up. "You," Dylan breathed, half smiling as he gazed at the woman from his dreams. She was standing before him. "I know you," Dylan whispered.

She nodded slowly. "I know you," she agreed in a puzzled voice. "Who are you?" she asked. She looked deep into his eyes as if she could find the answer somewhere in there.

"Who are you?" he asked.

She shrugged and shook her head. "I don't remember," she admitted.

"Neither do I," Dylan agreed.

She leaned forward and placed a kiss on his aching forehead.

"I know that I love you," she whispered.

"I love you too."

She smiled sweetly.

"What's your name?" he asked, but before his eyes she disappeared. She was gone, but so was the emptiness deep inside. The loss of Sunshine was still there, but an older loss that Dylan didn't even know existed was gone. He felt almost whole again.

Dylan jumped up and ran into the hallway. "Where is she?" he asked. "Where did she go?"

"What are you talking about?" Josh was looking at him like he was insane.

"The girl! Where did she go?" Dylan demanded.

'What girl?" Josh snarled, getting angry.

"You didn't see her?" Dylan's heart fell. His thoughts were filled with doubts; maybe this girl wasn't real, maybe he'd just imagined it all.

"Dude, you're tripping. There was nobody here, but us," Josh assured.

"Hmmm, oh well."

"Dylan, are you sure you're alright?"

The word: Dylan. It cut like a knife. He was filled with an intense sadness that seemed to come from somewhere deep inside of him.

"Dylan was my husband's name," Dylan whispered in a voice that wasn't quite the same.

"You told me that already." Josh reminded him.

"He died. Four years ago. I don't know why I picked that name."

"I don't know either," Josh commented, but Dylan could tell that he didn't care anyway.

Dylan shook his head, trying to clear it of all the foreign words and emotions that seemed to fill him. "So, what now?"

"Let's go ask around for this Tori person."

"OK, but let's go make sure Erik's alright first,".

"What for?" Josh asked impatiently.

"Sometimes you're such an ass!" Dylan snapped and stormed past Josh. He walked back to the room where Angel's body lay with Erik's soul inhabiting it.

"Is she going to be alright?" he heard Josh ask a doctor.

Dylan didn't need to know the answer. He already knew what happened. He had felt Erik's soul trying to break free from Angel's body. He would have succeeded too if Dylan hadn't grabbed him and pulled him back into the body. All of this happened in the three seconds that his skin had brushed against Angel's. That's when he somehow caught the Rejection reverb that ached through his body. Then *she* came and took all his pain away. Did he really do those things? He remembered them happening, but he didn't seem to be in control of it at all. What was happening to him?

Dylan placed his hand on Angel's forehead. He lowered his head and his voice so he was barely whispering in her ear.

"Erik, listen to me. I know you're in there. I know you're Erik. You need to stay put and remember what I said before." Dylan paused, what had he said before? "Erik, I know you can hear me. We're trying to fix this, have faith and, hopefully soon, everything will be back to normal." Dylan removed his hand and kissed her on the forehead gently.

"Dylan, don't leave me," Erik whispered with Angel's voice. "Please."

"I have to…," Dylan started, but Erik cut him off.

"I can't hold on much longer," he whispered.

"I'm sorry. I have to go. I have to find a way to save us," Dylan assured him. "I'll come back. I swear."

"I saw her too," Erik whispered.

"Who?" Dylan demanded.

"The girl…the woman," Erik sighed. "She took the pain away."

"Did she tell you her name?" he asked.

"It was…," Erik started. He was getting too weak to talk. He turned his head and slipped back into the darkness.

"DAMMIT!" Dylan shouted louder than he expected too.

"What was that all about?" Josh asked as Dylan walked out of the hospital room.

"Something happened to me during that rejection thing," Dylan explained. "It's so strange, I feel whole. I guess that's the only way to describe it," he sighed. "I guess I just connected...in a way...with Erik. It's quite hard to explain."

"Then don't," Josh snapped impatiently. "You keep tripping out on me. Are you sure you're sane?"

Dylan thought for a moment before answering him. "Actually, no, I'm not sure. But hey, what can you do, you know?" Dylan laughed.

Josh turned and walked away. Dylan followed him in silence. He was quietly mulling over the question in his head. Was he sane? Could anyone remain sane when going through something like this? It was true that he felt more complete than he had before, but he wasn't sure if he felt particularly sane or not. He still couldn't remember any of his past or even the name of who he used to be.

He leaned against the wall, lost in thought as Josh talked to the nurse who had shown them to Angel's room.

"She's not here," Josh informed him as he returned from his mission.

"What did you tell her?" Dylan asked.

"Apparently, Erik and Angel were the prom king and queen of this hospital. They were both nurses here, everyone here knows them. I just told her that Angel was asking for Tori and then I asked if she knew where Tori would be," Josh related as he stabbed the button for the elevator.

"Did she know?"

"She told me that Tori was a nurse here, but she quit a while ago, but she also said that Tori is a total party girl and she gave me this." He held out a party flier towards Dylan. "She said Tori might be there. She even gave me a picture of Tori that was hanging in the lounge."

"Great. So I guess we're going to a party,"

"Who said we? I'll go find her. You can stay in the cabin," Josh instructed, referring to the cabin that they had made their temporary home. It belonged to Erik's mother.

"Why can't I go?"

"Because you're acting crazy, I want you at home sleeping and taking care of my body."

"I'm not a fragile child! I can take care of myself!"

"No, you're not a child," Josh agreed. "You're an intruder and human bodies were not made to take the strain of all this switching," Josh explained as he hailed a cab.

"Then you stay home! You've been in there longer then I've been in here. If anyone needs rest, it's you," Dylan retorted.

"How can I trust y...?" Josh began, but was cut off by the pain that filled him.

"See, you're having the Rejection pains even more frequently than I am," Dylan pointed out smugly. He was going to have to learn to quit goading Josh. Josh punched him in the stomach. He was not at his usual strength, but it still hurt all the same. Dylan gritted his teeth and opened the cab door. He helped Josh into the cab and shut the door. "And I'm not entirely sure that you're sane," he said as he walked around the cab to get in the other door.

"I heard what you said," Josh whispered as soon as the pain went away.

"How did you hear me?" Dylan asked, just as the words came out he realized the windows of the cab were down.

"Do you really think I'm crazy?"

"Sometimes, but look, I don't think anyone would be sane in our situation," Dylan rationalized, looking around for something. "Your nose is bleeding," Dylan pointed out, trying to remain calm. Erik's body seemed to be winning the battle it raged against Josh's spirit.

"Is it?" Josh asked, sitting up. He lifted his fingers tentatively up to his nose. He saw the blood on his fingers and finally believed his nose was bleeding. He reached into his pocket and pulled out a bandana. He shook it out and squeezed his nose shut with it.

The two men sat together in uncomfortable silence for a little while and then Josh spoke up.

"I think that you are supposed to forget who you were," Josh suggested softly. Erik's body looked pale and weak.

"Don't say that, we won't forget."

"I think that's his plan," Josh ignored Dylan. "He wants you to forget who you are. That's what makes the body more willing to accept the soul."

Dylan glanced up at the cab driver. He was staring at them in the rearview mirror. He seemed to be getting uneasy.

"Shh, don't worry about it now," Dylan soothed. He wanted to put his arm around Josh to comfort him, he looked so scared and vulnerable, but he knew Josh would never allow that.

"How are we going to fix this now?" Josh asked miserably, ignoring Dylan again. "When I was chasing you…him… I had a purpose; I had a plan; something to do, someone to follow. Now…now I have nothing."

"Nothing to hide behind?" Dylan supplied softly. "Nothing to help keep away the truth of what's going on? You were in denial before, now you have to face it." Dylan guessed at what Josh was feeling. "That's what happened to me after Sunshine died. She was my denial. She helped me to pretend that nothing was wrong. She made me believe that this whole crazy thing had never happened," Dylan admitted truthfully, amazed that Josh was actually lowering his walls enough for Dylan to peek inside. Just as quickly as they came down, Josh slammed them back up.

"BULL SHIT! It's not denial. I know what's going on. In case you've forgotten, the issue was pretty much forced on me. I had to face it. He purposely did it to me, so I would get arrested instead of him. I know the severity of the situation. I've experienced it first hand and I'm not trying to hide from it," Josh snapped at him. He calmed a little bit. "It's just that, I don't know where to go from here. Revenge took up all of my thoughts before and it still does, but I don't know how we are going to find this guy now. We've got nothing; nothing, but a wild goose chase. Seriously what is tracing the tattoos back going to accomplish? We're not going to find him by going backward. We need to go forward. You need to remember who you were."

"I'm trying to remember." Dylan said desperately. "We can find other survivors by tracing the tattoos back,"

"Survivors? SURVIVORS?" Josh yelled. "How many have we found so far? Let's see one of them is dead and the other is in a coma because he can't face the fact that NOW HE'S A WOMAN!"

The cab driver looked back quickly with a stricken look on his face. Dylan gave him a sympathetic look and tried to hold back his tears. He was beginning to hate Josh and his anger.

"That's what makes me think you're insane," Dylan whispered. "Your anger is so intense."

"My anger is all that I have left of me," Josh admitted calmly. "It's my anchor. Unlike you, I'm fighting inside to remember myself, to remember my roots. I have to remember me. I have to remember Lauren. Right now, after all this time, my anger is all I've got. So quit trying to take that away from me!" Josh demanded as the cab finally arrived at its destination.

"I'm not trying to take anything from you," Dylan argued, getting out of the cab. He walked up to the front porch and waited while Josh paid the cab driver. When Josh finished, he turned and walked toward Dylan.

"Then what do you want?" Josh looked at Dylan as he unlocked the door.

"I just want to help you. We're in this together, now. You're not alone," Dylan assured him as they both walked into the living room. Josh sat down on the couch.

"We are not in this together! We are in this alone! Lauren's gone! Sunshine's gone! We are all alone." Josh was near hysterics. "They're both gone and nothing is going to bring them back! Don't you get it? No matter what we do; it will never be the same again! Even if we do get our bodies back, it will NEVER be the same."

Dylan stared at Josh in shock. The walls were gone completely. There was Josh, plain, vulnerable, lonely Josh sitting before him.

"I don't know if I even want to live like that. Why are you doing this to me?" Josh begged. He was crying now. "Why did he take her from me?"

He looked at Dylan, wanting answers. Dylan could only shrug.

"How can you stand to be around me? I'm such a wuss. Look at me sitting here crying like a baby." He sniffled and wiped at his now blood free nose.

Dylan handed him a tissue. "Don't be ashamed about showing your emotions. You went through a great loss, two great losses really. You've been through so much. You have a right to cry; to mourn," Dylan soothed softly, wanting so badly to hug him. But he wasn't sure if Josh was ready for that.

Tentatively, Dylan placed his hand on Josh's shoulder. Josh's walls shot right back up as he shoved Dylan's hand violently away.

"Don't touch me!" he cried out. "Don't touch me with my hands! Don't ever touch me! Leave me alone! I can't stand looking at you. Looking at me…" Josh ran into his room and slammed the door.

"We've got to fix this and fast. Josh is losing it," Dylan stated to no one in particular. "So am I," he amended softly. He sat on the couch in silence, trying not to think about what was happening. He couldn't stop himself from estimating how long he thought Josh had left. Dylan wondered when Josh's body would reject his soul.

He started violently as Josh opened his bedroom door and stuck his head out.

"We're both going to the party, we've got about five hours. I'm taking a nap. I suggest you do the same!" He slammed the door, making Dylan jump again.

Josh had the right idea. Dylan was exhausted too. He got up and headed into his designated room. He took off his clothes and climbed under the covers in his underwear.

29

The Rave:

Dylan, Josh, & Trance

In his dream Dylan was doing what he loved the most. He was riding his motorcycle. He felt another person's arms around his waist. They were a man's arms. He recognized the feeling of those arms, but he couldn't quite place them. Maybe this was his husband. He tried to turn around and look behind him, but he could barely see. It was foggy all around him. He tried to concentrate on the road, but the familiar arms kept tugging at his memory. He had to know who this man was. He pulled quietly over to the side of the road. The passenger behind him took off his helmet. Dylan found Josh's face staring back at him.

"Josh?" Dylan asked.

"Zach," the voice replied, "it's important that we get going. Here, let me drive."

Confused, Dylan climbed back on the bike behind Zach. He put his arms around Zach's waist and felt a familiar ache fill him. He kissed Zach's neck seductively.

"Not now, love, we've got to hurry," Zach insisted, nudging his lips gently away.

He started up the motorcycle and they were off. They were tearing through the back roads at speeds that made Dylan uneasy.

"Slow down!" Dylan yelled, but the only response he got was the screeching of the bike tires as Zach applied both brakes to avoid hitting a tree. Unfortunately, it didn't seem to work and they crashed.

Dylan's broken body was filled with excruciating pain.

***

Dylan woke up screaming, hoping it was all a dream, but the pain was still there.

The pain dimmed for a second, then there was even more pain, blindingly bright. He couldn't stop screaming as the seemingly endless pain continued to rip through his body. He opened his eyes to find Josh standing over him shaking him.

"STOP!" Dylan screamed. "Don't touch!" Dylan groaned through clenched teeth.

"Dylan?" Josh removed his hands and the pain cut off abruptly. Breathing deeply Dylan slowly began to relax.

"Zach?" Dylan was still muddled from the strange memory dream.

"No, I'm Josh," Josh's words were slow as if Dylan were stupid or something.

"Where am I?" Dylan was afraid to move his body; afraid the pain would come back.

"The cabin,"

"I had the strangest dream," Dylan rubbed his eyes. He looked up at Josh in wonder. "There was a man named Zach and he had your face…this face." Dylan placed a hand on his borrowed face.

"Get up. It's time to go," Josh's voice was cold and Dylan knew he wasn't listening.

"I died. In my dream, I died."

"I'm sorry." Josh threw some clothes at him. "But not now, we've got to go."

"I died," Dylan said quietly, pulling the clothes on.

***

The party was loud and scary to Dylan. He wanted to cower in a corner and wait for this to be over with. He had too much on his mind to concentrate on the job he was supposed to be doing. He couldn't stop thinking of the dream he had. How could he be dead and yet still alive?

Josh left him with instructions to meet at the water table in a half hour. He was supposed to be asking people about Tori, but everyone he tried to ask just ignored him. Finally, he gave up and found a hidden corner far away from the music. He lowered himself down and sat on the floor. He was thankful to be away from all those people.

"Are you having a bad trip?" a voice asked. Dylan looked up to find the sweetest, softest male face staring down at him. He fell in love with the face instantly.

Dylan shook his head.

The boy sat down next to Dylan. "You look so scared or sad. Are you?"

Dylan nodded.

"Well which is it?"

"Both, I guess," Dylan sighed, if only he could tell this boy the truth.

The boy placed his hand on Dylan's knee in silent support. Then he jerked it away as if he were in pain. "Maggie," the boy whispered looking into Dylan's eyes.

Dylan was filled with joy at the sound of the name that had eluded him since he had awakened tied up in the cabin. "Do you know Maggie?"

The boy shook his head. "You're looking for her and you don't even know it. You're looking for her, but she doesn't want to be found. I can't help you with that, but I know where Tori is."

"Tori? How do you know about Tori?"

"Trance," the boy offered his hand to Dylan.

"Trance?"

"That's my name."

"Oh…OH…" Dylan took the proffered hand. "I'm Dylan," he shook Trance's hand.

"You're trying to find someone else too…a man…he took something of yours and you want it back," Trance spouted.

Dylan was staring at him in shock. "How do you know all this stuff?"

"That's easy, I'm a psychic," Trance revealed.

Dylan shook his head. "I don't believe in stuff like that."

Trance laughed. "In your situation, I figured you'd be a believer. Anyway, we better get going. We don't want to keep your friend waiting." He stood up and walked away, leaving a flabbergasted Dylan to scramble up and chase after him through the crowd.

Somehow he managed to make it back to Josh before Trance did. "I found someone who knows where Tori is," Dylan stammered out to Josh, just as Trance arrived next to him. "Trance, this is Josh... Josh, this is Trance," Dylan introduced them to one another.

Josh held his hand out to Trance.

Trance shook his head. "No touching," Trance warned. "If you don't want me to know what you're hiding, then don't touch me. You'll do well to remember that."

"How do you know I'm hiding something?"

"It's written all over your aura. I'm psychic and yes I know that you don't believe in that. I also know that you think I'm crazy."

"I don't think you're crazy," Josh admitted. "Lauren was psychic too."

"Well then, here's the deal. I know where Tori is, but it doesn't open until tomorrow morning. If you guys take me someplace safe where I can eat and sleep, then I'll take you to Tori in the morning. Do we have a deal?" Trance asked.

"You're sure you know where Tori is?" Josh asked.

"Positive."

"Then let's go." Josh said, accepting Trance's terms.

30

The Hospital:

Erik & Lilly

Lilly walked quietly through the almost empty hospital. She was wearing clothes that Emmy had brought for her. Emmy was so nice and sweet. Lilly was not surprised that Maggie and Emmy were such close friends.

Lilly paused, standing in front of the elevator. She should check on the two survivors that were at this hospital before she left. She climbed into the elevator and hit the button for the floor that Erik was on.

"Erik?" She stood next to the bed where Angel's body lay. She wasn't expecting an answer. Erik hadn't woken up since Eon switched them, but as always she wanted to make sure he was all right. "Erik?" she asked again.

"Maggie?" the woman lying in the bed asked. How did Erik know Maggie?

"No, Erik. My name is Lilly," she explained.

"You look like Maggie," Erik pointed out.

"I know," she sat down on the side of his bed.

"Did he do that to you?" Erik asked. "He did it to me and Angel," he said sadly.

"Yes, he did," Lilly nodded. "How long have you known about what happened?"

"I woke up yesterday or the day before. I'm not sure. I kept trying to tell them I was Erik, but no one would believe me. Except..."

"Who, Erik?" Lilly was intrigued. "Who believed you?"

"The man in my...body," Erik was growing weaker and his voice was getting softer.

"Stay with me Erik, this is important. When did he come here?"

"Today," Erik answered.

Lilly was in awe. There were survivors.... survivors that were looking for Eon. They had to be tracing the tattoos backwards. Tentatively, she reached forward and moved Erik's nightgown aside.

"Tori," she read out loud.

"Maggie did that too," Erik told her sleepily. "But she was a man and they were both in another man's body."

"Both?" Lilly asked in shock.

Erik nodded, "Two souls, one body." He held up his hand illustrating with his fingers as he spoke.

"That's when you met Maggie?"

Erik nodded again. "She stopped me from leaving. She showed me her true self. She showed me you," Erik whispered.

"You were leaving?" Lilly brushed back a piece of Angel's hair.

"Yes, I'm so tired. I just want to go home."

"Stay here. Please, don't leave. I'm going to fix this. I'll get you back into your body," Lilly promised.

"Maggie said that too," Erik reminisced smiling. "I'll stay as long as I can, but I really just want to go home,"

"Sleep now,"

Erik nodded once more. He smiled at her. "You *are* just like Maggie."

Lilly returned his smile. She stayed and watched as Erik fell back asleep.

Lilly stopped in front of the mirror and stared at Maggie's face. "You seem like a good person." She smiled and Maggie's face smiled back at her. "If I can't stop him, maybe you can."

Lilly walked back out towards the elevator. She had one more survivor to visit before she escaped.

31

The Cabin:

Dylan & Trance

Dylan sat silently in the darkness watching the boy sleep peacefully. He envied him for that. Dylan always slept fitfully, his mind full of nightmares and memories. He wondered what would happen if he just leaned forward and kissed the boy. He wondered what it would be like to kiss him tenderly.

"How long have you been sitting there?" Trance's voice whispered in the darkness.

"All night," Dylan replied truthfully.

"Did you want something?"

"No," Dylan lied. "I was just looking at how beautiful you are," Dylan admitted, getting closer to the bed. He reached out to caress Trance's cheek, but stopped just before he actually touched him. He pulled his hand back slowly, regretfully.

"I don't want you to know what I'm hiding."

"Well, then you shouldn't touch me," Trance warned sadly.

"But I want to,"

"And I want you to."

"Can I lie next to you?" Dylan's voice was pitiful and childlike.

Trance nodded and smiled. He lifted the covers, but then thought better of it and laid the covers back down. He patted the bed next to him. "Above the covers, sometimes that helps block out the visions," he instructed. "Sometimes I wish I couldn't *see* so well," he whispered, as Dylan lay down beside him. "Everyone tells me it's a gift, but not being able to touch people makes it a curse, especially, people as beautiful as you." Trance closed his eyes.

Dylan tried to close his eyes and sleep, but he couldn't.

"I don't want to hide things from you," Dylan whispered and kissed Trance gently on his forehead. Then he got out of the bed and left Trance to sleep alone.

***

Trance woke up out of his nightmare trying to grab onto Dylan and hold him, but Dylan was gone. He looked around the room, but Dylan was not there. Had he dreamt the whole encounter with Dylan last night?

He threw back his covers and stood up. He padded softly into the living room, where he found Dylan sleeping on the couch. He walked quietly over to the couch and knelt down beside Dylan.

"I don't want you to hide things from me either," Trance whispered softly and kissed the man gently on his lips. He saw flashes of a motorcycle; felt the wind in his hair. Someone was there with him. It was someone Trance knew and it wasn't Dylan.

Trance stumbled backwards blindly and tripped over a coffee table. He threw a frantic glance towards Dylan, but he had not woken.

He felt a presence in the small kitchen. He walked in to find Josh in there cooking breakfast.

"I hope you like eggs," Josh said in lieu of a greeting.

"Why do you hate him so much?" Trance nodded an answer to the egg question. "What did he do to hurt you?" Trance prodded, "Why did you beat him so badly?" He guessed at what happened between the two of them.

"Why are you so annoying?" Josh cracked another egg into a glass dish. He stirred the mixture with a fork and dumped it into a pan.

"I'm sorry, sometimes my curiosity gets the best of me."

"You seem pretty cocky for someone as young as you are."

Trance smiled oddly at the comment. "I'm sorry."

"Listen kid, you don't know what you've gotten yourself into and you don't want to know. So from now on, don't touch me. Oh yeah, and you can keep your hands off of my b.... Dylan too," Josh cautioned, catching himself.

'Was he just about to say boyfriend?' Trance wondered. "So, you guys are a couple then?" Trance asked.

"NO!" Josh yelped. "You can keep your nose out of our business and our minds too. If I...If we want you to know something we'll tell you."

"Fair enough," Trance gave in, throwing his hands up in the air. "I won't look anymore." He put air quotes around the word look.

"Good morning," Dylan yawned as he entered the kitchen.

"Eat up, so we can go find Tori," Josh set a plate of scrambled eggs in front of each of them. "I'm getting dressed." He walked out of the room.

Trance looked up at Dylan and smiled. "What a jerk. Is he always like that?"

"Since I've known him he has been. I guess I should warn you, he's a very violent person."

"I can tell. Did he do that to you?" Trance stared at Dylan's bruised face.

"That was a misunderstanding," Dylan explained. "Seriously, Trance, don't piss him off. He's unstable. He just recently lost his fiancé. Whatever you do, don't mention her."

"Lauren?" Trance smiled. "Oops, I forgot I'm not allowed to do that anymore."

"What did he say to you?"

"He just told me to stay out of your business."

Dylan nodded. "It's probably best that way."

32

The Hospital:

Dylan, Josh, & Trance

"St Louise's, please," Trance requested of the cab driver after they all piled into the back of the cab.

"We were just looking there yesterday," Dylan pointed out.

"Apparently, you weren't looking hard enough," Trance smiled shyly at Dylan. Trance was silent for the rest of the ride. He was trying miserably to block out the images that were bombarding his mind.

The main image that kept repeating was the vision of the motorcycle. He whimpered softly as he watched the motorcycle collide with the tree over and over again.

"Trance, you OK?" Dylan asked.

Trance nodded, quickly trying to hide the horror that filled his eyes. He wanted to ask Dylan how he had survived the accident, but he couldn't; not after Josh warned him to keep his mind out of their business.

When they arrived at the hospital, Trance was the first one out of the cab. He left the two men to deal with the money. He waited, just inside the door.

"Follow me," he said as they entered the lobby. He led them to the children's ward of the hospital. They followed him down hallways filled with children's laughter and sometimes they could hear children crying. He stopped at an open door and pointed at a bed with a teenage boy laying in it.

"Now, this is the part where you'll think I'm crazy," Trance explained nervously. "This is her." He walked into the room and stood next to the bed.

"How do you know she's in there?" Dylan stared at the body in the bed.

"I'm psychic, I told you." Trance shook his head, tears in his eyes.

"Are you sure that's Tori?" Josh asked.

Trance nodded, "Yes, I'm sure, I saw him do it to her," he paused. "Now, you're really going to think I'm off my rocker," he paused again, swallowing, "that's my body she's in."

"You're one of us," Dylan whispered in shock.

"What do you mean 'one of us'?" Trance asked.

"You're a victim like us," Dylan explained excitedly. "We're not in the right bodies either," he whispered.

"Dylan!" Josh scolded. "Don't tell him that."

"Why not? He's one of us!"

"How's Tori doing? Can we talk to her?" Josh asked.

"Let me check," Trance took hold of the hand that used to be his. He closed his eyes and mentally reached outward towards the body lying in the bed.

Instantly, he found himself in the between place. It was a place that only existed between sleeping and waking. This was the place where Tori had been hiding. She wasn't there. "Tori?" he called out softly into the silence and darkness of the between place. "Tori?" His mental voice rose. "TORI!" he screamed, but she was no longer in the between place. His mind began to panic as he tried to flee back to the body he was stuck in only to find he couldn't get back in. He tried again to get back in his own body, but like all the other times something stopped him. He was in a panicked state, ramming his soul against the barriers that kept him out. When he was completely exhausted, he stopped fighting and closed his mental eyes, holding back tears he wasn't even sure he could cry in the between place.

"Trance, TRANCE WAKE UP!" He heard a voice calling him from outside the between place.

"I CAN'T!" Trance screamed as loud as his mental voice could. Trance collapsed onto the ground and curled up in the fetal position.

"What do I do? What do I do?" he repeated violently to the emptiness of the between place.

"Trance?" he heard a different voice calling him and this voice was female.

"Tori?" Trance asked, opening his eyes. A woman stood before him. It was another woman he had never met before, but he knew who she was from Dylan. It was the woman Dylan was searching for.

"Maggie," he breathed softly. She looked like she was an angel. She wore a white dress that made her look soft and delicate; like a lily. The dress had gossamer sleeves that trailed behind her as if blown by a breeze. Her hair looked odd with the dress. It was light green with stringy-looking dreads.

"Are you an angel?"

"You have to go back," she urged softly.

"How did you get here?" he inquired, still not moving.

"I can't hold it open anymore; we have to go back now! Take my hand!" Maggie begged him.

Trance jumped up and ran to her.

"Hold on, this is going to hurt," she warned. Her voice faded into pain as she led him past the wall back into the body he had been in before.

"No!" Trance screamed. "I want to go back to mine!" he screamed, fighting against Maggie.

"I can't do that! I don't know how. PLEASE! I'm losing you," she screamed.

Finally, Trance relaxed and let it happen.

"What the hell are we going to do now?" Josh asked.

Dylan shook his head as he stared down at the lifeless body that sat in the chair next to the hospital bed.

"I don't know, Josh. This is all just too messed up to even comprehend what's going on anymore."

"Quiet, Dyl. I think he's coming around."

"I'm sorry, Maggie," Trance whispered softly and then his entire body went rigid. His already pale face turned white. Dylan started to shake him again, but Josh stopped him.

"Leave him be," Josh instructed. "You'll only make it worse."

"What if it's not Rejection?" Dylan asked.

"It is, he's coming out of it," Josh pointed out.

"Ugnh…," Trance groaned. "What the hell was that?" he asked, looking around.

"How the hell are we supposed to know?" Josh replied.

"Where's Maggie?" Trance looked around.

"Who's Maggie?" Josh also looked around perplexed.

"She's my wife," Dylan supplied, not thinking about it.

"I thought you had a husband and his name was Dylan?" Josh asked.

"No, Maggie's husband's name was Dylan. I'm her husband," he said, trying to work out what was going through his head.

"But Dylan's dead," Trance whispered weakly.

"If Dylan's dead…then how can you be him?" Josh asked.

Dylan was suddenly filled with a horrible rage that he couldn't seem to control. He violently pushed Josh up against the wall and held him there with his forearm.

"I DON'T KNOW!" Dylan screamed and then lowered his voice to a growl. "Do you think I don't know how crazy it sounds? Do you think I don't know how crazy it makes me? Fuck you both! Fuck all of this! I don't need it anymore. I can't take it anymore," he spat out. That thing that had once made him feel so complete only made him feel empty now. Something deep inside of him had snapped. His hatred for Josh was multiplied ten-fold. He couldn't contain it. He wanted to kill Josh right here and now. He wanted to smother the life right out of him. Those thoughts frightened him horribly. He had never before experienced such all-encompassing rage. He had to get away from Josh and Trance before he hurt someone.

Dylan released his hold on Josh and spun for the door.

33

The Past:

Dylan, Maggie, & Zach

ylan headed out of the hospital, and then he did one of his and Maggie's favorite things to do. He began to run. He ran to get away from his feelings for Trance. He ran to get away from Josh and his fists of fury. He ran to get away from the emptiness that had settled inside of him. He kept running until he was out of breath. When he finally stopped, he found himself standing just outside of a forest on a lonely stretch of road.

Something about this spot of the road brought his memory back. At first it came in flashes and then in waves. He fell to his knees in front of the tree that killed his body.

His motorcycle... his night of passion... infidelity... Maggie alone... she was waiting... the tires screeching... Zach's caressing voice that was somehow inside his head... his best friend Gary's words...

"Don't do it, Dylan," Gary warned him over beers one night. "Don't ever cheat on Maggie. If you do, that will be the end of it."

Then he was there that night. The first night, the only night he had been unfaithful to Maggie. It was two weeks after their wedding and he was out driving his new motorcycle.

Zach was a beautiful hitchhiker. Dylan fell for him immediately and stopped to pick him up.

They ended up in a hotel room together. One night of passion was all they had and then it was all over. The next morning, as they were getting ready to go, Zach pulled a gun out of his backpack. Zach held the gun up to his own head.

"Kiss me quick," Zach whispered softly.

"Don't do it," Dylan begged.

"Just kiss me," Zach demanded. "I won't kill myself, if you kiss me."

Dylan complied.

He felt queasy and then a pain like no other. He was spinning in a sickening vertigo that he couldn't seem to stop. He felt his body tensing with pain as the spinning sensation slowly subsided.

The horrible sound of the gun going off was almost worse than the pain that ripped through his head. Zach had shot him instead. He opened his eyes to stare at the gun in his hand. Dylan was holding the gun. How had he gotten the gun? This wasn't his hand; it was Zach's.

"What?" he gurgled as blood poured out of his nose. The Dylan standing in front of him smirked.

Dylan closed Zach's eyes and felt himself slipping away. Zach's body fell backwards onto the bed, but somehow Dylan was still standing there staring at his own body. He was filled with rage that anyone could do that to him. He wanted to attack Zach. He wanted to kill him. Dylan ran towards Zach, ready to strike, but instead of colliding with him, he seemed to sink back into his own body.

That was the last thing Dylan remembered, until the night of the motorcycle accident. He woke up, inside his own body, that night a little more than three months after his failed encounter with the body snatcher. He got dressed, not realizing how long it had been since his affair with Zach. He went out and got on his bike. He drove the bike until, he felt Zach's arms wrap around him. They weren't actually there; Dylan was still alone, but he felt them, nonetheless.

Zach took over then, they never got off the bike; Zach just pushed Dylan's soul out of the way. He pushed Dylan's essence back into the depths of their shared mind. Dylan watched helplessly as Zach made him commit suicide for the second time.

After that it was just darkness and an occasional glimpse of Maggie sleeping or Maggie jogging. Somehow, he hadn't died.

He was still alive and now Maggie was missing. He had to find her again.

"Where are you, Maggie?" he whispered as he drifted into sleep, curled up under the tree that his body finally died under.

***

"Dylan?" Trance's voice called out to him. The sweet voice pulled him out of his nightmares. He awoke, shivering violently in the crisp autumn air.

"Here, put this on him," Josh's voice instructed and then Dylan felt a warm coat cover him up.

"How'd you know where to find me?"

"I remembered this spot from a vision I had when you...shook my hand." Trance didn't want to tell either man that he had kissed Dylan.

"Where's Maggie?"

"Don't worry, she's safe," Trance assured him.

"We hope," Josh said smugly

"What do you mean? Where is she?" Dylan begged.

"She's um...," Trance paused, not knowing how to explain what happened. "She's in my body at the hospital," he finished slowly with a guilty look on his face.

"What? Is she OK?" Dylan asked, struggling to get up.

"I think so," Trance replied.

"How did it happen? What about Tori?" Dylan questioned.

"Later Dyl, we need to get in the cabin. It's really cold out here." Josh shivered.

"Come on, the cab's waiting for us," Trance urged, helping him stand.

"Is she awake? Can I see her?" Dylan inquired desperately.

"No, not anymore, the shock was too hard on her. She's unconscious again. You can see her tomorrow when visiting hours start again."

"I need to see her," Dylan insisted. "I know what happened to me now," Dylan revealed. As the cab drove them back to the cabin, he closed his eyes and went back to sleep.

***

The rest of his past came back to him in a dream while he slept in the cab.

Dylan was lying on the shoulder of the road, calling for Maggie in his mind. He knew he was dying, but he needed to see her again. He needed to kiss her lips once more. He needed to touch her hair.

As if by some miracle, Maggie appeared.

"I heard you calling me," she whispered in his ear as she cradled his head. Dylan looked up and saw tears rolling down her cheeks.

Zach tried to take over then, but Dylan couldn't let him. He shoved Zach violently away.

"I....love...you...Magpie," he struggled to say using the nickname he always called her.

"Shh...shh! Dyl, don't try to talk. You'll be OK, I promise," she sobbed to her husband.

"No!" he said violently, coughing up blood. He shook his head painfully. "Kiss me, please," he begged.

"No, Dyl, no," she sobbed, wiping away at his lips. "You can't die, you can't."

"Kiss," Dylan growled, "KISS!" he shouted, more blood rushing between his lips.

Maggie shook her head, but bent down anyways and she kissed him passionately, trying to overlook the taste of his blood on her lips.

Dylan took a deep breath and jumped. He felt something pulling him back into the corpse behind him. Zach was still in there; he was trying to pull Dylan back. Zach wanted Maggie, Zach wanted to be Maggie. That angered Dylan and anger gave him strength.

Suddenly, he felt Maggie; she was pulling him in. She was accepting his soul into her own. Then it was over. He tasted his blood on Maggie's lips and went into shock. He receded so far back into Maggie's mind that he almost lost himself. She couldn't know he was inside of her mind. So he hid from her and slept. He slept until he felt her sorrow. Until he heard Josh's voice screaming for Sunshine. That's when he woke, but he didn't take over Josh's body until Maggie fled from the pain that Josh-in-Erik's-body inflicted on her.

***

"Dylan, wake up!" Josh's voice ripped him from his memory dream. "Get out of the cab!"

Dylan stumbled out of the cab and ambled slowly up to the cabin. His legs were sore and his lungs were on fire.

"Dylan," Josh called out to him as the cab drove away. Dylan turned to look back at him, only to find a fist grinding into his stomach.

"Don't ever try that shit again," Josh threatened.

"Look ASSHOLE! I don't know who the hell you are, bossing everyone around like you do. I haven't had a body of my own in about four years and I'd be more than happy to keep this one. So, I'd watch who I was hitting if I were you, or else one morning you'll wake up to find me and Trance gone. I don't need you and I'm not going to take your shit anymore!" Dylan shoved him angrily. "You better hope to God that Maggie makes it through this, because if she doesn't, then I'm out of here and so is your precious body," Dylan hissed.

"It must not be that precious to him. The way he keeps using you as a punching bag," Trance added as he leaned against the wall, just outside of the door.

"FUCK YOU BOTH!" Josh shouted and stormed into the cabin.

"Thanks, Trance."

"No prob," Trance gestured that they go inside. "We need to work with each other, not against each other."

"Exactly,"

"You are going to tell me everything aren't you?" Trance asked as he followed Dylan into the cabin.

"Definitely," he turned back to Trance and flashed him a smile.

34

A Theater:

Eon & Lilly

Lilly pushed past the crowd of people leaving the theater. She had to go somewhere she could hide. Somewhere Eon couldn't find her, but where? She used the crowd of people leaving the theater to slip inside. Just before she disappeared into the empty theater, a hand closed around her elbow.

She jumped, but tried to remain calm. It was probably just a theater worker stopping her from theater hopping. She turned to find a man in a theater uniform holding her arm.

"I've been watching you," the man revealed. "Two movies already and now you're going for a third. I don't think so."

She let out a sigh of relief. If they arrested her, she would be safe. She would be away from Eon.

"Are you going to arrest me?" Lilly asked.

"No, I'll just let you off with a warning this time," the man replied, leading her to the door of the lobby. "A very stern warning, Lilly," his voice turned maniacal as he dragged her out into the night.

"Oh God, no," Lilly cried, struggling to get away. "Leave me alone, Eon."

"I can't. You know too much."

"I don't know anything." It was a pitiful lie, but it was all she could think of to say.

"Don't lie to me, Lilly."

"Help me," Lilly begged the crowd that surged around them. Eon pulled her down an alley. "HELP ME!" she screamed louder.

"Shut up!" Eon commanded, slapping his hand over her mouth.

Lilly brought her knee up and kicked his shin with the back of her heel. He dropped his hand and let her go.

"HELP ME!" she screamed. The crowd seemed to not be able to hear her. Eon grabbed the back of her shirt and pulled her back towards him.

"Leave me alone," she begged. "You're not my Eon," she accused, spitting in his face.

Eon punched her face. Lilly opened her mouth in shock. "You are not my Eon," she repeated. She screamed as loud as she could. Finally someone heard her.

"Hey!" a man from the crowd shouted "Leave her alone!" The man ran towards them with three of his friends following him.

"Thank you. Thank you," Lilly gasped gratefully as they attacked Eon. She ran away from the alley. She ran as fast as she could into the night. They couldn't stop Eon for long, but maybe it was just long enough for her to disappear.

35

The Bedroom:

Dylan & Trance

"Trance, what happened at the hospital?" Dylan asked in a small voice as Trance tucked him into his bed.

"Honestly, I don't really know, but I'll try to explain it to you. There's this place…," Trance started.

"It's like a dark non-place?" Dylan asked, remembering all the time he spent there, wondering if it was heaven or hell.

"You've been there, I take it?"

"For a very long time," Dylan affirmed sadly.

"I would usually go there and talk to Tori. I thought if she wasn't so alone, then maybe she'd stay in my body and it wouldn't die. So, I went there to ask her how she was doing, but she was gone." He paused for a moment, thinking. "Then I tried to come back here to Elliot's body, but I couldn't get back in. I tried to get back into my body, but I couldn't do that either. I was stuck in that place. I totally panicked. That was when she came to me. She was so beautiful. Dylan, she looked like an angel. She took my hand and calmed me down. She started leading me back to this body and I freaked out. I don't know what came over me. I just didn't want to come back here into Elliot's body. I pulled away from her. She pulled back, warning me to hurry. She couldn't keep the link open for long. Then I finally gave in and followed her back to this body. As I settled in, I watched her and she was going towards the light; she was giving up and leaving the between place. I couldn't let her do that. I just couldn't. So I grabbed her with all of my essence and shoved her into my body…my real body. She didn't want to go, but I know how much she means to you. I couldn't just let her leave. You have to understand, Dylan, I had to do it."

"I understand. I would have done the same thing. Is she OK?"

"I don't know. I hope so. She never seemed to come out of the coma, at all. We didn't really stay that long; we had to go find you. Hopefully, she'll be awake tomorrow and you can finally see her."

"I hope so," Dylan whispered with a sleep weary voice.

"Goodnight," Trance said, placing a small kiss on Dylan's forehead and, for once, he didn't get a vision.

"That's weird," Trance told a half-asleep Dylan. "I didn't *see* anything."

36

The Hospital:
Eon & Maggie

Maggie opened her eyes to find herself staring at a ceiling that was painted to look like a blue cloudy sky. It was hard to remember where she was or even why she was there.

She heard footsteps coming towards her bed. She tried to turn her head, but she felt so disconnected. Her body didn't want to respond…until the nurse touched her.

That was when the pain started; a pain so horrible that she couldn't even cry out. She couldn't remember ever feeling anything like this pain. Then the visions started. They bombarded her mind with such speed she could barely make sense of them. Then, on top of the pain and the visions, came voices. Thousands of whispering voices came out of the darkness and filled her head.

Maggie cried out with a voice that was not her own and she didn't recognize the voice.

"Andrew, you're awake," the nurse said, still touching Maggie's arm.

Maggie wailed in pain and horror at the total assault against most of her senses. She struggled to push the nurse's hand away. Then she struggled to get out of the bed. It was so difficult for her to move, but she had to make the voices stop.

"SHUT UP!" she screamed, pounding at her head with her fists.

The nurse tried to grab her to calm her down, but the nurse's touch made everything amplified. She pushed the nurse away screaming. She pushed so hard she toppled out of the bed. She closed her eyes to block the visions, but that only made it worse. She felt more hands closing around her and lifting her back into the bed. The hands turned her onto her stomach. She felt a needle shoved rudely into her butt cheek. Then she felt nothing…bliss…. silence…darkness again.

***

Maggie struggled to open her drug-hazed eyes.

"I knew this was coming," a voice close to her ear whispered. She turned her head which was easier than opening her eyes. "I honestly didn't think you would wake up at all, most of them don't," the voice laughed. "Most of them don't have the guts."

Maggie's eyes finally opened and she saw the man who was talking. He was pushing her on a stretcher down a long hallway. He was bent down so low that his head was beside hers. Maggie caught a glimpse of a sign that read 'Men's Ward'.

"Not a man," Maggie struggled to get out. The man's smirk grew into a grin.

"So the way I see it…," the man started again, ignoring her, "you have two options. You can adapt and live a perfectly normal life as Drew or you can die in here, in 'hell', by trying to fight it," he laughed. "Choose well my friend."

He caught Maggie's eyes staring at his nametag. She was trying to read it.

"Don't even think about it, Drew." he said, stressing the name. "Even if you do survive this place, I'll be long gone and this body will have some other poor schmuck in it."

"Not Drew," Maggie insisted as she finally realized who was standing next to her. It was Josh…not Josh… It was the man…the thing that had stolen her body, who now had stolen this orderly's body.

"See Tori, I know that, and you know that, but they don't and I'm not saying a word. You can tell whomever you want; in here they'll just think you were sent here for the right reason." Eon laughed. "I'm ditching this body as soon as I get out of here. I don't need it anymore, now that I know where you are." Eon was silent for the rest of the walk down the long hallway.

Eon wheeled her into a plain white room. "Well, I guess we're here. It's time for me to go." He bent down next to her stretcher and placed a gentle kiss on her lips. Not knowing if it would work or not she pushed with all her might, trying to change places with him. He pulled back quickly.

"Whoa, where'd you learn that?"

Maggie closed her eyes and sobbed, all her energy was spent now.

"Too bad you aren't even close to being strong enough." Just then, Eon's borrowed eyes took an icy glaze. "So you want to be me now, huh?" he asked. "You want to be just like me?"

Maggie cried out in fear as Eon's hand grabbed her hair and pulled. He lifted her head up, towards his face. "Just in case you feel ambitious enough to try that again, let me give you a little taste of what it's like to be me," he spat into Maggie's ear. "Unfortunately, it will be painful and it may bring on insanity." He pulled himself back so Maggie could see his face. He clenched his teeth and his seemingly gentle face turned into a mask of pure anger and hatred. He covered the side of her face with the palm of his hand. His fingers twined through her hair.

"Josh, no," Maggie used the only name she knew him as. It was too late. She could feel the heat radiating from his palm. Then the hospital was gone, all that was left were the images; images of a thousand different faces, a thousand different kisses. There were memories too, so many memories, from thousands of lives. She saw so many faces and strangely she recognized more than a few of them. She saw Dylan's face; saw herself in Dylan's memories. She whimpered at finally seeing his face again. "Dylan," she whispered softly. Suddenly, everything stopped. She opened her eyes.

The man was down on his knees next to her stretcher. Tears were welling in his eyes. "Oh God, you can't be Maggie."

"I am," she whispered with conviction.

"No, Maggie, what have I done? I never wanted to hurt you. I love you. I love you, Maggie." Maggie was still in shock from all the memories.

"What did you do to me? Why?" she breathed. It was difficult for her to talk. Her mouth was dry and her tongue felt too big for her mouth. "Why?"

"I...I...didn't mean to," he stammered. He jumped up quickly from the floor as footsteps sounded in the hallway. He wiped a stray tear off of his face and all of his sadness appeared to be gone.

"Help me," Maggie begged. "Get me out of here,"

"I'm sorry, Maggie," she heard him whisper as he squeezed her hand. She took advantage of the touch of skin against skin and tried again. He jumped and looked back at her lying on the stretcher. Her hand felt like it was on fire. She lifted it up to see if it was burnt. She was not surprised to see smoke rising off of it.

"Don't leave me," she whispered with pleading eyes.

"I'm sorry, Drew, there's nothing I can do.," the man replied, walking out of the room.

"DON'T YOU LEAVE ME AGAIN, YOU ASSHOLE!" Maggie screamed. The man disappeared down the hallway.

"Well, I see our newest patient is awake," a doctor announced as he walked into the room. "We don't need to sedate you again, now do we, Mr. Maxwell?"

"No, but I'm not Mr. Maxwell," Maggie insisted.

"Well, we'll get all that straightened out later. For now, your parents are waiting to see you," the doctor said as an orderly walked in pushing a wheelchair.

"My parents are dead." Maggie said sullenly. She tried to sit up, but she couldn't get very far. Her body was still slightly drugged.

"Well, according to the lovely couple in my office, they're not," the doctor explained as he quickly wrote things down on his clipboard.

The orderly scooped Maggie up as if she were a rag doll. She felt like one. He placed her gently in the wheelchair. Maggie began to shiver. Why were hospitals always so cold?

"Can I take the blanket?" Maggie asked softly. The orderly picked up the blanket from the bed and laid it across Maggie's lap. He wheeled her down to the doctor's office. Maggie tried to remember the path he took, but she was still foggy and sluggish. A woman stood by the window fussing with her hair. She turned when they entered the room.

The orderly parked the wheelchair between the two chairs in the room.

"Drew!" the woman gasped and ran over to Maggie. She threw her arms around Maggie. Maggie had no choice but to hug her back.

Images filled her mind with the contact: the mother nursing a baby, a small boy skinning his knee, the feeling of the mother's panic when she found out her son was in the hospital.

'*I hope my baby's not crazy,*' the mother's voice echoed through Maggie's head.

Maggie shook her head, trying to clear the voice away. She didn't want to hear the voices or see the visions again.

"No," Maggie shook her head and pulled her arms away from the woman. "Don't touch me." The mother pulled back, a look of hurt filling her eyes.

"I hurt all over," Maggie lied to her. She didn't want to be the cause of any of the pain in the woman's eyes.

"What happened to his hair?" Drew's mom asked, turning to the doctor.

"My hair?" Maggie asked confused.

The mother pulled out a mirror and handed it to Maggie. Maggie stared in recognition at the faded purple-haired boy staring back at her.

"Trance," she gasped out.

"Yes, honey, that's what all of your friends call you."

"No." Maggie fingered the white spot in Trance's hair in the exact spot where 'Josh' had touched her.

"No, I'm not Trance."

"Honey, listen to me," Trance's mother began talking. "While you were in a coma you turned 18 and we need you to sign these papers for us, OK?"

"What for?" Maggie demanded.

"We want you to stay here in this hospital, until you get better." the father answered. He seemed very distant and awkward.

"OK," Maggie agreed. The orderly who was still standing behind her pushed her over to the desk. What did she care? This wasn't her body. She'd find a way out of here. Maggie leaned forward and placed her hands on the desk. The top of the desk shimmered and rippled as if it were covered with water.

"What the hell?" Maggie asked in Trance's voice.

"What is it, honey?" his mother asked.

"Nothing," Maggie shook her head.

She tried to pick up the pen and it happened again. She dropped the pen. "No. This isn't real. None of you are real," Maggie argued, quietly beginning to panic. "How did I get here?" she whispered softly. The last thing she remembered was Sunshine dying. Sunshine died when Maggie was Josh and then Maggie fled into the darkness. Somehow Dylan had taken her place.

Dylan. The word was like a breath of fresh air. Dylan was alive! The thought brightened her, but then she saddened just as quickly. Dylan was alive and in Josh's body. From the looks of it Dylan-as-Josh was nowhere around. Maggie was alone in another unknown body.

"No...no...no," she started mumbling. "I can't do this again. I can't do it alone." Maggie looked around at the dumbfounded faces around her. Quickly, she jumped out of the chair and ran to the fence-covered window.

"DYLAN!" she screamed. "WHERE ARE YOU?" She grabbed the fence around the windows and started shaking it. She was in total panic mode.

'*What's wrong with my son*?' the mother's voice sounded inside Maggie's head.

"I'm not your son," Maggie retorted, turning towards the mother.

'*He's possessed*,' the father's voice sounded in Maggie's head.

"I'm not possessed," she argued, turning back to the window. She began yelling out the window, calling to Dylan again. The sun was just rising over the horizon. All Maggie could see for miles was a forest.

"No...No...NO!" she yelled as the voices started to fill up her head again. "Shut up! SHUT UP!" she screamed, falling to the floor. Maggie watched as the ripples flowed around her body. She wished that they would somehow swallow her up. She just wanted to die. She was so close; so close to escaping and then that spirit named Trance pulled her back. When had that happened? She couldn't remember, but she could remember the light and how beautiful it was. "None of you are real. You're not real," she mumbled as the freshly injected drugs took hold of her and pulled her back into the darkness.

37

The Cabin:

Dylan, Josh, & Trance

Trance woke up, screaming in horror, at the nightmares that plagued his sleeping mind.

His screams woke up Dylan, who was sleeping in the next room. Dylan jumped out of his bed and ran into Trance's room. "Are you OK, Trance?"

"I had this nightmare, this horrible, horrible nightmare. I dreamt that I was blind. Oh God, I can't shake the feeling. I'm afraid, Dylan." Instinctively, Dylan ran to him and put his arms around him.

"Oh my God," Trance gasped, terror saturating his voice.

"What?" Dylan asked in fear.

"I *am* blind," Trance admitted quietly with a haunted look in his eyes.

"What do you mean? You can't see?"

"No…no…no…I can see, but I can't *SEE*. There's no visions; no voices, nothing. It's all gone!" Trance babbled urgently. "Everything is so different. Is this how normal people live? There's nothing… OH SHIT!" he shouted, cutting himself off.

"Trance?"

"Maggie… What if she has my *sight*? It will drive her crazy. It's driving me crazy without it. We have to save her. We have to go now!" Trance urged as he jumped out of bed and started getting dressed.

"I'll go get Josh," Dylan, who was already dressed, offered. He ran into Josh's room, but Josh was not there.

"JOSH!" he yelled out. There was no answer.

"I can't find him," Dylan informed Trance.

"Hold on, let me try." He tried to reach out with his mind, but there was nothing. "I forgot it's gone," he whispered, the haunted look returning to his eyes.

"Trance, it'll be OK. I swear. We just need to get to Maggie."

"No," Trance disagreed. "I can't get it back, unless I go back and no one knows how to do that."

Dylan put his arms around Trance again.

"I'm so sorry," Dylan whispered.

Trance looked up into Dylan's eyes. Dylan couldn't stop himself from placing Josh's lips onto Trance's borrowed lips.

"Thank you," Trance whispered.

"So what, are you two a couple now?" Josh asked. He was standing in the doorway.

"Maybe we are," Dylan retorted. He expected some rude comment about fags, but Josh said nothing. That was when Dylan realized how bad Josh looked.

"Are you OK?" Dylan asked.

Josh nodded slowly. "Not great, but I'm still fighting." He paused. "I rented a van since someone stole Erik's car. It'll help us get around faster…and it's cheaper than taxis." He leaned against the doorframe he seemed unable to support himself.

"Let's go make sure Maggie is OK," Dylan suggested.

Josh and Trance nodded.

***

"What's wrong with Maggie?" Josh asked as soon as they were on the road.

"Trance lost his powers. He thinks Maggie might have them."

"Dammit, Trance. Didn't I tell you not to leave your powers lying around?" Josh joked, laughing nervously.

Dylan's eyes widened in surprise, He exchanged a look with Trance; Josh had never joked with either of them. "Are you sure you're OK?"

"No, Dylan, I'm not OK. I'm losing the battle. I don't know how much longer I can fight," Josh sighed sadly. "I'm sorry I was such an ass to you guys. I just don't want to die like this. Not in here." Dylan was completely shocked. This was Josh. The real Josh: no masks, no anger, no walls. "Is Maggie going to be alright?" Josh asked, with genuine concern, directing his question to Trance.

Trance shook his head. "I don't think so, but there really is no way to know. If she has my powers, it could...destroy her." He closed his eyes and rested his head back on the seat. The void of nothingness in his head was giving him a headache. Though it was strange, because when he had his powers, he sometimes longed to just be 'normal'. Now he was just a 'normal' guy and all he wanted was to hear the soft murmur of other people's thoughts.

"Is it really that bad?" Josh turned the van.

"It could be. There's no way to know. I grew up with my gift. I didn't ever know what it was like to be normal. But if this is normal... this void, this emptiness, if this is what normal people feel, then it will be bad for her, very bad."

Josh said nothing, but Dylan felt the van accelerate.

38

The Asylum:

Cody & Maggie

Maggie awoke to the loud clamor of voices echoing inside her head. One voice in the clamor stood out above all the others.

"Lady?" a small child-like voice kept asking. She kept feeling a tugging on her sleeve. Trying to pull herself out of the darkness, she focused on the child's voice and reached out to it, hoping it could lead her back to sanity. Instantly, she regretted it.

She saw flashes of three people: a child, a mother, and a man with a gun. The mother and child were running from the man with the gun. He caught the small boy and kissed him full on the lips. Maggie saw the exchange happen. The little boy was pushed into the man's body and the man was now in the child's body. The child's body fell to the ground and started quivering. The mother ran to her baby's body. She was screaming. The child sat up and kissed the mother's lips. She watched again as the mother's soul went into the child's body as it lay on the ground dying.

The mother's body stood up and went over to the man with the gun. She took the gun from his hand. She shot the child's body and turned and shot the man. "Mommy, no!" the man begged in the same childlike voice Maggie heard earlier.

"Get out of there!" the childlike voice cried out. She felt a wall come down blocking her from those memories.

Maggie opened her eyes to see the man who had been holding the gun in the memory standing next to her bed. His face frightened her, but her eyes locked onto the eyes of a child.

"Cody?" Maggie asked. The name was supplied to her from the voices inside her head. The man nodded and then shook his head violently.

"No, I'm Nathan," he corrected.

"But you are Cody? The little boy from…," Maggie began.

"Not anymore," the man interrupted her. "I have to pretend that I am Nathan or they give me shocks. You have to do what they tell you to do or you get shocks," the boy explained with a frightened look in his eyes. "What's your name?" He sat down on his bed, sticking his thumb in his mouth.

"Maggie," she replied.

"Not your girl name. What's your boy name?" he sighed in frustration. "If I call you Maggie…"

"I know you get shocks," Maggie finished.

"And so will you," he warned.

"Fine, it's Drew, my boy name… My name is Drew." She looked around the room she was in. It was a sparse and sterile-looking room. There were some posters hanging on Cody's side of the room. Maggie laughed at the clichéd kitten hanging on to a rope with the words "hang in there" written across the bottom of it.

"West got me that. He knows that I like kitties." Cody smiled.

The other posters were of women in tight bathing suits. Maggie gave the boy a questioning look. "Those are my shocks protection. I'm not supposed to act like a little kid. I get shocks if I do."

"But you are a little kid?" Maggie asked.

Cody nodded. "Not anymore though, now I'm a man."

Maggie almost laughed, but she could tell how proud he was of himself.

"Where are we?" Maggie asked, looking out the window. It had the same fence on the inside of it as the one in the doctor's office did.

Cody smiled brightly. "I know that! I know the answer to that one. Woodview Re-hab-il-ation Hospital for the criminally insane," he said proudly. "And I even got the middle one right. That's the hardest one of all. I can spell it too want to hear me. R-E-H-A...," he started.

"No, that's OK," Maggie whispered, but he continued spelling. The last words hit Maggie hard. "Criminally insane," she repeated.

"Yeah, but don't worry. We're just in the crazy ward." He wrinkled his nose in disgust. "We're not in the meanie ward. My mom is in there, but it's not really my mom. It's someone else now, but it's not the bad man who did this to us. The meanies are locked up behind bars over there; on our side the doors are open."

He gestured at the door and it seemed to open on its own. Cody giggled as the doctor walked into the room.

"Andrew?" the doctor asked. Her voice was soft and sweet.

"My name is...," Maggie began glancing at Cody, who was shaking his head with a mask of pain on his face. "Drew," Maggie finished.

"Drew, I'm sorry I couldn't get here any sooner. We had an incident. I'm very busy. So, I'll leave Nathan to show you around. You can do that, right Nathan?" Her voice changed to the tone of someone who was speaking to a child.

"I can drive a car," he announced. Maggie knew he was lying, shocks-protection he called it.

The doctor laughed. She turned and left the room with a worried look on her face.

"She's crazy," Cody whispered after she was gone.

"I wonder why she seemed so worried,"

"An orderly went crazy. He's talking like us. Can't you hear his thoughts?"

"I can," Maggie said sadly, finally listening to the voice that was screaming in her mind. "It's not me! I'm not me!" It repeated over and over.

"Come on!" Cody called as he ran out of the room. Maggie jumped up and chased after him.

39

The Hospital:

Dylan, Josh, & Trance

"**H**urry up!" Dylan called out to Trance as they ran through the almost empty hospital. Dylan stopped short in the doorway to the room where Trance's body was. "Where is she?" he gasped as he took in the empty bed.

"Maybe they moved her," Trance suggested.

"Where is she? WHERE IS SHE?" Dylan screamed. Trance grabbed him and tried to cover his mouth with his hand.

"Shh! Shh! Please, Dylan, please. Stop screaming," Trance urged soothingly. He kept struggling to cover Dylan's mouth, but Dylan kept pulling away. He just kept screaming her name and "Where is she?"

"You better shut him up before they take him away too," Josh's voice said from the doorway. "I talked to the doctor, they transferred her to Woodview."

"Woodview?" Dylan's voice was raw from screaming.

"Why'd they take her there?" Trance asked.

"Apparently, she woke up and tried to kill one of the nurses."

"She tried to kill a nurse?" Dylan asked.

"She definitely has my powers then," Trance rationalized. "What are we going to do now?"

"I don't know," Josh shrugged. "Let's get him out of here," he gestured to Dylan, who was sobbing into Trance's shoulder. "We'll go look into this Woodview place. Maybe we can get her there."

40

The Asylum:

Cody & Maggie

"Drew? Please wake up." Cody shook the body of his new friend, but Drew wasn't waking up. Drew couldn't be sleeping, he was standing up; people don't sleep standing up. His eyes were open and Cody didn't like the way they were rolled back into his head.

Drew's eyes shut and Maggie opened them again. "Oh God, Dylan!" she collapsed into a sitting position on the floor. "I could hear him calling me," she whispered to Cody, who had sunk to the ground next to her.

"NATHAN!" an orderly screamed. "He's been in a coma! Why didn't you use a wheelchair?"

Cody started shaking. "I'm sorry," Cody apologized. "I didn't know. Nobody told me."

"Well then, it's not your fault, now is it?" the orderly said, checking Drew's vital signs. "I'm sorry I yelled at you."

"I saw Dylan," Maggie whispered to the orderly.

"Oh, did you?" the orderly patronized her.

"He needs me," Drew's voice whispered Maggie's words. "I have to find him. He needs me," she repeated and let the darkness take her again.

41

The Rental Van:

Dylan, Josh, Lilly, & Trance

"**I** have to find her," Dylan whispered hoarsely, from the front seat of the rental van.

"We will," Trance assured him softly. They'd been driving around half the day not knowing what to do next.

"We could keep going back," Trance suggested, from the backseat.

"What's the point?" Josh asked. "What is it going to solve?" He paused. "We don't need to know where he's been; we need to know where he's going."

"I could find him easily....if I had my powers," Trance rubbed his temples. His headache had turned into a migraine.

"Maggie?" Dylan asked softly.

"Will you two quit whining? I have to think, and all you guys can do is moan about your losses," Josh scolded.

"NO!" Dylan shouted. "That's Maggie! Well, it's her body anyway. Pull over!"

The van screeched to a halt in front of a bruised and dirty young woman.

"Maggie?" Dylan called, jumping out of the van.

The girl shook her head and started to run, but Dylan was faster. The girl struggled against his grasp, but he held her steady.

"Listen," Dylan started in a calming voice. "I know you're not Maggie. I know what he did to you." she froze.

"How could you know?" she demanded.

"Because, he did it to me...us," he admitted, gesturing to Trance and the van. "We're looking for the bastard who did this. We're trying to fix it," Dylan babbled. "We can help you," he assured her, letting her go. "I'm Dylan. What's your name?" he asked.

The woman's eyes seemed to become less wild. She dusted herself off and smiled shyly. "I'm Dr. Lillian Reynolds," she introduced herself, shaking his outstretched hand. "You can call me Lilly." She looked at Dylan suspiciously. "How do I know you're not Eon?" she asked softly. Even though, she could tell by looking in this man's eyes that he was not Eon.

"Who's Eon?" Dylan asked.

"The man who did this to me...to us," Lilly explained.

"I guess you'll have to trust me," Dylan told her softly.

"I do," Lilly said, in a voice barely above a whisper. "We have to get out of here. He'll find us," she warned. "He always does."

42

The Asylum:
Maggie & West

"Wake up, Drew." A familiar voice woke Maggie. She opened her eyes to find the orderly that had helped her yesterday. "It's time for physical therapy," the man said, locking the brakes on the wheelchair that he brought in with him. "We got to get those muscles working again."

"Where's Nathan?" she asked softly.

"Don't worry about him. He's watching TV," the orderly answered as he lifted her out of the bed and into the wheelchair. "I'm Weston, by the way," he said, pointing at his nametag, "but you can call me West." He released the brakes on the chair and pushed her out into the hall.

"Have I told you I like your hair? I'd do it like that, but my parents would kill me," West babbled. For the first time Maggie noticed how young he was. He couldn't have been more than 20.

"You're so young."

"I'm two years older than you." West ruffled her hair.

Maggie grunted. If only someone would listen to her, they'd know. They would know that she wasn't a man. They would know that she wasn't supposed to be in this body.

That's when it started again. The floor around the wheels began to swirl around as if West were pushing her through water.

"This can't be real," she murmured softly, barely above a whisper. West didn't hear her as he was too busy showing her the sights.

When they arrived at the room for rehabilitation, West began to help her into a standing position. More flashes came with his touch, but this time they weren't too unpleasant. They were flashes of West and a woman having sex. Maggie tried to push the memories away, but they wouldn't stop. They just kept repeating over and over.

"Stop touching me! STOP TOUCHING ME!" she screamed and immediately he let go. "I'm sorry, I'm sorry," she apologized losing her balance. She reached for him. He grasped her hand to steady her. This time the images were different: a funeral, voices, and sadness, so much sadness.

"YOU CAN'T TOUCH ME!" she screamed, pushing him away again and running away across the room.

"Drew, calm down," West soothed. "You do not want a doctor to see you like this," he warned, moving slowly towards her. "Listen, Drew, let me touch you. Let me put you back in the chair."

"I'm not Drew." Maggie shook her head, losing her balance again. She grabbed onto the counter, a plethora of images poured into her head just from touching the counter. She couldn't even concentrate on one of them, to separate it out from the rest. Then West's arms were around her. "Why can't you see me as I really am?" she asked staring into his eyes.

West stared back at the woman in his arms. Instead of holding Drew, West was holding Maggie. It was Maggie: her face, her body, her hair. "Who are you?" West whispered in shock.

"DON'T TOUCH HER!" West called out. The other orderlies, who had heard the commotion, were creeping towards West and Maggie. "I GOT IT!" he called out. She had gone limp in his arms.

"West, be careful, that boy is dangerous," another orderly warned, confirming Maggie's theory that it was only West that could see her for who she really was.

"Don't let them touch me, West," Maggie begged. "Please don't let them."

"What just happened?" West whispered in her ear.

"You saw me?" Maggie asked in a frightened voice.

"I see you," he carried her back over to the chair and set her down in it, not once taking his eyes away from hers. He was looking at Maggie, not at Drew.

"Who are you?" he whispered again.

"I don't know, anymore." Maggie answered, staring into his eyes. As soon as he removed his hands from her, more visions filled her head. She was getting visions from the chair. She sprang up from the chair and ran over to the corner again.

"DREW!" West yelled.

"He died in there!" she screamed in an accusatory tone. "You put me in that chair where he died. Who was he? How did he die? Did you guys kill him? Which one of you did it?" She spun around to look at the orderlies. "WHY CAN'T YOU JUST LEAVE ME ALONE?"

West tried to make it back over to her, but another orderly got there first. He closed his arms around her. She howled in pain at the visions that assaulted her brain. She swung her elbow backwards and caught him under his rib. He fell backwards groaning in pain.

She was surprised at her own strength. "Stay away from me!" she threatened, grabbing the syringe from the felled orderly. She held the syringe out in front of her and made her way over to West. "I'm sorry, I can't stay in here," she whispered softly. Then she gently kissed his lips. She forced her soul towards him and into him, but hands closed upon her and pulled her away from West. West collapsed to the ground.

"NO!" she screamed in anger at her failure. She struggled against the hands, but they continued to hold her. "NO! NO! NO!" she screamed, expecting them to give her another shot, but they didn't.

"The only way you're ever going to learn is if you feel it, so, no medicine for you," The orderly closest to her explained. They carried her out of the room and down the hall. She was screaming and kicking, but nobody cared. The patients looked up, but the nurses and other orderlies looked away.

They carried her into a room and placed her on a table. Three of the orderlies had to hold her down while one strapped her down on the table.

"NO!!!" Maggie screamed as she realized what they were doing. Wasn't electro-shock therapy banned? She couldn't remember. Maybe she could still get out of this body. She reached for the closest orderlies arm and clasped her hand around it. She tried to force herself across the gap, but it was too late, the electricity flowed through her. All she could feel was pain and then finally, thankfully, she fell back into the darkness again.

43

Outside the Van:

Dylan, Josh, Lilly, & Trance

The sound of someone collapsing onto the ground stole Dylan's attention away from the newfound victim. "Josh!" Dylan yelled, running over to Josh who had just stumbled out of the van and collapsed to the ground clutching his stomach.

"Trance! I need your help!" Dylan called out, glancing back to where Trance had been standing, ready to greet Lilly. He too was doubled over and Lilly was reaching out to touch him.

"LILLY! No, don't touch him," Dylan yelled. "Help me with Josh, he's bleeding."

Lilly ran over to Josh. "He's not breathing," Dylan pointed out. "Don't you give up, Josh!" Dylan screamed, grasping Josh's shirt in both hands and shaking him.

"Stop," Lilly placed her hands on Dylan's shoulders. "Let me look." She knelt down beside Erik's body. "He's breathing, but it's shallow," Lilly informed Dylan. "Help me take off his shirt. We need to stop the blood. He must have cut himself when he fell."

Dylan ripped Josh's shirt and gently peeled it open. There were half-healed scars all over his chest and stomach. "What the hell?" Dylan asked. He was sure he had never seen them there before.

"The pain," Josh reached up and clasped his hand on Dylan's wrist. His voice was barely above a whisper. "Don't you see? It's the pain that kept me here."

"We're not going to lose you. Whatever you do, stay in the between place," Dylan begged with tears streaming down his face.

"Even if this body dies?" Josh whispered tears filling his eyes. He was not ready to die.

"You're not dying!" Dylan assured him.

"But this body is. Besides, what do I have to live for? My girl is gone; my body is occupied. Maybe it's just better this way," Josh rationalized softly.

"Dammit Josh, DO NOT GIVE UP!" he screamed.

"I can't fight anymore, Dyl. Erik won," he said, coughing up blood.

"I can't stop the bleeding," Lilly cried. Dylan didn't hear her. He was looking at the blood on Erik's lips. It was Josh's blood, but it reminded him of his own blood...so long ago... He remembered what Maggie did.

"Josh?" Trance's voice asked. "Dylan, what's going on?" he asked.

"Your friend is dying," Lilly replied. "I'm calling 911."

"No," Trance gasped, falling onto his knees beside Erik's body.

"Not if I can help it!" Dylan said, lowering his head towards Erik's face. "Josh, don't leave," he whispered softly.

"Trance?" Dylan called out, before he could bring himself to try what he was going to do.

"Yeah?" Trance asked.

"I love you. When you find Maggie, tell her that I love her too," Dylan instructed, staring directly into his eyes.

Trance was shaking his head. "Don't do it, Dylan."

"I have to. I'm not supposed to be here. I'm not supposed to be alive...he is."

"Dylan, NO!!"

Before Trance could stop him, Dylan pressed his lips against Erik's in an awkward kiss. He forced his way into Erik's body at the same time pulling Josh's essence back into its original body.

"DYLAN!! NO!!" he heard Trance howling out. "NO! NO! NO!"

Dylan's soul moved towards Trance's voice. He had to see him once more. He couldn't leave without giving him a kiss.

44

The Asylum:

Cody & Maggie

"No...no...no...no...no," Maggie repeated between twitches. She rocked back and forth hugging herself, not because she wanted to, but the straightjacket was making her.

She felt Dylan go; she felt him slip away. She had nothing left to live for now. Dylan was gone and she was locked up in a tiny padded room unable to move her arms. "No...no...no...no" This isn't real, she told herself. This can't be real. It's all a big nightmare. "Wake up...wake up...wake up."

"*This is not a dream*," a quiet voice in the back of her mind soothed. The voice calmed her, but it also added to the clutter in her mind. It made her think that she really was crazy. Maybe she was just a teen-aged boy who was making this all up.

"*Don't give up! Don't think that!*" the female voice told her. It was her mother... No, it was Sunshine's voice.

"Sunshine?" she cried out, but there was no reply.

"Drew?" a familiar voice called out. Maggie was afraid that it too was only in her head...his head; it was slowly getting hard to remember which it was anymore. "Drew?" the voice called again. She didn't answer. She wasn't Drew, she was...

"MAGGIE!" the voice shouted.

She snapped her head around to look at the door. A familiar face was poked between the padded bars of the door.

"NATHAN!" she shouted back and scooted over to the door. "Cody!" she whispered, still twitching a bit.

"They gave you shocks?" he asked.

She nodded, shivering at how casually he said the word.

"They're going to have to put you in the mean people place now. You killed one of the orderlies," he informed her quietly. "I don't want you to go."

"I don't want to go," she shook her head. "Is West alright?" she asked.

His silence told her everything.

"He's dead?"

Cody nodded.

"Oh God," she sobbed, "everyone I've ever loved is dead." She leaned her forehead against Cody's.

"I love you," he breathed softly. Maggie was surprised to hear him say that, since they really hadn't known each other that long, but that's how children are. They love quickly and deeply.

"I love you too."

"I'm not dead," he pointed out.

"No, you're not, Cody. Thank you." She kissed him on the forehead.

He looked quickly to the left. "I've got to go," he blurted out. Then, just before he left, he whispered, "I wish you were my mommy."

Maggie started crying softly. She was just as bad as the man that did this to her. In fact, she was worse. Instead of changing places, she killed the person. Unless somehow West was inside of her like Dylan had been. 'West?' she called into her own mind. There was no answer, but the normal persistent voices. 'Dammit, West, please say you're in here!' she demanded to herself. "I don't want you to be dead," she spoke the words out loud hoping he would respond.

She needed to free her arms. She struggled for a moment, but the jacket seemed to be loosened already. Cody couldn't have untied it for her, could he? She shrugged the jacket off and looked for something sharp. All she could see was a window that was too far above her to reach, but this had to be done. She focused on the swirl-covered watery-looking surface covering the glass. She closed her eyes and shoved with all of her will power. The glass shattered inward and rained down upon her. An alarm rang out; she had to work fast. She took a shard of the glass and opened the veins on both of her wrists. She heard Cody screaming, he must have come back when he heard the glass shatter. She fell backwards to the floor, but instead of hitting it, she sank down into it and the swirling jetties of energy swallowed her up.

45

The Rental Van:

Josh, Lilly, & Trance

Trance rocked back and forth as he sat in the front seat of the van and waited for Lilly to come back from running into the shopping center. He stared at the unconscious body lying in the back seat of the van. He wondered when the body woke up, who would be inside it. He hoped to God it would be Dylan. He couldn't lose Dylan, not after her had just found him.

The body began to stir.

"Am I dead?" the voice asked. It was the voice Dylan had always used. Trance's heart jumped. It had to be Dylan…it just had to be.

"Dylan?" Trance asked, not really wanting to hear what he knew was coming.

"No, I'm Josh."

"Dylan," Trance cried out.

"Hey, I'm me. I'm not dead," Josh pointed out as he checked his body.

"Duh,"

"How?" He sat up and looked at Trance.

"I don't know. Dylan did it."

"Where is he?" Josh sat up and admired his real face in the mirror.

"He's dead, Josh. He went into Erik's body. He said you belonged here and he didn't. So he did it and now he's gone and we just left him lying there in that alley." Trance closed his mouth and stared out the window, trying not to cry.

"Look, I'm sorry about the way I treated you and Dylan. I was an ass. I can't apologize enough."

Trance turned to look at Josh with the coldest glare in his eyes. "That doesn't bring him back," he growled through clenched teeth.

Lilly opened the sliding door to the van. "You're awake," she handed Josh some grocery bags. He set the bags on the floor at his feet.

"I am." He nodded and then he realized he had never actually met this woman, except for when she was trying to save Erik's body. "I'm Josh." Josh extended his hand.

"Lilly," she replied, shaking his hand. "So Dylan…" She glanced at Trance.

"Is dead," Trance finished sadly.

"I don't know." Josh shrugged.

Lilly shut the side of the van and walked around to the driver's side.

"OK, Guys. I got one more stop to make, and then we can figure out how to get Maggie," she admitted, climbing into the van.

"How do you know about everything?" Josh asked.

"Trance told me, while you were sleeping." Lilly chewed at her lip. "though, I haven't been quite honest with you," she admitted, directing the statement more to Trance then to Josh. "I'm not just Eon's victim. I'm…his accomplice, I guess. Well I was, until he turned on me."

"What?" Josh exclaimed. He was defensive, but something about this woman made him want to trust her.

"I'm sorry. I felt that I had to be honest with you," Lilly explained. "We need to go to my apartment. Why don't I explain on the way?"

Josh nodded in agreement.

"Whatever," Trance responded. "I'm going to take a nap." He climbed over the seat and pushed past Josh.

Josh took Trance's now vacant place in the front seat. "I have a few questions."

"Yeah?"

"What happened to Erik's body? Why was it dying? Was it sick? Is it going to happen again, is my body going to reject me? Who did this to us? Why? How is it even possible?"

Lilly laughed. "Slow down, Josh. Let me see if I can explain but, you need to understand, what I'm about to tell you is only a theory I have. It's based on observing Eon and what he does. I've also done extensive research in parapsychology, psychology, medicine, anatomy, and basically anything remotely related to whatever it is that he does.

"The way I see it, the body and soul are two separate and completely different organisms. They have a symbiotic relationship where one cannot exist in the human realm without the other. The body needs the energy the soul provides and the soul needs the home that the body provides. The body cannot live without the soul and, although the soul can live without the body, it has no power to exist in the human realm and it must move on to another realm where it can exist without relying on a body.

"Before I go on, I have to explain that all things have energy. Everything in the universe has energy. Some people can see these energies and some can even manipulate them. Eon is one of those people. He's been studying how to use energy for as long as he's been alive. God only knows how long that is. He knows so much about the energies that he is able reach inside a body and detach the energy that lives within. He takes the soul, gathers it up and pulls it out. He can then jump into that body and release the energy of the soul into the body he just left.

"If you think of the soul as a vine you can imagine once it is inside the body it spreads out and controls every part of the body. So when Eon does what he does and the soul is released into the new body, it winds its way through the body and takes it over completely. The body senses that something is wrong, but it doesn't know what, so the autoimmune system kicks in to fight whatever is intruding on the body. It doesn't seem to know exactly where the soul resides, so it begins to systematically destroy every organ within the body that is controlled by that new soul. In essence, the body is trying to destroy the interloping soul, but it ends up destroying itself. The pain you feel is the pain of the body trying to destroy your soul. If you give in and give up, the brain convinces the soul that it belongs there, supplying memories and a personality that are programmed into the brain after years of living together. It's how your body functions when you are on autopilot. The body knows what to do so it does it without the soul being involved. The only way the body will not attack its soul is if it is a blood relative of the original soul… HOLY SHIT!"

"What?"

"That's his plan. That's been his plan all along. He's been talking about the 'one'. The one is his descendant. He's planning on staying in one body."

"The one?"

"It's some evil plot that he's been conceiving since God knows when, probably since the dawn of time. He never explained the details of it, but he told me that one day, he would find The Vessel that could hold him for longer than a couple of years. He tried to act compassionate. He told me that once he found the 'one', he would go back and put everyone back. He wanted to fix everything. That was a line of bullshit if I ever heard one. I guess, at one time maybe, he wanted to fix everyone, but now…"

"That's why he's been doing the tattoos so he can keep track and put the bodies back, if he can. He wants to fix us."

"He can't fix us," Trance spoke up, in a small voice. "If a dish breaks, it's easy to fix, just slap on some glue and everything is fine –cracked– but still usable. If the dish is shattered, you pick up the pieces and throw them away. You can't fix shattered. That's what happened to us. Our lives; our loves, everything was SHATTERED! IT'S GONE! You can't fix shattered." Trance lay back on the bench and closed his eyes.

"No, he doesn't control the tattoos." Lilly was saddened by Trance's loss of hope, but she continued talking. "The tattoos just happen. He thinks it's a conspiracy, but I think it's his subconscious keeping track. Deep down, he knows what he is doing is wrong, but he needs to do it to survive."

"We have to stop him." Josh couldn't stop staring at Lilly as she drove and talked. She reminded him so much of Lauren. Not her looks, but the way she carried herself. It was the strength and confidence in her movements; the way she held her head high and her back straight.

"Josh, there's something else. It gets weirder."

"Weirder than body switching?"

Lilly nodded. "In some bodies he has this ability, this power, magic if you will. He doesn't always have it. I guess it depends on the innate abilities of the person he becomes. He tries to remember which body has the power, so he can go back later and steal the power. I didn't believe him at first, but he showed me once how they work. All he does is manipulate the energy and he can control things. He can make things appear, make things change. He could kill a man with his mind if he wanted to."

Josh shook his head. "I don't want to believe you, but I feel like I have to with everything I've been through. So," Josh began thoughtfully, "he's got your body then?"

"No, after Eon saw what was on my laptop, he um did it again. He put me in here." She gestured to the body she now wore. "He attacked me and tied me up. I didn't know what to do, it was all so sudden. After that, he disappeared for a while. It seemed like he was gone for hours and hours. When he finally came back, he was a teenage boy." She paused, trying to swallow back tears. "I didn't know how twisted he was until he did this. Eon made me watch him. He used the energies to force my eyes to stay open. The boy's soul was in my old body. He used the boy's own body to rape and torture him. He did things to that boy I didn't think were humanly possible. I can't...I can't... I don't even want to think about it. He mutilated the poor boy. I can't get the boy's sobs out of my head. How nightmarish and horrible would that be to watch your own body rape, torture, and mutilate you? After Eon was done 'playing', as he called it, he turned his attention to me. Thank God, he didn't torture me like that." Lilly was sobbing now. "He raped me. The sickest part was, the whole time he was doing it; he kept calling me Maggie and telling me how much he loved me. I thought he was going to kill me too, but he didn't." She took a deep shaky breath, getting her tears under control.

"So, can anyone do what he does?"

"If the conditions are right, the person needs to know how to manipulate the energies. Also the body has to be willing."

"Who in their right mind would be willing to let that happen?" Josh gasped.

"That's where the kiss comes in. He warps your mind so badly that the body cannot help but to willingly give in."

"You sure seem to know a lot about him." Trance piped in.

"I should. He was my husband for a very long time."

"Was?" Josh asked.

"Yes, it's been over for about 50 years."

"What happened between you two?" Josh couldn't seem to stop asking questions, he was mesmerized by Lilly.

"I'm not ready to talk about that right now, besides we're here." She pulled the van into a parking lot. "He wants to kill me," Lilly admitted, pulling the keys out of the ignition. She turned to face Josh. "I did something bad. Well good, but bad in his eyes. You see, when he left me, I started tracking him. I followed his movements and tried to help the ones he left behind. I knew that was the only way that I could redeem myself. I'm the one who paid for Erik's bail, not his mother. I knew you were innocent. I knew you weren't Erik."

"Thank you."

"You're welcome. I just wish I could have gotten the money together sooner." She paused to take a long swallow of the water bottle she had purchased at the store. "Eon found my journal," Lilly continued. "He was furious. He totally lost it. That's what set him off. It's my fault, what he did to that boy; all of it. It's my fault.

"I'm really sorry for what's happening to you guys. I wish I would have tried to stop him sooner. I could have killed him in his sleep or something. I honestly didn't think he was this crazy. I was so dumb not to see it," Lilly babbled.

"You're not dumb. He's a liar; he's a charmer too. It's hard for anyone to see past that," Josh reassured her, thinking of Lauren.

"He needs to be stopped," Lilly growled.

"I'll kill him," Trance offered softly.

"No, I have to. It's my responsibility," Lilly said solemnly.

"He's all of our responsibilities now," Josh corrected her.

46

A Bedroom:

Shadow

A soul, floating in oblivion, lost in the ethereal mists of one's own mind. *The soul* struggled for clarity; searched for reality. Finding nothing, it continued to float. It was ageless, sexless, lifeless, colorless. Nothing existed and nothing had any meaning.

There was no meaning until *the soul* heard a voice drawing *the soul* closer, nearer to reality. Then the voice was gone, but the music was still there, leading *the soul* back to reality.

Gradually, *the soul* began to feel a body again. Then the voice came back, the voice that sounded familiar. The voice, that had led *the soul* home, was so familiar. The voice was familiar, but *the soul* had never heard it so angry, so passionate.

The words began to entangle *the soul* and drag it back into *the body*.

Then it clicked, *the body* knew whom the voice belonged to: Robert Smith of The Cure.

"Robert," *the body* whispered. It's first attempt at speech. "Robert," *the body* repeated, listening to the sound of its own voice.

The body opened its eyes, to find itself staring at a poster of Robert Smith. *The body* moved its hand to touch the picture. Black painted fingernails followed *the mind's* instructions to trace the outline of Robert's face. *The body* felt so much love for this man. More love then it had ever felt before.

A question occurred to *the soul* with such violence, that it made *the body* quiver. 'Male or female?' *the mind* begged. The black finger-nailed hand traveled across *the chest* to answer.

"Male," *the mouth* answered. "Who am I?" *the mouth* asked, but no memories came rushing in to answer the question. "Where am I?" he asked. *The head* began to shake. "Home?" he asked.

The body pushed itself up and looked around the room at the unfamiliar surroundings. Black and red were the two most common colors. Black walls with red velvet curtains.

He stood up from the bed and crossed the small room to a mirror above the dresser. The mirror was covered with writing; black permanent marker covered the entire thing. Song lyrics, poems, and quotes were obscuring every part of the mirror. Along the edges of the mirror were pictures. He could see his face clearer if there wasn't writing under those pictures.

He took down one of the pictures not even looking at it and moved closer to the mirror. *The face* in the mirror was Robert Smith's...no, it wasn't Robert's. It was a boy's face in Robert Smith's hair and makeup. Goth. *The body* was a Goth kid.

The body looked down at the photo in his hand. It was a picture of a girl with purple hair and black clothes. She was clinging to a smiling boy. *The body* reeled in shock; he was the boy in the picture. It couldn't be, could it? It didn't feel right, but somehow, strangely it did.

Suddenly, memories began to fill *the mind*. *The body* sat back on the bed moaning at the sheer volume of memories filling *the mind*. He couldn't concentrate on just one; they were coming in too fast. He pressed *the palms* of his hands into his closed eyes, trying to keep the memories out.

"Alex?" a woman's voice called out. "Are you alright?" *The body* felt hands soothing his back. "Alex? What's wrong?" the woman asked.

"Who's Alex?" *the ears* heard *the mouth* ask. Everything seemed to be working independently of each other.

"I'm sorry," the woman sighed in a defeated way. "Shadow, what's the matter?" the woman asked emphasizing the name. Something from a memory pulled at him at the sound of that name.

"You called me Shadow," *the mouth* whispered. "Is that my name?" The raw aching tone of *the voice* brought tears to *the eyes*.

"If that's what you want me to call you. I'll call you Shadow," she said, putting her arm around *the body*. *The body* sagged into the woman's body. "Shadow, what's wrong? You can tell me, I'm your mother."

"I'm OK," Shadow replied in a tiny voice, still clinging to the mother. Everything would be all right if he could stay in the mother's arms and listen to Robert's voice forever.

"Dinner's ready. Are you hungry?" the mother asked.

Shadow paused a moment, consulting *the stomach*. "Not really." He looked around the room; he wanted to leave this depressive room. "I need to go for a walk."

"OK, but be careful and just remember I love you," the mother said and softly kissed Shadow's head.

"I love you too, Mommy," Shadow whispered.

Shadow could see the mother's eyes filling with tears. "Are you sure you're OK?" the mother asked again.

"No," Shadow replied truthfully. "But I will be," he assured her.

The mother stood up and left the room, wiping tears from her eyes.

This wasn't right. He didn't belong here. He'd hurt the mother without even trying. Everything seemed to point out that this was his home, but he knew deep inside that he didn't belong here.

He had to leave. He had to go and find the place where he did belong, but he wasn't going to go without Robert's voice. He filled a backpack that he found at the foot of the bed with five or six Cure CDs that he found lying around. He grabbed the CD Walkman off of the dresser and stuffed some clothes into the bag.

He took the CD out of the radio and placed it gently into the Walkman. He wanted to finish listening to it. He felt like this was the first time he was ever hearing it.

He wanted to stay here with the mother. He wanted her to comfort him some more, but he knew he had to find out where he really belonged, even if it meant never seeing the mother again.

The feet walked and lead him to the sidewalk outside of the house.

He had to find out who he was.

47

The Between Place:

Maggie

Maggie opened her eyes slowly. She was afraid that she would find another hospital room.

This time, Maggie found herself in a forest. She stood up and looked around. It was the most beautiful place she had ever been. She saw a river nearby and she ran over to it. She felt as free as a child. She looked at her reflection and was overjoyed to see it was her real reflection. She smiled the biggest smile she could ever remember smiling.

The smile faded as a face appeared beside her. It was Dylan's face. She hadn't seen his face in so long.

"Dylan," she breathed. The smile returned to her face, as she turned to look at him. He smiled back and circled his arms around her waist.

"Maggie," he said, lifting her up and spinning her around.

"Dylan, I love you," she declared as he set her back down.

"I've been searching for you everywhere," he informed her. "I love you too."

He kissed her passionately.

"I've missed your kiss," she whispered softly.

"I can't understand why people keep separating us," he mumbled in her ear as he hugged her once again.

"What?" she asked, pulling away from him.

"I'm just so glad we're finally together."

"Who separated us, Dyl?" she asked, concern crossing her face. Something was wrong.

"You don't remember, do you? You don't! You don't know me," he accused and turned to walk away. "You don't love me, you love him."

"Dylan, what are you talking about?" she walked over to him and put her hand on his shoulder.

"You don't love me."

"Yes I do, Dylan. I do," she reassured him smiling, but her smile faded as he turned around. This man was not Dylan. A familiar looking man stood before her. It was her first love, before Dylan.

"Don't you recognize me?" the man asked her.

"Max?" she guessed.

"Think hard, Maggie. Try to remember," he urged softly.

"No!" Maggie cried. She didn't want to remember.

"Maggie!" he commanded. "What did I tell you back then?"

"NO!" she screamed, not wanting to face the memory. It was all so clear to her now.

Before there was Dylan, she dated Max. He was her first; her first love, her first everything and she loved him, but she also feared him. His temper was too erratic for her.

Maggie closed her eyes, trying to shut it out, but the memory came back to her. That night Max got shot and he kissed the guy who shot him. That was the soul transfer. He tried to tell her what happened; he tried to tell her he was all right, but she didn't believe that the killer of her first love, was in fact her first love's soul inside the killer's body. That was a preposterous thing to think. You can't exchange bodies. So, she did what anybody would do. She called the cops and had him arrested.

"It's amazing what you can make yourself forget," he snarled in a sinister voice.

"Where am I?" she demanded, staring deep into the eyes of her first love.

"Good question; easily answered. All you have to do is open your eyes."

"They are open!"

"Open your real eyes."

"My real eyes...," Maggie began confused, then she felt it...another body. She was in someone else's body. "No," she said in a voice that was deep and masculine. She opened her new eyes and found herself looking in a mirror. She was a young man with black hair and pale skin. His eyes were dark like Max's eyes.

"No!" she exclaimed, closing her eyes again. When she opened them, she was in the forest again.

"Where am I?" she asked again.

"You're with me," he replied. This time the man was in the body of the boy she had just seen in the mirror. He was standing before her wrapped only in a towel. She ran her hand down his chest.

"Who are you?"

"Eon," he replied simply.

"What are you?"

He remained silent.

"What are you?" she demanded.

He shook his head.

"Am I dead?"

"I couldn't let you die."

"Why? I just want to die," she begged.

"Because, I love you," he replied softly, shifting his body to the form she recognized the most: Dylan.

"I don't love you," she insisted softly, turning away from him. "I love Dylan," she declared defiantly.

"I WAS DYLAN!" he shouted at her.

"No," she argued.

He placed his hand on her shoulder and she saw what had happened between Dylan and Zach.

"NO! NO! NO!" she screamed.

"You're very fond of that word."

"Who are you?" she screamed. "What do you want from me?"

"I just want you to love me," he replied sadly.

"I will never love you!" she growled at him. "Why can't you just leave me ALONE?"

Eon's eyes filled with rage and his face was a mask of anger.

"YOU WANTED TO KNOW WHO I AM?" he *screamed at her. "I'll show you."*

The forest around her disappeared and they were left standing in the darkness of the between place. Eon had a cloak wrapped around him, a hood covering his face.

"You want to see my real face?" he growled. "Go ahead, look at it."

Undaunted, Maggie stepped forward and pushed back his hood. She gasped at what she saw and backed away. "What the hell are you?" she asked in a tiny voice.

He smiled and dropped the cloak letting it fall to the ground.

What stood before Maggie was an abomination; it was a demon. His entire body consisted of patches of skin, each a different shade, a different texture. They were all pieced together in mottled patchwork pattern. Each piece of skin had a name tattooed on it. Every piece except for the two pieces that made up his face. She sobbed as she stared at his face. She wanted to scream or cry out in rage, but she was speechless. His face was half Dylan's face and half Max's face.

She shook her head.

"I don't want to be here with you," she told him finally. "I want to die. Please, just let me die," she begged.

"I can't let you die, you must understand."

He pulled her close with his patchwork-skinned hand. She whimpered softly, shaking her head. He kissed her with his split lips and she was reminded of all the kisses they had shared. She pulled away from him, still shaking her head. She turned and ran from him into the darkness. She stumbled and fell, instead of landing on the ground, she kept falling.

Maggie understood now, he had given her a choice. Leave with him or fall into this oblivion. Maggie knew this was the right choice and she'd choose it again if she had to.

48

Lilly's Apartment:

Josh, Lilly, & Trance

"What in God's name happened here?" Josh exclaimed as he took in the blood all over Lilly's apartment. They had snuck into Lilly's apartment, which was still considered a police crime scene. Trance was standing watch, out near the van.

"Trust me, you don't want to know," Lilly made her way to her bedroom. "It's not here," Lilly whispered as she came back into the living room.

"Maybe you left it somewhere else?" Josh suggested.

"No. He took it, probably to destroy it."

"Well, let's get out of here before we get caught." Quickly, they headed back out to the van.

"What are we going to do now?" Trance asked quietly through a pinched nose. He had just had another rejection attack that left his nose bleeding.

"We need to get you back in your body," Josh handed him a tissue. "You're falling apart."

Trance nodded. "I think my abilities were keeping me safe," he speculated. "I never felt that pain thing until after I lost them."

"Wait, you never told me you had abilities," Lilly exclaimed. "What kind of abilities?" She turned to look at him.

"I used to be psychic," Trance explained. "I could see things about people's past. I could leave my body. I could see spirits; feel their presences. I could see the energy in everything, just like you said. I miss that the most. Everything is so boring without the little swirls of energy," he told her wistfully. "Now there's nothing, nothing at all. We think that when I shoved Maggie into my body she somehow took my powers with her."

"Shit! So, she's in another new body and she has your powers? All of that at once would drive someone insane," Lilly whispered.

"I know," Trance agreed softly. "I'm going to try something, if it doesn't work... I might die. Elliot might die."

"Elliot?" Josh asked.

"This body's real name," Trance replied, taking a deep breath. Before either one could stop him he concentrated and put himself into the trance that earned him his nickname. It was going to work. 'Maggie,' he whispered in his mind, but nothing happened. Did it actually still work? He shifted his energy and concentrated on stepping forward. It definitely worked. He stood in the van outside of the body he had occupied.

Lilly and Josh were both turning back towards Elliot's body calling his name. Trance's soul walked out of the van, without opening the door. He turned and looked back at the van; Josh was just about to start shaking him, if he did that...too late. Trance felt himself being pulled back into the body.

"It worked," he whispered, barely able to talk. "Not with the results I wanted though," he said softly and passed out.

"Astral projection," Lilly breathed in awe. "It's also known as an out-of-body experience," she explained. "He's got enough control and discipline to still do it, even though his abilities are gone."

"Is he going to be OK?" Josh turned to look at Lilly.

"He should be. It's rather taxing to go out-of-body, but when you're as drained as he was. I don't know" Lilly sighed. "We can only wait."

49

The Asylum:

Cody & Drew

rew opened his eyes in response to the sound of mumbling in the room with him. No, the mumbling wasn't in the room with him; it was in his head. He tried to lift his hand to rub his eyes, but they were tied down. He screamed in pain as the restraint rubbed against his newly healed scar.

"Drew!" a voice called.

He looked over to find a familiar face. "Cody?" he asked. The man nodded. It was strange, he could remember the events of the past week vaguely, but anything before that was a blank.

"What am I doing back here?" he asked Cody. "I thought they were taking me away."

Cody shook his head.

"Maggie, West is in my head," Cody informed her happily.

"Who's Maggie?" Drew asked. He was reminded of the dream he had. He had been a woman in that dream. Maybe that woman's name had been Maggie. There was a creature in the dream too. That human being made up of another person's skin; lots of other people's skin. He shivered. He never wanted to see that man again.

"You told me you were Maggie. It's your girl name."

Surprised, Drew looked at Cody. "I don't remember that." He closed his eyes. "I think I have amnesia or something."

"West is in my head," Cody repeated.

"The orderly that I killed?" Drew asked.

"No, you didn't kill him. He had a bad heart. It worked too hard and it got broken."

"He died of a broken heart," Drew said sadly. A flash of the woman with West whipped through his mind. "She loved him too much," he whispered.

"Maggie?" Cody asked.

"I don't know."

"West says we have to get out of here," Cody announced. "He says we have to find others. He says that you're his only hope."

"Me, what can I do?"

"You can do magic," Cody whispered softly in the darkness.

"Magic?" Drew asked in disbelief.

"Yes, magic," Cody insisted. "He says you made him see you as you really are. You made him see Maggie."

"That was real? Maggie is real? Why don't I remember her?"

"You don't need to remember her. You are her."

"No, Nathan. I'm not. I'm Drew." Drew stressed the name that Cody had to go by. He could not see himself as a woman. He was Drew and only Drew.

"Goodnight, Drew," he scooped up his teddy bear from off the floor and deposited his thumb in his mouth. Drew watched the man-child fall asleep. He wondered about his past. Why couldn't he remember anything? What about that dream with The Patchwork Man? He couldn't seem to get it out of his mind. Eventually he fell into a fitful sleep.

50

The Rental Van:

Josh, Lilly, & Trance

"Trance said that he could communicate with spirits," Josh began as he and Lilly walked down the street across from the parking lot where the van was parked. "Do you think...if he gets...when he gets his abilities back, he can talk to Lauren?" Josh asked softly.

"I was wondering when you were going to bring her up," Lilly shrugged her shoulders. "I don't know. You need to talk to him about that."

"He won't talk to me," Josh pointed out sadly. "He blames me for Dylan."

"You have to put yourself in his shoes," Lilly suggested softly. "How did you feel when Lauren died?"

"I wanted to die," Josh admitted. "But Dylan did this, not me. I had nothing left to live for. I wanted to die," he repeated.

"We should go check on Trance," she said, pulling out of the eye lock that they had ended up in. "He's awake, you two need to talk."

"I know," he agreed, following her to the van. He still couldn't believe he was back in his body again.

"How long was I out?" Trance was up and walking around outside the van.

"A couple of hours," Lilly replied. "You look better."
"I feel a lot better."
"What did you do?" Josh asked.
Trance ignored him. "I'm hungry," he stated to Lilly.

"We'll go get some food," Lilly replied. "As soon as you and Josh talk, go talk in the van. I'll wait out here."

"So," Josh said nervously as they sat down in the van.

"So what?" Trance said angrily.

"Why are you so upset with me?"

"You know why."

"No I don't! I didn't choose this. I wanted to die. Dylan chose this." He glanced at Trance. "Not me!"

"Then why are you still here?" Trance asked through his tears. "Why don't you just leave? You got what you wanted. You got your body back and Dylan is dead. You hated him. You wanted him dead," Trance accused.

"I never wanted Dylan to die," Josh said in outrage. "Most of the anger I had came from Erik's body. I cared very much for Dylan. We were a team and I know I treated him like shit, and you too, but it's over now and I apologized already."

"But you're, STILL HERE!" Trance screamed and ran from the van. He stumbled and fell. Lilly rushed over to him.

"Trance?" she asked.

"Leave me alone," he choked out, but she couldn't leave him alone. She sat down next to him on the ground and put her arms around him. He nestled into her shoulder.

"I can't stand looking at him," Trance gasped. "I can't stand looking at him and knowing that Dylan is not in there," he cried. "I just want him to hold me...Dylan, not Josh, but I can't have that ever again."

Tears ran down Lilly's face as she rocked the young man gently in her arms.

51

The Asylum:

Drew

Drew woke up to a flash of pain ripping through his body. He opened his eyes, but all he could see were the visions bombarding his mind.

"Drew, it's time to see the doctor," a voice close to his ear said. "You better not try anything."

Drew could hear the voice, but he could only see the visions. He tried to move his arms, but he felt so heavy. Drugs…he was drugged. It felt so euphoric, but still the visions wouldn't go away.

"No touch," he managed to mumble out.

"I know, but I got to get the restraints off, just one more…there, all done. Now I have to get you into the wheelchair."

"No," Drew demanded with conviction. "I can do it,"

"Are you sure?"

Drew nodded. He had to do it. The visions were so much stronger when people touched him.

Shaking with effort, Drew lifted himself into a sitting position. He was a lot stronger now, even though he feigned weakness. He lowered himself into the chair.

He recognized the orderly as the one he had shoved across the room. "I'm sorry that I pushed you,"

"It's no problem. Just don't do it again, OK?"

Drew nodded. "I won't."

The murmur of voices in his head was giving him a headache. He dozed a little on the way to the doctor's office.

"Hello Drew. You're looking well," the doctor greeted when he was wheeled into the office. "How are you feeling?"

"Surprisingly enough, I feel pretty good," Drew replied.

"You do?"

Drew nodded.

"OK then, let's talk about this fixation you have. Do you still believe that you are a woman named Maggie?" the doctor asked after consulting his notes.

Drew shook his head. "No, and to tell you the truth, I can't even imagine why I told you that."

"Can we talk about your wrists?"

"These?" Drew asked, gesturing to the bandages on his wrists. "I don't even remember doing it." Drew pursed his lips. "Could you maybe tell me how I did it, maybe then I'll remember something."

"It's quite an odd story," the doctor began, touching his pen to his lips. "It seems that a tree branch broke the window open in your isolation room and you used a piece of glass to slit your wrists," the doctor explained slowly. He pushed his glasses up his nose. "See, the thing I can't quite figure out is how you go the straightjacket off."

"Nathan... He did it."

"No, I watched the video tape. Nathan didn't do it."

"I don't know how it happened."

"I think I do," the doctor nodded and closed Drew's folder. "Drew, there is reason to believe that you have a rare ability called telekinesis." He placed the folder on his desk and leaned on his elbows on the desk.

"tele-kah-what?"

"Telekinesis," the doctor chuckled. "It's a rare ability to move things with your mind."

"That's crazy," Drew scoffed. "I can't move things with my mind." He laughed, but he wondered about it. Could he actually move things with his mind? He had never tried, maybe he could. Was that what Cody was talking about? Was that the magic?

"I would like you to undergo some testing, nothing too difficult."

"I don't want any more tests done. I'm sick of tests."

"Nonsense, you signed the papers, you are obliged to have any tests done that we deem necessary."

"But…," Drew protested.

"No matter, we can discuss this later," the doctor cut him off. "I would like you to tell me why you wanted to kill yourself."

"Well," Drew tried hard to remember that moment. "I was sad and afraid," he explained truthfully.

"Why were you sad?" the doctor asked.

'Lie, Drew, lie,' a little voice whispered in his head. "The orderly….West, I thought I killed him," Drew said. It wasn't exactly lying.

"Well, it was his heart that killed him. It turns out he had a bad heart, that's all. It could have happened at any time."

"I know that now."

"Do you still feel that the world is unreal to you?" the doctor asked.

"No, it kind of feels that the past week was unreal though, it feels like it was all a dream."

"Well, that's good. Do you feel up to some physical therapy now?"

"Sure. Doc, I wanted to apologize for what happened in there. I guess I just got scared."

The doctor looked taken aback.

"And also Doc…," Drew started. "I'm feeling a lot better. I don't feel all crazy inside anymore. Something is different though. I can tell; it's not the same as it used to be." He paused, laughing inwardly as the doctor's flabbergasted expression. "But I do have one small problem," Drew finished.

"What's that?" the doctor asked, intrigued now.

"I can't remember anything at all from before I got to this place."

"Nothing at all?"

"Nothing," Drew replied.

52

The Rental Van:

Josh, Lilly, & Trance

"He just wants to help you, Trance," Lilly whispered softly. "That's why he's still here."

"I don't want his help. I want him to go away!' Trance mumbled into her neck.

"Josh going away isn't going to bring Dylan back," Lilly reasoned.

"I know that," Trance pushed away from her. "Nothing is ever going to bring him back." Trance laughed sadly. "Do you know what the worst part is? I keep hearing him calling out to Maggie...not me...Maggie. I feel bad because I didn't want my body back because that meant that Dylan and Maggie would be together again and I would be alone,"

"I'm so sorry," Lilly sympathized. "If I had stopped Eon, none of this would have happened."

Trance immediately changed from the comforted to the comforter.

"No Lilly, don't say that," Trance sniffled. "This has been the best thing that has ever happened to me...EVER."

"Really?"

"Yes, if this hadn't happened, I would never have met Dylan at all." Trance wiped away her tears. "Come on, let's go get Maggie." He stood up and offered his hand to help her up.

"You're sure?"

"Definitely, Dylan wanted me to find her." They walked back to the van Lilly's arm around Trance's waist, giving him moral support, but also helping him walk.

She helped him into the back seat and closed the door. She walked to the front of the van where Josh was leaning.

"We have to hurry and get him back into his body," Lilly explained in a hushed tone. "He's latched onto his sadness as a way of keeping him here, much like you said you did with pain."

"Let's go do it then."

"It's getting late; we'll have to wait until morning now. Is there some place I can sleep? I'm exhausted."

"I thought you knew all about us," Josh laughed. "How come you don't know about the cabin that we've been shacking up in?"

"Shut up and let's go," Lilly handed him the keys. "You drive. I'm too tired."

53

The Street:

Shadow

"**S**hadow!" *The ears* heard a new voice calling out. "Shadow! Wait up!" The voice called again.

Shadow couldn't seem to make *the feet* stop walking.

"Dammit Shadow! Don't do this to me! I know you can hear me!" the voice called angrily as it grew closer.

The shoulder felt a hand close over it. *The body* stopped and spun around to face the newcomer.

"Shadow, where are you going?" The purple haired girl from the picture stood in front of him. Her hair was now a faded purplish pink.

"Kyle?" *The mouth* spoke. The girl nodded. Her name was Kyle, how did he know that?

"Are you feeling alright?" Kyle asked. With that question, Shadow felt connected for the first time to every part of his body. *The mouth*, *the feet*, everything was now controlled by Shadow.

"I'm OK," Shadow replied, testing his mouth.

"So, what, you're running away?" Kyle put her hands on her hips. "Everything we just went through and you're just going to leave," she demanded in anger.

"I have to," Shadow insisted, turning away from her. "I need to find out who I am."

"You don't need to run away." She grabbed his shoulders and spun him around. "I can tell you who you are."

"You don't get it. I'm not Shadow." He pouted at the girl.

"What do you mean? Of course you are."

"No," Shadow argued, shaking his head. "I'm not the boy you know. I am not the boy named Shadow."

"Well, then who are you?"

Shadow could see anger warring with sadness in her eyes.

"I don't know. I can't remember anything at all," Shadow admitted quietly.

"You have amnesia?" Kyle asked. "Shadow, you are so messed up!" The anger won out. "You always make up these stupid stories. How do you expect anyone to know when you're telling the truth?" she sighed. "Why do you think nobody believed you when you tried to kill yourself?" she asked, grabbing his arm and pushing up his sleeve.

He looked down at the angry red scar. It ran the length of his wrist, starting at the palm of his hand and ending just under his elbow.

"I didn't do that."

"Well, then who did?"

Shadow ignored her. "I'm dead," Shadow whispered. It was the only way to explain what was happening to him.

"You are not dead!"

"YOU DON'T KNOW!" Shadow screamed. He turned and ran away from her.

"SHADOW! WAIT!" she called after him.

He ran from her; ran from the house, ran from the mother, ran from the life he knew was not his.

54

The Bedroom:

Josh & Lilly

Josh woke up to a muffled screaming sound coming from Dylan's old room.

"Lilly!" He jumped from his bed and ran into her room. Lilly's sheets were wrapped around her head and she was struggling to get free.

Josh ran in and uncovered her head, but her struggling didn't stop. He shook her shoulders gently at first then with more force. "Wake up Lilly!" he shouted.

"Get off me! Don't touch me! I don't love you! I could never love you!" she screamed, swinging her arms wildly at him. Even though he knew she was still dreaming and she didn't mean it, it still hurt, for he had developed a crush on her.

"Lilly! It's me Josh!"

"Josh?" she asked, blinking her eyes against the brightness of the light. "Please, don't touch me," she whimpered.

"Does it hurt?" he asked softly, removing himself from the bed.

"No. I just…. I can't…. he raped me," she murmured in a small hurt-filled voice. "I thought he loved me. What happened to him? How could he do that to me?" She couldn't seem to stop asking questions.

"Shh!" Josh soothed softly. Lauren had gone through something similar once, so he understood why Lilly didn't want to be touched. He leaned down and kissed her gently on the forehead. She flinched. The best thing Josh thought he could do was leave her alone, so he walked towards the door.

"Please stay," she called out before he could leave. He walked back towards the bed, but then thought better of it and lay on the floor. He grabbed a blanket off of the chair and covered up with it. He fell asleep once he heard Lilly's rhythmic breathing.

55

The Asylum:

Cody, Drew, & West

"Drew, are you still awake?" Cody's small voice asked.

"Yes," Drew turned on his side to face Cody. The moon was bright, but the light that lit their room came from the fluorescent lights that illuminated the entire compound at night. The doctors here were pretty serious about security.

"Do you think I'll ever get to be a little boy again?" Drew could see sadness shining in the man's big, childlike eyes.

Drew shrugged, but said the first answer that came into his head. "No, probably not."

Cody's face bunched up, he looked like a four-year-old about to throw a temper tantrum, and then suddenly he stopped.

"West says I will!" Cody announced happily, "but he said that you have to get us out of here."

"Do you actually believe that an orderly is living in your head?" Drew asked rudely.

Cody's bottom lip quivered, but he said nothing. He rolled out of his bed and went over to Drew's bed.

"What are you doing?" Drew sat up.

"I don't want to do this, but West says I have to." Cody explained, lifting his hand to Drew's cheek. "Close your eyes,"

Drew obeyed.

"No," Drew breathed as Nathan's hand connected with his cheek.

"I'm sorry, but it's the only way for you to know."

"No, I don't want to know," Drew begged, but it was too late. The visions came to him quickly. The fight in the rehab room....him clinging to West...the memory wrenched his heart. He loved West. He loved him more than anything. He saw West as a means of escape, they kissed and West's spirit was inside of Drew's body for a brief moment. Then they were apart and West's soul started to float away, towards a bright light. Suddenly, it was ripped quite violently in another direction. It disappeared from the room, but Drew followed it. West's soul was heading straight for Cody, who was watching cartoons. Cody began to shake violently as West's spirit entered his body. Then he passed out.

The visions stopped then. Drew opened his eyes, tears rolling down his cheeks. "Why?" he asked, not really knowing what he was asking.

"Because, he loves you and I love you," Cody pressed his lips clumsily against Drew's lips. Drew, again, got the vision of West kissing a woman. The kiss turned passionate for a split second.

Cody pulled back. "That was from West."

Drew was still in shock as he lifted his hand to touch his lips. It wasn't all an act. Cody wasn't faking it. He really was a child trapped in a man's body and West was in there too.

"West told me to make a deal with you," Cody began, "I know how to make the voices and the pictures go away."

Drew perked up.

"But if I tell you, you have to promise to get me out of here."

Drew nodded enthusiastically.

"You promise?" Cody asked, holding out his pinky finger. "You have to pinky-swear."

"I promise," Drew hooked his pinky around Cody's and shook. "I pinky swear."

"OK. It's really easy. All you have to do is imagine yourself in a bubble. The bubble goes all the way around your whole body. It's like a body-shaped bubble. Then you just concentrate on making that bubble so strong that nothing can break through it."

Drew closed his eyes and imagined a large body shaped bubble encircling him. Instantly, the voices stopped.

"It can't be that easy," Drew exclaimed.

"It is, see," Cody put his hand on Drew's hand. Drew saw no visions what so ever.

"Cool. What about the swirls that I see everywhere?" Drew asked.

"Swirls?" Cody was confused at first and then his eyes got brightened in understanding. "The energies!" he practically screamed. "You can see the energies too?" He lowered his voice, knowing if they got caught talking they would be in big trouble.

"The energies?"

"Yeah, everything around us has energy and some people can see it, but most people can't." Cody explained happily. He was glad to be teaching someone something, rather than having it the other way around. "This is a bit harder. You're looking with your wrong eyes. You need to switch your eyes…turn them off."

Drew stared at Cody in disbelief. "What?"

Cody sighed. "Just smoosh your eyes closed as hard as possible without closing them at all."

Drew tried it. "It worked," He announced amazement filling his voice.

"There's something else," Cody whispered "something kind of bad. I'm not good at it, but maybe you will be."

"What is it?" Drew asked, lowering his voice to match Cody's.

Cody got down on all fours on the floor. "Come down here. We can't let anybody see."

Drew rolled off of his bed and knelt down on the floor beside Cody. Cody reached up and pulled a pen down off of his dresser. "When you look with your energy eyes," he placed the pen on the floor, "you can reach an imaginary hand into the energy and use it to move things." Drew watched in amazement as the pen moved across the floor.

He looked over at Cody's face. It was scrunched up in concentration. Drew was filled with the urge to smooth down the creases. A boy this young shouldn't have crow's feet around his eyes. He reached up and caressed Cody's cheek.

Cody looked over at Drew in shock.

"Can West feel that?" Drew asked. Cody nodded, smiling. "Can West talk to me?"

"He could, but he's too scared," Cody explained as he climbed back into his bed. "I think, he still thinks that this is all just a dream."

"I know how he feels," Drew commiserated, getting back into his own bed. He stared at Cody for a bit.

"You didn't try to move the pen," Cody reminded him.

Drew laughed. He turned his stare to the pen and concentrated hard. He saw the energies swirling around the pen. "So I just reach out and push?"

"That's all."

Drew did as he was told. The pen shot across the room and lodged into the wall just next to Cody's head.

"Oh my God, did I hit you?" Drew jumped off his bed and ran over to Cody's bed.

"I'm good," Cody assured him. "Why'd you throw the pen at me?"

"I moved it," Drew whispered. "I tried to use the energies. I didn't think it would work."

Cody looked at Drew with awe. "You have an amazing amount of power inside of you," he said in a small non-Cody-like voice. "I felt it when I was holding you. It was like electricity crackling through your body and into mine." Cody's hand lifted up and caressed Drew's cheek "Even now, can't you feel it?"

"West?"

"That was him." Cody nodded. "He's gone again."

"Do you think I can make fire?"

"If you had a match or a lighter," Cody responded innocently.

Drew laughed, "with my mind, Cody."

"I don't know."

Drew held up his hand. He adjusted the energies in the air above it and a tiny flame appeared above his hand. "Holy shit!" The flame wavered and grew stronger with his excitement.

"Put it out, Drew. They'll see."

Drew nodded. "You're right." He extinguished the flame with his mind. "Do you know what this means, Cody?"

Cody shook his head. Drew could see fear raging in his eyes.

"Getting out of this place just got a whole lot easier," Drew said, prying the pen out of the wall. He sat back on Cody's bed. "Let's make a plan. I need West to listen in too, OK?"

"OK, he's listening. We both are."

56

The Bedroom:

Josh & Lilly

Josh woke from his dream with a smile on his face. He had been dreaming about Lilly. His smile got bigger when he realized that Lilly had come down from the bed, onto the floor, at some time during the night. She was lying in his arms, facing him, with her face buried against his naked chest.

He shuffled his feet around trying to get them back under the blanket.

Lilly woke up with his movement.

"Sorry," he whispered, "I didn't mean to wake you."

She shrugged, tracing the tattoo on his chest.

"With these tattoos, you could follow his trail all the way back to the Dark Ages." Lilly spoke in a haunted voice. "Hardly anyone survives the process. If they don't die, the new body convinces them that they had always been in that body. When that happens, their original personality is gone, deleted, erased. It's almost as if that person never existed. You people, us people, we are the bravest people out there. We chose to fight. We know who we are and who we want to be," she whispered against his lips, looking up into Josh's eyes. Her heart was aching. It had been so long since she had kissed someone other than Eon. Would she have the guts to follow through?

The choice was made for her as Josh leaned forward and met her lips. Lilly kissed him with all of her heart. The kiss grew more passionate and more urgent. She pulled away as his hand traveled to unbutton her top.

"No, I'm not ready," Lilly cried softly. "Not yet."

"I know."

"I may not be ready for some time."

"I know," Josh smiled. "I can wait."

"After this is all over, will you still be here for me?" she asked tentatively.

Josh smiled and nodded, "Always."

"Why are you being so nice to me?"

"Because, you remind me of Lauren," he replied softly.

"I'm not her," Lilly argued, "and I will never be her. I don't want to be your replacement Lauren."

"Don't worry. You won't," he assured her softly, rolling unto his back.

"This one's different," she said, sitting up and placing her hand over her heart.

"Huh?" Josh said, rolling into a sitting position.

"The tattoo," Lilly stated as if that explained everything. "Do you want to see it?" she asked shyly. He nodded. She unbuttoned her top slowly and pulled it slightly to the side so Josh could see the tattoo. It was the name Josh written in the same writing as Josh's tattoo was, but hers had a heart around it. He reached his hand out to touch it, but again she flinched away.

"I'm sorry," she apologized.

"No, I'm sorry. I keep forgetting."

"Thank you," she whispered and kissed him gently on the lips. She lay back down and patted the floor next to her. "Let's get some sleep."

"I'm not tired." Josh lay back down next to her. "Tell me about your life," he suggested.

"I already did."

"No you didn't. You told me about what happened recently, but I want to know about your life with...," he paused. She was so quiet he thought she had fallen back asleep.

"You really want to know?"

"I do."

"I guess I should start from the beginning," Lilly began. "I met Eon. That's his real name; at least it was when I met him."

"Ian?" Josh asked.

"Actually it's E-O-N, like a measure of time," Lilly explained. "I can't remember what year it was when I met him. I know it was a long time ago… 100 or 120 years, maybe more. I was about 40 years old and I was dying. Of course, I didn't know it at the time. We fell in love and when we found out I was dying, he told me what he could do. I didn't believe him at first, but then he showed me. I was in utter shock, but he loved me and I loved him and this was a way that we could be together a little longer. So we did it.

We had a little fun, for a while. Switching body's like they were clothes. I saw what we were doing to the people we switched with and I couldn't do it anymore. I wouldn't do it anymore and I urged him to stop too. So he found me a young, rather good-looking female body and then he put me in it.

"I lost part of myself; I acclimated. I became that woman. He had to remind me about my past life and eventually I remembered it. Not everything, but enough to inflame my curiosity about Eon. I wanted to know what he was. I wanted to know how he did what he did. That's when I started studying, trying to figure out what he was and how he does what he does.

"After a while we settled down. We got married, bought a house, and eventually we had a baby girl. Our daughter never even thought twice about why her father always seemed to be a different person. She actually thought it was fun. Guess which one Daddy is today? She loved it.

"The body Eon had picked for me had diabetes and because I had it, so did Mae. We did very good managing both, until one day my blood sugar dropped. Eon couldn't find my insulin and I went into a diabetic coma." She took a deep shaky breath. Josh put his arm around her. "Instead of taking me to the hospital, he just did it. One day I was me and the next thing I knew, I was Mae, our 19-year-old daughter. He gave me our daughter's body, while I was unconscious. He let her die alone in the body I had previously occupied. I was furious with Eon. I told him to get out. I told him I never wanted to see him again.

"He left and stayed away for a time. He found me every once in a while. He'd convince me that he was sorry and that he loved me. I'd let him stay with me, but then after he got what he needed, he would disappear again. I was so in love with him that I was blind. I couldn't see that what he was doing was wrong. Then one day, a couple weeks ago, he came to my door in this body," she indicated Maggie's body. "He was filthy and wet. I took pity on him and let him in. We sat by the fire and talked. He told me he missed me, but I didn't miss him. There was too much evil in his soul. Too many innocent deaths on his hands and because I didn't stop him, those deaths are on my hands too. We had one lovely night together and then he found my journal, he snapped. He accused me of trying to stop him. He hit me, Josh. In all the years we had been together, he had never laid a hand on me."

"I'm so sorry, Lilly."

"Do you know what happened in that apartment? All that blood…"

"No Lilly. You don't need to tell me."

"But I do, Josh. You need to know how evil he has become. I told you about the boy, the one he tortured."

Josh nodded.

"The boy's soul was crushed. What did Trance say?"

"Shattered," Josh supplied.

"His soul was shattered. I mean, Eon obliterated it. The boy thought he was me. I saw an opportunity to have my baby back, so I took it. I told him he was Mae and instantly my baby girl was there. She was an old woman and I was in this young body, but she was my daughter. We tried to escape, but I forgot to pack my insulin, her insulin. She would die without it. We had to go back. When we arrived, I called 911 just in case Eon was there. He was." She stopped talking.

"Are you sure you want to go on, Lilly?" Josh rubbed her arm.

She nodded. "I have to say this. I have to face it. You have to know." She put her hand on Josh's chest. "You have to be careful of Eon. He's a monster. When the police arrived, he was so angry. He tried to kill me, but he killed one of the police officers. He threw the knife and it hit the man. He wasn't dead, he could have made it, but Eon ripped the knife out like it was nothing. The blood went everywhere. We tried to run. We tried but he grabbed Mae and he...he...he," she sobbed. "He slit her fucking throat. Josh, I had to watch her die again."

"Oh my God." Josh pulled her close.

"I kicked his ass." She laughed. "But he's stronger than a normal human. He knocked me out with one punch. I woke up in the hospital with Maggie's friends around me."

"We have to be careful."

"We will," Josh assured her.

"He won't hesitate to kill any of us, except maybe Maggie. He's got some strange obsession with her."

"I'll kill him before he hurts you again." Josh ground his teeth.

"I'll kill him if he ever lays a finger on you," Lilly vowed through her own gritted teeth.

"Thank you, for being so brave," Josh whispered.

"He needs to die." She shrugged. "Besides, you're the brave ones, you and Trance. It takes a lot to not lose your soul in someone else's body."

"Can Eon even be killed?"

Lilly shrugged again. "We may have some help with that, if I can get my laptop back."

"Can I kiss you?" Josh asked, quietly.

Lilly smiled and nodded. She leaned forward and Josh placed the softest, most tender kiss she had ever felt on her lips.

"I think I love you," he whispered. Despite his earlier claim of not being tired, his eyes were slowly closing. She stared at him as he drifted into an easy slumber. Just as she began to drift off herself, she heard a loud slam.

"Josh! Did you hear that?" Lilly whispered.

"It was just the wind," Josh reasoned sleepily.

***

Trance slid down against the door he had just slammed, hoping Josh and Lilly wouldn't investigate the noise. He didn't want to wake them; he was just so angry and jealous. He wanted Josh's eyes to look at him that way. He wanted to see Dylan's life flickering behind those eyes. He didn't want Josh and Lilly to fall in love. He wanted them to suffer like he was suffering.

How could she say they were brave? He wasn't brave. He wasn't strong enough to face life without his powers and without Dylan. He wasn't brave at all.

Trance sighed as he stood up and crossed the room. He sat down at the desk and pulled out a piece of paper and a pen.

He wanted to write a long note. He wanted to explain everything about how he felt. He put the pen to the paper, the words floating around in his head. He tried to write, but his hand didn't seem to want to work.

He shook his hand and tried again. This time he wrote his name Andrew 'Trance' Maxwell. The name came out perfectly, but now the words that were in his head were gone.

"Please, let me do this," he whispered to no one in particular. He wrote one simple phrase, and then he couldn't think of anything else to write. He set the pen down, folded up the paper shoved it into his pocket and went to bed.

57

The Asylum:

Cody, Drew, & West

"Come on, Cody," Drew whispered loudly, begging for Cody to catch up. He was going to ruin everything if he didn't quit lagging behind. Drew was waiting at the escape point, sitting in a wheelchair. No one in the hospital knew that he was at full strength again.

This was one of the rare evenings when most of the nonviolent patients were allowed to go outdoors. It was supposed to be so the patients could take in the beauty of the sun setting, but Drew saw it as a glorified recess. Still, he felt lucky to be counted among the nonviolent patients, considering his first few days at the hospital.

Drew ran his hand through his newly cut hair. It was now brown and spiky. He cut it last night as an effort to start his life anew. Cody kept stopping to talk to his friends instead of heading out to their point of escape. Drew hoped that the boy in the man's body had enough sense to keep their escape a secret. As soon as Cody stopped yapping and started walking, he could get things started.

"Nathan!" Drew called out.

Cody nodded and said goodbye to his friend. He walked over to where Drew was waiting.

"Do you think you can do it?" Cody asked as he approached.

Drew lifted his hand in response and concentrated on the energies. Suddenly, a small flame started in his palm. He blew it, but instead of going out, it flew towards the hospital.

"Just watch," Drew expected his bed to catch fire at any moment.

Instead of catching fire to the bed, the entire room exploded. Cody screamed and covered his ears. Drew just stared in awe at what he had just done with only the power of his mind. He stared for so long he almost forgot about the plan.

"Come on, Cody. It's time," Drew stood up from the wheelchair. "Let's go."

Cody nodded and followed Drew as he led the way. They ran through the open field surrounding the hospital, heading for the woods. It was full dark by the time they made it into the woods. So far everyone had been preoccupied with the burning building and they had escaped without anyone seeing them, but another obstacle blocked their path. A giant wall stood in their way.

"This must be the wall West was talking about," Drew surmised as he ran his hand across the surface searching for handholds. "There's no way we can climb this."

"Drew, somebody's coming," Cody whispered.

"Get down," Drew dropped down into the tall grass.

Cody fell down to the ground and stealthily slithered his way towards Drew. "Just like an army guy," he said, smiling.

"Do you like climbing trees?" Drew pointed at a nearby tree. Cody nodded and continued his army man slither towards the tree.

"Drew, that guy is going to see me," Cody whispered urgently. A guard was sweeping a flashlight slowly in the direction of the tree that Cody was trying to hide behind. His large stature didn't allow his entire frame to be hidden.

"Don't move!" Drew whispered from the ground at Cody's feet.

"He's going to see me!" Cody whispered, panicking.

"No, he won't," Drew closed his eyes. 'You don't see anything. You don't see anything,' he repeated forcing the energies towards the guard. The guard screamed and fell to the ground.

"Shit!" Drew grimaced.

"What did you do?" Cody asked in an accusatory tone.

"I don't know." Drew walked over to the guard who was laying a few feet away unconscious.

"What did you do?" Cody repeated, walking up beside him.

"I just moved the energies at him," Drew explained.

"Why is he crying blood?"

Drew gasped as he too noticed the blood dripping from the man's eyes. "I didn't want him to see anything."

"You turned him blind?" Cody asked in shock.

"I didn't mean to."

"Can you fix him, Drew?"

"What do you mean fix him?"

"Make him better. Make him not blind."

"I don't know."

"You have to try, Drew," Cody urged.

"What's happened to me?" Drew asked. "I could never do this shit before." He walked over to the guard who was lying unconscious on the ground. "I blinded this man. I'm a freak…a monster," he said with tears in his eyes. He knelt down and placed his hands over the man's eyes.

Drew closed his eyes and concentrated. He shifted the energies around the guard's eyes. "The bleeding's stopped, but I don't know if I fixed the blindness."

"You did what you could," Cody whispered, pulling him towards the tree. He climbed the tree next to the wall.

"It's too high, Drew. I'm scared," Cody whispered loudly from the top of the wall. "I can't do it."

"Cody, you have to," Drew said as he climbed from branch to branch.

"I can't, Drew. I want my MOMMY!" he screamed.

"Cody!" Drew yelled, but watched in amazement as Cody quietly turned and jumped from the wall. He howled in pain as he hit the ground and rolled beyond the barrier of the hospital.

Drew jumped down after him.

Cody was lying on the ground, still howling. "Shut up!" Cody scolded himself.

"West?" Drew asked the pain-filled man-boy.

"Yeah," the man answered. "I think it's broken," he whispered.

Drew rushed over to look at it.

"He wouldn't jump. I had to make him," West explained. "This is real, isn't it?" he asked in a small voice.

Drew nodded. He placed his hands on Cody's ankle.

"This may hurt a little," Drew warned.

"What are you going to do?" West asked.

"I'm going to try to heal it, like I did with the guard," Drew explained.

"For the love of God, don't blind me too," West begged.

"I won't," Drew assured him. Drew once again shifted the energies around and he could feel the bone growing back together.

"You did it!" West exclaimed. His eyes rolled back into his head.

"West?" Drew called out, afraid that somehow the healing went wrong.

"He's hiding again," the child's voice answered him as his eyes returned to their normal position.

"Cody?" Drew asked, using the boy's real name.

"Yes, I'm Cody," the boy replied smiling.

"We have to get out of here."

Cody nodded and stood up, tentatively testing out his foot. "Still hurts," he informed Drew. "But not as bad as it did. Thanks."

"Is West hiding because he's afraid of me?"

Cody nodded sadly.

58

A Restaurant:

Harper, Josh, Lilly,

& Trance

"**E**LLIOT!" Trance jumped violently as a female voice screamed out his body's name. It took him a moment to realize that she was talking to him. He turned slowly in the booth at the restaurant where Josh and Lilly decided they would eat.

"You look like shit," the woman stated "Are you OK?"

Trance shook his head.

"You don't know me, do you?" she asked.

Trance looked at her for a moment, "no, sorry."

"Of course you don't, how could you?" She lowered her voice. "It's me, Jack Harper. You always just called me Harper. Look, there's something weird going on here.'

"I know," Trance told the woman.

"How do you know?" Harper asked.

"I'm not Elliot." Trance revealed.

"But…," she started and then looked into his eyes. "You're like me?" she asked in astonishment. "What's happened to me?"

"So, who's your friend, Trance?" Josh asked as he and Lilly returned with a tray of food.

"This is Harper," Trance introduced them. "He's like us."

"You look familiar. Do I know you?" Lilly asked.

"I don't think so," Harper responded.

Trance stood up. "I need to lie down." He held out his hand for the keys to the van. Josh handed them to him and Trance went out to the van, leaving Josh and Lilly to explain to Harper what was happening.

He climbed into the passenger side door. Could he really go through with this? He was going to die soon anyway. He could feel this body rebelling against his soul. Dylan was gone. His powers were gone. What else could he do? He opened up the glove box. That was where Josh had stashed his knife. Josh told him that he bought the knife for protection, but Trance knew now that he had bought it to cut himself with.

Trance quickly wiped the tears away. He had to do this. He placed the knife between his knees and squeezed them together. Then he put a wrist on either side of the blade.

"The note," he whispered. He stopped and reached into his back pocket. He pulled out the note that read simply:

"I'm sorry, but I'm not as brave as you."

He placed the note on the dashboard ahead of him. He closed his eyes and did it. Pain raced through his wrists and pulsated upwards through his arms. He watched Josh's face for a brief moment through the window of the diner.

"Dylan, I love you," he whispered and as he closed his eyes and drifted into oblivion, he could have sworn he heard Dylan reply.

59

The Street:

Kyle & Shadow

"Please Shadow, stop!" Kyle's desperate voice broke through his panicked run. She was right behind him.

Shadow felt pain then. His lungs were on fire and his legs were aching. He stopped and collapsed to the ground, sobbing and trying to catch his breath. Kyle knelt down beside him. She put her arm around Shadow's shoulder.

"Don't you ever leave me," she demanded between breaths. "I'd die if I didn't have you."

Those words struck a memory in Shadow. He looked up at her with tears in his eyes. "You said that to me in the hospital when I tried to kill myself," he whispered.

Kyle nodded. "I knew you could hear me," she whispered back, kissing his forehead. "Come back to my house. You can take a nap, get cleaned up and stuff. You can wait for me to pack."

"Pack?" Shadow sat up.

"I'm coming with you."

"You can't."

"But I'm going to."

"Kyle…," Shadow began, but she cut him off.

"No Shadow, you're not leaving me in this shithole. I won't stay here alone. I'd rather kill myself."

"Kyle," Shadow whispered and fell into her arms. This was much better than the mother's arms, so much more relaxing. It was only then that Shadow realized that Robert's voice was no longer playing in his ears.

"Take me to your house," he managed to whisper through his sobbing.

It felt like an eternity before the sobbing stopped. Kyle held him, rocking him gently and whispering meaningless phrases into his ear.

"Don't ever leave me, Kyle," Shadow whispered hoarsely as she helped him stand.

"Don't worry, I won't," she assured him. "I can't. You're my best friend," she admitted, smiling, "my soul twin."

Those words brought tears back to Shadow's eyes, but he pushed them away. He had cried enough for one day.

In silence, they walked to Kyle's house. Shadow was clinging to the girl as if he was drowning and she was a life preserver.

What was wrong with him? Was he going crazy? Why did he believe so strongly that he wasn't the boy named Shadow?

The image of a small child appeared in his head and took his mind off of his questions. The image of the child turned and smiled at him. Shadow was filled with such love for the small boy, a mother's love. He watched as the boy chased a ball out into the street. He felt his lips calling out a name. He was scolding the boy. "Trevor, get out of the street." He heard a female voice call out the words he said.

Shadow shook his head, pushing the memory away. It wasn't one of his memories, was it?

"Shadow? We're here," Kyle stopped in front of a small mobile home. "Dad's not here, so we have the whole trailer to ourselves."

Shadow nodded. "Good, I don't want to be around people right now."

"Do you want to go take a nap in my bed?" Kyle offered as they walked into the living room. Shadow nodded again, waiting for Kyle to show him the way to the room. She didn't notice that he was waiting. She walked into the kitchen and started making lunch.

Sighing, Shadow walked down the hallway and opened doors. After looking in three different rooms, he finally found Kyle's room. It was almost identical to the room at the house he woke up in.

He crawled into Kyle's unmade bed and pulled the soft, black blanket up to his chin. He closed his eyes and was instantly asleep.

60

A Restaurant:
Harper, Josh, Lilly,
& Trance

Lilly was patiently explaining to Harper everything they knew about their unique situation. Josh was so bored he was almost drifting off, until he heard a frantic horn honking. He jumped up from his seat when the horn stopped. "Lilly, call an ambulance," he instructed, noticing the blood on the windshield.

"Trance!" Lilly called out in horror.

"I got him, you call 911!" Josh shouted as he ran out to the van. Trance was sprawled between the driver and passenger seats.

Josh tried to open the door, but it was locked. "SHIT!" he howled in frustration. "I'm not losing you too!" he vowed, picking up a large chunk of loose concrete. He moved to the back window. He didn't want to get any glass on Trance.

"They're on their way." Lilly informed him as she ran out to the van. "Josh, what are you doing?"

"He locked the...," he hit the window with the concrete, "doors," he finished as the window shattered. Josh reached in and opened the door. He hit the unlock button and he and Lilly ran to the sliding door. Lilly opened the door and Josh looked down at Trance's blood covered face.

"Help me," Trance whispered weakly. "Help me," he repeated, once more before his eyes rolled back into his head.

"We have to get him out of here," Josh urged Lilly.

"We have to stop the bleeding." Lilly instructed.

"Oh God, it's stopped!" Josh screamed. "I think he's dead!" Quickly, Josh pulled Trance out of the van. "Please don't die.... Please," Josh begged as he laid Trance's borrowed body on the sidewalk next to the van.

Lilly knelt down next to the body, holding a piece of paper in her hand. "You are brave enough, Trance. You're the bravest one of us all," she whispered. "You've held on longer than almost anyone." She brushed his hair back from his forehead.

"Trance, you son of a bitch! Open your eyes!" Josh yelled, thinking if Trance heard the old Josh he would respond.

"You have to help him," a voice whispered from Elliot's lips.

"Dylan?" Josh asked.

Elliot's head nodded. "I can't hold him here much longer. Please help him. I can't lose him, I can't," Dylan begged through Elliot's lips.

"Just a little longer Dylan, help is on the way," Josh assured.

The eyes of Elliot's body rolled back into his head, again, but this time the ragged breathing remained.

61

The Forest

Cody, Drew, & West

"Drew, we have to keep going," Cody whispered. Drew was stopping for some reason.

"Did you hear that?" Drew asked.

"I didn't hear anything."

Drew closed his eyes and concentrated on the voice that had stopped him. "Trance!" the voice called, but it sounded so far away. The voice was so familiar to Drew. "Trance, you son of a bitch! Open your eyes!" Drew opened his eyes.

A silhouette of a person was forming in the air slightly ahead of him. He walked towards it, ignoring Cody's pleas to keep going.

"Who are you?" Drew asked the silhouette.

"I'm Cody," Cody answered.

Drew shook his head. "Not you, him," he explained, pointing at the boy standing in front of him.

"Him who?" Cody asked.

"TRANCE!!" a voice called. This voice was different then the voice that stopped him, yet equally as familiar. "COME BACK!"

The silhouette was becoming clearer.

"Oh God, you're me, you're Drew." Drew whispered. "If you're Drew, then who am I?" Drew asked the specter of himself.

"TRANCE!" the voice screamed again, this time more desperate then before. The specter turned his head to look back towards the voice.

Drew stepped forward and reached out to touch the specter. The specter reached out to touch Drew's hand. As their hands touched Drew felt a strange, tingling, sensation in his hand. His wrist wounds began to ache again as if they had been reopened.

"Why are you here?" Drew asked, but the specter was suddenly, violently, pulled backwards. "Don't go!" Drew called out, but the specter was already gone.

"Drew, let's go NOW!" a more demanding voice came from Nathan's lips.

"West, did you see that?" Drew asked, staring at his bandaged wrists. He was surprised that there wasn't blood oozing from the wounds.

"No, I didn't see anything. Now let's get out of here. Someone's coming...or are you going to blind them too?" West's words finally convinced Drew to run.

"I didn't do that on purpose. I don't know what's happening to me," Drew said as he chased after West.

"Just shut up and run!" West replied.

62

The Hospital

Harper, Josh, & Lilly

"He's going to make it," Josh announced with relief. He walked into the waiting room where Lilly and Harper waited in uncomfortable silence.

"What about Dylan?" Lilly asked softly.

"I don't know," Josh replied sadly. "He never said anything else."

"Should we tell Trance?" Lilly asked.

Josh shook his head. "We don't even know what happened. If Dylan isn't in there and we tell Trance that he is…," he trailed off.

"You're right," Lilly agreed thoughtfully.

"We need to go get Maggie and Trance's body tonight. We can't wait anymore,"

"Well, let's go then," Harper, who seemed overly anxious to get his own body back, prompted them.

"Where is she at?" Lilly inquired.

"They took her to Woodview," Josh replied.

"Woodview?" Lilly asked shocked. "Do you know what Woodview is?"

Josh shook his head.

"It's the worst mental hospital ever. It's essentially a prison for the criminally insane. They don't care about the patients there. They don't even try to help them. Most of them have life sentences anyway. They were petitioning to have it closed down. I was one of the biggest advocates until Eon…," she stopped.

"Have you worked there?" Josh asked.

"No, I would never."

"Then how do you know what it's like there?" Harper asked.

"I have a friend in there," Lilly replied softly.

"Tell me how to get there, we'll get her out, right now," Josh commanded.

"How?" Lilly asked.

"We'll figure that out when we get there," Josh said, leading them out of the hospital.

63

The Forest:

Cody, Drew, & West

"West, I have to stop!" Drew called out. It seemed he wasn't in as good of shape as he thought. West slowed down and finally stopped. He collapsed to the ground, under a large willow tree. Drew fell into his arms.

"We can rest here for a little bit," West whispered. "It's pretty hidden."

"West?" Drew asked, after he caught his breath.

"Hmm?" West replied.

"Who am I?" Drew asked softly. "What am I?"

"I don't know."

"I didn't mean to hurt that man. I just didn't want to get caught."

"I know," West assured him.

"Are you afraid of me?" Drew asked nervously.

"No, not you. I'm not afraid of you," West sighed, "I'm afraid of what you can do." He shivered. "It's unnatural."

Drew looked up into West's eyes, only then realizing that West's arms were closed tightly around him.

"Do you love me?" Drew asked, feeling like a silly little girl.

West nodded, slowly with tears in his eyes. He leaned forward and kissed Drew's lips.

"I love you, I don't care who you are. I don't care what you are, I don't care about that," West proclaimed.

"Then what's wrong. Why are you so...sad?" Drew asked for lack of a better word.

"It's weird. Sometimes I feel like I don't know who I am. It feels like everything about my life before this is slipping away. I can barely remember who I was," West admitted.

"That's how I feel too, but back there, I saw…I guess I saw a ghost."

"A ghost?"

"Well, like you said, it's weird. He looked like a ghost, but it was my ghost. My ghost was standing right in front of me." Drew tried to explain. "If it was my ghost, how can that happen? If it was me, then who am I?"

"I don't know."

"What are we going to do now?" Drew's entire body was shaking with cold.

"We're going to get out of here."

"How? We're in the middle of nowhere," Drew pulled away from West's arms.

"There's a road. It's pretty far, but we have to try and make it. When we get there, we can hitch a ride or something," West suggested.

"And then what?".

"I don't know," West repeated. For a brief second his muscles tensed up. His face scrunched up and then Drew saw Cody looking out at him.

"Cody?" Drew asked.

Cody nodded. "We have to find Dr. Lilly. She'll know how to help us."

"Who's Dr. Lilly?"

"She's my friend. She taught me about the bubble and about the energies. If anyone can help us, she can," Cody said excitedly. "She knows who I am…who I really am. She believes me. She said it happened to her a long, long, time ago."

"How do we find her?"

"Let's worry about that later," West's deeper voice said. He was once again in control of the body. "Let's just get to the road for now."

64

Kyle's House:

Kyle & Shadow

This was the first dream Shadow ever remembered having. At first, he had trouble figuring out that it was only a dream. It felt too real to be a dream. It felt too real for him to be asleep.

He found himself walking down a darkened hallway. He felt disconnected, like he did when he first woke up with amnesia. Once again, he felt ageless and sexless.

He saw a figure standing in the light, at the end of the hallway. It looked like Kyle.

"Kyle?" he asked in an ethereal voice that was not his own. It sounded almost as if two voices were speaking in unison. "KYLE!" he called again. The figure turned to look at him. He could see now by the profile that the figure ahead of him was pregnant. She stretched out her hands to Shadow.

He moved closer to the woman. He could make out her features now. It was Kyle.

"Kyle?" he asked, but the woman shook her head.

"Who are you?" Shadow asked with a strange voice. He never saw the facial features change, but when he looked again the face was different.

"Are you my real mom?" Shadow asked. It was only then that he remembered he had been adopted. The woman shook her head. "Who are you?" Shadow demanded. She was so familiar to him.

"I'm you," she answered in the same voice he had used.

228

"You're me?" Shadow asked. This was what he was looking for, the answers he was searching for.

"NOOO!" a voice screamed. Shadow turned to see Kyle running towards him at full speed. "She's lying, Shadow, She's lying," Kyle screamed as she barreled into him, knocking him over.

"KYLE!" Shadow screamed as pain ripped through him.

Kyle started to growl as she stared deep into his eyes. "You can't have him bitch!" Kyle's voice had turned demonic.

"Kyle," Shadow struggled against her iron grip on his shoulders. Kyle's face was morphing slowly until Shadow was staring into his own face.

"He's mine," Shadow heard his real voice say. It came from the demon on top of him. "If I can't him, then no one can," the demon with Shadow's face declared. Shadow noticed the arms that were holding him down were made of a patchwork of skin. Each piece had a different name tattooed on it.

"What the...," Shadow's unison voice asked. Something inside of him raged and instantly, he was so much stronger than the abomination holding him down. Shadow wrestled the demon around, until he was holding the demon down with his knee on its back. He had both of the demon's hands pulled behind him in classic police fashion.

"Ow! Shadow!" Kyle's voice cried out.

"Who are you really?" Shadow growled, putting pressure on the demon's lower back.

"SHADOW! IT'S ME KYLE! I SWEAR!" Kyle screamed out.

Shadow opened his eyes to find himself in Kyle's room. He was holding Kyle down against the floor. "Kyle! I'm so sorry." He released his hold. "I thought you were he Patchwork Man," Shadow claimed, helping her to stand up.

"What?" Kyle yelped. It was one of the dumbest stories Shadow had ever come up with.

Shadow couldn't answer, for just behind her stood an apparition of The Patchwork Man. Screaming; Shadow backed himself into the corner of Kyle's small room. He pointed speechlessly at the apparition. Kyle looked behind her, but the apparition had disappeared.

"Shadow, what the hell is wrong with you?" Kyle asked.

Shadow shook his head. He reached for his backpack and dumped it out on the floor. He picked out The Cure's Disintegration CD and put it into the Walkman. He put the headphones on his ears. He curled up in the fetal position on Kyle's bed.

Kyle lay down in front of him like before, but this time she teased a piece of his hair between her fingers.

He smiled and just lay there, staring at her beautiful face. He lifted his hand and placed it on her neck, rubbing his thumb gently across her cheek. Together, they fell asleep.

65

The Forest:

Cody, Drew, & West

"My feet hurt. Can we rest now?" Cody whined.

"We're almost there," Drew pointed out, wanting to push forward.

"Cody's right. This ankle is killing me…us. We need to rest," West agreed, pointing towards another willow tree. The two boys crawled under the branches and curled up under the tree.

"I'm so hungry," Drew whispered.

"Us too."

"Here, let me take a look at your foot," Drew suggested, hoping he could somehow relieve the pain.

"No," West replied. "You don't have to fix everything, Drew."

"I know," Drew felt tears building in his throat. He felt like West was rejecting him. If he didn't have West and Cody, then what would he have? Nothing. He would be all alone, again. He couldn't stand being alone, not again. "Do you hate me?" Drew asked with tears in his eyes. He looked up at Nathan's face, only to find Cody looking back at him.

"I don't hate you," Cody assured.

"Where'd West go?" Drew asked.

"He said you were acting too much like a girl and he left."

"Left left?"

"No, not left. He's still there, he's just not around, now," Cody replied. He opened Nathan's arms and Drew settled into them.

"I love you."

Drew couldn't tell who had whispered it. He closed his eyes and tumbled into a deep dreamless sleep.

66

The Asylum

Harper, Josh, & Lilly

"It should be just around that corner," Lilly pointed towards a bend in the road.

"You mean right where all that smoke is coming from?" Harper asked.

"Oh my God," Lilly breathed.

"Shit," Josh gasped.

"What the hell happened here?" Lilly asked as they pulled into a parking lot that was bursting with people and cars.

"Let's go find out," Harper suggested.

"How are we going to do that? Just walk up and ask one of those police officers?" Josh asked.

"Leave it to me," Harper said and jumped out of the van.

"Do you think that blood will ever come out of the carpet?" Josh stared down at the floor of the van.

Lilly shook her head. "I don't even want to think about it," she rolled down the window to see Harper better. "What is she doing out there?"

"She's talking to a cop. I wish I could hear what they are saying," Josh answered her.

"Me too." Lilly nodded. "Here she comes."

"OK, here's the story," Harper began, after she shut the van door behind her. Both Josh and Lilly turned in their seats to face her.

"An explosion occurred for no apparent reason. They suspect it was arson. It started in a room in which both occupants are now missing and presumed dead. All attempts inside or outside to find them have failed. The missing patients are Nathan Sinclair and Andrew Maxwell."

Lilly gasped. "Maggie and Cody."

"Cody?" Josh asked.

"A victim from an earlier change, he was only five, but he's in a man's body," Lilly explained.

"Your friend on the inside?" Harper asked.

Lilly nodded, tears rolling down her face. "I promised him that I would get him out of there."

Josh placed his hand on her shoulder. "They may be still alive," he reasoned, even though he didn't really believe it.

"I hope so," Lilly whispered through her tears.

"How did you find out so much?" Josh asked.

Harper smiled. "Apparently, I am a police woman," she proclaimed, pulling a badge out of her back pocket.

"That's where I know you from!" Lilly exclaimed. "When Eon attacked Mae and I in my apartment, there were two cops there. You were one of them or your body was anyway," Lilly explained.

"Hmm," Harper said, looking thoughtful. "I don't remember that. I think it was before I got in here."

"How did you get in there?" Josh asked.

"I was just walking down the street minding my own business when this lady came out of nowhere. She tackled me and then she…kissed me," Harper explained with a puzzled look on her face. "I blacked out and woke up in the hospital in this body."

"At least he didn't play with you, like he played with us," Josh reasoned.

"So, what do we do now?" Harper asked.

"There's nothing we can do now," Josh replied. "It's all over."

"For you guys maybe, but what about me?" Harper asked. "I want my body back too," Harper rolled his head back in frustration. "You guys give up way to easily. Like Josh said, maybe they are still alive."

"I don't think they are. There's no reason to go on," Lilly whispered.

"Don't say that, Lilly," Josh answered without conviction.

67

Kyle's House:

Kyle & Shadow

"Are you awake, Shadow?" Kyle asked into the darkness of her room.

"Yes," Shadow whispered, running his finger down her arm. She shivered in delight.

"Shadow, I thought you said...," she began to remind him about their agreement to just be friends.

Shadow remembered, but he couldn't stop himself from kissing her.

"You don't know how long I've been waiting for you to do that," Kyle whispered, a tear rolling down her cheek. Shadow quickly wiped it away. Kyle bit her lip to keep more tears from falling.

"What about Paul?" Shadow asked.

"Paul dumped me about a week after you tried...," she stopped talking.

"Why didn't you tell me you were pregnant?" Shadow pressed his open palm against her almost flat stomach.

"Shadow, how do you... I just found out a little bit ago. That's why I was going to your house. I was going to tell you," Kyle was flabbergasted. "How did you know?"

"I had a dream." Shadow traced the line of her side back up to her neck.

"Just now?" Kyle kissed the inside of his wrist.

"No, before."

"Oh," Kyle pulled away. "The one you had when you tried to kill me?"

"Kyle, you don't understand. You weren't you. You were some kind of demon, but it wasn't you. It was…"

"Shadow, you're confusing me," Kyle interrupted him. "Tell me about the whole thing, from the beginning."

Shadow nodded and in hushed tones told her all about what happened in the dream. He described the woman who claimed to be him and how he believed that maybe, that's who he really was.

"You weren't really running away, were you?" Kyle asked, smiling.

Shadow shook his head, then changed his mind and started nodding. "I don't know. I just wanted to find out what the hell happened to me."

"So, what do you want to do now?"

"I don't know, I was thinking about kissing you again," Shadow said shyly.

A smile spread across Kyle's face. She leaned towards Shadow and they kissed.

Shadow groaned in pain as a ripping sensation tore through his body.

"SHIT!" Shadow screamed out in agony.

"Shadow, what's wrong?" Kyle asked, pulling away from Shadow.

Shadow curled up, once again, in the fetal position and started pounding his fists against his head.

"Stop, Shadow, Stop," Kyle begged, throwing her arms around him to stop him from hurting himself.

"Make it stop. Make it stop," Shadow begged.

"I don't know how," Kyle cried. "What's wrong? What's happening to you?"

68

The Forest:

Cody, Drew, & West

Cody woke to the sound of dogs barking in the distance. Fear struck panic into him. Someone was coming.

"Drew, wake up!" Cody whispered, pushing Drew off of him. "Please wake up," he whispered louder, shaking him gently.

'*Help me, West,*' Cody called into his mind.

'*What is it?*' West groggily answered him.

'*Dogs,*' Cody replied. '*I can't wake up Drew.*'

'*Let me try,*' West said, moving his essence forward. Cody's in turn receded.

"Drew, get up!" West said as loudly as he dared.

West pulled back Drew's eyelids.

'*He's in some sort of shock,*' West explained to Cody.

'*I could go in and try to find him,*' Cody suggested.

'*There's no time. We have to carry him,*' West demanded, but Cody's stubbornness won out. His essence rushed forward. '*What are you doing?*' West asked meekly, he hadn't realized Cody was so strong.

'*I'm going to try what the bad man did to me,*' Cody answered. '*If I can't find him, at least I can make him run.*'

Cody leaned Nathan's body forward and placed a wet sloppy kiss on Drew's lips. West felt Cody's essence surging forward across the link made by Nathan's lips against Drew's lips. West pushed Cody's spirit forward towards Drew's body.

"Thanks for the boost," Drew's voice croaked out when Cody was gone.

"Let's go, Cody," West whispered.

"I...I think we messed up," Cody's eyes rolled back into his head. He began convulsing suddenly.

"Cody? SHIT!" West started to panic, but stopped himself. "No, don't panic. The dogs are coming. You have to get them out of here," he whispered to himself as he assessed the situation. Drew's body was now lying still before him. He bent down and scooped up the skinny boy as if he were a patient. He held the limp body close to his own and started to run towards the road.

69

The Forest:

Cody, Drew, Harper, Josh, Lilly, & West

"Pull over," Lilly shouted, startling Josh who followed her direction and pulled the van over to the side of the road.

"What is it?" Josh looked at Lilly.

"There was someone back there. They looked hurt," Lilly explained, opening the door.

"Lilly, don't! We don't have time to worry about everyone we see. We have to figure out what to do about us," Josh scolded, but she didn't listen. She stepped out of the van and closed the door.

"Yeah Lilly, get back in the van," Harper called out in agreement.

Lilly stopped mid-stride as she was walking away from the van. She turned and headed back.

"Look," Lilly said through the open window. "If I'm going to be stuck in this body, then I want to use my gifts while I still remember that I have them. The only gift I have is the gift of healing and if you guys aren't compassionate enough for that, then too damn bad. Go ahead and leave me here!" She stormed off in the direction of the man she saw struggling to carry a young, injured-looking boy.

"We better go help her," Josh gave in.

"Why?" Harper replied nastily. "If she wants to do it, let her do it on her own."

Josh took the keys for safety and followed after Lilly. He didn't trust Harper. He was afraid that she would steal the van and leave them both stranded.

"Lilly?" Josh called out.

"Over here, Josh," she replied. "Josh, it's Cody!" she called excitedly, "and Maggie!"

Josh broke into a run. He found Lilly kneeling next to two men. One of them was Trance's body. It looked very pale. All of its hair was cut off and he had bruises on his temples.

"Maggie?".

"I don't know," Lilly replied.

"Is she alright?"

"She's just in shock," Lilly assured him.

"Please, help him," the older man said, still trying to catch his breath.

"Don't worry, Cody. It's me Dr. Lilly. We'll help her," Lilly whispered.

"It's not a *her*, it's a *him*." West whispered, still gasping for air. He couldn't seem to catch his breath.

"Cody, don't you remember what I told you?" Lilly asked.

"Look, I am not Cody. Drew needs help and there are guards chasing us with dogs. We have to get out of here," West growled, once he finally caught his breath.

"Josh, help me get Ma…Drew back to the van," Lilly requested.

Josh stepped over and scooped up the boy, while Lilly helped West hobble to the van. His entire body ached from carrying Drew's seemingly lifeless body. His foot felt swollen and aching.

"Shit!" Lilly heard Harper cry as she jumped out of the door and opened sliding door.

"It's Cody and Maggie," Lilly whispered, struggling to help Nathan's body into the car.

"I'm not Cody," West reminded her once again. "My name is West."

"Where's Cody?" Lilly asked in shock.

"I hope he's in there," West pointed to Drew's body.

"You said Drew was a boy, right?" Josh asked. "What happened to Maggie?"

"I don't know. It's all really hazy. First I was holding Drew down. He was struggling to get away. Then something strange happened. I was looking at Drew, but I saw her. I saw Maggie...I guess. She told me, she was sorry and she kissed me. The next thing I really remember is waking up in this body," West explained.

70

Kyle's House:

Kyle & Shadow

"Better now?" Kyle asked as Shadow finished the last bite of the sandwich she'd made.

Shadow nodded. "Much.'"

"So, what do we do now?" Kyle asked.

"I want to go talk to my mom."

"For what?"

"I want to ask her about my biological mother."

"If that's what you want," Kyle sighed. She didn't like his mother; she was a bit of a lush.

"I do," Shadow replied. "I'm not going back there to stay though," he assured her. Kyle nodded. "I just need to find my biological mother."

"Why?" Kyle asked.

"I want to know if she was the pregnant woman in my dream," Shadow explained. He was in a particularly good mood. "After that, let's go to a club,"

"We're not old enough. Duh."

"How old are we?"

"I'm 17 and you're 15."

"15!" Shadow barked. "I'm just a baby."

"I know."

"There's so much I can't remember," Shadow whispered sadly.

"It's OK. I'll help you remember," Kyle kissed him on the cheek. "Let's go to The Velvet and see if we can sneak in."

"The Velvet..." Shadow closed his eyes trying to remember. "I remember The Velvet. I remember we saw...we saw a band there."

"Right, The Crüxshadows!" Kyle finished excitedly.

"I remember...the latex dress you wore. That was the night that I fell in love with you," Shadow said quickly; glad to remember something.

"When you what?" Kyle sat back down at the table.

"When I fell in...love...with you," Shadow repeated.

Kyle smiled the biggest smile Shadow had ever seen. "That's the night I fell in love with you, too."

"I think I'm going to be OK," Shadow informed her and for the first time he really believed it.

"Better than OK," Kyle dragged him to his feet. "Let's go change and then go see your mummy."

71

The Rental Van:

Cody, Drew, Harper, Josh,

Lilly, & West

"I have a question," West whispered into the silence of the van. He looked up from where he sat on the floor holding Drew's hand.

Lilly opened her resting eyes.

"That's Maggie," West smiled and pointed at Lilly. Lilly nodded.

"Was that your question?" Lilly asked.

"No," West replied. He laid his head back down on the cushion next to Drew's limp body. "I was just thinking. When Cody left this body, he took his abilities with him. Are Cody's psychic abilities going to affect Drew's abilities?" West looked back up at Lilly. "Maybe that's what's wrong with them."

"Cody's powers weren't that strong," Lilly said thoughtfully.

"How strong were Drew's powers?" Harper looked at West.

West's face paled at the question, "too strong." He pushed back the sleeve of Drew's dirty shirt and kissed the bandage covering his wrist. West placed the hand on the back of his own neck and nuzzled into Drew's side.

"How strong is too strong?" Lilly asked.

"He caused the explosion in his room with his mind alone. He was outside when he did it. He blinded a security guard and he healed my broken leg,"

"Whoa," Harper exclaimed in an awestricken voice.

"Shit!" Lilly whispered softly. "If he wasn't insane before…,"

"He wasn't insane," West declared.

"This could drive Drew crazy and Cody along with him," Lilly speculated.

"No," West gasped.

The hand on the back of West's head started to move. It was comforting West.

"Drew?" West asked.

Drew nodded. "I've got a killer headache," he murmured.

"Are you alright?" Lilly asked.

Drew's eyes shut and then opened again, a child-like innocence shone brightly in them. "Dr. Lilly!" Drew's voice yelled.

"Cody?" Lilly asked.

"I knew you'd come back for me," Cody sat up and reached out Drew's arms for a hug. Lilly climbed out of the front seat and maneuvered her way around the inside of the van. She hugged Cody tightly.

"You are such a brave little man," Lilly whispered into his ear.

"I did exactly what you said," Cody stated, proudly. "I pretended I was Daddy and they were nice to me."

"Daddy?" West asked.

"Nathan was Cody's father," Lilly explained softly.

Drew waited patiently as Lilly and Cody reunited. All he wanted was for West to hold him.

"So, are we good to go?" Josh started the van without waiting for an answer.

Drew pushed Cody's presence back.

"West, hold me," he begged. West sat on one side of Drew and Lilly sat on the other. She wanted Cody to feel her closeness too.

"Where are we going now?" Harper asked.

"First, we'll go to the cabin to sleep, it's been a long day. Then tomorrow we have to get to the hospital and figure out how to get Trance back into his own body," Josh replied.

Horror chills ran through Drew's body. If Trance got his body back, then what would happen to him? Would he just disappear into that deep dark void that he came from?

He looked at West, sleeping next to him. He couldn't leave West, not again.

'*Cody?*' Drew called out tentatively into his mind.

'*I don't like that girl,*' Cody replied.

'*Harper?*' Drew asked, closing his eyes.

'*Yes,*' Cody answered as Drew imagined sitting in a field with a small child next to him.

"*She scares me,*" the child said.

"*Why?*" Drew asked.

Cody shrugged. He ripped out a piece of grass and began to tear it to shreds. "*We have to go away again, don't we?*" *he asked.*

"*Yes,*" Drew replied. "*I don't want them to take my body away.*"

"*That means I won't get a body, will I?*"

"*No, it means that I will find a way to get you into your own body,*" Drew replied.

"*YAY!*" Cody squealed. "*Can West come too?*" he asked.

Drew remained silent

"*We can't tell him anything about it. He'll try to stop us, won't he?*" Cody surmised.

Drew nodded.

"*When are we going to leave?*"

"*Tonight, while everyone is asleep,*" Drew reached forward and took Cody into his arms.

"*Good, the sooner the better.*" Sadness filled Cody's voice at the thought of leaving West behind.

"*We'll be better on our own,*" Drew assured the boy with the same sadness in his voice.

"*We don't need anybody,*" Cody agreed, trying to be brave.

72

The Cabin:

Cody & Drew

Drew rolled over in the bed that the strangers had given him. His mind was filled with anger. This was his body and no one was going to take it from him. It was time to go.

He lowered his shields just enough to make sure that everyone in the cabin was sleeping. He looked longingly at West sleeping on the floor next to the fireplace. He brushed West's mind gently with the feathery touch of his own mind. '*I love you,*' he whispered into West's mind. West smiled in his sleep, but didn't wake up.

Drew made his way over to the dresser next to the door. He opened it to find it filled with black clothes. He picked out a shirt and slipped it on. He pulled on a pair of pants, but they were too big and they kept sliding off. Silently, he searched for a belt, wishing that the pants were tighter. He watched in shock as a belt appeared on the top of the dresser. "What the hell?" he whispered. He picked it up and went to put it on only to find that somehow the pants had shrunk to fit him perfectly.

"This shirt needs to be tighter too," he said slowly, afraid of the results. They were the same, the shirt shrunk, before his eyes, to fit him.

"Cool!" he whispered, and slipped out the door. "Now, all I need is a pair of combat boots," he whispered, hoping that they could just appear. They did. "This is so awesome!" he exclaimed, pulling on the boots. He slipped out of the cabin and ran into the woods.

'*Cody, get up, I need to talk,*' Drew called as he continued to run through the forest.

'*I'm awake,*'

'*Did you see what just happened?*' Drew asked excitedly.

'*You're magic,*' Cody replied in a scared tone.

'*We're magic,*' Drew pointed out, crouching beneath a tree. '*Go ahead. Give it a try.*'

Drew pulled his essence back so Cody could try it.

"I want a Popsicle," Cody yelled and a Popsicle appeared in his hand. "Cool!" Cody shouted. "I want a pony!" he said, but nothing happened. '*Where's my pony?*'

'*I don't know let me try,*' Drew said, taking control of his body again.

"I need a pony," Drew commanded, concentrating as hard as he could, but still nothing happened. "Give me a car," he said angrily. "A motorcycle," he shouted.

'*It's not working now,*' Drew told Cody.

"I NEED A SKATEBOARD!" Drew screamed and a skateboard materialized on the ground in front of him.

'*We can only make little things,*' Cody pointed out.

Drew picked up the skateboard and ran towards the road.

'*Do you know how?*' Cody asked in fear.

"I will. I wish I knew how to skate," Drew shouted and his body automatically started skating.

'*Aren't you scared of the magic?*'

'*Why should I be? This is awesome and I am never giving this body up,*' Drew laughed into the wind as he skated towards town.

With a sinking feeling, Cody realized that Drew would never find him another body. He was too obsessed with the magic.

73

Shadow's House:

Kyle & Shadow

Shadow and Kyle stood outside Shadow's house. He was reluctant to go in.

"Let's just forget about it," Kyle suggested.

"No, I have to do this," Shadow disagreed. "You can wait outside, if you want."

"No, I don't want her to convince you to stay," Kyle laughed, kissing him on his cheek. "Let's do this." She rang the doorbell before he could chicken out.

"I could just walk in," Shadow pointed out.

"No, this isn't your home anymore," Kyle reasoned. "Your home is with me."

Shadow smiled, running his hand through his long black hair.

"How do I look?"

"Does it matter?"

"Not really." Shadow laughed.

The mother opened the door.

"Alex, why are you ringing the doorbell?" Mrs. Roderick asked.

"I forgot my key," Shadow lied. "Tell me about my mother."

"I am your mother."

"No you aren't. I saw the papers."

"The papers," she sighed. "Come in, come in." She ushered them into the kitchen. "You kids want something to drink?" she opened the fridge. "Coffee?" she offered, "Beer?"

"No, thank you," Kyle replied politely.

"I didn't come here to get drunk with you." Shadow followed his mother into the kitchen.

"What's that supposed to mean?" his mother sat down at the table, then gestured for them to join her.

"Nothing," Shadow sighed, biting his tongue. He didn't need to start a fight with her about her drinking again. Another memory had surfaced at the mention of beer.

He had drunk his first beer at the age of 11 and had been so drunk he'd fallen asleep at the dinner table. His mother and her boyfriend at the time teased him about it for weeks afterward. He hadn't had a beer since.

"Please, Mom, just tell me about my birth mother. It's important to me." Shadow sat at the table, Kyle stood behind his chair resting her hand on his shoulder, both showing support and staking her claim.

His mother smiled. "She was such a sweet little thing. She was only 14; such a sad story." Her smile turned into a frown. "She was raped, but she wouldn't even think about abortion. Your father and I, God rest his soul, wanted to adopt. She was willing to give us her baby." She took a drink of her beer. "It was all perfectly legal, you saw the papers."

"Do you remember her name?" Shadow asked.

"Her name... I can picture her sweet, sad little face." She paused. "Her name was Maggie."

"Maggie," Shadow repeated. The name meant nothing to him. "Do you have a picture?" he asked.

"Unfortunately, no, she didn't give us one." She looked at him. "Oh, did I tell you? That cop lady that dropped you off stopped by here again."

"Cop lady?" Shadow asked. "When did the cops drop me off?"

"Two days ago. She dropped you off here. She told me you were a witness to a murder or something. She was here yesterday looking for you."

"What?" Shadow exclaimed. "A murder? I don't remember that."

"I told you, I don't know what happened. She just dropped you off and left."

"Maybe that's why you can't remember," Kyle suggested. "Maybe you blocked it out."

"I blocked out my entire life?" Shadow asked.

"Let's just go, Shadow."

Shadow nodded and they stood up to leave.

"Where are you going?" the mother asked.

"To a club, I won't be home too late," Shadow lied.

74

The Street:

Cody, Drew, Kyle,

& Shadow

'*I'm hungry,*' Cody complained.

'*Um...yeah....so am I. Remember we have the same body,*' Drew thought angrily.

'*I wish we didn't have this body! I wish I had my body,*' Cody retorted, just as angrily.

Abruptly, a horrible pain ripped through Drew's body. For a split second, Drew thought he was going to explode. He was forced so far back into the mind, that he couldn't even feel the body anymore.

'*Drew! Help me! Where are you?*' Drew could hear Cody's frantic call, but he couldn't seem to answer. '*Drew, I want you back. I didn't mean to wish you gone. I'm sorry. Please come back.*'

Suddenly, Drew was back. He was staring at a close-up view of the sidewalk.

'*We fell,*' Cody started to cry.

'*Stop it!*' Drew demanded, pushing Cody's essence back.

He stood up and immediately he knew something was wrong. Everything seemed to be too big. He picked up the skateboard and it was almost the same size as he was.

'*Cody, what did you do?*' Drew stomped over to a storefront and stood in front of the closed store's window. The reflection that stared back at him was that of a five-year-old child.

'I'm sorry. I didn't mean it,' Cody moaned.

'Don't be, this may be something cool,' Drew reasoned. "I want my body," Drew said, out loud, closing his eyes to brace himself for the pain. When he opened his eyes, he was himself again. Drew smiled brilliantly. "This is so awesome!" Drew screamed out into the empty street. "Mirror!" he commanded and pointed at the wall next to the store window. He stood in front of the mirror that appeared there. "Woman!" he commanded and his body morphed into that of a woman. "Back!" He was Drew again. *'Let's go to a club, Cody.'*

'I don't want to. I want to go home. I want to go back to Dr. Lilly,' Cody begged.

"I'm never going back," Drew growled. "Older!" he commanded. His face grew wrinkled right before his eyes. "Too old. 25!" he commanded. He was having so much fun. "Jet black hair! Long spiky." He smiled at the older reflection of himself in the mirror. Those people who wanted to steal his body would never recognize him now. He laughed excitedly.

He noticed bruises near his temples. He didn't know where he had gotten them, but he wanted them gone. "Heal." He placed his hands over the bruises and they faded away. He pulled up his sleeves and tore off the bandages. "Heal," he commanded and both of his wrist wounds turned into thin white scars. The stitches came undone and fell to the ground at his feet.

'STOP!' Cody screamed.

'Why?' Drew asked. He was power hungry. He wanted more. He wanted to push the limits of his newfound powers. "Goatee," he said aloud.

'STOP!' Cody begged. *'It hurts. Can't you feel it?'* Cody screeched inside their head.

'STAY BACK!' Drew commanded. He didn't need a Jiminy Cricket around telling him what to do.

'NOOOOO!' Cody screamed as his essence faded away.

Drew looked up at the mirror. "Mirror gone," Drew commanded and the mirror disappeared.

"OK, I need a wallet, ID, and money," Drew mused and all of these things appeared in his hand. He stuck them in his back pocket. His nose was running, so he wiped it away with the back of his hand. Drew was startled when his hand came back covered in blood.

'*CODY! Come back!*' Drew called into his mind, but there was no reply.

"I need something to wipe this with," Drew said, out loud, holding out his hand, but nothing happened. His head was beginning to ache. He sat down on the curb and put his head between his knees.

"I need aspirin," Drew said, but nothing came. "I need this blood to stop!" he said fearfully, but nothing happened. "It's gone," he said softly. He was too tired to be angry. "And so is Cody," he thought sadly as he pinched the bridge of his nose.

"Hey are you OK?" a female voice asked him.

He looked up. Two Goth kids stood above him.

"Nose bleed," Drew explained.

"I have allergies. I'm the Kleenex queen." The girl handed him a Kleenex from her purse.

Drew chuckled. "Thanks, I'm Drew." Drew wiped his bloody hand on his pant leg and reached up to shake their hands.

"I'm Kyle and this is my boyfriend, Shadow."

75

The Cabin:

Harper & Josh

Harper woke up to the sound of distant noises. She couldn't tell if the noises were in her head or outside in the woods. She felt something else too. She knew something was wrong; it was almost as if an echo of power woke her up. She stood up and snuck into Drew's bedroom. West was curled up on the floor, but Drew was nowhere to be found. Harper gently shut the door.

"Shit," Harper whispered.

"What's the matter?" Josh's voice answered. He too had been woken up by the noises.

"Nothing," Harper replied.

Josh knew that Harper was up to something. He had never trusted this man trapped in a woman's body. Her current suspicious behavior didn't help him trust her more.

"Why don't I believe you?" Josh asked.

"I don't like being a woman," Harper admitted sadly. "Do you know why I don't like being a woman?" she asked seductively.

"No," Josh replied slowly. What was this girl up to?

"I don't like being a woman..." Harper started as she walked across the room and pressed up against Josh's half naked body. "Because, when I look at you, it makes me feel like doing this," she said, slithering her hand seductively down his pants. "It makes me want to kiss someone as sexy as you," she whispered, placing her lips on his.

By the time Josh realized what was happening, it was too late. He was spinning around and around, dizzy with an aching longing for this man. He hated this feeling. He hated Eon for fooling them all. Anger swept over him. He didn't want this to happen again. He fought and fought, raging against the force that was pulling him from his body. In the end Eon was stronger and he won out.

"Don't be alarmed if there's a little more pain this time around," Eon told him, using Josh's own voice. "You see, I booby trapped that body. The pain will only last for a short time, but it'll be worth it," he whispered into Josh's new ear; Harper's ear.

Josh struggled to open Harper's eyes. "You asshole!" Josh spat out. It was all he could do around the paralyzing pain that filled his new body.

"Too bad we don't have more time," Eon paused. "Well, maybe we do," he said, pulling down the pants on the body he was now in.

"No!" Josh managed to whisper. He hated hearing his new voice. He wanted his real voice back.

"I wish I'd had the time to do that sweet fiancé of yours," Eon whispered as he lowered himself onto the body that Josh now occupied.

"Fuck you!" he growled.

"I thought that's what we were doing. Can't you feel it? You want it harder? You must like pain."

Josh tried to get any part of the body to respond to him, but the only part that seemed to work was the mouth. Every time he tried to move any other part there was so much pain Josh thought he would die. He whimpered, tears falling down his female face.

"Come to think of it," Eon started, "maybe I did rape your girlfriend... What was her name? Lauren? She put up a little bit more of a struggle then you are."

"Bastard!" Josh cried out in a pitiful voice.

"Shut up. I'm having fun," Eon said, smacking the woman's face. "Oh, and by the way, this time I did it JUST TO PISS YOU OFF! You SON OF A BITCH! YOU RUINED EVERYTHING!" Eon said, getting angrier. His anger was making him more brutal.

Josh felt as if his insides were tearing.

"Please, stop," he begged.

"SHUT UP!" Eon screamed, smacking Josh again and again.

Thankfully, Josh finally slipped into a deep oblivion.

***

West awoke to the sound of Harper screaming bloody murder. He could tell, by that scream, that something was terribly wrong. He ran into the living room to find Harper, her nightgown covered in blood. She was running around the living room of the cabin throwing anything she could get her hands on.

"Lilly!" West screamed. "DREW, HELP!" Where was everyone? Lilly ran out of her room tying a bathrobe shut.

"Grab her," she called out.

West ran over and tried to grab Harper. Harper panicked even more, punching and kicking at him, until he finally backed away.

"Harper, calm down," Lilly soothed. "Where's Josh?"

"Where's Drew?" West replied.

"JOSH!" Lilly shouted. Harper stopped her tantrum.

"Lilly?" Harper asked.

Lilly nodded.

"Help me Lilly, help me," Harper ran over to Lilly's arms.

"What happened, Harper? Where are Josh and Drew?" Lilly asked holding the woman and soothing her.

"He raped me. It hurts so bad!"

"Who raped you?" Lilly asked.

"Did Josh do it?" West asked.

"No, NO, Lilly. Eon did. I'm Cheyenne," Harper's desperate voice told her.

"Josh...," Lilly fell to the floor still holding Harper's body. Eon put Josh in this body and because of what he did Josh was giving up. She had to reach Josh. She couldn't lose him not like this. She had to get him back, but first she had to get Cheyenne to trust her. She started sobbing and Cheyenne sobbed with her. The two clung to each other desperately.

"I'm so sorry. I should have known Harper was actually Eon. I should have sensed it or something. I can't believe how blind I am," Lilly sobbed.

"From what I've heard, there's no way you could have known," West assured her as he cleaned up the living room.

"You're bleeding," Lilly pointed out.

Cheyenne nodded.

"Let me take a look at it," Lilly offered.

Cheyenne shook her head.

"It's OK, I'm not going to hurt you," she said softly.

"My baby," Cheyenne whispered. "Is my baby alright?"

"You're pregnant?" Lilly asked.

"Three months." Cheyenne replied, smiling a small smile.

"I'm a doctor. I can check on the baby for you," Lilly assured her, as she led her into the bathroom.

76

The Street:

Drew, Kyle, & Shadow

"You look really sick, Drew," Kyle pointed out.

"Do you need a place to crash?" Shadow asked.

Drew nodded his vision blurring.

"My house is a couple blocks that way," Kyle pointed in the direction they were headed.

Drew nodded, letting them help him up. They walked one on each side of him helping him walk. He was completely drained. He could barely walk, let alone see straight.

"Had a little too much to drink?" Kyle asked.

Drew nodded. Let these strangers believe that if they wanted to. "Sorry if I'm ruining you guys' night," he murmured.

"Don't worry about it. We couldn't get into the club anyway," Kyle laughed.

"Why not?"

"We're not exactly old enough."

"Me either," Drew replied forgetting about what he had done only moments ago. "I can't find Cody,"

"Is that your boyfriend?" Kyle asked.

Drew laughed. "No, he's like my brother. He was crying because we fell."

"How old is he?" Shadow asked.

"He's five," Drew replied.

"We should go look for him," Kyle stopped walking.

"Nah, he's alright, I don't think he was really here. I'm just a little confused" Drew replied, realizing how bad what he said must sound to them. He closed his eyes and couldn't seem to open them again.

"I think he passed out," Kyle said over the guy's head.

"He sounds really drunk, but I don't smell anything on him. Maybe he's high on something." Shadow observed.

"Maybe he's just crazy," Kyle suggested. "Hold him up while I open the door," she laughed. "I'm opening the door to let in a crazy drunk."

Drew tried to tell her he wasn't crazy or drunk, but he was too weak to move at all.

77

Outside the Cabin:

Eon

Eon snuck around the back of the cabin, where he knew from Josh's memories that a motorcycle was hidden. He pushed the bike out to the road and walked with it for a bit before starting it.

This was right around the area where he tried to kill Dylan. Dylan, if he could get his hands on that one, he would make him suffer. Dylan just would not die. He'd tried to kill him at least three times and each time he survived somehow. He just stayed alive, making things bad for Eon.

If only Dylan would have died the first time he tried to kill him, before he married Maggie. Then Maggie would have been out of the picture, long before Eon had gone all soft inside for her. Now he couldn't imagine forcing Maggie to die in her boyfriend's body, but before he knew her, it could have been fun to watch. Especially now that he knew she was Nessa; that betraying bitch. Who'd have thought she'd be reincarnated. Nessa was supposed to be immortal.

Maggie: the name cut through him like a knife. How could one woman, one soul, make him so soft inside? And how could he ever forgive her for what she did when she was Nessa? Hell, how could he forgive her for what she did as Maggie?

He needed to stop thinking about Maggie. Thinking about her just brought up the pain of her rejecting him. He was glad she was gone. She could have been his downfall.

He struggled to push her out of his head. He had to stop thinking about her. He had other things now that he had to concentrate on. Somehow, he had to get to Drew and keep him away from Lilly and her do-gooder friends. Lilly: another bitch that betrayed him.

He had to kidnap Drew and lock him up somewhere until his Vessel was ready. Then while he waited, he would devise a plan to get HIS powers away from Drew.

First he had to find The Vessel, and then he could work on getting Drew.

78

Kyle's House:

Drew, Kyle, & Shadow

"When is your dad coming home?" Shadow asked Kyle. It was in the early afternoon and they had just woken up.

"He's in California for two weeks on a business trip," Kyle replied.

"Does he know about the baby?" Shadow asked.

"Hell no! He's the last person I would tell. He's going to beat the shit out of me when he finds out," Kyle answered fearfully.

"We'll be gone before he gets back."

"So we really are going?" Her voice rose with excitement.

"Yes, we'll go somewhere safe and raise our baby," Shadow tucked a piece of her hair behind her ear.

"Really?" Kyle asked.

"Of course," he smiled. "I will love it as if it were my own."

Kyle smiled and kissed him passionately, then pulled away. "Should we be doing this?" she asked, running her hand up his chest.

Shadow shrugged. "It's too late now." He laughed. "I don't think we could stop now."

"I agree," Kyle told him. "Can I ask you a question?"

"What?"

"Who's Mae?" she asked, running her fingers across the fresh tattoo on his chest.

"I don't know," he said, glancing down. "I didn't even know that was there," he said, running his own fingers across the tattoo.

Both were startled as they heard screaming coming from Kyle's dad's bedroom.

"Drew!" Shadow jumped out of bed and pulled on his pants. Kyle jumped up and threw on her oversized tee shirt pajamas. Together, they ran into Kyle's dad's room.

Shadow ran over to the struggling form on the bed. He grabbed the man's shoulders and tried to hold him down. Pain ripped through his body as his hand came in contact with the man's bare flesh. He broke the contact and the pain subsided.

"WAKE UP DREW!" Shadow called out, not wanting to risk touching him again.

Drew sat up, but to both Kyle and Shadow's surprise, it wasn't the man they brought home late last night. It was a boy about the same age as they were.

"Where am I?" the boy asked.

"You're at my house. I'm Kyle," she whispered softly.

Recognition filled the teenager's eyes. "Thanks for letting me crash here,"

"Who are you?" Shadow asked.

"I'm Drew."

"You're not the Drew we brought home last night," Kyle could not believe her eyes.

"Hmm," Drew said thoughtfully. "Is there any way I could take a bath? I can explain after that, but right now, I feel very filthy. I must have landed in something when I fell"

"You are the Drew we brought home?" Shadow asked.

The boy nodded.

"The bathroom's just down the hall on the right," Kyle directed. "Towels are in the closet just before the bathroom." She pointed down the hall. "I'll go make some lunch." She went into the kitchen and Shadow followed.

"What the hell is going on?" Kyle began filling a pot with water.

"I have no idea," Shadow said, sitting down at the table. "Do you remember yesterday when I had that really bad pain?"

Kyle nodded.

"I got that same pain when I touched that boy."

"That boy who is claiming to be the man we brought home last night," she sat next to him at the table. "Do you think it could have been a disguise?" She laid her hand on top of Shadow's.

"I don't think so," Shadow placed his other hand on top of hers. "It could've been, but I don't think so."

Kyle nodded in agreement. "What the hell is going on here?" Kyle repeated. She was very frightened.

"I have a feeling that we are just skimming the surface of something much bigger."

"How do you know?" Kyle asked.

"I don't know. I think…," Shadow started, but lost his nerve. "I think," he tried again, "that it has something to do with The Patchwork Man." Fear filling his eyes as he finished.

"Who is he?" Kyle asked.

"When I was younger, I used to have these nightmares about him all the time. They were horrible, horrible nightmares in which he'd be chasing me and I would run and run, trying to escape. When he finally did catch me…" Shadow's voice shook as a sob wracked through his body. Kyle wrapped her arms around him. He began again when he could. "When he would catch me, whatever part of me he touched would slowly turn to patchwork skin. He would keep grabbing me, until I was just like him and then I would fall into darkness forever.

"As I got older, the nightmares went away, but in there…," he pointed to Kyle's room, "they came back."

He looked up into Kyle's face with tears rolling down his cheeks. "I think he's real and one day, he's going to catch me and when he does, I'm going to die."

"No," Kyle gasped.

"Kyle, he's pure evil," Shadow whispered, clinging to her.

Without warning, they both heard a strangled cry and splashing sounds coming from the bathroom.

"Drew," Shadow cried jumping up and running to the bathroom.

He knocked on the door, but there was no answer. "Drew, are you alright?" he asked. The only reply was more splashing. He pushed the door open.

"DREW!" Kyle screamed.

It looked like Drew was being held under the water, but no one else was in the room. Shadow reached his hands into the water and struggled to pull Drew out.

"Something's holding him under the water," he explained looking at Kyle, who was standing by the door frozen in fear. "Help me," he begged.

As soon as Kyle started running towards the tub, whatever was holding Drew under, released its hold. Drew came out of the water gasping for air. He fell out of the tub on top of Shadow.

"It wasn't a dream," Drew kept whispering between breaths.

"I guess you don't need me," Kyle said, stepping out of the room and closing the door.

Drew rolled off of Shadow onto the floor, still gasping for air.

Shadow went to the hall closet and pulled out some towels. He handed two to Drew and kept one to dry himself off.

"So you're the one he wants," Drew said after he was dried and had a towel wrapped around his waist.

"Who?" Shadow asked.

"You already know who," Drew replied mysteriously. "Well, he doesn't want you particularly. He just wants the body that you're in; the body that you are in now, not your actual body. Who knows where that is?"

"It's right here. This is my body," Shadow demanded.

"You don't know? You don't remember?" Drew asked cryptically.

"What are you talking about? Know what?"

Drew stood up from his seat on the side of the tub, his right hand held against his chest as if he were still in pain. He walked towards Shadow, who was backing away from him.

"He did it to me too. I didn't remember it until you touched me." Drew moved his hand away from his chest to reveal a tattoo just like Shadow's, only his said ELLIOT.

Drew reached up and smoothed down an errant piece of Shadows hair. "This is going to hurt, I'm sorry, but you need to know."

"No...," Shadow whispered, but it was too late. Drew placed one hand on Shadow's cheek and the other on Shadow's chest.

Shadow screamed and clenched his eyes shut as the memory overtook him.

***

Shadow walked slowly down a corridor, to what looked like an apartment. No, he wasn't Shadow. He was Cheyenne Beswick and she was walking down the hallway with her partner, Brad. She pointed towards apartment 5C. "Open up, this is the police!" Cheyenne shouted at the door. "Eon Reynolds, open up," she yelled.

She watched the murder as it replayed itself in her mind.

"Brad!" Cheyenne screamed. She ran over to her fallen partner. Cheyenne lifted her hand to her radio; she needed a bus. A hand closed around her hand and squeezed it.

"I wouldn't do that if I were you," Eon warned. He pulled the knife out of Brad and wiped it on Cheyenne's uniform.

"What are you?" she asked, staring into Eon's eyes.

"I'm your worst nightmare," Eon replied.

"Lilly, grab that boy before he gets out," Eon instructed. Why did he keep calling the old woman a boy? Cheyenne watched as the younger woman tried to escape with the older woman. She watched as Eon slit the old woman's throat.

The woman had him down on the floor. This was Cheyenne's chance to cuff the murdering bastard. She lifted the still sobbing woman off of the teenager. She turned the teenager over and started to cuff him, but with surprising strength, he broke free and pinned Cheyenne to the ground.

"I was hoping for a man, but I guess you'll do," the teenager told her. Then curiously he kissed her full on the lips. Cheyenne was ripped out of her body so suddenly that she felt no pleasure, only pain.

"What?" Cheyenne asked, but her voice was wrong. She opened her eyes and found herself staring into her own eyes. Her eyes, but someone else was looking out of them. It was the boy, but not the boy. Cheyenne started to panic.

"Now, we've got no time for that," her own voice whispered to her. The girl named Lilly ran at him. He shoved her against the wall so hard that she crumpled to the ground, unconscious. Cheyenne struggled to get out of the iron grip that the man in her body had on her.

"What are you?" Cheyenne asked, a male voice speaking her words. She cleared her throat. "What...?" she tried again, but stopped as she noticed her reflection in the mirror next to the door. She was the boy. She reached up and touched a hand to her face. In the mirror the boy's hand responded. She started to scream and felt a hand clamp down over the boy's mouth, her mouth.

"I already told you, I'm your worst nightmare," he repeated. "Let me clarify this situation for you," he said, speaking slowly, as if Cheyenne was too dumb to understand. "You just beat and raped two people. You also murdered two of them, including a cop. You killed my partner."

"Brad is my partner and I didn't kill him. I didn't kill anyone," Cheyenne protested.

"I saw you do it. I'm a witness."

"But I'm not...I...I didn't," Cheyenne stuttered.

"Here's a tip for you: people tend to believe the police over street urchins," he told her.

"But, I am the POLICE!" Cheyenne screamed out in a pitiful voice. The man in her body slapped her.

"One more time: Me—police. You—cop killer," he sighed. "I can help you or I can screw you over, which one will it be?"

"Help," Cheyenne replied meekly, wiping the tears away from her eyes with black-painted fingernails.

***

"No more, No more," Cheyenne begged, opening her eyes. Where was she? She was in Kyle's bathroom with Drew. The Patchwork Man, he did this to her. The Patchwork Man was one of Shadow's memories. How could she still remember his memories, when she could also remember hers?

"You!" she accused. "You did this to me!" She screamed with Shadow's voice. "Who are you? WHO ARE YOU?" she screamed.

"I didn't do it. I'm just another victim, I swear," Drew bit his lip. "Actually, I've got another victim with me in here," he said, tapping his head.

"Cody?" Shadow asked, remembering the name that Drew mentioned last night.

Drew nodded.

"I'm not Cheyenne anymore," Shadow said in a low whisper. "I don't want any of her memories in my head."

"Then you can get rid of them, but at least this time, you have a choice," Drew explained solemnly as he began to put his clothes back on.

Shadow remembered Cheyenne's voice whispering in his ear the night she brought him home. *"I'll be seeing you again. Don't think you can hide from me, I'll find you."*

"It's never going to be the same again, is it?" Shadow asked thoughtfully.

Drew put his arm around the younger boy's shoulder. "No, nothing will ever be the same again."

"Is Cody OK?" Shadow asked in a small voice.

"I don't know," Drew replied sadly. "Like I said before, I can't find him." He paused for a moment. "I'm not Maggie anymore, but I can still remember some of her memories. Let's go get some food and I'll tell you my story and Maggie's too."

"My mother?" Shadow looked up at the boy.

"Shadow's birth mother." Drew nodded.

"You're her?" Shadow looked at him desperately.

"I was, but like you, I chose to survive. I let her go so I could live."

"So she's gone?"

Drew nodded. "Let's go eat and I'll tell you everything."

79

The Cabin:

Lilly, Josh, & West

"Who am I?" Cheyenne's voice whispered in the darkness. She was wrapped in Lilly's arms, content in her knowledge that her baby was safe and sound.

"I think you're Josh," Lilly answered.

"I don't remember being Josh. I just remember being Cheyenne."

"Do you remember Lauren?" Lilly asked.

Cheyenne's heart stopped at the mention of the name. A vision of a woman's face flashed across her mind.

"I loved her," Cheyenne replied.

"She was your fiancée," Lilly explained.

"I feel like I don't belong in here. It's just this constant feeling that something's not right," Cheyenne whispered. "I don't want to be Cheyenne I want to be who I was."

"What do you remember?" Lilly asked.

"I remember Trevor," she paused. "It's a Cheyenne memory. He was my son. He got hit by a car," she thought some more. "I remember Isabel. She was my lover after my husband left me." She paused; the word husband drew her attention. "I remember DYLAN!" she said with joy. "He was in my body, not this body, but the one Eon took from me again."

"Yes," Lilly said, smiling, happy that she was helping Josh come back.

"I remember a scar, right here." She pressed her finger against her stomach. "I got it when I was in prison."

She paused. "Cheyenne was never in prison. She was a cop. She put people in prison."

"Josh was in prison," Lilly clarified.

"No," Cheyenne disagreed.

"Josh was in prison when he was in Erik's body," Lilly explained.

"My head hurts," Cheyenne complained.

"Don't worry, sleep now. We can remember more later."

There was a knock on the door. Cheyenne looked scared, but Lilly knew it was West.

"Come in," Lilly called.

West entered.

"I know I don't know you guys too well, but would you mind if I slept in here? It's lonely without...," West asked, choking back tears.

Lilly nodded.

"Thanks." West was content to curl up on the floor where Josh had been laying the night before. Lilly smiled. She considered all of Eon's victims her children. All of them but one, she thought, as she stared at the woman sleeping in the bed with her.

She would have to keep a better eye on her children. She was slowly losing all of them.

80

𝕾𝖍𝖆𝖉𝖔𝖜'𝖘 𝕳𝖔𝖚𝖘𝖊:

𝕰𝖔𝖓

𝕰on smiled as he took Josh's license and slipped it in with Cheyenne's badge. It wasn't the greatest cover, but as long as no one examined it too closely it should work.

He swung off of the bike and walked up to Alex's front door. He had visited this house a few times both as Alex and as Cheyenne, even as someone completely different once just to meet Alex to make sure he was the one.

Eon had followed the line of his descendants very diligently, even at times nudging certain ones to procreate. This boy was a direct descendant of his only son; that he knew of anyway. He may have fathered many children over the centuries, but this boy was the only descendant of his original body.

He knocked on the door and waited as patiently as he could under the circumstances.

A moment later, Mrs. Roderick opened the door. "Can I help you?"

"Evening, Ma'am," Eon began in his best police tone. "I'm looking for Alex Roderick," he held up the police badge, but snapped it closed before she could look too closely at it.

"I'm sorry officer, but he's not here. He never came home last night," she told him.

"I just needed to ask him a few questions about the, um, incident," Eon said.

"Sorry, I don't know where he is." She paused looking very thoughtful. "I know who he may be with though."

"That would be great, ma'am,"

"I can't remember her name," she replied. "It's a boy's name, I know that. I think I might have a picture of her."

"A picture is better than nothing," Eon rationalized.

She opened the door. "Come on in. Have a cup of coffee," she invited, letting him into the house. This was just what he wanted. He needed to be alone in her kitchen.

She poured him a cup of coffee. "Cream? Sugar?" Mrs. Roderick offered, sitting down at the table.

"No thanks. I'll take it black," Eon replied. "You said you had a picture of the girl?" Eon prompted after a few moments of awkward silence.

"Right," she said, jumping up so fast that her chair almost fell over. "I'll be right back." She hurried out of the room.

Eon stood up and righted her chair. He peeked out of the kitchen and, when he was sure she was gone, he reached his hand up above the cupboard over the table. The camera was so much easier to retrieve than it had been to set up. When he set the camera there, he had been in the teenager's much shorter body. He had to climb onto the chair to reach it then. He slipped the micro camera into his pocket and sat back down at the table.

He sighed in anger. If he still had his powers, he wouldn't need to stoop to such unsophisticated tactics. He could just read the energy stored up in the area around him. Now all of his powers were gone. It happened like that from time to time. Sometimes his powers would stay with him after the switch and sometimes they would go away. It was especially hard to lose them now, because for the past fifteen or twenty switches he had been gathering some rather amazing powers.

"Here's the picture I was telling you about," Mrs. Roderick said as she entered the room holding out a picture for Eon.

***

Eon laughed in excitement as he reviewed the video. The Vessel had returned home and learned who his birth

275

mother was. He had also given away where they were going to be. The club's name he remembered from the time he spent in the boy's body: The Velvet. He would find the boy there and kidnap him.

81

Kyle's House:

Cody, Drew, Kyle, & Shadow

"I don't believe you!" Kyle spat out as Drew finished up his story.

"I didn't ask you to believe me. You don't matter," Drew retorted blatantly. "You're not part of this, only Shadow matters."

"Kyle does matter!" Shadow turned back to look at Kyle. "I believe him Kyle. I know who I am…was. I was that police woman."

"Shadow, no," Kyle disagreed. "It can't be true."

"I guess the only way for her to believe is to show her," Drew reached out his hand towards Kyle.

"NO!" Shadow yelled. "Not that way." Drew stopped just before he touched Kyle.

"Well then how am I supposed to show her?" Drew asked.

"Remember how you looked older when we found you?" Shadow asked.

"That's easy enough," Drew replied, shrugging, he lifted his hand towards his face.

"Not you, me," Shadow corrected, stopping Drew once more. "I want to look older," he whispered.

"How much older?" Drew asked.

"Just a couple of years. I want to be twenty or twenty one," Shadow answered slowly.

"That's it?" Drew asked.

"That's old enough to get us in to the Velvet," Kyle explained, laughing. She still didn't believe that Drew could do magic. How ridiculous was that?

"I can do that, I think," Drew said thoughtfully. He placed his hands over Shadow's face.

'Older, 21 years old, 21 years old,' he repeated in his head over and over again.

Shadow groaned and fell forward almost falling off of the couch they were sitting on.

"SHADOW!" Kyle screamed in concern.

Shadow stuck out his arm out to stop her from rushing to his side. "I'm OK," he told her in a voice slightly deeper than it had been. "How'd you do the trick with my voice?" he asked.

Drew shrugged.

"Are you sure you should be messing with powers that you know nothing about?" Kyle asked.

Shadow looked up at them. His hair was longer and he had a full beard.

Drew laughed. "You look like the Wolf Man. I can fix that too." He put his hands over Shadow's face again. He repeated the words 'clean-shaven' in his mind. When he took his hands down, the beard was gone.

"That rocks," Shadow whispered, rubbing his hands across his cheeks.

"Now it's Kyle's turn," Drew announced.

"I don't know," Kyle said skeptically.

"It doesn't hurt that much," Shadow assured her.

"Hold on." Drew covered his face with his hands. "Watch!" When he withdrew his hands he was the same age as he was when they first met. This time his hair was in a green Mohawk.

"OK," Kyle gave in reluctantly.

Drew turned to Kyle. "How old do you want to look?" he asked.

"25," she pointed at her hair, "with pretty blue hair."

"OK," Drew lifted his hands to her face the same way he had done for Shadow.

"STOP!" Kyle screamed seconds after he had started. She was in horrible pain. "YOU'RE KILLING MY BABY!"

"Baby?" Drew asked, pulling his hands away.

"PLEASE STOP!" she screamed.

"I did!" Drew assured her.

"Why does it still hurt? You're crushing it!" she said, opening her eyes. Her stomach had grown considerably.

"It's not Drew, it's your pants that are crushing it," Shadow explained.

"Wait! I got it," Drew said as he placed his hand over her pants. They suddenly grew to fit her swollen belly. "Oh Shit! I'm so sorry."

"You keep your powers away from me!" She shouted, swatting at his head. "WHAT DID YOU DO TO ME?" she screamed.

"JUST LET ME THINK!" Drew screamed back at her. Shadow took her hand, trying to calm her down.

"Shadow, let me try something," Drew requested. "I'm going to make you look 15 again."

"OK," Shadow agreed, clearing his throat. He was still not quite used to his new voice.

"Back," Drew said aloud. Nothing happened. "Younger." He tried again still nothing. "15!" he demanded, still nothing happened.

"You didn't make us look like we were older you made us older!" Kyle accused her voice getting louder with every word. "MY BABY IS OLDER!" Kyle screamed. She began to punch Drew repeatedly.

"STOP!" Drew screamed backing away from her fury.

"YOU CAN'T MAKE IT GO BACK! WHAT ARE YOU? HOW COULD YOU DO THAT TO US? YOU'RE A MONSTER!" Kyle screamed.

"I'M NOT!" Drew screamed back at her. "I AM NOT A MONSTER!" he screamed, wishing she were closer so he could stop her from screaming. She started to move slowly across the room as if pulled by some force. Her mouth was still moving, but no sound came out.

Kyle grabbed at her throat and looked back at Shadow helplessly.

"Let her go!" Shadow demanded, but Drew had already released his hold. Kyle's voice was back and she was screaming again.

"Oh God, I am a monster," Drew whispered, sliding his back down the wall until he sat on the floor. "I am a monster," he repeated.

"You're not a monster." Shadow comforted him, his motherly instinct from his past self kicking in. He moved across the room and sat down next to Drew. Tentatively, he put his arms around the sobbing boy.

"LEAVE HIM ALONE!" Kyle screamed. "He deserves to suffer."

"No, he doesn't. Can't you see how scared he is?" Shadow scolded her. "Why are you so angry anyway?"

Kyle sighed and lowered herself awkwardly onto the couch. "I was...," she swallowed back tears. "I was going to get an abortion," she explained, the tears rolling down her cheeks. Before it was OK, I could justify it in my mind. It wasn't really anything before, but now...," she said, placing her hand on her swollen abdomen. "Now, it's a baby."

Drew stood up slowly and walked towards her. "I could..."

"You're not killing my baby. You're not touching me again,"

"I'm not going to hurt you," Drew said softly. "I swear; I will never hurt you again. I just want to make sure that the baby is OK," he said soothingly.

"You can do that?" Kyle asked as Drew placed his hand on her belly. He nodded and closed his eyes.

The first thing he felt was fear, Kyle's fear and the baby's fear of its own insanely rapid growth.

He gasped in horror. The baby was exactly eight months and three weeks old. If he hadn't stopped when he did, he could have killed both mother and child.

"I am so sorry," Drew apologized again. "I nearly killed you both. The baby is scared, but otherwise OK and healthy. It's almost nine months along. If you hadn't stopped me..."

"The baby would have torn me apart," Kyle supplied.

"Maybe," Drew acknowledged.

This time, Kyle's maternal instinct took hold as she started to lecture him.

"Why don't you think about the consequences before you act? You don't know the limit of your powers. You shouldn't play with them, like they were a toy. They're dangerous. Look what you almost did to my baby and me. Look at Shadow; he's lost five years of his life."

"Six years," Shadow corrected.

"Six years that now he can never get back," Kyle amended.

"I don't want to hear this."

"But you need to hear this, Drew. You need to think about what could happen before you act."

"Give him time to breath," Shadow whispered in her ear.

"God, you're beautiful," Kyle turned to look at him. "You're still basically the same; just older and more masculine."

"Come with me to look," he suggested helping her stand up. "I'm afraid to do it alone." He led her towards the bathroom.

"I guess I'm still in…," Shadow stopped talking as he finally caught sight of himself in the mirror, "…shock." His makeup was gone and his hair was lying flat against his head.

"Where did Robert Smith go?" Shadow asked, tracing his finger along his jaw line.

"He grew up, Shadow," Kyle looked up at him. "You're taller." She caressed his cheek. "I just want this to be over; I don't like this adventure anymore." Her hand flew to her stomach as she felt the oddest sensation. "I think the baby's kicking."

Shadow kissed her forehead. He knelt down and pressed his ear against her belly. "Calm down, baby. I won't let anyone hurt you," he whispered. The baby stopped kicking. He rubbed his hand across her belly.

"I'm afraid of Drew," Kyle admitted as she placed her hand on Shadow's head.

"So am I," Shadow admitted, "but I'm more afraid of The Patchwork Man. We need Drew and, as much as I hate to say it, Kyle, he could protect us."

"Yeah, when he's not trying to kill us," she joked.

"What is he doing out there?"

Drew seemed to be singing tunelessly.

"I don't know," Kyle led the way back into the living room. "What the hell?" she stopped short of the living room. A small boy sat on the floor drawing on a piece of paper. He was surprisingly good for such a small boy.

"It's you," he held up the paper to show Kyle the sketch he'd done of her.

"Who are you?" Kyle asked.

"You must be Cody," Shadow surmised.

"Where's Drew?" Kyle directed the question to Shadow, but Cody answered.

"He's sleeping. Don't tell him I made myself little again," he pleaded. "He doesn't like when I do that."

"I would never," Kyle slowly sat down on the couch. "You know, he's very worried about you."

"I know, he told me to go away...so I did. Then he wanted me to come back, but I was still so scared, so I hid."

"What were you scared of?" Shadow asked.

"I don't like the magic. It comes from a bad place in Drew. It makes him a meanie."

"I don't like the magic either," Kyle admitted.

"The magic can help us against The Patchwork Man." Shadow put his hand on the boy's shoulder. He wanted to know that the boy was real. Cody shrugged. "Aren't you afraid of The Patchwork Man?" Shadow asked.

"Nope," Cody replied, casually going back to his drawing.

"Why not?" Shadow asked.

"He doesn't want me, he wants you."

"Why? Why does he want me?" Shadow begged of the small boy.

"You're his son. Didn't you know that?"

"How do you know these things?" Kyle asked the boy.

"I have magic too, other than Drew's magic." He paused, showing her the drawing of Shadow he had just finished. "He doesn't know about it. There's a lady. She comes to me. She tells me things. Her name is Maggie."

"Maggie?" Kyle asked. "Is she...?" she started

"Yep, she's Shadow's Mommy," Cody interrupted.

"Can you draw a picture of her?" Shadow asked, with tears in his throat.

"Yes, and if we ever find her again, you can see her face. Dr. Lilly is in her old body."

"Dr. Lilly?" Kyle asked.

"She's my friend. She helped after The Patchwork Man killed my mommy and daddy. She could help us now, but Drew won't let her. He ran away from them."

"Why did he run away?" Shadow asked.

"They want to fix us. He is afraid they won't give him a body. He's not Maggie; he's Drew. He's not Trance; he's Drew." Cody's mouth opened in a huge yawn.

"Who's Trance?" Kyle asked.

"I don't know," Shadow replied, rubbing his head. He was starting to get a headache.

"This is your mom," Cody handed the picture to Shadow. "I need to sleep now, too. Using the magic makes you very tired. He curled up on the couch and a teddy bear appeared out of nowhere. He cuddled into the teddy bear and fell asleep.

Shadow and Kyle watched in awe as the body slowly melted back into its original form.

82

A Restaurant:

Lilly, Josh, & West

"Do you think Eon got Drew?" West asked as he and the two women ate dinner.

"Why would he do that?" Cheyenne asked. She was still having trouble believing that she was really Josh.

"With all that power, he could...," West began.

"SHIT!" Lilly screamed, slamming her fist against the table, startling Cheyenne. "Sorry, Josh... Cheyenne. I didn't mean to startle you, but with all that power, he could destroy anyone who crosses his path. We have to find him. We have to stop him."

"How are we going to do that?" West asked.

"We could find this Harper that he was claiming to be," Cheyenne suggested.

"Good idea," Lilly said, pausing as she stared at the paper that West was thumbing through.

"That's me," Cheyenne said as she pointed to the paper. "And that's you, Lilly."

"The real me...," Lilly whispered as West spread the newspaper out on the table.

The headline read: "Bizarre double homicide leads to mysterious disappearances." Lilly scanned the article. "This is all about what happened at my apartment. 'This incident led to the death of one police officer and the disappearance of another.' That's you," Lilly read.

"'Police believe that the killer is still at large and abducted all the witnesses of the slaying of Dr. Lillian Mae.

Among the missing are Alex Roderick, Maggie Kenyon, and Cheyenne Beswick. Kenyon has been missing for almost a month. After the slaying, she was hospitalized, but was abducted from the hospital. Beswick is a police officer, a 12-year-veteran of the force, who never missed a day of work. She disappeared two days after the vicious murder.'

"Why didn't I see this before? Of course Eon would switch into the cop. He could get away with so much stuff," Lilly said in anger.

"Plus, it's easier to earn the trust of people as a cop," West pointed out.

"We have to go to Alex's house. I need to see his room," Lilly whispered.

"Why his room?" Cheyenne asked.

"I have to find my laptop. Maybe he left it there."

"What's so important about this laptop?" West asked.

"I have an email saved on it, from someone who I think can help us."

"Who?" Cheyenne asked.

"I don't know the person's name or even how they got my email address. All I know is that Eon is deathly afraid of them," Lilly explained.

83

Kyle's House:

Cody, Kyle, Maggie,

& Shadow

"Shadow?"

Shadow stopped mid-bite as he heard a voice calling to him from the living room.

"Cody?" Kyle asked.

Shadow shrugged.

"Shadow, please hurry. I can't hold this much longer." The voice sounded distinctly female.

Kyle and Shadow exchanged glances and then they ran into the living room. They were both surprised to find a woman sitting on the couch where Cody had been only a few moments ago.

"Are you my mother?" Shadow asked.

Maggie nodded with tears in her eyes.

"I always regretted giving you up," she whispered.

"But you were only fourteen," Kyle reasoned.

"Still…," she said, smiling sadly. She held her arms out to hug him.   After a brief hug, Maggie pulled away. "I came to warn you."

"About The Patchwork Man?" Shadow asked.

"Yes," Maggie nodded. "Cody was right he is your father. Not only that, he has spent hundreds of years planning and carefully archiving. You are a direct descendant of his original body. You, and only you, have the capability of…," she paused, swallowing. "immortality."

"Immortality as in living forever?" Kyle asked.

"Yes, but only if he has the powers that have been combined within this body." She gestured to the body that held Cody & Drew's souls. "We must, at all costs, keep these bodies away from him."

"What are we supposed to do?" Shadow inquired.

"You must hide, and if he finds you, you must run," Maggie sighed. Her voice was growing weaker. "You were supposed to be safe until you turned eighteen." She caressed his cheek.

"And Drew made you older," Kyle pointed out.

"Now my body can hold his soul," Shadow whispered in shock.

"It's not safe here," Maggie softly. She kissed Shadow's forehead again. "Don't let him get you, please."

"I'll try my hardest," Shadow assured her.

"Goodbye and stay away from The Velvet. He's waiting for you there," she whispered as the body melted back into Drew's shape.

"Drew?" Shadow asked. The body didn't answer. "Maggie?" Shadow tried.

The body shook his head. "It's me, Cody." He smiled. "You saw Maggie? She's nice, isn't she?"

"Yes, she's very nice," Shadow told him. "Where's Drew?" he inquired.

"Drew is Maggie. Maggie is tired, so Drew is tired too," Cody explained.

"So, there are three of you in there?" Kyle could not believe what had just happened, even though she had seen the transformation with her own eyes.

"No, it's just me and Drew. Maggie was Drew, but she didn't want to be any more so she went into the light. Drew took her place. It's very confusing."

"I'll say," Kyle laughed.

"OK, Cody, Maggie told us we have to leave here," Shadow explained.

"Where are we going to go?" Kyle asked.

"I know a place," Cody told them. "The Patchwork Man won't find us there."

"What are we waiting for?" Shadow asked.

84

Shadow's House:

Lilly, Josh, & West

Lilly rang the doorbell of Alex's house.

"Officer Beswick was it? So nice to see you again," Mrs. Roderick opened the door for the trio to walk in. "Come in, come in," she ushered them inside. "I just started a pot of coffee."

"No thanks, ma'am," Cheyenne said in a shaky voice.

"Any word on my son?" Mrs. Roderick asked. "I know your partner was just here a while ago, but I would like to know if my son is alright."

"My p-partner?" Cheyenne asked.

"Yes, lovely man, about six foot three, maybe four, beautiful blue eyes."

"Did he give you a name?" Lilly asked.

"Yes…um… Reynolds, I believe he said."

"Eon," Lilly whispered. "What was he asking about?"

"He wanted to know where he could find my son."

"What did you tell him?" Lilly asked.

"I told him I don't know where Alex is. He ran away."

"Ma'am," West piped in, trying to sound like the cops on Law & Order. "We have reason to believe that this officer Reynolds is in fact not an officer at all."

"Are you serious?" Mrs. Roderick asked.

"Very. We also believe that he is the prime suspect for the murder of Lillian Mae. We strongly advise you not to talk to this man,"

"But he had a badge," she whispered in disbelief.

"He stole my badge," Cheyenne said quietly.

"He's going after my son," she whispered in horror, grabbing onto a side table for support. "He's going to kill my son."

"Not if we can help it ma'am," West said reassuringly.

"I told him to find Kyle. Alex is probably with her."

"Do you know this girl's last name?" Lilly asked.

"No, I just gave him a picture of her. I didn't even tell him her name because I couldn't remember it at the time."

"That is a very good thing," Lilly told her. "Do you know if your son had a connection with someone named Jack Harper?"

"I don't know about the Jack part but," She glanced at Lilly suspiciously. "My name is Harper."

"He played us," West practically growled.

"My son?" She turned back to look at West so quickly she almost fell over.

"No ma'am, the killer. He was using your name."

"What? Why would he do that?"

"That's what we'd like to know," Lilly agreed. "This guy is a psycho, he needs help."

"Is there any way my associates and I could look in your son's room? Maybe we could find clues to his whereabouts," Cheyenne suggested.

"Sure…Sure… Right this way." She led the way to Alex's bedroom.

"Maybe I will take you up on that coffee," Cheyenne told Mrs. Roderick.

"Oh OK, I'll go get it. Anyone else for coffee?"

"No thanks," Lilly answered absently as she searched the room for her laptop.

"Does your son have a computer or a laptop?" West asked.

"No, I don't think so," Mrs. Roderick said. "Oh wait, he was borrowing his friend's laptop," She pushed past West and walked towards the closet. "He usually keeps it in here." She opened the door and pulled out a padded messenger bag.

She placed the bag on the bed and headed towards the door. "I'll be right back with your coffee," she said as she disappeared through the doorway.

"Is it yours?" West asked as Lilly pulled out the laptop and set it on the desk.

"This is it," Lilly confirmed, "but there's some kind of lock on the screen. I need a password."

"Try Reynolds," West suggested. It didn't work.

"Maggie," Lilly recommended as she typed it in. She tried her name, Mae's name, the name of their first pet together, but none of them worked.

They had just about exhausted all of the possibilities when Cheyenne spoke up. "MacLeod," she said softly.

"That's it. Why would it be MacLeod?" Lilly pondered.

"I'm Duncan MacLeod of the clan MacLeod," West answered cryptically.

"What?" Lilly asked.

"It's a TV series…'Highlander' The guy in the show is immortal," West explained.

"Lauren and I used to watch it," Cheyenne said sadly. "Who's Lauren?" she asked.

"Josh's…your fiancé," Lilly explained.

"Why does it make me feel so sad inside to think of her?" Cheyenne asked.

"She died," Lilly explained sadly.

"No," Cheyenne corrected. "Eon killed her."

Lilly nodded. "OK, here's the email." Lilly clicked on the reply button and began to type a quick email.

`Eon's killing people. Please help. Meet in the place you mentioned last time we talked. Lilly.`

She clicked the send button and then back to delete everything in the mailbox.

"Do you have an Internet server email?" she asked West.

West nodded and supplied the address. Lilly attached a copy of the journal she had kept describing Eon's exploits in detail and sent it to West's email. Then she proceeded to erase everything she possibly could.

"Sorry to take so long," Mrs. Roderick apologized as she entered the room with a tray and four cups of coffee. Lilly shut the laptop with a snap.

"I am so sorry, Mrs. Roderick. We've got a lead on your son. We've got to be heading out."

"When you find him, please tell him that I love him and I want him to come home," she requested, setting the tray on the desk.

"We'll do that," Lilly assured her.

85

Shadow's House:

Eon

Eon put the stolen car in park on the street outside of Alex's house. He watched in amazement as Lilly, West, and Josh-in-the-woman's-body walked away from the house. He could not believe the sheer audacity of his ex-wife (although technically they were still married) and her newfound friends.

He waited and watched as the group got into their van and sped off.

What were they up to? Did they get the laptop before he could?

He stepped out of the car and walked stealthily towards the house, hoping Lilly and the rejects wouldn't drive by again.

He knocked on the door, but no one answered. He knocked again.

"Go away or I'll call the cops," Mrs. Roderick shouted through the door.

"I am the cops," Eon announced.

"No, you're not. You stole that badge. You killed that lady," Mrs. Roderick accused.

"Lilly," Eon whispered in anger. "OK, I'm leaving. Don't call the cops," He turned and walked towards his car. He could feel her eyes on him the whole time. He climbed into the car and started it.

He looked back at the house. There she was, still watching him from the window. He put the car in gear and drove away.

He could wait; he was good at that. He had waited over 500 years for the immortality that he had earned so long ago; the immortality that was stolen from him.

He had waited for that and he could wait for one drunken, coffee-obsessed housewife to fall asleep.

86

A Playground:

Cody, Kyle, & Shadow

"Cody, this is a playground," Shadow pointed out.

"I know." Cody smiled. "The bad man will never think to look for us here. We can hide inside the tunnels," he said, pointing to the gigantic play structure in the middle of the playground.

"He's got a point," Kyle struggled to pull herself up the rung ladder. Shadow helped her up.

"Fine," Shadow conceded. "We can stay here until morning, but then we have to get out of Dodge."

"Where's Dodge? Why do we have to get out?" Cody asked.

"It's a figure of speech. It means run away," Kyle explained patiently.

"Oh, I'm good at that," Cody assured her.

"Where's Drew?" Shadow asked. "Is he still sleeping?" As much as Shadow hated to admit it, he missed his newfound friend.

"He's grounded," Cody told them. "Maggie said he was bad and now he has to stay in the darkness."

"Can't you wish him out?" Kyle asked.

"No, I tried," he said sighing. "It's lonely in here," he said, tapping his head.

"I'm so hungry," Shadow whispered as he sat down next to Kyle on the bench inside the playhouse at the top of the tunnel structure. "Can't you wish us something to eat?" he begged as Kyle dug through her backpack.

"Maggie says if we use the magic then The Patchwork Man can find us," he said quietly.

"We don't want that," Kyle stated, pulling something out of her pack.

"What is that?" Shadow asked.

"Granola bars," Kyle replied, handing one to each of them. "I brought water too."

"Thank you," Shadow said as he gobbled down his granola.

"Why don't you two try and get some sleep?" Kyle offered. "I'll keep watch."

"OK, but wake me at the first sign of anything," Shadow said as he took of his jacket and balled it up to use as a pillow.

87

The Playground:

Lilly, Josh, & West

"Are you sure this is where he said to meet us?" West asked, looking around at the empty moonlit playground.

"Yes," Lilly replied. "The playground was built on some sort of holy ground. He'll be here as soon as he gets my email."

"So, then I guess we wait," Cheyenne sat down and began to swing casually back and forth on the swing.

"We could be finding Drew," West complained.

"No," Lilly disagreed. "It's too late for that. If he doesn't have them already, he will soon. Now we need to find someone who can stop this. We need someone more powerful than we are who can stop it."

"But…," West protested.

"Trust me," Lilly told him. "Eon is not someone we want to be messing around with by ourselves."

"He's ruthless," Cheyenne added softly.

88

Shadow's House:

Eon

Eon parked the car slightly down the street, away from Alex's house. It was a different stolen car this time. He didn't want Mrs. Roderick to remember his car and call the police. If he had the time and the patience, he would have taken another body, but he really just wanted to get Lilly's laptop and be gone.

He walked around to the back of the house. People always seemed to lock their front door, but they usually forget to lock their back door. Eon tried the door, but it was locked. He pulled out his lock picking kit and set to work on the lock. This was so much easier when he had his powers. Then, he could just unlock the door with his mind.

He was a bit rusty at picking locks, but he finally got it done. He tried to open the door, but the chain lock was set.

He was beginning to get a little angry; all he wanted to do was get the laptop. He should have gotten it when he retrieved the camera.

He aimed and kicked the door with more force than was actually necessary.

"I'm calling the cops!" Mrs. Roderick screamed and ran from the kitchen.

"I wouldn't do that if I were you," Eon warned. He grabbed for her and missed. She swung her elbow back and hit his stomach. He bent over in pain and she elbowed him in the mouth.

"Oh, you're going to pay for that, bitch," Eon spat through his bloodied lips. He grabbed a butcher knife off of the counter and took off after her.

89

The Playground:

Josh, Kyle, Lilly,

Oliver, & West

Kyle closed her eyes listening to the sounds of the empty playground. Something was odd. She thought she could hear voices. She climbed slowly down the ladder and started walking forward following what seemed like three separate voices.

She stopped, ducking behind a tree as she saw three people standing around the swing set. One of them looked a lot like the picture that Cody drew.

"Dr. Lilly?" Kyle called out quietly.

"Who was that?" the woman with Dr. Lilly asked fearfully. Kyle started walking towards the swing set.

"Is that The Guardian?" the man asked. He too looked familiar from one of Cody's drawings.

"I'm a friend of Cody and Drew's," Kyle explained. "They're sleeping…"

"You're Shadow's girlfriend, aren't you?" Lilly asked.

"How do you know that?" Kyle asked.

"He called out your name when Eon…," Lilly stopped talking.

"Is Eon The Patchwork Man?" Kyle moved closer to the woman. Lilly nodded. "What did Eon do to him? Where's Shadow…the real Shadow?"

"He's gone Kyle. I'm so sorry. I had to help him let go. Eon destroyed his soul. It was better for him to let go. He died believing he was my daughter." Lilly hated the look on Kyle's face, the mixture of hatred, sadness, and confusion.

"But the Shadow I'm with…is that why he has amnesia? Because he's not my Shadow?"

"If the soul inside of him gave up, then the Shadow you knew is there." Lilly purposely avoided mentioning Cheyenne's name.

"So, this is all real? Drew and Shadow were both women before?"

"Where are they, Kyle? We need to keep them safe from Eon."

"They're right over…"She stopped talking as she noticed a light in the sky.

"What is that?" Cheyenne asked, pointing to the light. Lilly and West turned to look at what appeared to be a meteor streaking directly towards where they were standing.

"I think it's The Guardian," Lilly breathed.

"What is that?" Kyle echoed Cheyenne's question. West ran forward and pushed Kyle gently out of the path of the meteor.

"The correct question would be: who is that?" a voice answered the question.   The meteor stopped just before it hit the ground and a ball of light the size of a tennis ball hovered above the ground for a split second before it began to grow. It grew larger and larger until it took the form of a man.

"Oliver O'Keefe, at your service," the man standing in front of Kyle introduced himself. Oliver sniffed a bit and blew his nose into a handkerchief that magically appeared at his fingertips. "I do apologize," he said, making the handkerchief disappear. "Aerial travel always seems to make my nose run."

Kyle stood there open-mouthed, staring at him. She was still in shock that a man had just fallen out of the sky.

"I am The Guardian," he announced, "one of them anyway. Do you have a problem?" he asked Kyle.

"I think I'm hallucinating, but other than that, I seem to be problem free at the moment," Kyle assured him.

"You are Dr. Lillian Reynolds, are you not?"

"No, I'm Kyle," she explained. "I'm a friend of Cody and Drew's."

"Cody Andrews. Can't say that I know him, but I'm sure he's a nice fellow,"

"No, Cody and Drew are two people. Well, I guess they are one person, but…," Kyle tried to explain.

"I'm Dr. Reynolds," Lilly stepped in to rescue the poor girl. "Please call me Lilly."

"Ah, Lilly, our informal informant," Oliver said, pumping her hand up and down. "What is our errant son up to now?"

"It's bad Oliver, very bad," Lilly replied.

90

Shadow's House:

Eon

Eon wiped the bloody knife on the dead woman's dress. She couldn't call the cops with her throat slit. He had been so angry with her that he had almost decapitated the poor woman. He dropped the knife next to her, not worrying about the fingerprints that were not his anyway.

He stood up and walked into Alex's bedroom. The laptop sat on the table; Lilly had definitely been using it. He opened it up and waited for it to boot up. He tried to open Lilly's journal, but it had been deleted. He went to her email box, but it was completely empty.

"DAMN IT!" he screamed, pounding his fists against the desk. He had wanted to read about his own exploits, but it was all gone. Everything deleted. He checked the recycle box: empty.

He switched back to her mailbox to see if she had received anything. Nothing, it too was empty, but there was one letter in her Sent Items box. He opened it and read the betraying bitch's words. There was no doubt now that Lilly was working with The Guardians.

Eon stiffened as he felt the buzz of energy filling his body again. This time the energy was powerful, more powerful than he had felt in a long time. He drank in the feeling of it, not realizing how much he missed the feeling of it. That would be remedied shortly, as soon as he found Alex or Drew.

This power being used was probably Drew or Maggie, whatever you wanted to call the spirit that inhabited that body. He could follow the trail of energy while it still echoed through the air.

Eon slammed the computer shut so hard he almost broke it. He picked it up and stuffed it into the messenger bag.

He had to find Drew and get his powers back, especially if The Guardians were coming for him.

91

The Playground:

Cody, Drew, & Shadow

"**S**hadow, wake up!" Cody begged. He shook Shadows arm. "Wake up! He's coming!"

Shadow stirred in his sleep.

"The Patchwork Man is coming to get you!" Cody whispered urgently.

Shadow sat up. "Where's Kyle?"

"I don't know. She's gone."

"We have to find her," Shadow begged him.

"She'll be fine! He doesn't want her," Cody tried to pull Shadow into a standing position. "He wants us! We have to leave!" Cody put his arms around Shadow and wished they were at his home.

Shadow gasped as his body was pulled into a void. He felt like he was falling, but when he opened his eyes he was back on solid ground.

"What the hell was that?" Shadow asked, as he gasped for air.

"I made us disappear," Cody answered. "I didn't know if I could."

"Well you did. Where are we?"

"This is my home. Well, it was my home," Cody explained.

"How far away from the park are we?" Shadow asked, glancing at the empty street.

"Not far. We used to walk to the park," Cody reminisced, "my Daddy and me. I miss him."

"Why is that car driving so slowly?" Shadow asked warily.

"Why is it even driving down the street at three in the morning? That's a better question." Cody's voice had changed a few octaves.

"Drew?"

"Yeah, it's me," Drew affirmed. "Whatever Cody did set me free. I can't believe she did that to me."

"Guys, that cars coming back," Cody's voice chimed in.

"It's him, run!" Shadow screamed. He grabbed Drew's hand and pulled him into the yard behind the house.

***

Eon couldn't believe his luck; The Vessel was with the boy who had Eon's powers. This was going to be easier than he thought. Just as he stopped the car, the two boys started to run.

"You can run, but you can't hide!" Eon called out. Instead of chasing after them, he turned onto the next block. He cut the pair off as they were running across the street. The Vessel was slightly ahead of the boy with the powers. The Vessel made it to the other side of the street, but the boy with the powers was still crossing. Eon floored the gas the pedal and aimed the car at him. He clipped him with the corner of the car and knocked him to the ground. Hopefully, the boy was unconscious so that he couldn't use his powers.

Eon climbed out of the car just as The Vessel ran to the aid of his friend.

"It's very surprising to see you both together," Eon snarled as he towered over the two boys.

"Leave us alone!" Shadow said meekly. Eon could smell the fear oozing off of The Vessel.

Eon reached down and grabbed the boy's chin. He turned Shadow's face from side to side so he could study it in the light of the car's headlights.

"You look…," Eon paused. "Older."

"I'm not. I'm only 15," Shadow tried to convince him.

"No, you're not," Eon told him. "You're mature, ripe for the picking," he laughed. "Drew couldn't resist playing with my powers, could he?"

"I don't know what you're talking about!" Shadow shouted. "You have the wrong man."

Eon reached down and grabbed his arm. Shadow tried to pull away, but Eon's grip was too strong. Eon turned the boy's wrist over and revealed a birthmark on his arm that looked almost like the letter A.

"What is that?" The birthmark was beginning to glow.

"It's your brand," Eon explained. "It tells me that you belong to me."

"No, I don't!" Shadow pulled his arm away.

"Get in the car and lock the door," Eon commanded.

"NO!" Shadow defied him.

"Do it or your girlfriend dies," Eon lied.

"Kyle?"

"That's right, you do as I say and she will be free to go. I only want the two of you."

"Fine, but if you go back on your word, I will kill myself," Shadow threatened.

"I would love to see you try," Eon laughed. "Now, get in the car."

"Take me to Kyle!"

"I will," Eon lied. "Just get in the car."

Shadow stood up and walked towards the car. Something about the way Eon was acting was strange. Something told Shadow that he was bluffing. Still he got in the car and locked the door.

Eon picked up Drew's unconscious body and put him in the back seat of the car.

92

The Playground:
Josh, Kyle, Lilly
Oliver, & West

"This is where they were hiding," Kyle explained as she showed the play tunnels to Dr. Lilly and her friends.

"Well, they're not here now," Weston called from inside the tunnels.

Oliver sniffed at the air. "Sulfur," he announced. "That, combined with a massive amount of remnant energy, tells me that they must have teleported out of here."

"Can you trace the power?" Lilly asked.

"There's no way to tell where they teleported too," Oliver explained.

"Let's get somewhere safe until morning," West suggested, shivering.

"What about Shadow and Drew?" Kyle asked.

"There's nothing we can do for them." Lilly said sadly.

"What about your precious Cody?" Kyle demanded. "He's in there too."

"She's right," Cheyenne agreed. "We have to try to save them."

"If they teleported themselves out of here then there is still a chance that Eon hasn't got them yet," Oliver offered.

"How do you know they did it to themselves?" Kyle asked.

"The amount of power used. Only an amateur would waste that much power for something as simple as teleportation," Oliver answered.

Kyle felt an unusual pain rip across her stomach muscles. She doubled over as far as she could. West grabbed her around her waist, supporting her.

"Was that a contraction?" Lilly asked.

"I hope not," Kyle said meekly.

"Time them, please, just in case," Lilly instructed.

Kyle nodded.

"How far along are you?" Oliver asked, placing his hand on her stomach.

"Just over three months," Kyle explained through clenched teeth.

"Are you having multiples?" West asked in shock.

"No. Drew messed with me. He made me age, which made the baby age too. It better not be coming now," Kyle said with a sigh as the pain finally subsided. "I'm OK now," she assured West, pushing his hands away.

"Are you sure?" Lilly asked.

"The pain went away," Kyle said lamely. She paused and then picked up the conversation again. "He did the same thing to Shadow."

"The same thing?" Lilly asked.

"Made him older," Kyle clarified. "Now The Patchwork Man, Eon, is going to steal his body and when he does, he will be immortal."

"What?" Oliver asked. "Who told you that?"

"Maggie did. She came to us. She's Shadow's real mom and The Patchwork Man is his real father. Shadow is a direct descendent of The Patchwork Man."

"This is bad," Oliver announced. "Very bad."

"Where would Shadow go if he needed a place to hide?" Cheyenne asked.

"I know a few places where he would go," Kyle nodded.

"Well then, let's go find Shadow before Eon does," Oliver instructed.

93

𝕰on's 𝕾tolen 𝕮ar:

𝕮ody, 𝕯rew, 𝕰on,

& 𝕾hadow

Shadow turned his head as something glinting in the moonlight caught his eye: the keys. Eon had left the keys in the ignition.

Shadow waited until Eon tucked Drew in all nicely into the backseat and shut the door. He climbed over the gearshift and locked the doors.

As Shadow he had never learned to drive, but Cheyenne had. So, he concentrated and tried remember his years of driving as Cheyenne. He turned the key and the engine came to life. Stepping on the brake he put the car in gear and floored the gas. The engine revved and he shot forward as he took his foot off of the brake.

"Please let him be bluffing. Please let him be bluffing," he prayed as he looked back at Eon stranded in the street.

"Shadow?" Drew's voice came from the back seat.

"Drew," Shadow exclaimed. "You're OK!"

"What happened?" Drew was in a daze. "Why do I feel like I got hit by a car?"

"You did. Eon ran you down," Shadow clarified.

"That explains it."

"I'm taking you to the hospital."

"No need," Drew announced as he hopped over the seat to sit next to Shadow. "I've already healed myself."

"What do we do now, Drew?"

"I don't know, just keep driving. Where's Kyle?" Drew inquired looking around.

"I don't know. She was gone when I woke up. Cody took us away too fast for me to look for her," Shadow explained sadly. He slowed the car down to match the speed limit sign he noticed on the road.

"We have to find her," Drew insisted. Shadow was surprised by Drew's urgency to find her.

"Cody said she's better off without us," Shadow stated.

"No way, if she's not with us, The Patchwork Man can use her against us," Drew rationalized.

"If he doesn't have her already," Shadow whispered.

"Why do you say that?"

"He told me that he has Kyle, but the way he said it, I didn't believe him."

"I hope you're right."

"Me too," Shadow murmured sadly.

"Let's go back to her house and see if she goes back there," Drew suggested.

"If he doesn't have her,"

"He doesn't," Drew assured him.

94

The Street:

Eon

Eon screamed out in rage as the two boys drove off. His scream set all the neighborhood dogs barking.

"SHUT UP!" he yelled. He knew full well that it wouldn't do any good, but he had to let his anger out somehow.

A car blew its horn as the driver slammed on the brakes to avoid hitting Eon. Eon turned his rage onto the driver of the car.

"Turn off the car!" he commanded, standing in front of the car.

"Chill out, man!" the driver yelled back to him. "I stopped in time."

"Turn it off!" he screamed.

"OK, OK." The driver obeyed him.

"Now get out!" Eon demanded, using as much of *the voice* as he had left.

"No way," the driver called out, but couldn't stop himself from exiting the car. "Calm down, dude," the man soothed; trying to avoid a scene.

"Hand me the keys," Eon demanded.

"I left them in the car," the man's eyes were so full of fear that Eon was surprised he hadn't pissed himself.

Eon walked towards the car door.

"You can't take my car, man," the man followed him to the car door.

"I can and I will," Eon turned towards him. "Consider yourself lucky that I don't have time to play."

"What?" the man asked

Eon drew back and punched the man just hard enough to knock him out.

"I have to find those boys before The Guardians find me," Eon explained to the unconscious man as he climbed into the car.

95

Shadow's House:

Josh, Kyle, Lilly,

Oliver, & West

"That one, right there, is Shadow's house, I don't know that he would go there, but he might." Kyle pointed to his house.

"OK, you stay in the van; Oliver and I will check it out," Lilly instructed her.

"No, that won't work. If you go in there, Drew will bolt and he'll take Shadow with him. He's afraid that you guys won't give him a body. I need to go in there first and tell them that it's all right," Kyle explained. "Plus, I have a key," she smiled. She climbed slowly out of the van as another pain overcame her. "Twenty minutes apart," she announced.

"Once they are five minutes apart, we'll have to take you to the hospital," Lilly informed her.

Kyle nodded. "I know. I just hope we find them before then." She waited for the pain to subside and then walked up to the front door. She unlocked the door and walked in. It took her a moment to take in the scene that lay before.. Shadow's mom was laying in the living room, just outside of the kitchen. Her head was pulled back as if someone had tried to cut it off completely. There was so much blood everywhere. She fell to her knees, gagging.

"Take her outside," Lilly instructed West.

West nodded thankfully and led Kyle to the bushes where she proceeded to vomit. When she was done, West buried the vomit and led Kyle back to the van.

"Eon," Lilly affirmed as she read the wall on which Eon had written, 'Only through his children can man be truly immortal,' in Mrs. Roderick's blood.

Oliver picked up the phone and dialed 911. He placed his hand over Mrs. Roderick's throat and when he spoke next, he spoke with her voice.

"Help me," he begged when the 911 operator picked up the line. "There's an intruder in my house and he's going to kill me. Oh God, he has a knife, help me!" he screamed. He disconnected the line and wiped his fingerprints off of the receiver. He pressed the receiver into Mrs. Roderick's lifeless hand. He wiped the prints off of the knife and turned to face Lilly.

"Let's go find this bastard," Oliver said in his own voice.

96

The Street:

Drew & Shadow

"Ditch the car here, it's probably stolen," Drew commanded.

"But we're nowhere near Kyle's house," Shadow protested.

"Exactly. I can just zap us there or whatever Cody did before."

"OK. At least this time I'll be ready for it," Shadow rationalized.

"Are you ready?"

Shadow nodded.

"Hold on tight," Drew put his arms around Shadow.

Shadow took a deep breath and was suddenly plunged back into the dark, icy nothingness. It seemed to take longer this time as he felt himself slipping out of Drew's grasp.

'*I'm falling,*' he tried to scream out, but his voice didn't seem to work in this void.

'*Hold on!*' Drew's voice echoed through his head. He grabbed onto Drew's wrist, but he still felt himself slipping further and further into the void.

'*Drew, HELP!*' he screamed in his mind. He curved his fingers to fit into Drew's curved fingers.

'*Don't let go,*' Drew begged him. '*Something was blocking us, but we're almost there now,*' Drew explained.

'*I can't hold on!*" Shadow screamed with his mind voice.

97

Shadow's House:

Josh, Kyle, Lilly,

Oliver, & West

"**W**hat was that?" West asked as a sickly vertigo feeling swept over the van and everyone in it.

"That was an amateur using the power that he knows nothing about," Oliver explained.

"Drew," Kyle breathed.

"Turn left here, we can follow the energy and find him," Oliver instructed.

"But, so can Eon," Lilly reasoned.

"Drive faster," Kyle begged.

98

Kyle's House:

Cody, Drew, & Shadow

Just as Shadow thought he couldn't take it anymore, he felt Drew let go of his hand. He panicked until he realized Drew had only let go briefly so that he could get a better grip.

Shadow fell to the ground in Kyle's living room, gasping for air.

"Shadow?" Drew asked. He had tears streaming down his face. "I thought I lost you."

"I think I'm OK," Shadow affirmed when he could finally breathe again.

"What are we going to do?"

"We're going to fight back."

"No," Shadow whispered. Even though deep down he knew it was the only way The Patchwork Man could be stopped.

"We've got to do something," Drew implored him.

"I know," Shadow reluctantly agreed. "I just don't think I can do anything."

"Neither can I," Cody agreed. "I want out. I don't like the magic anymore. It scares me."

"Cody, there's no way," Drew explained.

"Yes, there is," Cody corrected. "I can go into Shadow."

"I don't know," Shadow whispered nervously.

"Just do it," Drew pressed. "He'll only hold me back."

"What do I do?" Shadow asked.

"Just relax and let me do it," Cody instructed. He leaned forward and placed his lips on Shadow's in a clumsy kiss. Shadow felt strange as if something was trying to push him out of his body.

"*Stop fighting it*," Drew told him. Shadow didn't know if the voice was inside of his head or out.

Shadow tried to relax, but the feeling was so strange he couldn't help but fight it.

'*Let me in*,' Cody begged.

'*I'm trying*,' Shadow thought, realizing then that all communication was in his head for their lips were still connected.

'*I'll help*,' Drew offered.

Cody tried once more, but this time Drew pushed and Shadow pulled. Shadow screamed in horror and pain as he was ripped into darkness again.

99

Kyle's House:

Eon, Lilly, & West

"It's him!" Lilly screamed as she slammed on the van's brakes.

"I got him!" West yelled; jumping out of the van before it came to a complete stop. He chased after Eon. West made it to the door right on Eon's heels. He lunged at Eon, trying to tackle him, but Eon jumped out of the way.

"Leave them alone, Eon!" West demanded.

"Shut up, REJECT!" Eon screamed out as he slammed and locked the front door. "You're not even supposed to be here!" Eon shouted, grabbing West by the collar. "But since you are…" he pulled West close to him.

"NO!" West screamed in horror. He knew what a kiss from Eon meant. He tried to get away, but Eon had him tight in an iron grip. He lost consciousness after one kiss from Eon.

100

Outside Kyle's House:
Drew, Josh, Kyle,
Lilly, Maggie, Shadow,
& Oliver

"**S**hit!" Kyle said as she dropped her keys again.

"Give them to me!" Lilly snapped.

Kyle stepped back so Lilly could retrieve the keys from the ground.

"West!" Lilly called out in response to his scream.

"West," Kyle said in a pitiful voice. Lilly unlocked the door and ran into the house.

"I got him!" Lilly yelled as she grabbed Josh's body. "Guys! I got Eon!" she rejoiced as the others entered the house.

"That's not Eon," a strange voice spoke up from the hallway. "That's West."

"West?" Lilly asked.

"Eon switched with him," the stranger told her.

They all looked up at the approaching stranger. It was a man; a young man that none of them had ever seen before.

"I'm sorry, Kyle," the stranger apologized, falling to his knees in front of Kyle. "I messed up again."

"Drew?" Kyle asked.

The young man nodded. "Shadow too," he replied, tears streaming down his cheeks. "Cody wanted out," Drew explained, "so we tried to put him into Shadow and somehow

320

this happened. Somehow we melted together and became this...became one. I'm so sorry that I messed up again."

Rage filled Kyle's eyes and she smacked Drew as hard as she could.

"Kyle, I love you," the man whispered.

"Shadow?" Kyle asked. The man nodded. "You have to fix this!" she demanded of Oliver.

Oliver remained silent, staring in awe at the man in front of them.

"You can fix them, can't you?" Kyle begged.

Oliver shook his head sadly. "I can't fix this, this is beyond my abilities,"

"Then, what the hell are we going to do?" Kyle asked.

"There is only one person who can fix this," Oliver said thoughtfully. "We need to get to Maggie."

"But Maggie's gone," Lilly whispered as she placed a pillow under Josh's body's head.

"No," Oliver disagreed. "Maggie is still there; just like Josh is still inside of Cheyenne."

"I am Josh," Cheyenne whispered. "I'm remembering more and more of me and less of her.

"Drew won't let Maggie out," Kyle pointed out.

"He won't be able to stop her," Oliver assured her. "Once I show her the memories, she will know who she was, who she is."

Oliver stepped forward and placed his hand on the strange man's cheek. Drew fled back into the darkness away from the man who was trying to destroy him.

'*He's trying to help*,' Shadow spoke into the darkness.

He grabbed on with a mental hand and pulled Drew forward. Cody joined Shadow and helped to pull Drew's essence forward.

'*TRAITOR! LET ME GO!*' Drew screamed, even though no one in the living room of Kyle's house heard the struggle.

'*They want to help us*,' Cody explained.

'They want to help you. They want to kill me,' Drew cried as Oliver finally got a hold of him.

Suddenly, Drew's essence relaxed as Maggie's memories washed over him.

"I know who I am," Maggie said aloud, using the voice that the three boys shared.

"Maggie?" Lilly asked.

"Yes and no," Maggie replied. "I am Maggie, but I was also someone else a long, long time ago."

Oliver nodded. "Those are the memories you need to tap into. You must tap into your memories from when you were Nessa. That is where the knowledge about using your powers will come from," he said in a smooth, even voice. "Go back to that time."

"Yes," Maggie replied. "My name was Nessa. I was chosen as a Guardian. I was given immortality. I protected the powerless until he found a way to kill me. The man now known as Eon, back then his name was Azriel."

"Go on," Oliver prompted.

"I was sent back to stop him," she looked around the room at the poor shattered souls around her. "I was sent back to put right what was torn apart." She sighed and took a deep cleansing breath. "I was a Guardian." She paused, looking again at everyone. "I am a Guardian!" she announced with excitement. The body she now wore was a woman's body, but not the body she wore as Maggie.

"I can fix this, Cheyenne," She reached out her hand to Cheyenne.

Cheyenne stepped forward and placed her hand in Maggie's. Maggie took Josh's body's hand and closed her eyes.

Maggie used her powers to filter Josh's soul back into his own body. She tried to find a soul inside of Josh's body, but if West was there, he was hiding somewhere deep where she couldn't find him. Cheyenne's body collapsed to the ground.

"West?" Kyle asked.

"No," Maggie replied. "I couldn't find West. He must have been hiding."

"Josh?" Lilly asked.

Josh opened his eyes and sat up. He nodded and smiled at Lilly.

Lilly threw her arms around Josh. "I'm so glad you're back."

"Me too," Josh rubbed his eyes. "I just hope he doesn't do it again."

"He won't, I've anchored your soul into that body. No one will ever be able to force it out again," Maggie assured him. "Now you must take me to the boy named Trance."

101

The Forest:

Eon

Eon took off in the new body he was in. It felt so strange, yet familiar. He ran out the back door of the trailer and out into the woods behind it. He couldn't let The Guardians catch him now.

Then again, if they only sent Oliver, he would be safe. Oliver wasn't very powerful at all. He knew this because Oliver had been his apprentice for many years. Oliver would never do anything to hurt him.

For now, he ran. He ran as fast as he could. This body had some power in it. He could once again see the energies swirling around him. He couldn't seem to manipulate them in anyway, but at least he could see them now.

He felt joyous for what Drew's meddling had done. Now The Power and The Vessel were one. He could easily take over that body and then he would be powerful and immortal. Once that happened, he could do anything. He would be a god.

Seeing Oliver standing there (looking like he had over 500 years ago) filled him with mixed emotions. On one hand, he was glad to see his protégé, but on the other hand he was angry; angrier than he had been in years. Oliver's powers were nowhere as powerful as Eon's had been back then. Yet they had given Oliver the gift of immortality and not Eon. What was so special about Oliver? Why wasn't Eon so special? Why was Oliver given the gift that Eon had been denied?

Eon ran with rage clouding his vision. He didn't see the log until he tripped over it. He landed face down in the water and sank into darkness.

102

The Hospital:

Dylan, Lilly, Maggie,

& Trance

Lilly and the woman known as Maggie walked through the hospital unnoticed.

"Why can't anyone see us?"

"I am using the energies to shield us from their eyes and ears," Maggie explained.

When they arrived in the room, Lilly pulled back a curtain to reveal Elliot's body. "You're in Trance's body," Lilly reminded her.

"No, this body is a genetic mutation. Trance's body is over there." Maggie pointed to the empty bed next to Elliot's body.

"There's nothing there." Lilly looked at Maggie.

"Look again," Maggie replied.

Lilly looked back at the bed and Trance's body was lying there.

"How did you…?" Lilly started.

Maggie cut her off. "No one should ever have powers this great. Humans were not made with the capacity to handle powers like this," Maggie explained, walking towards the beds. "Not even Guardians have powers such as these," she admitted.

Maggie took one of Elliot's hands and one of Trance's hands. Once again Lilly watched as Maggie filtered Trance's soul back into his own body.

"Take him out of here," she instructed.

"Trance, get up," Lilly whispered.

"My powers, I don't have them," Trance whispered back.

"You will," Maggie assured him. "I need them for now. Leave now, please."

Lilly helped Trance out of the bed and the two left the room. As soon as they were gone, Maggie's body shifted into that of Maggie's original body.

"Dylan, honey, wake up." she urged gently. Dylan's eyes fluttered open.

"Where's Trance?" he asked in fear.

"He's safe, back in his own body," Maggie informed Dylan.

"Maggie?" his voice whispered softly.

She nodded. "You do deserve to live," she whispered kissing his forehead. Elliot's face changed to that of Dylan's own face. "Rest now," she instructed as she turned to leave.

"Maggie, don't go!" Dylan called out.

"I have to stop him," she insisted, her body slowly changing to that of Nessa The Guardian's again.

"Don't leave me here," Dylan begged.

"I would never," Maggie extended her hand, smiling. "Let's go see Trance,"

"Trance," Dylan breathed, a smile spreading across his face.

103

The Hospital:

Eon & Kinsey

Eon opened his eyes to find himself staring at a white ceiling. "Where…" he started to say, but stopped as he realized how badly his throat and lungs hurt. "What happened?" he growled.

"You almost drowned," a young woman told him. "You're lucky I was hiking in the woods. If I hadn't found you, you would have been dead."

"Drown?" Eon asked, laughing quietly to himself. It would have been just his luck to die just as everything was finally coming together.

"You must have tripped and hit your head on a rock or something. I found you face down in less than a foot of water," the girl explained. "My name is Kinsey."

"Eon," he introduced himself. "I have to get out of here," he announced, struggling to get up.

"The doctor hasn't even seen you yet," Kinsey informed him.

"It doesn't matter. I'm fine," Eon declared.

"No," Kinsey disagreed. "You're not fine." She pointed to his wrist. A handcuff chained him to the bed.

"What? What is that?" he said, trying to free his hand.

"They know you escaped from that mental hospital," Kinsey explained. "I'm sorry," she whispered. "I wouldn't have brought you here if I'd have known."

Eon brought his free hand up to his eyes. "I don't believe this shit," he groaned softly.

"I know," Kinsey agreed. "I'm so sorry."

"It's fine. I just need to find a way out of here," Eon whispered, looking around the room. "Do you know where the key is?"

"No," Kinsey whispered back. "The policeman took it with him."

"Too bad," Eon sighed. He glanced at Kinsey again. "You're really beautiful, you know."

"I'm all dirty and wet," Kinsey pointed out.

"Makes you more beautiful," Eon flirted.

Kinsey blushed furiously. She batted her eyelashes, looking away from Eon.

"Well you saved my life. The least I could do is give you a kiss," Eon offered.

"Sure, why not?" Kinsey smiled and nodded. She leaned forward and placed her lips on his.

Eon smiled a wicked smile as he kissed her and leapt into her body.

"What?" the man in the bed croaked out. Kinsey cleared her throat. "What happened? What did you do?" she begged.

"I believe I just made my daring escape," Eon informed her, using her own voice.

104

The Hospital:

Cody, Lilly, & Maggie

"This is Cody," Lilly announced as she led Maggie into the boys hospital room. "His body grew a little bit since he was last in it," she explained as they both stared down at the 12-year-old body.

"Who is inside there?" Maggie asked.

"His mother was, but I think she left long ago," Lilly surmised.

Maggie lifted her hand up to the little boys face.

"What are you going to do?" Lilly asked in fear.

"You don't want to watch this," Maggie warned as she pulled the sheet over the boy's head.

"Don't hurt him!" Lilly begged.

Maggie smiled. "I wouldn't dream of it, I only want to give him back what he's lost." She closed her eyes and transferred Cody's soul back into his body. Lilly watched in awe, as the body seemed to shrink underneath the covers.

"What...?" Lilly began, but stopped as she realized how useless the question was.

Maggie pulled down the sheet to reveal the body of a five-year-old child. The boy's eyes were open and he was smiling the biggest smile Lilly had ever seen.

"Dr. Lilly!" he screamed. "I'm back! I'm me! I'm a little boy again!"

Lilly held out her arms and Cody jumped into them. "I've been dreaming about this day for seven years," Lilly said through tears as she held the small boy closely.

"Me too," Cody agreed.

105

The Hospital:

Eon & Kinsey

"I'm feeling a bit generous right now," Eon whispered. "I'm going to give you what you couldn't give me." He looked around the room, searching for something.

"Are you going to kill me?" Kinsey asked, clearing her throat again and again.

"It's not going to help," Eon informed her. "Clearing your throat, it won't help. There's nothing wrong with your voice," he clarified. He ran Kinsey's hands through Kinsey's hair. "Ah-ha," he said as he pulled out a bobby pin.

"Please don't kill me,"

"I'm not going to kill you," Eon laughed. "I'm going to set you free."

"Why set me free?" Kinsey asked, fear filling her new eyes.

"Like I said, I'm feeling very generous. I mean, after all, you saved my life, didn't you?" Eon smiled. "Besides, I want to see your face," he explained as the handcuff clicked open.

"My face?" Kinsey asked.

"Your face," Eon agreed. "I want to see your face when you look in the mirror. I so often miss that. It's my favorite part."

"Your favorite part of what?" she asked as he led her to the bathroom.

"Life," Eon answered cryptically. "My favorite part of life." He couldn't stop smiling at the girl trapped in the man's body.

"No," Kinsey cried as she caught her reflection in the mirror. "No...No...No," she chanted, getting louder.

"Typical," Eon said, disappointment filling his voice.

"What did you do?" she screamed. She turned on Eon and started hitting him.

"That's better. Don't get too loud though. You don't want to get caught. Authorities frown upon men beating up poor defenseless women," Eon warned.

"I'm not a man!" Kinsey argued.

"Yes, you are. Just look in the mirror," Eon pointed out.

Kinsey stopped attacking him and turned to look at the mirror. "This is a trick," she stated.

"It's not a trick," Eon disagreed.

"It is. This isn't real. This is a nightmare," Kinsey rationalized.

Eon chose not to respond. Instead he swung his arm and slapped her hard across the face. "Did that feel like a nightmare?"

Kinsey stared at the mirror in horror.

"Finally... Acceptance," Eon growled.

Kinsey opened her mouth as if to scream.

"Don't scream," Eon warned, so happy he was almost laughing. "If you scream they'll come running. They'll cart you off back to the mental institution where you belong."

The scream died in her throat. "I-I don't belong there, do I?" she asked in confusion. Eon knew the body and the soul were trying to fuse.

"You don't, Kinsey, but that body does," he laughed.

"No...no...no...no...no," Kinsey began chanting again. She ran her fingers across her new face. "This isn't real. This is a trick," she repeated.

"Oh, it's real all right and they are coming for you," Eon assured her.

"Who?" Kinsey asked.

"The police, the doctors in white coats—all of them," Eon answered. "But what they will do to you pales in comparison to what the others will do if they find you."

"Others?" Kinsey asked. "What others?"

"Maggie, Lilly, Oliver, and all of their little friends," Eon spat out.

"What will they do to me?" Kinsey asked in fear.

"They will do things that you can't even imagine," Eon whispered evilly.

"No."

"Yes. Stay away from them if you value what little life you have left," Eon warned.

Kinsey nodded.

"Now, it's time for you to go," Eon commanded, opening the door leading out of the shared bathroom into the adjoining room. "I'm giving you to the count of five," Eon warned.

"For what?" Kinsey asked.

"That's when I start screaming, so you better run. One... Two...," Eon began counting. He had no intention of screaming, but he wanted to see her panicked run.

Kinsey turned and ran.

106

The Hospital:

Everyone

"Are there anymore?" Maggie asked.

"Just West. Eon took his body… Well, the body he had been in," Lilly sighed. "The rest are either dead of resigned to the situation." She paused. "What about me?"

"You can keep that body," Maggie said softly. "I won't need it anymore."

"You're not staying?" Dylan asked.

"No. I'm sorry, sweetheart. I don't belong here. I know who I am now and I am needed elsewhere."

"What about The Patchwork Man? We need to stop The Patchwork Man," Cody reminded them.

"Why do you call him The Patchwork Man?" Lilly asked.

"Because that's how he sees himself," Cody answered.

"Patchwork?" Lilly asked.

"I've seen him like that," Maggie agreed sadly.

"He has all these different patches of other people's skin. He looks yucky," Cody described as he climbed into the van.

"West's not looking too good," Trance informed them as they arrived at the car.

Lilly climbed into the van and lifted the eyes of the woman's body where West should have been. "That's odd," she stated. "His eyes look so vacant."

"Let me see," Maggie closed her eyes. After a few moments she opened them again. "West isn't in there," she pronounced.

"Then who is?" Josh asked.

"No one," Maggie replied.

"We have to take…this body into the hospital," Lilly whispered.

"I'll do it," Oliver volunteered. Oliver laid his hand on the woman's head and they both disappeared.

"If West isn't in there, then where is he?" Cody asked, tears filling his eyes.

"I don't know, honey," Lilly answered truthfully.

"Is he… dead?" Trance hesitated slightly, not wanting to mention death in front of Cody.

"He wasn't even supposed to be alive," Maggie whispered.

"I saved him!" Cody cried. "I caught his soul. I made him stay."

"I know you did, honey," Lilly hugged the small boy. "But maybe it was his time to go."

"No, he was my friend," Cody sobbed.

"Sometimes friends have to leave," Lilly explained.

"Oliver is coming back," Josh pointed out.

Everyone turned to see Oliver running towards the car. "Eon's here!" he announced as he jumped into the van. "I saw him, he's someone else now…a girl."

"Which way was he headed?" Josh started the van.

'That way, towards the park," Oliver pointed.

"You're sure it was him?" Maggie asked.

"I'd recognize his energy signature anywhere," Oliver replied. "There, that's him." He pointed at a figure entering a junkyard through a locked fence.

"Follow him…her," Trance yelled.

Maggie reached her hand forward and moved the energies around the gate. It swung open, startling Eon into a run.

"What are we going to do when we catch him?" Kyle asked fearfully.

"I'm going to give him what he wants," Maggie replied.

Josh followed Eon through the junkyard. Eon dodged down an aisle of stacked cars. Josh stopped the van at the end of the aisle.

"EON, STOP!" Maggie roared as she stepped out of the van. She threw up her hand again, creating a force field. Eon ran directly out into it and bounced backwards.

"BITCH!" Eon screamed. He stood up to find Maggie and all of her friends standing outside of the van. "This isn't about you, whore. I just want the boy!" he demanded.

Maggie let her body morph back into Shadow's original body.

"Now I am the boy. You'll have to go through me to get to him," Maggie retorted.

"Easy enough," Eon answered in confidence.

"And me," Oliver stated, taking his stand next to Maggie. Trance, Josh, Dylan, and Lilly also joined the line. Kyle and Cody stayed by the van. The group began to advance upon Eon. He snaked around Maggie and went after the most vulnerable one in the group.

Kyle screamed out in fear as Eon latched onto her. He kissed her and forced his essence forward and into her, but nothing happened.

"It won't work, Eon," Maggie informed him. "I've protected all of them from you."

Eon looked around at the crowd closing in on him, fear and rage filling his eyes. He stared at each one of them in turn and saw on each one of them a force field of energy, blocking him. He noticed one person was not protected properly.

"No," Eon whispered. "You didn't protect them all," he said as he kissed Kyle's lips again.

"NOT MY BABY!" Kyle screamed out in pain as Kinsey's body collapsed to the ground.

"NOOOO!" Shadow screamed; taking control over the body he was sharing. He ran over to Kyle and kissed her lips. He jumped into the baby's mind, trying to push Eon's presence out. He fought with Eon for control of the tiny body.

Kyle continued to scream out in horror and pain, as her labor seemed to jumpstart. A warm liquid spilled down her legs. "I think my water just broke!" she cried out.

"That's not her water," Josh whispered.

"Get her to the hospital!" Lilly demanded. "Teleport her there, Oliver!"

"I can't. It will kill the baby," Oliver explained.

"Shadow has to get Eon out of the baby," Maggie explained. She was trying to quiet the baby, whose soul was now in the woman's body. "I have to get your baby's soul back in there."

Maggie took one of Kyle's hands and filtered the baby's soul back into the fetus inside Kyle's belly. At the same time, Shadow finally succeeded in forcing Eon out. Then he sank down into the warm depths of darkness inside the baby's mind.

"Shadow?" Kyle asked through tears and pain.

"Shadow's gone," Maggie informed her. "I think he's inside your baby. Don't worry, I can get him out." Maggie's face suddenly went rigid with pain. "No," she cried with a vacant look in her eyes. She fell to the ground beside Kyle.

"What is it?" Trance asked.

"Eon," Maggie whispered. "He's here, inside me."

"Maggie?" Trance called out. "Maggie? I think she passed out."

"What does that mean?" Josh asked, turning to Lilly. But Lilly was too preoccupied with Kyle to answer.

"It means Eon is now inside of The Vessel," Oliver explained. "With a power far greater than any person has ever known."

"How do we stop him?" Dylan asked.

"We don't," Oliver answered. "It's up to her now. She has to fight him off on her own."

"There's got to be something we can do," Josh whispered.

"There's nothing," Oliver responded sadly.

"I may know something we can do," Trance whispered hopefully.

107

The Between Place:

Eon & Maggie

*M*aggie opened her eyes and found herself in a familiar forest.

"Finally," Eon murmured, caressing her cheek. "Alone at last."

"No," Maggie whispered softly.

"Yes," Eon corrected. "All alone. You fixed everyone clearing the way for me to be in this body."

"No!" Maggie argued.

"Yes! You want this," Eon assured her. "You and I together in here for eternity." He kissed her lips against her will.

"NO!" she screamed and slapped him across the face. She tried to push him away using the energies, but nothing happened.

Eon laughed. "You may be experienced with magic outside of the body but I, on the other hand, am the master of magic within the mind," he scolded her. "Your magic doesn't work here. Mine does."

Eon threw out his hand and a straightjacket appeared.

"No." Maggie whispered futilely as Eon put the straightjacket on her. "NO!" she screamed. "Not this, not again," she cried, pulling back deeper into the mind to escape the horrors that Eon was about to perform on her.

"Stop that!" Drew's voice called out. Eon dropped the unconscious body of Maggie to the ground.

"Ah... The enigma... The boy who shouldn't exist." Eon smiled wickedly. *"You defend her even after she tried to steal your body?"*

"You can't have something stolen if it isn't yours to begin with," Drew rationalized. *"I didn't exist before and I don't exist now. I'm only in your head."*

"What are you talking about?" Eon asked, moving closer towards Drew.

*"What are **you** talking about?"* Drew asked him.

"Who are you?" Eon demanded.

"It's just like you said... I'm an enigma. I don't exist... or do I?" Drew asked cryptically.

Eon grabbed a hold of his shirt. *"What are you talking about?"* Eon began shaking him. *"Who are you? What are you doing? Why are you bothering me?"* Eon screamed.

"I'm not bothering you," Drew replied insolently.

"Then what exactly are you doing?"

"Stalling," Drew answered truthfully.

"What?" Eon asked, looking around. Maggie, Trance, Oliver, Josh, Dylan, Drew, and Cody were surrounding him again.

"How?" he began.

"I may not have as much experience in mind magic as you, but unlike you, I have friends," Maggie laughed.

"You're not the only one who knows about mind magic, Eon," Trance argued.

"Where's Lilly?" Maggie asked.

"Delivering a baby," Dylan answered.

"We can do this without her," Trance assured her.

"We have to do this all at once," Oliver instructed them.

"Do what?" Eon begged. *"What are you doing?"*

"PUSH!" Oliver commanded. They all pushed Eon backwards and out of the body that he was in.

108

The Junkyard:

Everyone

"Maggie?" Trance asked again. Everyone had woken from the trance he had led them in, except for Maggie.

"I'm here," a voice whispered out of Kinsey's body.

"Maggie?" Dylan asked, staring deeply into her eyes.

"Did it work?" Drew's voice came out of the body that Maggie had inhabited.

"Yes," Maggie whispered through tears. "Now it's time for me to say goodbye."

"No," Dylan begged.

"Yes," Maggie argued. "I was reincarnated for one reason and one reason only. I had to stop Eon. Falling in love with you was just a bonus."

"What about me?" Drew asked. "What happens to me?"

"What about Shadow?" Kyle asked. She was holding her brand new baby.

"Everything will be set right," Maggie assured them. "I need to hold the baby."

Kyle nodded and handed Maggie the baby.

Maggie took Drew's hand and led him away from the others. "Don't worry. This won't hurt at all."

"Well, goodbye everyone, it was fun while it lasted," Drew said with tears in his eyes.

"I love you all," Maggie whispered with tears equal to Drew's.

Maggie seemed to glow brighter and brighter until the entire group was forced to look away. When the light finally dimmed, Lilly could make out three figures sitting on the ground where Maggie and Drew had been.

Lilly walked over to the bodies sitting on the ground. A pair of young boys looked up at her with identical eyes. One of the boys was holding Kyle's baby. Lilly stared at them in awe. "Twins," she whispered. The boys looked at each other and back at her, smiling.

The twins didn't look like Shadow or Drew; they looked like a mixture of both boys. They looked to be about 17 years old.

"I'm alive," the one holding the baby said.

"Me too," the other one agreed.

"SHIT!" Lilly screamed as the other body grabbed at her ankle, she pulled it away.

"Eon?" she asked, but the face that looked up at her answered all her questions. The skin on the woman's face was made up of patches of different colored skin. Each piece seemed to have been sewn together haphazardly. The woman grabbing at Lilly's ankle was The Patchwork Man, now trapped in a woman's body.

He saw the horror on Lilly's face and raised his hand to touch the face he now wore. "What did she do to me? WHAT THE FUCK DID SHE DO TO ME?" the woman screamed. She kept running her fingers across the patches of skin covering her face. She ran her fingers down her neck and found what seemed to be a collar. "What is this? What is this?" she begged.

"It's what is keeping you in there," Oliver explained. "Now, sleep," he commanded and Eon fell asleep instantly.

"Kyle?" the twin holding the baby called out.

"Shadow?" Kyle called out, reaching her hand out to him.

Shadow nodded. He stood up and walked over to Kyle. He handed her the baby and sat down next to her putting his arm around her.

"Cody, she let me live," Drew said happily, holding his arms out to the little boy. "She gave me a body."

"I knew she would, silly. Maggie's a nice lady," Cody ran to him.

"She gave me my powers back," Trance said ecstatically.

"She gave you all powers," Oliver informed them.

Drew suddenly stopped tickling Cody and sat up straight. "The Guardians have decided it has been far too long since they took on new blood." Drew spoke with a voice that was two voices blended into one.

"Maggie?" Dylan asked.

"Yes." Drew's head turned to look at him. "Oliver and I will teach you to become Guardians and you will protect the non-magical world from the world of magic and you will be jailers to Eon. Eon will live forever now as the monstrosity he has made of himself. Each one of you will live for as long as you choose to be a Guardian. Your children will live and grow, and will one day choose whether or not they too wish to become Guardians."

"And so a new generation is born," Oliver whispered.

"I will come only when I am needed, for I have many other children who need me now," Maggie smiled. "Goodbye, my friends."

"What?" Drew asked, looking around at everyone staring at him. "Why's everyone staring at me?"

"You were Maggie for a second." Cody explained.

"Great. I get a body and a job: mouthpiece to the Guardian." Drew laughed.

Kyle nuzzled deeply into Shadow's warmth.

"She feels feverish, Lilly," Shadow pointed out. "Is she going to be OK?"

"We all are Shadow. We all are," Lilly said softly. She gently placed her hand on her stomach. She knew that Maggie somehow took the fetus out of Cheyenne's body and placed it in her own.

The End
(or is it?)

Shattered Souls is a fictional novel, but it deals with some very real problems. If you are suffering from any of these problems there is help. There is a light. Suicide is never the answer. If you are contemplating suicide or if you suspect someone you know is, please call the National Suicide Prevention Lifeline any time 24/7…

     1-800-273-TALK (8255)
or visit their website..
     http://www.suicidepreventionlifeline.org/

     If you or any one you know is struggling with drug or alcohol abuse Call Substance Abuse and Mental Health Services Administration or SAMHSA any time 24/7 …
     1-800-662-HELP (4357)
or visit their website…
     http://www.samhsa.gov/find-help/national-helpline

     Self Injury or Cutting is a very real disease. It is not a healthy way to deal with your feelings. I should know I used to do it. I conquered this disease with therapy and a book called:
'Bodily Harm: The Breakthrough Healing Program for Self-Injurers' by Karen Conterio and Wendy Lader, Ph.D.

For more information on S.A.F.E. (Self Abuse Finally Ends) Alternatives. Call…
1-800-DONTCUT (366-8288)
or visit their website
www.selfinjury.com

Coming Soon....

The Phoenix
by Patti Keno

Blinking, Jezebel stepped out into the sun and reveled in the sweet warmth it provided. It was a welcome relief from the chilly studio apartment where Evan lived. Evan was one of those strange people who actually enjoyed the cold. Jez hated it, but put up with it because Evan was her best friend.

"Are you sure you're going to be alright Jezzie?" Evan asked, leaning tiredly against the doorframe. His was pouting his supple lips at her.

"Quit pouting," Jezebel laughed. "I'll be fine, it's a beautiful day. I don't mind the walk." She smiled brightly at him. The truth was she did mind the walk. Ann Arbor wasn't a bad city and she usually felt safe walking through its streets. Unfortunately, recent events had left her feeling weak and vulnerable everywhere she went.

"I'm sorry Miles took off with the car." He apologized, as if he knew what she had been thinking.

"It's fine, really," she insisted, "just go get some sleep. I wouldn't trust your driving right now anyway." She paused watching him yawn a massive yawn. " I'm sorry I kept you up all night." She laughed. "I didn't think that game would last as long as it did." She lied again. She knew the game would last forever that is why she chose it. The fact was she didn't trust herself being alone anymore. If she had her way she would stay with Evan all the time, but she knew Miles wouldn't appreciate that.

"Neither did I." He agreed yawning again. "But I had lots of fun."

"Me too, tons of it," she replied truthfully.

"Good, you needed it." He reached out and hugged her tightly. "Be careful, Jezzie." He cautioned her kissing her forehead. "Don't do anything stupid." He lifted her chin forcing her to look him in the eyes. "If you get sad again, call me." He begged, gesturing to her arm. The white webbing of scars on her forearm shone brightly in the sun.

"I don't cut anymore." She declared truthfully, although she had been playing around with the idea.

"That's not what I'm worried about." Evan whispered.

"Evan!" She exclaimed at his boldness.

"I'm sorry, I just worry about you." He rubbed her arm. "I mean after everything can you blame me?"

"I know." She replied instead of answering his question.

"I'm just so afraid I'm going to lose you." He explained.

"You won't." She assured him, staring into his crystal blue eyes. She couldn't look into them very long without that familiar longing, filling her. She looked away. "I'm too much of a chicken for that." She laughed a little through her tears. She was trying to make light of her past suicide attempt. She wouldn't do anything drastic now, not with Evan around.

"Don't laugh about it Jez, I'm serious, I can't lose you."

"Sorry. I promise I won't try it again." She assured him

"Ever?"

"Ever." She agreed.

"I love you Jezebel." Evan pronounced her name as if it were an insult.

Jezebel smiled. It was amazing how those words could lift her spirits.

"I love you too, Harlot," she giggled at their longstanding joke. "Now go to bed, so you can be well rested when Miles gets home." She demanded.

"Now that sounds like a plan." He said with a sly grin. He opened his arms to let her go.

"See ya!" She said beginning to walk away.

"Hey Jezzie?" He called as she reached the corner.

"Yeah?" She answered, turning around.

"Be careful, there are a lot of loonies out there."

"Like you?" She joked.

"Ha ha," he replied, his face was serious. "Worse than me, just be careful please."

Jezebel sighed. "I will!" She called looking back at him. "Besides, what could happen? Its broad daylight out here," She laughed. "The Vampires are all nestled in their coffins." She spun around still laughing.

"Get some sleep!" He shouted to her.

"You too!" She shouted back, without turning around.

It was always so hard to say goodbye to Evan. She loved being with him and he loved being with her. He always told her that they were two halves of the same soul. To which she would laugh, "Unfortunately we both got the female halves of it." He would laugh and hug her and she would revel in it. It was her way of having the feeling of a man's touch without ever having to worry about anything. Evan was gay and totally in love with and committed to Miles. That was why she needed to keep her longing for him hidden deep inside.

She glanced back at his apartment to make sure he wasn't still watching her. He wouldn't approve of what she was going to do. She wasn't entirely sure that she herself approved of it, but it was the quickest way across town to the parking structure where her car sat waiting for her.

Even thought there was a parking structure just across the street from Evan's loft, Jezebel refused to park in it. Just over five years ago, she had been attacked in that structure and even though the original structure had been demolished and a new structure stood in its place, she still couldn't bring herself to park there.

She pushed those memories out of her head. That incident happened at night after the bars had closed. Like she told Evan, it was broad daylight, what could happen?

Finally she took a deep breath adjusted her purse for a better grip and stepped into the shadow darkened alley. She tried to reassure herself that nothing would happen at 10 am, but she didn't believe it. She pulled out her car keys and hooked her fingers around them so that the longest one stood out between two of her fingers like a tiny little Wolverine claw.

She walked through the alley feeling more relaxed as she went. She smiled as she reached the end of the alley. She faced her fears and nothing had happened to her.

She looked both ways and quickly crossed the street. She started into the next alley more confident than the last. She even slowed down so she could admire the graffiti that covered the brick walls. She chuckled at a particularly funny drawing.

The smile disappeared quickly when she heard footsteps echoing into the alley. She looked behind her and back towards the front again. She was directly in the middle of the alley. She was frozen in fear, from the footfalls it sounded like a jogger. She stood completely still, hoping that's all it was.

She barely had time to register the man that appeared in front of her, let alone realize he wasn't looking where he was going. He was headed straight for her at breakneck speed. She tried to move out of the way, but she wasn't fast enough. At the last second she threw her arms up to block her face.

The man collided with her and knocked her to the ground. She screamed out in horror, but her scream died when she opened her eyes and looked up at her attacker. He was standing above her with his hand was stretched out to help her up.

"I'm so sorry Belle. I wasn't watching where I was going." He apologized.

Jezebel gasped; did he know that was her name or part of it anyway? She sat for a moment just staring up into his eyes; they were the deepest brown eyes she had ever seen. She took a moment to look over the rest of him. He was definitely a homeless man; of questionable age. His dark hair was so dirty and matted it almost looked like dread locks. His face was covered with a matted beard. He looked down at her the same way she looked up at him, judging her intent.

The homeless man worriedly glanced behind himself. "Don't worry Belle, I won't hurt you." He assured her in a voice that made her believe he would never hurt anyone. "Are you hurt?" He asked.

"No I'm fine." She answered as she took his hand. She noticed he winced in pain as her hand enclosed his. "Are you ok?" She returned with real concern in her voice.

"Just a little scrape." He pulled her to her feet with one arm.

She looked at his other arm. He was cradling two loaves of bread, they looked quite fresh.

"Hot out of the oven." He stated noticing how she stared at the bread. "Are you sure you're alright?"

"Yes I'm fine." She replied, dusting herself off. "Just a little shaken, thank you for asking," she smiled tentatively.

He returned her smile with teeth that didn't quite fit in with his homeless attire. "No Problem, I'm just glad you're alright, Belle."

"Do I know you?" She asked in shock. How did he know her name?

The homeless man didn't answer. He was standing still listening. He lifted a finger to his lips. Jezebel longed to feel the warmth of his hand on hers again. She lifted her hand reaching out to touch him, but a sound echoing down the alley stopped her. She heard more footsteps coming towards them.

She gasped in shock as he reached out with his other hand dropping the bread to the ground. She was sure that he was reaching out to take her outstretched hand. Instead he used both hands to push her as hard as he could. She stumbled backwards falling down and sliding almost five feet away from where she had been standing. She stared back in horror and fear at the homeless man standing a few feet away.

He was staring back at her and she saw the look of sorrow in his eyes. She knew as two policemen tackled him that he had just wanted her clear of the fight. Something in his eyes told her he would never hurt her intentionally. Maybe it was the way he knew her name. He had called her Belle, that's the name her parents used to call her.

The homeless man looked at her pleadingly, but he knew there was nothing she could do to help. He elbowed the cop holding him and broke free. He tried to move towards her, but after a few steps one of the policemen tackled him again.

She watched as the cop who had been elbowed pulled his gun. "Stop fighting or I'll shoot!"

"I'm not going back!" The homeless man screamed.

The cop cocked his gun. The homeless man looked directly at Jezebel his eyes wide. "Don't let them take me." He begged her, futilely; there was nothing she could do to help him.

"I'm sorry," she mouthed, staring into his eyes. She was fascinated by their color. They seemed to be fading from dark brown to light brown to an unnatural orange color. The color reminded Jezebel of fire. The whites of his eyes were turning the same light blue color as the base of a flame.

One of the cops had him in a headlock and was struggling to put the handcuffs on him. The other cop kept his gun trained on the homeless man, but he couldn't shoot because his partner kept getting in the way.

The homeless man screamed out in pain as his body seemed to ignite. The cop holding him let out a scream of his own as his uniform caught fire. His partner uncocked and holstered his gun. He rushed over to help his partner put the uniform out. Both of the cops were too busy to notice the suspect they had been chasing was now a blazing inferno.

Jezebel watched in horror as the man burned. She had never seen a person be burned alive before. She had thought he should be screaming and trying to put out the flames, like the cops were now doing. Instead he just knelt there staring at her with his flame colored eyes. Together they stared neither wanting to look away, until there was nothing left of the man but ash. It was as if someone had constructed a statue out of ash shaped to look like the homeless man had.

Jezebel was filled with deep sadness, that this man she had only known for a few moments was gone. She blinked away tears and gasped as she caught the sight of movement within the ash statue. No way, he could not be alive, not after that inferno. The ashes seemed to fall away revealing a smaller form. She watched in amazement as a small child crawled out of the flames and hid between two dumpsters. Once he was hidden the inferno mysteriously went out. It was as if they had never been there in the first place. All that was left of the homeless man was a pile of ashes, a red hot puddle of melted metal, off to the side, two blackened loaves of bread, and a strange, small boy cowering between the dumpsters next to Jezebel.

Neither of the officers seemed to be injured, not even the one whose uniform had been on fire. The sleeves of his uniform were burnt, but his skin was untouched.

Now that the fire was cleared Jezebel could see their name tags.

"What in God's name was that?" The one whose name tag read Barker asked. He was gingerly touching the still warm fabric of his burnt sleeve. "How the hell?" He asked, examining the arms under the fabric.

"Spontaneous Combustion?" The other one named Fortuna suggested, he was just as puzzled. He toed the pile of ashes. Jezebel whimpered as his toe spread what used to be the homeless man across the ground.

Surprised Fortuna looked up and saw Jezebel. "Are you alright?" He stepped over the ashes and moved towards Jezebel.

Barker was now poking through the ashes with the butt of his flashlight.

Jezebel nodded, still in shock. She couldn't stop her eyes from looking back and forth between the ashes and the small boy. He was still hiding, shaking with fear. She looked in his panic filled eyes and as she watched the faintly glowing orange eyes turned back to brown. He was watching the cops in utter fear.

"I have no idea how we are going to write this one up." Barker contemplated. "I think I found my cuffs," he prodded the quickly cooling metal.

"What the…" Fortuna started, but them he trailed off. He was looking back at the metal puddle. "We have to think of something. No one will believe us if we walk into the station talking about a homeless bread thief bursting into flames."

"How about," Jezebel began. "He started a fire to escape and you had to put it out to save me and that's when he got away from you." She suggested, not believing the words that were coming out of her mouth. She wanted to tell them exactly what she saw. They would believe her. They saw pretty much the same thing she did, except for the little boy. She wanted to tell the officers about the boy, but she couldn't.

"That's a pretty good story." Fortuna offered her his hand.

"And he made off with my cuffs." Barker added.

Jezebel reached up and took his hand. She flinched at the pain she felt then, pain she hadn't felt before.

"That looks pretty nasty." Fortuna pointed out after helping her up. He turned her hand over to examine the scrape. "You might want to get that looked at." He suggested. "I can get you an ambulance."

"Oh no, there's no need for that." Jezebel answered. "I can drive us to the hospital." Us? Why did she say us?

"Us?" Fortuna asked looking around.

Oh God, was she really doing this? "My son and I." Jezebel answered. Yep, there it was. What was she thinking? She didn't know the homeless man…boy. She knew this was the way to make up for not being able to help him before. She had to get him away from these cops

"Where is he?" Fortuna asked. "Is he hurt?"

She pointed to the dumpsters where the little boy was still hiding. He looked back at her in shock. Slowly his shock turned to relief and gratitude.

"It's ok Johnny, you can come out now." She soothed, pulling the name out of the air. She still had no idea why she was doing this, but the boy/man seemed to be in series trouble. If what she saw was real and not some sort of illusion, she had to keep his secret.

The boy crawled out from between the dumpsters and ran to her side. She fell to her knees to hug the small boy like a mother would. They both played their parts perfectly.

"Thank you, Belle" The boy whispered into her ear. She shivered at the softness and gratitude she heard in his tiny voice.

"It's going to be ok now, the bad man is gone." She soothed running her hand through his clean soft hair. She looked up at Fortuna. "Do you need to take my statement or something?"

"Um." Fortuna replied, he had taken off his head and was scratching his head.

"No," Barker answered. "I don't think we're going to report this." This time Barker offered his hand to help her back up to her feet.

"Yeah, this never happened." Fortuna agreed.

"I lose my cuffs all the time." Barker laughed.

"And it's not the first time he burned his uniform." Fortuna laughed.

"Or the second." Barker admitted his face reddening a bit.

"So, It's ok if I…if we leave?" Jezebel asked.

"Yeah, you might want to stay out of alleys with a little one in tow." Barker squatted down in front of the boy and reached out to scruff his hair. The boy jerked violently away from the cop.

"Sorry, he's shy." Jezebel explained.

"Don't worry little buddy, I won't hurt ya, I'm your friend." Barker assured him, not realizing that he had earlier tackled him to the ground. "It looks like he's took quite a knock to his head." He pointed to the bump on the boy's forehead. It was identical to the bump that was on the man's head before he burst into flames.

"I better get him to the hospital." Jezebel said in a motherly tone. She reached her hand down to take the boy's hand. When he didn't automatically take her hand she shook it at him. She looked down and glanced from the hand back to him again. He finally understood and took her hand. Together they walked away leaving the cops still shaking their heads over what just happened.

Patti Keno lives in Belleville with her family and her two fur babies. She has been writing since she was ten years old. She has written many poems and many stories waiting to be turned into novels. Check out her debut novel A Murder of One available on Amazon.com. When she isn't writing she likes crafting, bowling and ghost hunting. She is a spirit medium who can speak with the dead. She likes creating her own cute crochet stuffie patterns.

Follow her on…

Twitter:	@PattiKeno
Facebook:	www.facebook.com/authorpattikeno
Blog:	www.pattikeno.com

Contact her at:
pattikeno@gmail.com

To check out her ghost hunting group visit:

www.facebook.com/michiganghostswatchers
or
www.michiganghostwatchers.net